TRAITOR TO THE CROWN

THE PATRIOT WITCH

TRAITOR TO THE CROWN

THE PATRIOT WITCH

C. C. FINLAY

BALLANTINE BOOKS • NEW YORK

The Patriot Witch is a work of fiction. Names, characters, places, and incidents are the products of the author's imagination or are used fictitiously. Any resemblance to actual events, locales, or persons, living or dead, is entirely coincidental.

A Del Rey Mass Market Original

Published in the United States by Del Rey, an imprint of The Random House Publishing Group, a division of Random House, Inc., New York.

DEL REY is a registered trademark and the Del Rey colophon is a trademark of Random House, Inc.

This book contains an excerpt from the forthcoming book *A Spell for the Revolution* by Charles Coleman Finlay. This excerpt has been set for this edition only and may not reflect the final content of the forthcoming edition.

ISBN 978-0-345-50390-9

Cover design by Jae Song. Inset illustration by Craig Howell.

Printed in the United States of America

www.delreybooks.com

OPM 9 8 7 6 5 4 3 2 1

For Rae
from start to finish

Chapter 1

April 1775

Proctor Brown stopped in the middle of bustling King Street, close enough to Boston's long wharf to smell the fishing boats, and wished he hadn't worn his best linen jacket. He rolled his shoulders to loosen the fit, but it still felt too tight. His mother had given him the linen jacket two years ago for his eighteenth birthday, and he'd already outgrown it. Taking over all the work on the farm hadn't made his shoulders any smaller.

The elegantly lettered sign of the British Coffee-House swayed over him, above the door of a narrow bay-windowed building squeezed between aged storefronts. Emily Rucke waited inside. He would be excited to see Emily again except her father was going to be there too. It figured—the first time he was to meet Emily's father, and he would show up in a jacket that was two years too small. A fine impression that was going to make.

He tugged the sleeves down one last time and stepped resolutely toward the door. A rattling cart loaded with barrels of molasses careened toward him, and Proctor jumped out of the way to keep his feet from being crushed by the wheels. His elbows bumped into someone behind him.

"I beg your pardon—" Proctor began to say as he turned.

A bright flash cut off Proctor's sentence and made him avert his eyes. When he blinked them clear, four men in the red coats of the British marines blocked his way, two bullies and two officers. The senior officer glared at Proctor;

the flash had come from something at his throat, but the light faded and Proctor no longer saw it. The marines snickered, mistaking Proctor's averted eyes for fear. The largest one loomed over Proctor, shoved him.

"Watch where yee're goin', and watch yeer manners," he said in a thick Scots accent.

Proctor's urge to strike back surprised him by its violence, but he mastered the feeling in an instant, not wanting to ruin his best jacket before meeting Emily's father. He lifted his head and met the big Scot's eyes.

"Come, be good fellows now," the senior officer said, his accent similar but not as strong. "There was no harm done."

The marines brushed past Proctor as if he were nothing. Proctor stared at the senior officer's back. The light at the man's throat had faded as suddenly as it had flashed. Proctor couldn't even say what he'd seen, as there was nothing unusual about the officer's uniform or its embellishments.

As they entered the coffeehouse, he saw Emily wave to him through the panes of the window. She shimmered like a mirage through the uneven glass. A similar ripple rolled through his stomach when he returned the greeting. He tugged at his collar, which felt as tight as his jacket. Meeting Emily's father couldn't be any worse than dealing with his own mother, could it? He stepped up to the entrance and pulled on the handle.

The door opened onto laughter and clattering crockery and the scent of pipe tobacco. Dozens of chairs and benches crowded the long, narrow building, with brass candlesticks on every table, though only a few of them were lit. The walls were bare, not that you could see much of them with all the people gathered—a variety of British officers, periwigged officials, and ambitious merchants, all talking over one another. Two black slaves, one laden with cups, the other with platters, ran from table to table. The British marines Proctor had bumped into moved to the back of the room.

Emily sat at a table up front. She had arranged her cap so that her black curls spilled out of it; the yellow silk ribbon in the back matched the piece she had given Proctor as a keepsake. He reached into his pocket and brushed it with his thumb. Although she sat with her hands folded delicately in her lap, her large eyes were bright and mischievous. Proctor couldn't help himself and grinned back at her.

The man sitting at the table rose and cleared his throat. Thomas Rucke, sugar merchant. Emily's father. The resemblance was remarkable for the way it transmuted her own features: her black hair matched his in color, but her curls were his unruly tangle, her round face became jowls and a second chin, and her pink cheeks reddened into his veins and sunburn. Emily's butter-colored silk dress was even outmatched by her father's sumptuously tailored jacket and ornate lace cuffs.

Rucke's thick eyebrows curved down in a disapproval that mimicked the shape of his mouth. "Emily," he said. "You didn't tell me that you planned to introduce me to a mute."

Emily's cheeks flushed. Proctor tore off his hat and stepped forward, offering his hand. "I'm sorry, sir. My name is—"

"Proctor Brown. Yes, I know. I've heard entirely too much about you already." Rucke ignored the offer of a hand and sat down impatiently, waving his plump fingers at Proctor to take the third seat. "Let's get this over with."

Proctor bumped the chair against the table, shaking the candelabra as he sat.

"It's good to see you again, Mister Brown," Emily said, more formally than Proctor had ever heard her speak.

"And you also, Miss Rucke," he replied, in the same tone but with just a hint of mockery. He could see her suppress a grin.

"I'll be blunt with you, Brown," Rucke said. His hands were spread flat on the table and he stared at them as if he had a point of argument for every finger. "One of the reasons I sent my beloved Emily away from Boston to the more rural climate and estate in Lexington was that I wanted to remove her not only from the tumult and mobs of the city, from the precipitous actions of those pernicious Sons of Liberty, but also, with so many officers and other gentlemen about, from the temptation of liaisons that would be ill advised because of her relative youth. But for three months now, she's done nothing but talk about you until I finally agreed to arrange this dinner."

Not exactly the cheerful welcome Proctor had hoped for. He spread his own hands on the table. "I'm flattered that she thinks so well of me, sir."

"Daddy, I think once you get to know Proctor—"

Rucke's stern look made Emily wilt under her bonnet and fall silent. Turning back to Proctor, he said, "You understand that it will be best if we get this all out in the open and put an immediate end to this unsuitable courtship."

Proctor leaned forward and matched Rucke's expression. "Sir, I came down to Boston to visit my aunt and for the honor of meeting you. But for Emily's sake, I would have walked all the way to Georgia. I'm willing to undertake whatever is necessary to convince you of the seriousness of my intentions."

Emily blushed again. Proctor would have given her a wink, but Rucke watched him directly, so he held the older man's gaze.

After a moment, Rucke looked away, raised his hand, and shouted across the room. "Hannah!"

An older woman made her way to their table, wiping her hands on her greasy apron. "Good afternoon, Mister Rucke, and the young gentleman, and the young lady," she said. "What may I bring you?"

"What would you like to drink, dear?" Rucke asked his daughter.

"Since this is the Coffee-House, I would dearly love to have a cup of coffee," Emily said brightly.

"The young lady will have tea," Rucke grumbled. "Some Madeira for myself. What do you want, Brown?"

"Beer. Pale ale if they have it."

Hannah ducked her head. "As you wish, sir."

"Beer?" Rucke sneered when she had gone. "That's a farmer's drink."

"That might be because I'm a farmer," Proctor answered.

Rucke glanced at Emily and then leaned forward. "Which is exactly my problem with this youthful fancy."

"Daddy!"

"No—I did not raise my daughter to become a farmer's wife." Turning to Proctor, he said, "Do you think a farmer could keep her in the manner to which she has been raised?"

Proctor leaned forward in response. "Sir, she knows how I live and it doesn't seem to frighten her exactly."

"Which is what I've already told him," Emily said.

Rucke waved this off. "That's the foolishness and inexperience of youth. Your farm would start to look very small to her—like a cage, Emily—with the passage of time."

"Oh, it won't always be such a small farm, sir," Proctor said.

Rucke leaned back and studied Proctor again, as if there might be more to him than a too-small jacket. "What exactly do you mean by that?"

"We've got more than sixty acres. With only the three of us there—my father, my mother, and myself—there's room to grow. Next year, I'll buy two heifers for the pastures. And with the fields fallow much of these past ten years, they'll yield a better harvest of corn to take them through the winter. The stand of trees at the back of the farm has been untouched for a long time too. They're big enough now that I can cut them down and mill them for a new barn first, and then, in a few more years, a new house."

"You can only get so far with sixty acres, boy, no matter how you use it," Rucke said. But he was interested.

Proctor stole a glance at Emily, and she gave him a small, encouraging nod.

"I plan to sell the beef here in Boston and save the money," Proctor said. "Old man Leary lives just over the hill, and his daughters moved off to Connecticut. Once I've saved enough, he'll sell his farm to me and go live with them. Then I can rent out his house and expand my herd into his fields. I'll be the richest farmer in Lincoln inside five years."

"Ten years at the least, with that plan," Rucke said. He leaned out of the way as Hannah returned with their drinks. Rucke told her to bring them plates of chicken and whatever else was fresh in the kitchen.

Emily poured her tea, saying, "I'd much rather have a cup of coffee."

"It's a foul liquid. The colonials would never drink it if there wasn't this nonsense over the tea stamps," Rucke said. He patted her hand. "Coffee is beneath you,"

Proctor sipped his beer and found it dark and bitter. Voices rose in argument behind them, chased by the scuff of feet and furniture. Proctor twisted in his seat to look, just in time to see a golden light flash so bright it made his head ache and his hand knot into a fist. The light faded the instant the scuffle broke up, and Proctor saw that it came from the same British officer he had encountered outside.

"Do you know who that man is?" Proctor asked.

"That's Major Pitcairn, John Pitcairn," Rucke said. "One of the best officers we have in the colonies. Completely and utterly fearless, would charge a line of bayonets with no more than a butter knife. His men love him. Why do you ask?"

"We bumped into each other once," Proctor said absently. He could have sworn he'd seen a gold medallion flash at Pitcairn's neck, but when he peered close, there was nothing. The big marine caught him staring, and Proctor glanced away.

Rucke refilled his glass of wine. "You're thinking too small, Brown."

Proctor was shaken out of his thoughts. "What do you mean?"

"With the cattle," Rucke said. "Think bigger. Do you think Boston's a big city, Brown?"

"Biggest I've ever seen, though I hear Philadelphia's twice the size."

Rucke laughed heartily. "Boston has fifteen, maybe twenty thousand people, and that includes every jack-tar who jumps off a boat to get drunk in the taverns. Now, London, London she's a city—seven hundred thousand people living there, Brown. You could drop Boston down whole in the London docks and not find it again for three days."

Emily caught Proctor's attention and rolled her eyes. The greatness of London was one of her father's favorite topics.

"You don't say, sir?" Proctor replied.

"I do say. That's why these Sons of Liberty are spouting nonsense when they talk about breaking free from England. The world's a big place, but the empire makes it small. We're all part of one big English family, and we'll all profit more if we stand together." He swallowed his wine and thumped the glass on the table. "You're on to something with the cattle. Massachusetts already ships beef to Virginia and the Carolinas, even to Barbados and some of the other islands. They're too busy growing tobacco or sugar to raise beef, so they pay top pound for it. That trade's going to grow, and a young man poised to take advantage could make himself a fortune."

"And end up richer than the richest farmer in Lincoln?" Proctor asked.

Rucke laughed heartily. "Perhaps." With that, he started in on everything he knew about the business end of beef, from butchering to salting to shipping to markets. Emily seemed pleased. She sneaked smiles at Proctor, which he returned as surreptitiously and enthusiastically as possible. His beer turned out not to be so bitter after all, and before he realized it the pint was gone and he excused himself to visit the necessary house, not just to relieve himself but to relax and collect his wits. If Rucke meant to help him trade beef, Proctor could advance his plan by years, and he and Emily could get married that much sooner. That was even better than making a fortune.

He pushed his way between sharp-elbowed men smoking long-stemmed pipes and junior officers quaffing rum or sipping bowls of chocolate. He smelled the privy as he passed through the back door.

"Look 'ere, it's the runaway apprentice," said a thick Scots voice behind him. Proctor spun. The four marines had followed him out the door.

"The one too big for his wee jacket," mocked the huge Scot.

They all laughed, except for Pitcairn, who said, "Bring him to me."

The huge Scot and another man with bushy red sideburns seized his arms. Proctor was strong—you didn't plow and cut wood and harvest grain without being able to take care of yourself—but he didn't react. The last thing he wanted was to return to Emily and her father after a dunk in the privy.

Pitcairn stepped in close. "Why were you staring at me inside?"

Proctor glanced at the spot on Pitcairn's chest where he thought he'd seen the medallion. "I wondered who you were."

"He's one of His Majesty's officers," the big man grunted in his ear. "That's all ye need to ken."

"You have the general appearance," Pitcairn said, "and, dare I say, the particular arrogance of many of these so-called Sons of Liberty I've seen around Boston since my arrival."

"Sons of something is right," the huge Scot said.

"I'm the son of Prudence Brown, and no one else," Proctor replied.

"See, he's not shaking or trying to bargain for his freedom," Pitcairn told the others, almost respectfully. He pulled off his gloves. To Proctor, he said, "I want to show you something. A friendly demonstration."

Proctor tried to pull his arm free, on the chance he could escape inside, but the big man tightened his hold. The other grabbed his right arm with a grip like iron.

"William," Pitcairn said to the fourth marine, the pink-cheeked officer in the brand-new coat, who had so far avoided Proctor. He bore a striking resemblance to the older man, with a similar widow's peak and aquiline nose—very likely they were father and son. "Be so good as to lend me your knife."

"Sir?" William seemed surprised.

"Your knife, *damn* it."

He reached inside his jacket and unsheathed six inches of steel. Proctor struggled to get away, but the huge Scot behind him clamped one hand over his mouth and squeezed him in a one-armed bear hug that pinned his left arm at his waist.

With a nervous glance at Proctor, William flipped the knife in his hand and passed it hilt-first to his father. Pitcairn pressed the tip into his thumb until it drew blood, then held up his bloody thumb for Proctor to see.

"Don't worry," he said. "The knife is for you to use."

Fear knotted Proctor's stomach. He struggled to get away without striking the huge Scot or doing anything more to provoke the marines. He looked at William, who dropped his gaze and stepped away.

A cold smile crossed Pitcairn's lips. He pried Proctor's hand open and pressed the hilt into his palm, then squeezed Proctor's fingers closed around it. The marine with the red whiskers chuckled as he clamped his rough fist over Proctor's hand. The knife edge gleamed in the sunlight.

Pitcairn licked the blood off his thumb and held his arms open nonchalantly, stepping closer.

Twisting his head from side to side, Proctor tried to talk through the big Scot's suffocating paw. He tried to push himself away, but his toes barely touched the ground. No jury would convict him for attacking a British officer, not under these circumstances—but he doubted any jury would believe his version of events.

Pitcairn nodded to his men. The big Scot held him tight as Red-whiskers pulled Proctor's arm back and thrust the blade at Pitcairn's stomach. Proctor struggled to divert it, but the knife was already moving toward the officer's white waistcoat.

Proctor's forearm felt as if it had slammed into stone. The tip of the blade snapped off, flying away to nick the sleeve of Proctor's jacket.

Pitcairn stood there with his arms still open, one eyebrow curled up like a question mark.

Proctor panted through the big hand clamped over his mouth. What had just happened?

The circle of light glowed at Pitcairn's throat again. Proctor detected the outline of a chain at his neck and a medallion of some sort under his shirt.

Pitcairn pried the knife out of Proctor's hand and returned it to William. "I'll replace it with a better one," he promised.

"There's no need, sir," William mumbled.

The big Scot released Proctor from his bear hug and shoved him aside.

The door opened behind them, and Hannah stuck her head out into the alley. Seeing the expression on Proctor's face, she glanced quickly up at the marines and said, "Has there been some trouble here?"

"No, ma'am," Proctor said. He tugged his coat back into place. "These gentlemen were just giving me a demonstration in the superiority of London knives."

She looked puzzled. Major Pitcairn said, "We were trading opinions. We both learned a few things."

"As long as all the gentlemen are satisfied and none of the other customers are disturbed," she said, and then she tossed a plate of bones and garbage over the side of a small fence, where a pig roused itself from muddy slumber and starting rooting through it.

The door closed behind her. Pitcairn studied Proctor judiciously. "It's essential for you colonials to realize that you can't hurt us."

"I had no desire to hurt you," Proctor snapped. He would have added *before,* but he was still shaky.

"You're full of spirit, but that spirit ought to be aimed against the French and Spaniards and other godless papists, not against your fellow Englishmen."

"My father fought against the French in the last war," Proctor said. "We're not afraid of a fight."

"Don't be so eager for one either," Pitcairn replied. "You are fools to think that you're better off without the empire. Spread that word among your fellows."

The big marine shoved Proctor aside, and the four of them peeled away to exit through the gate. Proctor turned away to go inside when a hand gripped his arm. It was William, the young officer, and he held his other hand open in a gesture of peace.

"The knife was just tinfoil," he whispered.

Proctor snorted in disbelief. "Tinfoil?"

"Yes, that's all," he said. "A joke, no harm done."

Proctor shrugged his arm free from William's grip. "No, no harm done."

"We're all one people, Englishmen, no matter which side of the ocean saw our birth. There's no need for us to start fights with one another."

For people who didn't want a fight, they did an awful lot of provocation. "I don't recall starting anything," Proctor said. "Now, if you'll excuse me."

His blood was still racing as he returned to the coffeehouse, squeezing up against the wall to let another man pass on his way to the privy. He threaded his way through the crowd and returned to the table where Emily sat alone.

"Where were you so long?" she asked. "And what's the matter? You look upset."

He slid into his seat. "I'm fine."

She reached under the table, her fingers finding his hand. He was looking over his shoulder at the back door when he felt her give his hand a little squeeze. "I think Daddy likes you," she said.

"Of course he likes me."

He had answered more than half distracted, still trying to understand what he had just witnessed. He realized he'd made a mistake the instant Emily's hand yanked free of his. She pushed her chair back and sat up straight.

"It's nice to see that you're not *too* full of yourself," she said. "Humility is such a rare trait in young men."

"I'm sorry, Emily, it's just . . . just . . ."

"Just what, Mister Brown? Spit it out."

"It's just that it wasn't a tinfoil knife." There. He'd spit it out.

"What are you talking about?"

"The knife that British marine had, it wasn't tinfoil." It had nothing to do with the knife, Proctor realized. Major Pitcairn had been wearing a protective charm about his throat. That's what Proctor had seen. It shone actively anytime the major was threatened, even by so little as a bump in the street. "It was magic."

"Magic?" Emily's face was puzzled, as though she were trying to figure out if he was joking.

Proctor opened his mouth, but no explanation formed on his lips. He'd said too much.

"Hannah said she saw you talking to Major Pitcairn," Rucke interrupted, returning to the table with a plate of roasted chicken, which he thumped down on the table. "Dig in. She thought there might have been a problem, but I see that you're fine."

"I bumped into the major again," Proctor said. "We talked about London and steel."

"Good." Rucke squeezed his large body into his seat. "That's a smart lad. Always make use of all your connections. If you can sell beef to the beefeaters, you're well on your way to making your fortune." He cleared his throat. "Emily tells me you serve in the colonial militia."

"Not just the militia, Daddy, but the minutemen," Emily said. Though her voice was cooler than it had been before.

"I don't understand the difference," Rucke said.

"The minutemen are required to do additional training," Proctor explained. "We have to be able to scout trails, run longer distances, reload and fire faster. And we have to be ready to fight at a moment's alarm."

"It sounds like the sort of foolishness that takes time away from honest work," Rucke said. "And it's the kind of thing that the rabble-rousers in this colony—Otis, Adams, Hancock, their sort—are using to raise up the folks against the royal governor. I'm concerned that you would be part of that, Brown."

Though she sat perfectly primly, Emily pressed her toe against Proctor's foot to let him know this was an important question to her father.

Proctor pulled a drumstick off the chicken, tearing off a piece of the meat. "My father served in the militia, during the last war with the French and their Indian allies. They didn't have the minutemen then, but he was a ranger, which is similar. If I'm going to do anything, I want to do it to the best of my abilities, just like he did. And he'd be disappointed in me if I didn't do my duty to the colony as he had done. So that's one reason."

"And the other?" Rucke asked, following Proctor's example and tearing off the other drumstick.

Proctor put the meat in his mouth and chewed it a moment to give himself time to think. He swallowed, saying, "All the men in my community belong to the militia. Not just in Lincoln, but in Concord and Lexington, and all the towns around. So it's a great means to reinforce connections. That's how I came to find out that old man Leary was interested in selling his farm."

Rucke chewed on his own food before he finally nodded, if not in approval then at least in understanding. Emily relaxed, taking her foot off Proctor's.

"When you get ready to move your cattle toward Boston market," Rucke said, "you might want to begin by contacting a man named Elihu Danvers. Danvers has a house near the mouth of the river, across from Cambridge. Though he's no great sailor anymore, he moves goods around the bay—"

As he continued with his advice, Proctor grinned at Emily around his mouthful of chicken. Of course her father liked him.

She smiled back, but with tighter lips; beneath that smile lingered worry over his unexplained comment about magic.

Eventually, Proctor would have to figure out a way to explain the magic. He wouldn't be able to keep it secret from her, not if they were going to be together. He reached under the table, wiped his fingers on his breeches, and then stretched his arm to try to touch her hand. A huge ripping sound stopped Rucke in the middle of his description of the harbor shipping lanes.

"What was that?" he said.

Proctor looked over his shoulder at the torn seam in his linen jacket and sighed. "That is what happens when you grow more than you expected."

Chapter 2

Proctor dreamed he heard a gunshot and it woke him, or else a gunshot stirred him from his dreams.

Either way, he lay half awake in bed. The full moon was past its apex, shining down through the gap in his curtains, so it was a few hours before the break of dawn. He thought of Emily and the next chance he might have to see her. As he tugged up the wool blankets and rolled over to go back to sleep, a horse galloped down the Concord Road. The hoofbeats grew closer, and a voice shouted across the spring fields.

"The regulars are coming! The regulars are coming!"

The Redcoats were marching.

Sleep sloughed off him. When Proctor had returned from Boston a few days ago, his militia captain had passed the word to be ready. The Redcoats were planning on taking the supplies from the armory in Concord. Proctor jumped from bed and dressed in an instant, tugging suspenders over his shoulders as the door creaked open below. He ducked his head when he came to the narrow steps and ran downstairs. Outside, the chickens cackled in their coop.

A candle flickered in the kitchen. His father sat shut-eyed in the corner, propped in a high-backed chair, wrapped in blankets. Light snagged on the pale scar across his forehead from when he'd been scalped and left for dead during the French and Indian wars.

There'd be no chance of anything like that tonight. The

regular army and the colonial militia, they were all Englishmen at root. A show of force would remind the royal governor of that, just as it had in February at Salem.

Proctor retrieved his father's old doglock musket and tin canteen from the cupboard. Powder horn and hunting bag went over his left shoulder, hatchet in his belt, hat in hand. He reached for the door, but it swung open in his face.

His mother barged in with a lantern in her hand. She unloaded two eggs from her dress pocket into a bowl on the table. "Where're you off to in such a hurry?" she asked.

"To muster—the Redcoats are marching on the armory."

"Not without a scrying first you aren't."

"Mother, there isn't time."

"I've been awake all night with worry, because I knew something was coming. Now that I know what it is, I'll not risk you dying from the guns of the Redcoats without a glimpse of the future first." She blew on her hands and rubbed them together for warmth.

Prudence Brown was ten years younger than her husband, but years of labor had aged her like a tree on a cliff. She was deeply rooted and could withstand any storm, even if she was too weather-worn to bear much fruit. Nothing could dissuade her once she had a notion to do something.

Truth was, Proctor wanted to see what was coming too. He propped his musket against the door and put down his hat. "Let's be quick about it."

She fetched another bowl, a pitcher of water, and moved the candle to the center of the table. Proctor held the chair for her. Wooden legs scuffed across the floor as he pulled his own seat catty-corner to hers.

She nudged the broad shallow bowl to the middle of the table and poured water in it. Drops splashed cold and sharp onto the back of Proctor's hand.

One by one, she retrieved five small candle stubs from her pocket and handed them to Proctor, who arranged them in a circle around the bowl. She frowned, made minor adjustments in their position, then lit them with the candle. A honeyed scent spread across the table.

Proctor tapped his shoe impatiently, then forced his foot to still. The other minutemen would be marching without him, and scrying didn't always require any candles or rituals.

His own talent had appeared by accident, no rituals required. He'd been carrying in the eggs and dropped one—it'd practically leapt out of his hands, an egg near to hatching that left the tiny chick inside sprawled dead, wet in the dirt. Without knowing why he said it, Proctor announced that his friend Samuel was dead. The next day they heard that Samuel had been shot by Redcoats during a riot in Boston. That's when Prudence Brown finally told her son about the family talent for witchcraft, passed down generation to generation from their roots in Salem. His mother's maiden name was Proctor; one of her ancestors, John Proctor, had been hung as a witch during the trials.

He'd have to tell Emily about the magic too. He was determined to do it sooner rather than later, in case someday their children, if they should be blessed that way, showed the talent.

Prudence Brown turned the two brown eggs over in her hands, squinting at the specks.

"I'm surprised you could find any eggs this time of night," he said.

"The hens lay more at the full moon." She pursed her lips, selecting one, and had it poised to crack on the edge of the bowl.

Over in the corner, Proctor's father moaned and rocked so hard his chair banged against the wall. Proctor winced—his father hadn't been the same since his apoplexy.

His mother switched eggs. She tapped the second one on the edge of the bowl, letting the white drain from the cracked shell into the water.

Her free hand sought Proctor's, gave it a squeeze. "Holy Father, who art in heaven, hallowed be Thy name," she prayed.

Proctor leaned forward to study the picture formed by the egg white.

"If I have found grace in Thy sight, then show me a sign that Thou speakest with me. Be Thou a light in the darkness of days, showing us the way forward, that we might know the path Thou wishest us to take."

A shudder ran through her arm. The eggshell crunched in her palm, and the yolk splashed out into the middle of the bowl.

They both flinched. Proctor didn't know if it meant anything or was just an accidental spasm. She didn't say.

The yolk floated in the center like the sun reflected in a pond. Candlelight slicked off its thick bulge as egg white filmed over the surface, forming ghosts in the water. A streak of red blood trailed off the yolk into the white.

Hairs went up on Proctor's neck. He could feel a vision gathering, like bees to a hive, in the back of his head, but he wasn't ready for it yet.

His mother flicked the eggshell pieces onto the table and wiped her hand on her apron. She licked her right forefinger and traced the name of the angel Gabriel across the circle of water. Gabriel, the messenger, revealer of the future.

The yolk swirled around, off-center, as reflections from the candles danced with one another. A sharp intake of breath and his mother pulled her hand back to the edge of the bowl.

She swallowed, then tugged Proctor's finger up to the bowl. "Take a moment to sweep your mind clean," she said.

He nodded acquiescence, but the broom in his head chased futilely after the stray thoughts. The other minutemen would already be on their way, and he didn't want to look like a Johnny-come-lately. Then a tightness formed in his chest, the way it always did when the sight was coming on.

"Heavenly Father," he said. "If it pleases Thee, give me a sign, so that I may better know Thy will."

His eyes drifted shut.

He saw a militiaman, an officer, on the green in the pale before dawn. A horse stamped through the grass—its flanks, the rider's boots, blocking his view of the militiaman's face. This vision was clearer, more vivid than any Proctor had ever scryed. He saw the mounted Redcoat officer's face flush with anger. A golden coin of fire burned at the Redcoat's throat.

Pitcairn.

Pitcairn leaned over and aimed a pistol at the militiaman's back. He was going to shoot—

A sudden bang made Proctor's eyes blink open, but it was only his father's chair cracking into the wall. The old man moaned as if he'd been wounded.

Proctor breathed deeply and fell back into the vision. At first everything was white, like fog, only dry and sharp—the smoke from musket fire. The bitter taste of black powder ran across his lips. A single line of red bled through the white haze. Then more lines of red, slashing across the back of his lids until they resolved into shapes of men, marching—no, running—away. The backs of the Redcoats. A sense of their fear, of his own elation, flushed through him.

His eyes opened.

"And what did you see?" his mother asked quietly.

Pulling his hands away from the bowl, he said, "I saw the Redcoats, Mother. Marching back to Boston, in a fine hurry."

"Is that all?"

He nodded firmly.

Her mouth tightened and she jabbed a finger into the yolk, breaking it. She whipped the egg into the water, mixing it all together.

"I heard gunfire," she said. "And I think I saw men shot and dying."

"That last part is your fear talking. I didn't see anything like that, only the Redcoats marching off."

"It would gratify me deeply if you were not to muster," she said. "Let other mothers with children to spare send theirs, and not ask me to risk my only child."

Proctor couldn't blame her, not with his father all but gone. But he had to do his duty. "I'm on the roster, Mother, so I have to muster. Don't worry, we just need to show the governor our resolve to stand up for our rights. It won't come to shooting."

Maybe a single round of warning fire, just for show, like in his vision, and the Redcoats would march back to Boston. If only he knew what the golden coin at the Redcoat officer's throat meant. If only he could be sure it was Pitcairn.

He rose to go. His mother leaned over and blew out the five candles in one breath. "Be cautious," she said. "The future is a blank road to me like it has never been before."

"I won't do anything to put myself in harm's way," he said, picking up his hat and musket. "Besides, you know what Miss Emily would do to me if I got myself hurt."

His mother smiled, just as he'd hoped. She was almost as fond of Emily Rucke as Proctor was. The two of them were a bit young to be getting married yet, at only twenty and nineteen. But in truth, he expected to rightfully take over the farm soon if his father's health continued to fade, and he and Emily could live there with his mother.

"You best hurry on then," his mother said. She wrapped an end of bread and a slice of cheese in cloth, and tucked it in his pocket. "You wouldn't want them to muster without you."

"No, ma'am," he answered. He paused at the door and looked back to see his mother fussing with the blankets around his father's shoulders. He tipped his hat to her and ran out into the night.

The wind gusted, the air chillier than he expected. He stopped at the well to fill his canteen. When he was done, he pulled Emily's yellow ribbon from his pocket and tied it to the canteen buckle. Smoothing the silk through his fingers made him eager to see her again.

He crossed the pasture toward the road, his path broken by boulders. Lights flickered like stars in distant windows, forming a constellation of his neighbors. Shadows moved through the moonlight on the road ahead.

"Hold up," he shouted.

Someone called back, and the shadows paused. Proctor ran across the pasture, his horn, bag, and canteen banging against his sides. He climbed the stone wall that lined the road. The moon was bright enough to illuminate the faces of the men. There was old Robert Munroe, carrying the same heavy Queen's Arm musket that he carried during the last war when he fought beside Proctor's father. Square-jawed Everett Simes and his nephew Arthur were also there. Arthur had turned fifteen back in January, but he was small enough to pass for twelve. Although he was too young to be enrolled on the official militia rosters, he showed up to every muster.

"Good morning, Proctor," old Munroe said, tugging at his beard. "Your father not coming?"

"No, sir," Proctor answered. "His health won't allow."

"No, didn't think so. It's too bad. He was always a good un in the thick of it. Sure hope you take after him some."

"I could do without seeing the sharp end of an Indian tomahawk," Proctor said, and the other men chuckled. He started one way and they turned the other. "Shouldn't we be headed into Niptown to muster?" he asked.

The locals called the new town of Lincoln Niptown because it had been made from a nip of Concord, a nip of Lexington, and a nip of Bedford, sitting in a spot amid all three. Proctor still went to church at the meetinghouse in Concord, because that's where his family had always gone, and he served with the militia in Lincoln because that was where he was assigned. In a way he felt like part of all three towns, and like part of none of them. Someday he would have to choose a spot and make it his own.

"Cap'n Smith says that a few of us ought to fetch back a firsthand report of the situation from Lexington," Arthur explained. "So that's where we're going."

"Well, all right then," Proctor said, and he started in the other direction.

"Say, Proctor, we'll march right past the Rucke place, won't we?" Everett asked.

"Hadn't really thought about it," Proctor said, "but you may be right." He tried to sound as if he were talking about the weather, but he was eager to change the subject before they started teasing him. Arthur carried a long fowling piece for his weapon, so Proctor said, "You going bird hunting there, Arthur?"

"Sure," Arthur answered back, deadpan. "Plan to shoot some redbirds if I see 'em."

Robert Munroe and Everett Simes laughed, so Proctor chuckled with them, but the remark made him uncomfortable. Sure, there'd been some conflict between the soldiers and the colonists. Despite his unpleasant encounter with Pitcairn, though, they were all Englishmen in the end. Just like Emily's father said. They might squabble with one another the way a large family always did, but in the end they'd set aside their differences and make things right because it was better for everybody. It wouldn't come to shooting.

The other three began to chatter about how many Redcoats might be marching out of Boston, and how many militiamen would show up to fight them. Proctor walked in silence, slowly drawing ahead. As they passed through the swampy land west of Lexington, the wind played odd tricks with sounds, bringing snatches of voices from homes too far away to see. Every farmhouse between Cambridge and Salem was awake by now, having the same conversation about Redcoats and militia.

When Proctor rounded Concord Hill and came in sight

of the rooftops of Lexington, the large, familiar house ahead was lit up bright as day. Even from a distance, he recognized the feminine silhouette in the main window.

As he ran ahead and up to the porch, the silhouette disappeared. He was reaching for the brass knocker when the door flew open. A heavy brown woman stood there in a dress thrown hastily over her shift.

"Sorry to come calling so late, Bess," Proctor said, addressing the house slave Thomas Rucke had brought with him from a voyage to the West Indies. "I wondered, if Miss Emily was awake, if I might have a brief word with her."

"She right here, be out in a second." Sleep filled Bess's eyes, and she frowned as somebody behind her nudged her gently aside. It was Emily, in one of her best dresses, despite the hour. More dark curls than usual tumbled out from under the edges of her cap.

"Well, this is certainly an unexpected visit," she said. She glanced at his weapons and her face turned cool. "I can't imagine what you're grinning at."

Proctor dropped his gaze and his smile. "Might be because I'm looking at the sweetest woman I know."

"You only say that because my father is in the sugar trade."

"I'd think you were the sweetest woman in the colonies if your father traded lemon rinds." She still wasn't smiling back. Bess pushed past them, a drowsy-eyed chaperone, shawl over shift, carrying a basket of darning. She grunted as she eased herself into the porch rocker, spreading the work on her lap as the wood creaked rhythmically. Proctor said, "I think I made a good impression on your father."

"You did," she said. "The only thing that concerns him is the militia business."

"Emily—"

A faint voice down the road called, "Brown?"

Proctor looked over his shoulder. Turning back to Emily, he said in a rush, "You must believe me, there's nothing to fear."

"Oh, Proctor," she said, wringing her hands. "There was another incident in Boston after you left. Father says those rebels, that mob behind that tea party and everything since, they want to start a war."

He shook his head. "No, no one wants to start a war."

"Brown!" The voice was stronger as the other three militiamen marched around the bend.

"I have to go, Emily."

She stared meaningfully at the yellow ribbon tied to his canteen. "If my affections mean anything to you at all, Proctor Brown, you will not be part of any mob tonight."

The creaking on the porch had stopped. Bess sat with her chin on her chest, the darning egg naked in her lap. Impulsively, Proctor took Emily's hand and leaned close to her. "You remember how I mentioned magic to you, when we were at the Coffee-House," he said in low voice.

"Yes," she said, more puzzled now than angry.

"Sometimes I can see a short ways into the future. You might call it scrying."

"It sounds like you mean witchcraft." She tried to pull her hand away, but he held on tight.

"It's not like that," he said. "It's like . . . like the parable of the talents. God gave me this talent, and He meant me to use it, not bury it. I used it tonight, and I saw the Redcoats marching back to Boston. So there won't be any shooting, and there won't be any war."

Emily yanked her hand away. Her eyes were startled wide.

"You done courting there, Brown?" Everett Simes's voice said right behind him.

"Yes, sir, I am," Proctor said. He straightened up, slid his thumb under his powder-horn strap to readjust it, and gave Emily a firm nod. "I was just telling Miss Rucke here there's nothing for her to worry about."

"Good eve, Miss Rucke," Everett said, squinting toward the east to see if dawn had poked its nose over the horizon.

"Or maybe it's good day. It'd be best if your father didn't come out to visit you. With his support for the governor and all, he might find a welcome made of tar and feathers."

"It's so pleasant to be threatened on my own front porch. I see the kind of company you've decided to keep, Mister Brown. Be so good as to call on me again when you can come alone." She went over to the rocker and shook the slave awake. "Come, Bess, we should go inside. It's too dangerous to be out here. Good day, gentlemen."

"It won't come to shooting," Proctor assured her.

She closed the door behind her without looking back.

Chapter 3

Proctor hopped off the porch and crossed the little yard to rejoin the militiamen. As they resumed their march toward Lexington Green, he considered whether he needed to go back to repair his understanding with Emily. She was high-spirited—he loved that trait in her, though it meant she upset easily. Likely she'd be fine in a day or two, once the current commotion had passed and she saw that he was right.

The conversation of the other men turned to the spring planting, and to Everett's trouble with one of his plow oxen, and from there to the milk trade with Boston. The air grew colder, and the men's breath frosted as they spoke. When the conversation came back around to the British, it shoved Proctor's thoughts from Emily to Pitcairn. The scrying confirmed his earlier sense: the gold medallion was definitely some kind of protective charm. He didn't know how it worked or what it meant, but the rest of his vision was clear enough: the Redcoats would march back to Boston.

They passed the Lexington burying ground, with its grave markers thrust up from the darkness like tripstones. The four men fell into a natural silence. Cattle lowed uneasily in the common pen as they came to the green.

Lexington Green was a triangle where two roads combined to go into Boston. They passed the schoolhouse at the wide end of the triangle and crossed the open grass toward the meetinghouse that sat at the point. A few small groups of militiamen moved like shadows across the green.

Maybe a dozen others, their faces lit by lanterns, were gathered around a cask of ale outside one of the houses that faced the green.

"Don't look like they're ready for the Redcoats," Munroe muttered. "If the Redcoats are truly coming."

"Don't look like there's more'n fifty men here total," Everett said.

"And that's with a thousand Redcoats marching from Boston," Arthur said. "How will we fight 'em?"

"There won't be any fighting—" Proctor started to say, but he was interrupted by a ragged volley of musket fire east of the green. He fumbled for his powder horn.

Old Munroe laughed at him, planted the butt-end of his weapon in the ground and leaned on it. "I think that's them as made up their minds to enter Buckman's tavern."

That's when Proctor heard casual whoops and laughter from the same direction. But of course—you couldn't carry a loaded weapon into a tavern. He relaxed, laughing at himself.

"We could go to the tavern," Arthur suggested hopefully, and his uncle glared at him.

"That'll be the best place to find Cap'n Parker," Munroe said. "He uses it as his headquarters when the militia drills."

They walked toward the tavern, passing the big oak tree and the bell tower. As they did so, a man came out of the tavern and crossed the road toward the green. Proctor would've walked past him in the moonlight, but Monroe stopped and lifted his chin in greeting.

"Good evening to you, Cap'n. We were just coming in search of you."

Parker stopped. He was a tall man in his mid-forties with a large head and high brow. He coughed into his fist, sick with consumption—his eyes and his cheeks were sunken from it, dark shadows even at night. "Good evening, Robert. Who're your friends?"

"These are the Simeses, cousins from up by Lincoln," Munroe answered. "And this is Brown. We picked him up on the road in."

"We're grateful for your hike, but it doesn't 'pear as though we'll see any Redcoats tonight after all," Parker told them. "I was just giving men permission to disperse to their homes, though a few decided to go into the tavern to warm themselves first."

Everett sighed loudly. "But if I go home now, I'll have to plow, and my ox isn't fit for it."

Parker chuckled and excused himself to take the same message over to the men gathered around the keg of ale. Arthur yawned and stared down the road toward Boston. "Guess we wasted our time."

"Not Proctor," Munroe said. "At least he had the chance to visit his sweetheart."

"And next time I see her, I can tell her I was right, that nothing happened," Proctor said. He was relieved. With luck, he could stop by Emily's house for breakfast and find some way to make her understand what he was trying to tell her about the talents.

He was shifting the bag and horn on his shoulder for the march back home when a man ran onto the green from the Boston Road.

"The regulars have passed the Rocks," the newcomer shouted. "They're only half a mile away!"

"What do we do?" Arthur asked.

"Keep a cool head," Proctor told him. "This'll be peaceful."

"Let's find Parker and see what he wants us to do," Munroe said.

The warning spread faster than their conversation. Before they could find Parker, a man ran out of the tavern and sprinted to the belfry. In seconds the bells were clanging. The sound drew Captain Parker and everyone else.

"Cap'n," Munroe shouted as he headed across the green. "Hey, Cap'n."

"Seems I was mistaken after all," Parker said, hurrying toward the noise. "The Redcoats are marching, and we mean to show them our resolve. Would you gentlemen be so good as to parade with my company?"

"That's why we came," Munroe said, and Everett said, "Guess I'll miss that plowing after all."

"What about the young gentleman?" Parker asked with a nod toward Arthur.

"I can stand in line," Arthur said.

Everett put a hand on his shoulder. "And do exactly as he's told."

"I thank you," Parker said, turning immediately away and yelling, "Billy! Billy, get your drum and beat to arms!"

The other three ran off to join the rest of Parker's gathering company. Munroe stopped and looked back at Proctor, who still hadn't moved. "You coming?"

There was still time for his scrying to come true, Proctor told himself. The Redcoats would march up, see the militia making their stand, and they'd turn around and go home, just like they had at Salem. If he was lucky, he'd still get to eat breakfast with Emily and make things right with her.

"I'm coming," he said, and he followed after them.

For the next few moments, Lexington Green reminded him of an anthill stirred up with a stick. Men ran in every direction at once. The coming dawn cast a pale gray twilight, so that everything took on the aspect of shapes emerging from a mist. Captain Parker shouted at the men to form a line at the wide end of the green. Men from the tavern reloaded their weapons as they ran to obey. Proctor and the other three took a spot on the far end of the line, closer to the Concord Road.

Captain Parker paced up and down the line, shouting, "Form up, form up!" A young boy was beating the drums, the bells still sounded in the belfry, and families, drawn by the noise, gathered by the schoolhouse, where they called to their husbands and sons for an explanation.

One of the militiamen left the line to go speak to his wife. Parker ran him down and shoved him back in line. "The time for second thoughts is done," he said, loud enough for everyone to hear him. "Now form up, just like you trained."

Munroe loaded his musket and fitted the ramrod in place under the barrel. He nudged Proctor. "You might want to feed that weapon if you plan to empty its guts."

"I'll wait," Proctor said. He looked down the line of men and made a quick count. "If it's sixty of us against a thousand Redcoats, there won't be any shooting."

Arthur finished loading his fowling piece. "Here they come," he said, his voice shaking. "Here they come now."

The Lexington drum was drowned out by the sound of the approaching drummers, and the first Redcoats marched around the bend beyond the meetinghouse. To judge by the brogue, it was an Irishman who set the pace, his accent carrying across the green as he yelled the soldiers on. They came fast, for all their delay in getting this far, and once they started they seemed to keep on coming, a long line of red uniforms stretching as far as the eye could see. Proctor tried to count them too, but the dawn twilight blurred their numbers. His heart began to pound—there were hundreds, maybe even a thousand of them. In contrast with the militia, they formed a line with startling alacrity, several ranks deep, as wide as the green, and not more than seventy yards away. A deadly range for massed fire.

They would march back to Boston. He had scryed it.

Three British officers on horses rode onto the green and galloped at the center of the colonial line. One of them waved a sword and yelled, "Throw down your arms! You rebels, throw down your arms, damn you!"

Pitcairn's voice. Unmistakable.

A flame of anger jetted through Proctor, a reaction to the protective charm that Pitcairn wore. He reached into his hunting bag for a ball to load his musket. The militia might have to make just one volley, so the Redcoats could save face when they returned to their barracks in Boston.

He had his ramrod in the barrel when Captain Parker approached the British officers. Parker met them eye-to-eye, speaking quietly. The officers blustered back, shouting orders at him to disarm his men.

A cry came down the line. "Don't fire unless fired upon."

Everett took up the order and repeated it to Arthur. "Hold your fire—we're not to start any war."

"But if they start it, we'll give it back to them," Munroe said. He put his flints and his lead balls into his hat and set it on the ground in front of him for quicker reloading. After a second, Everett followed suit.

Proctor finished loading his weapon and looked up to see that the situation had quickly deteriorated. Two of the mounted officers cantered across the green while Pitcairn continued to shout at Captain Parker. The mass of Redcoats had grown so deep, it was impossible to see if more were coming. Meanwhile, flashes of brown and russet appeared behind the stone walls surrounding the green, where men too cowardly to join the line of the militia took cover. Women and children bunched by the cattle pen and between the houses that lined the commons, straining for a view.

The Redcoats took up their battle cry, shouting, "Huzzah! Huzzah! Huzzah!"

The roar made Proctor's skin goose-pimple. Everett swallowed nervously.

"There won't be any shooting," Proctor told him.

Captain Parker finally turned away from Pitcairn, who was left mouth open in mid-rage, and walked back toward his company of militia.

"They won't listen to reason and mean to disarm us," Captain Parker shouted down the line. "And we'll have none of that. So take your arms and disperse. Go home at once."

"What do we do?" Arthur asked his uncle, looking more like twelve than fifteen.

"We'll disperse, that's the order," Everett said.

Proctor breathed a sigh of relief. He would stop by and talk to Emily on the way home, make things better there.

As the other men in the line started to break away in groups of two and three, Munroe pointed across the road behind them. "Let's stay off the main road. We'll circle the burying ground and cut back through the trees."

"That sounds good," Everett said, and he bent to pick up his hat and flints.

But the British regulars would not let them go.

Pitcairn had chased after Parker, circling his horse around him. "Order them to lay down their arms or by God every man on this field will end the day dead," Pitcairn shouted.

He pulled his pistol and aimed it at Captain Parker.

"Damn you, I order you to surrender."

That was when time slowed down, and Proctor felt like a fish swimming beneath the frozen surface of a winter pond. Pitcairn's horse stamped and whinnied, blocking Proctor's view of Captain Parker's face. Proctor felt a knot of tightness in his chest. Pitcairn leaned over and aimed his pistol at Captain Parker's back, clearly intending to shoot. A golden circle of light was spinning on his chest.

It wasn't right: a man who couldn't be stabbed with a steel knife, who couldn't be shot, shooting another man in the back at point-blank range.

"Hey!" Proctor raised his musket.

He heard a bang, like a chair slamming into the wall. When the smoke cleared from the end of his muzzle, Pitcairn stared at him. Untouched.

"Boy, what did you just do?" Munroe asked.

Time rushed forward again, like a mountain cataract when the ice melted. Scattered popping echoed around the green and a second later the Redcoats' line erupted in a wall of smoke shot with flame. Proctor turned to answer

Munroe just in time to see the old man's head split open by a lead ball, flinging him backward in a spray of blood.

What *had* he done? Proctor's training kicked in and he started to reload. The jumbled Lexington line, in the middle of dispersing, responded to the Redcoats with ragged shots. When the second British rank fired, men all around Proctor threw themselves to the ground.

Some of them went down for a different reason. Everett had taken a ball through his leg and was trying to stanch the flow of blood. Arthur stared at his uncle; his shaking hand spilled gunpowder everywhere but into his barrel. Behind them women screamed and children shrieked, some running forward through the gunfire to check on their husbands and fathers, while others scattered to their homes.

Across the green, British officers shouted for the next rank of soldiers to step forward while the others reloaded. Proctor tugged on Arthur's sleeve. "We best be on our way."

"I'm staying! I'm—"

"You take him," Everett said through gritted teeth.

Proctor didn't need permission. He grabbed the back of Arthur's coat and dragged him across the road toward the cemetery. They ran with their heads down as the guns cracked and another round of lead buzzed over their heads. The Redcoat order to fix bayonets and advance came from behind as the two of them passed the smithy and ran among the crosses and headstones.

"We aren't going to take that," Arthur said, twisting to get free. "We aren't just going to let them march in and tell us what to do and shoot us. We have to get my uncle!"

Proctor tightened his fist on the boy's jacket and kept running. He glanced at his musket—the firing pan was empty, the hammer down—he'd shot a second time but he couldn't recall aiming or pulling the trigger.

What he did recall was the way the Redcoats concentrated their fire around him, because he'd been the first to shoot. And Robert Munroe, who had survived the French and Indian wars alongside Proctor's father, was dead.

How was he going to explain himself to his father?

Or to Emily?

He'd had to do something. He knew his shot couldn't hurt Pitcairn. He couldn't just let Pitcairn shoot Captain Parker.

How was he going to explain himself to anyone who saw him take the first shot? He wouldn't be able to tell anyone how he knew Pitcairn was safe, or Parker was in danger. Not without bringing magic into it.

Shouts behind him were followed by more scattered shots. Proctor pushed Arthur's head down as they ran into the cover of the trees. "Left," he said, guiding the boy with a shove. They'd have to get back to the road before they stumbled into the swamp.

Proctor's vision from the scrying came back to him again. He hadn't just lied to his mother, he'd lied to himself.

The smoke of muskets.

The taste of black powder.

The Redcoats running.

Why had he assumed they were marching back to Boston? They were chasing the militia.

"We need to find our company and report," he told Arthur, who was too stunned to respond. And then with certainty unrelated to his particular gift, he added, "The real battle is only beginning."

They clambered over the stone wall when they came to the road. There was a light on in Emily's house.

Out of reflex as much as purpose, he headed toward her door. They'd have heard the shooting out this far, and she might be worried.

"Proctor?"

He stopped, turning at the sound of Arthur's voice.

"I thought we had to find our company and report," Arthur said. His face was still clouded by anger and fear.

Behind them, a musket shot echoed over the trees from the direction of Lexington—the Redcoats could be coming this way any moment.

"Right," Proctor agreed. "We better hurry."

As they jogged past Emily's house, Proctor took one last glance over his shoulder. He made a promise to himself to come back later today, as soon as things settled down, and talk to her then.

Assuming that things could settle down in one day.

Chapter 4

Arthur tugged on Proctor's sleeves. Warning beacons lit the hilltops to the west, alerting other towns. A moment later, the fitful wind carried snatches of church bells ringing the same message north and south. The countryside was rising against the British.

They lost those signs when they rounded Fiske's Hill and passed under the shadow of the high bluff that lined the road. Arthur stumbled, and Proctor hooked an arm under his shoulder and hauled him along. The poor kid was probably exhausted, but before Proctor could say anything encouraging, hoofbeats sounded on the road behind them.

"Let's hide, in case it's the Redcoats," he said. The road was lined with boulders and loose stones, topped with logs. Proctor banged his knee on a stump end as they vaulted a low spot and crouched where they wouldn't be seen. Arthur tried again to reload his fowling piece.

Proctor reached out and stopped him. The rider was a boy, a colonial, galloping hard toward Concord.

"Hey!" Proctor shouted, standing up to wave his arms. "Hey, come back! What's the news?"

The boy reined in, kicking up dirt as he turned around. "The Redcoats shot the militia at Lexington. Now they're marching for Concord!"

"We were at the green when they started shooting," Proctor said. "We saw them shoot Robert Munroe in the head."

Arthur pushed forward. "Do you have any word about

Everett Simes? He was injured—we had to leave him behind."

"I don't know all the names," the boy replied. "But they bayoneted some of the injured men, speared them like they were fish, and they shot Jonathon Harrington on his own doorstep, right in front of his wife."

Proctor's jaw dropped open. Arthur started back for Lexington, and Proctor grabbed him.

"I need to carry the warning ahead," the boy explained as his anxious horse spun in circles, and Proctor said, "God speed."

As the hoofbeats faded down the road, Arthur tried to pull free of Proctor's grip. "We've got to go back."

"There's no help for your uncle now." His own voice sounded hard to him despite the evenness of his words. "There'll be plenty to do ahead."

Arthur's lips rolled into a grim frown, and he set off for Concord at twice the pace he'd had before. Proctor jogged after him, but his thoughts trailed behind. How could his gift have been so wrong? Why hadn't he seen the Redcoats firing at the militia?

He hated the true answer. He had seen it in his scrying, but he hadn't wanted to believe it. He'd taken his ability for a gift before this, but now he had doubts. It could get men killed.

The fields and farmyards along the road were empty. At Hartwell's place, a trunk full of books and silver had been left by the barn. When Proctor and Arthur crossed the bridge at Tanner's Creek, even the tavern was empty. Closer to Concord, at Merriam's Corner, three generations of Merriams had gathered to barricade the road.

"The British killed men at Lexington," the youngest Merriam shouted as they approached. "They shot Robert Munroe's head off and stabbed Everett Simes— Oh, hey, there's Arthur."

"We were there," Arthur said. He looked over his shoulder, as if the bayonets might still be right behind them.

Proctor's glance shifted from face to face. Maybe fifteen men, all brave and angry. He tensed, wondering what they would say if they knew he'd been the first to shoot. He felt like he carried a stain on him, as if they already knew.

The youngest Merriam, outside without a hat, handed them cups of fresh water.

"They shot Jonathon Harrington in front of his own home, with his wife and children begging the Redcoats to spare his life," Michael Merriam told them. "He bled to death on his doorstep, and none of the regulars did a thing to help him."

"They'll do the same thing to you," Proctor said, wiping water from his chin. "There's no way you can stand against them."

"We don't mean to," Michael said. "We're just watching the road until they come. When we see their numbers, we'll fall back and join the militia in Concord."

"We'll see you there then," Proctor said. "We have to muster and report what we saw."

They said their good-byes and continued on toward Concord. The last stretch of road ran beneath the shadow of Arrowhead Ridge. "We could pick them off from up there," Arthur said, squinting up at it. "While they were marching below."

"Reckon we could," Proctor replied, though he had reservations. Picking off a few of them wouldn't make any difference to Robert Munroe or Everett Simes, but it might make the Redcoats slower to shoot the next time. Or quicker. That Major Pitcairn meant business, and he had nothing to fear.

Drums and fifes played in the distance. Several companies of militia were marching out of Concord. Proctor and Arthur stepped to the side of the road to let them pass. He only saw young faces in their ranks. It was the minutemen. His company from Lincoln brought up the rear.

Proctor saluted Captain Smith, who was only a couple of years older than himself. "Brown," Smith said as Proctor fell in beside them. "We marked you down absent at muster."

"I went into Lexington with Munroe and Everett Simes," Proctor said. "Saw the shooting there."

"I'll correct the muster. Was it as bad as we heard?"

Proctor swallowed hard, thinking again that it might all be his fault. "As bad, or worse, depending on what you heard. There must be close to a thousand Redcoats, and the major of the marines is fearless. He means to take our guns or kill us."

Smith nodded. "We're bound to see more fighting today now that they started it. You better find your place in line."

"Sir, can I keep Arthur Simes with me?"

Smith glanced back at Arthur, trailing doggedly behind Proctor, and must have seen the intensity in his eyes. "You can. But Arthur?"

"Yes, sir?" His voice trembled.

"You're not to put yourself in the way of any exceptional danger. Your mother would have my hide."

"It's a bit late for that," Arthur said. Proctor took his arm and let the column pass. They exchanged nods of greeting with the rest of the men as they went by until Proctor saw the face he was looking for: sandy hair framing ice-blue eyes above a sharp nose and cleft chin.

"Amos Lathrop," he said, falling in beside his friend. "It's good to see you."

"I understand you already heard the British guns," Amos said, and when Proctor shrugged an affirmation, he said, "Do you have to be so impatient to do everything?"

Proctor smiled from habit, though he didn't feel it inside. Being the only one to work their farm, and not having much family on either side, Proctor didn't have many close friends, but Amos was the closest.

Proctor made a quick count of the line. There were only a hundred minutemen present. "Where's the rest of the militia?" he asked.

"The militia captains voted to guard the town center," Amos said, more than a little disgust tinting his voice. "The minutemen companies thought it better to meet the Redcoats on the road, so we voted to do that instead. Here we are."

He sympathized with the minutemen's sentiment, but he thought it madness to divide their forces. "Do the captains know how many Redcoats there are?"

"We've heard there's a thousand," Amos said. "But it wouldn't matter if there were ten thousand. These are our homes. Somebody's got to go out to meet 'em."

Proctor sank into silence as they marched. It wasn't going to be a fair fight, not with one of the British officers using sorcery to protect himself. Proctor wondered if Pitcairn was the only one, or if others carried similar charms. There was no way to know, not from any distance.

And he was the only one who knew about the charm. He didn't know how to defeat it—it was becoming clear to him how little he knew about magic at all—but he had to atone for the harm he'd brought on Robert Munroe and Everett Simes and all the others. If he had a chance to take it from Pitcairn, he had to do it.

The companies left the road, threading their way among the weeds and rocks to take up a position along the hilltop overlooking Tanner's Creek, where they were joined by a dozen or so Merriams. Proctor reloaded his musket. All around him men arranged their lead, powder, and flint in the manner they preferred for fast reloading. Proctor kept his ready for another quick retreat. There was no way a hundred and ten men could stand against that many Redcoats.

The sun was up now, the sky blue and clear, with a brisk wind drying off the last of yesterday's rain. Birds flitted through the air, singing their spring songs. Proctor reached for his canteen. He curled the yellow ribbon around his finger while he sipped, thinking of the curls in Emily's hair.

Would it make any difference if he explained the magic to these men? He doubted that they would believe him, or that it would change their resolve if they did. Here they stood, outnumbered, in full knowledge of their choice, ready to face the most efficient and deadly military force in the world.

The "deadly" aspect was chief in his mind.

The sound of drums came over the hills ahead of the Redcoats. Some of the birds fell silent.

"Let's bow our heads in prayer," Captain Barrett called out. Proctor realized the deadly aspect wasn't chief in his mind only. He put both hands around the barrel of his musket, propped butt-end in the soil, and bowed his head.

"Heavenly Father," Barrett said. "You bring these tribulations upon us as a chastisement because we fall away from Your Holy Word. Use Your rod to guide us back into Your safe pastures. And beat off the English wolves. Amen."

"Amen," Proctor said, echoed by a hundred other voices.

He knew what some of the men would say; they'd say that talents like his, skills they'd call witchcraft, were part of any falling away from the Holy Word. Were they right? If he knew how to fashion a charm like Pitcairn's, would he make it for himself? Was it a Christian gift, made with God-given skill, like his mother insisted their talents were? Or was it made with some other kind of magic?

Sunlight glinted sharp off movement at the far edge of the horizon, and the faint sound of drums strengthened into the rattle of a quick march. The double line of British regulars crested the road. The morning sun behind them turned their coats as red as blood.

Amos didn't change his expression, but he let out a low, appreciative whistle.

"Them's the ones who stabbed my uncle," Arthur said.

A British officer rode ahead, twisting in his saddle to shout orders. Pitcairn. The drummers changed their cadence and the Redcoats spread out over the fields, forming a skirmish line opposite the minutemen. Men around Proctor began to speak up.

"Cap'n, there're too many of them."

"We could hold this hill for one or two rounds, Cap'n Barrett, but they'll flank us for certain."

"Don't care for the looks of that, sir."

Proctor agreed with them. His first resolve to do something to make amends melted away like the dew.

"We'll stay here until they get within a hundred rods," Barrett said finally. "Delay them that long, give more men time to muster in Concord. Then we'll make an orderly retreat back to the other companies."

Proctor tightened his fist on his weapon, and he saw Amos and a few other men nodding. They could do that much without feeling like cowards.

If the British gave them the chance to do it. The skirmish line came at them steady, eager to engage and expecting to win any contest of arms. They were less than a quarter mile distant when Barrett signaled to the drummer and the colonials began their slow, deliberate retreat. The militia drummers matched the rhythm of the British drummers, beat for beat, with the fifers playing similar tunes. It would have felt like one of the parades Proctor had seen in Boston, mixing regular army with the colonial militia, were it not for the deadly circumstances earlier that morning.

They marched into Concord with the British holding firm a quarter mile behind them. The rest of the militia companies were lined up in formation on the high hill across the road from the meetinghouse. The liberty pole stood behind them, a thin reed stark against the pale sky, next to a pole flying the town flag. The minutemen hurried up the hill to join the other companies.

The Redcoats still outnumbered the militia two to one.

They slowed down as they entered the town, but still they swept down the road with the practiced ease of a scythe at reaping.

Along the hilltop, townswomen had been carrying food to the men. Proctor snatched a warm piece of buttered bread from a pale, determined girl he'd never met. She glanced down at the Redcoats and hurried away with her basket before he could thank her. Arthur started after her, but Proctor put a hand on his shoulder and handed him the bread. While Arthur devoured that, Proctor reached in his pocket, crumbled off a piece of the cheese his mother had given him, and slipped it in his mouth, savoring the sharp taste. He hoped she wasn't too worried, though she must have heard the shots or the news by now. By the time he swallowed, the British forces were forming their own line. Behind Proctor, the Concord militia officers debated their course of action.

"What are we waiting for?" Arthur said. "Let's shoot them."

Eleazar Brooks, a gray-haired veteran from Lincoln and another friend of Proctor's father, stood near them in the line. "Careful, now. It will not do for us to begin a war."

"The war's already begun," Proctor said. He told Brooks what happened to Munroe and Everett.

Brooks sucked his teeth. "That's unfortunate. Munroe was a good man. But it's not a war yet, just some scattered shooting. If it's going to get worse, we must make sure the regulars are the ones as start it."

Could Proctor take comfort in that? That he hadn't started it, that it was up to the Redcoats? He wasn't comforted. Somehow he had to make things right.

Up and down the line, the older men were cautious and wanted to wait, while the young men were all for meeting the British and giving them a whipping. Captain Smith, of the Lincoln minutemen, ran toward them, mopping sweat from his forehead. "More militia are coming in," he said.

"We're going to retreat across the North Bridge to Punkatasset Hill, until our strength is equal to theirs."

"Another retreat?" Arthur asked. "Why?"

"The hill's a good choice," the veteran Brooks said. "It'll give us a clear view to see them coming. And it's a bigger field for us to make formation."

"It doesn't matter if we have a bigger field, if they've got the bigger force," Proctor said.

Then the drums and the fifes kicked up a tune, and Proctor retreated again through the town. Their double file stomped on the wooden planks as they ran across the North Bridge, drowning out the sound of the drums. They climbed Punkatasset Hill, a broad field that looked over the Concord River into the center of town.

The British force followed their retreat, occupying the abandoned bridge. Now they were blocking the way back to Emily's house, Proctor realized, and he still needed to go talk to her, to make things right somehow, so they could have the life together that they planned. Seeing the Redcoats marching so near called back his memories of the men shot at Lexington, the sharp smell of their blood mixed with black smoke, and all his plans with Emily felt as fragile as a man's life. One musket ball could destroy them.

Down below, the British commanders sent several companies across the bridge and north toward the mill. That drew angry exclamations from several of the men. "They know exactly where we hid the munitions," Brooks said. "That means there's been Tory spies among us."

One of the other Lincoln men said, "I hear that Rucke up from Lexington is one of them. He moved out here with his daughter just so's he could spy on the militias."

"That's a damned lie," Proctor snapped.

"Says who?" The man had a lopsided mouth that made it look like he was ready to bite someone.

Proctor balled his fist and stepped up to punch that ugly mouth. "Says me."

Eleazar Brooks shoved between them, holding up his hand for peace. "Save it for the Redcoats, boys. We'll be needing both of you afore the day is out."

The other man backed away. "That's fine with me," he said. "There'll be time to deal with Tory spies and their friends after the day is over."

"You make sure you know what you're talking about," Proctor said. A cold knot tightened in his chest, different from the one he had when scrying. The worse things got today, the harder it would be to make things right with Emily. He turned back to his place in line and tightened his grip on his musket.

"I haven't ever heard anything like that about Miss Emily's father," Arthur said quietly.

"Because it's a damned lie," Proctor growled back. Immediately he regretted it. "Forgive my language, Arthur. It wasn't meant to be directed at you."

"We'll show those damned scoundrels," Arthur replied, trying to match Proctor's tone. "And we'll give them something back for what they did to my uncle. If I see any of them lying there injured, I'll bayonet them myself."

Proctor swallowed his first real laugh since sunrise. "But you don't have a bayonet."

"Then I'll just use a hatchet," the boy said in deadly earnest, looking at the one in Proctor's belt.

A barking dog slammed into Proctor's leg, knocking him off-balance, before it chased another dog up the hill and into the mass of confusion there. Men's dogs had followed them from their homes and farms and frolicked as if it were a picnic.

In many ways, the hillside did resemble a church picnic. Laundry hung from the lines outside the house atop the hill. Besides the dogs, women and children ran back and forth from town with food and news. Old faces mixed with young, the black faces of slaves and former slaves mixed with the white. The officers gathered there were dressed in ordinary clothes; the colonel in charge wore an old coat, a flapped hat, and a leather apron. The Reverend Emerson, Concord's minister, was present in his dark coat, moving among the crowd to offer words of encouragement and prayers. He carried a musket instead of a cross.

"You don't look well, Proctor," he said.

"I saw some things at Lexington this morning, Reverend," Proctor answered, though he meant to say *did* instead of *saw*.

"Your Miss Emily lives up that way, doesn't she?" Emerson asked.

How like the Reverend. He seemed to remember everything about every member of his congregation as easily as other ministers remembered their Bible verses. "Yes, she does," Proctor said.

Emerson clapped him on the shoulder. "You get her away from her father and make an honest patriot of her."

Before Proctor could reply to that, Arthur tugged at his sleeve. "Look!"

A column of smoke rose from the town below.

"That's the town hall," Emerson said in alarm.

Everyone saw it. Before the Concord men charged down the hill on their own, the drums started beating, calling them to order. As they fell into a double line, Proctor realized there were at least two full regiments gathered, more than enough to take the bridge. With volunteers still coming in from outlying towns, they had almost a thousand militiamen now, as many men as the British force. Proctor felt a pride in his countrymen. They had no lack of courage or discipline.

He braced his feet as they marched down the slope. The colonel, in his leather apron, stomped along the length of the line. "Do not fire first," he reminded the men every few steps. "Don't be the first to open fire."

Proctor looked away, unable to meet his eyes.

Down the line someone called out, "What do we do once they fire on us?"

The colonel paused to answer him. "Then you remember your training and fire as fast as you can. Aim low for their bodies."

By that time, they had reached the bottom of the hill. The British soldiers guarding the bridge saw that they were badly outnumbered and retreated across the river. As soon as the last ones were safely across, they began to pull up the wooden planks, rendering it impassable.

The colonel ran ahead to the bridge, leather apron flapping against his legs. "Stop that! Stop! That's our bridge, to our homes—you leave it be!"

In town, the column of smoke grew larger and sparks shot into the air. No direct order was given, but a consensus was reached, and the militia began to move with all the rapidity and force of a nor'easter.

The minutemen from Acton went first because they had bayonets and boxes loaded with cartridges for a faster rate of fire. Their fifer, a blond boy as young as Arthur looked, played "The White Cockade," a quick little Jacobite song the British thought seditious. The Concord minutemen followed after them. Proctor and the Lincoln minutemen came next, finishing the front ranks.

Most of the casualties would be there in front. Everyone knew it but no one held back. The militia companies filled out the middle ranks behind them, followed at the rear by the unorganized volunteers who answered the alarms.

As the formation swept down the hillside, the Redcoats fled the bridge and collided with a second company coming up from the town to support them. While they milled, confused for a moment, frantically sorting out their order on the western bank, the militia column spread out along the eastern causeway across the river. Close enough to exchange fire, but out of range of the British bayonets.

The Redcoats finally began to form a three-deep firing formation. When their flankers ran toward the end of the militia lines, Proctor and others aimed their muskets.

"Hold your fire," Captain Smith bellowed. "We're not to start it."

But I already did start it, Proctor thought.

And then he pushed that thought aside. Pitcairn had been ready to shoot Captain Parker, knowing that he was in no danger himself. And that shot would have started a war as sure as Proctor's had. Now he would do whatever he had to do to make things right again.

"Once they do start it," Smith ordered, "aim for the brightest coats first—that'll be their officers."

"The crossed white straps make for a nice target," Amos whispered to Proctor.

Proctor's heart pounded. He'd already faced their guns once. Waiting was harder, now that he knew what was coming. A gun cracked and a puff of smoke went up from the front of the outnumbered British line. Proctor swallowed, but kept his own finger frozen.

Two more British shots went off.

Still the militiamen around Proctor held their fire.

Then the front row of Redcoats let go with a ragged, unordered volley. One of the Acton minutemen went down, his chest burst open, spurting blood. The fifer dropped, his tune cut off in mid-note. A second volley came from the British line and a few more soldiers fell around Proctor. Still, the minutemen waited for the order.

"Fire! For God's sake, fire!"

Chapter 5

"Fire!"

The cry spread from one end of the militia line to the other. Proctor aimed for the reddest coat and squeezed the trigger. For the next few moments, all he was aware of were the men beside him, the men he aimed at, and the mechanical process of reloading his musket. Dense clouds of bitter smoke obscured both sides of the river. Before the third ball left his musket he became aware that he no longer heard lead whizzing past him.

The British lines had broken.

Men were down around him. Some of the militia retreated from the carnage to regroup, while others ran toward the bridge to secure it. Proctor stood frozen.

The musket fog began to clear; the harsh taste of gunpowder filled his mouth. Across the river, the Redcoats were in full retreat toward Concord Green.

Just like in his scrying.

The British dead sprawled awkwardly in the road, while the wounded cried out in pain. One Redcoat clutched his belly and crawled on hands and knees after the retreating column, until he fell on his face and lay there moaning, gut-shot, bleeding to death. One of the militiamen crossed the bridge, pulled out his hatchet, and calmly split the Redcoat's skull. Proctor was not sure if it was cruelty or mercy. You killed a chicken in the yard that way, but not a man. And yet, didn't he want the British dead? Hadn't they done the same to Everett Simes?

While he stood there unsure of his own feelings or next action, men began to carry the colonial dead and injured toward the farmhouse on the hill.

"Proctor," a small voice said beside him. "Proctor?"

He looked over and saw Arthur standing there, pale and trembling. His chin was slick with vomit. "Arthur?" Proctor asked, his heart lurching. "Have you been shot?"

"No. But I don't feel so good."

Proctor grabbed Arthur's shoulder, turned him side-to-side to make sure he wasn't hurt. "Maybe you should go home and check on your mother and your sisters."

"You sure that's proper?"

"I'm sure. The bridge is ours now. But don't go through the center of town. Cut through the pasture and go around behind the ridge, until you come to the Bedford Road. If that's clear, then take the road on home."

"All right."

"If you have to tell them about your uncle Everett, you do it straight-out, without details or embellishment," Proctor said. "You don't want to upset them more than need be."

Arthur nodded, but he continued to stand there. Proctor reached out and used his sleeve to wipe the spit off Arthur's chin. That made Arthur jerk his head away and scowl.

"I know what to do," he said, wiping his own chin.

He ran off, leaving his hat on the ground with shot still in it. Proctor didn't have the heart to call after him, so he put the lead in his hunting bag and tucked the cap in his belt. When Arthur reached the bridge, he sprinted across, past the Redcoat who'd had his skull split open. Proctor watched him climb over the far hill and head off through the woods behind town.

He wasn't the only one to leave. Here and there, other men headed off in other directions, ignoring calls to return.

Proctor didn't understand. The work here wasn't done yet—you didn't plow a field without planting it too. There were still plenty of Redcoats on both sides of the bridge. He found Captain Smith making sure the last of their injured were removed uphill.

"What're we to do next, sir?" Proctor asked. "The Redcoats haven't exactly packed their kit for home yet."

Smith looked past the bridge. "No, they haven't. Gather as many men as you can before they scatter more. We're caught between four British companies still on this side of the bridge, and the rest in Concord. Could be a hammer and an anvil if we're not careful."

"I'll go do what I can," Proctor said.

He went along the causeway and up the hillside, calling the men from his company and telling them to report to Captain Smith. He grew bolder as he went and started commanding other men to report to their officers too. "The fighting's not done," he said again and again. "The Redcoats're coming back for another try at us."

He wasn't sure if it was true, but he had to do something, anything, to make up for his decision on the green. The companies hadn't even re-formed when the order came to split their force, with the minutemen holding the eastern side of the river and the other militia the west.

Proctor ran across the bridge, skipping over the gap where planks had been pried up. The minutemen took up a position behind the stone wall on the hillside. Proctor double-shotted his musket when he reloaded. He wanted to do as much damage with that first volley as possible.

Smoke still rose from the center of town, but it was a smaller column now, more like a bonfire than a house fire. "What do you think they're burning?" he asked.

Amos Lathrop crouched next to him. "The carriages for the cannons, that's what one of the girls said. At least the cannons are safely hidden."

"We can build new carriages in pretty short order," Proctor replied. "But the cannons would be harder to replace."

"The Redcoat officers have to be thinking the same thing."

They were also thinking of retaking the bridge. The routed Redcoats had rejoined the rest of their troops, and they all marched back in fighting formation. When they saw the militia lined up behind the wall, they halted just outside range of the muskets. The officers rode forward of the troops for a better look.

One officer rode out farther than the others, well within range of their guns. Proctor again saw the spark at his throat, even though he had the sun behind him. Pitcairn.

Proctor sighted his musket at him, just as he had on the Lexington Green. Then he lowered the weapon. It would be wasted lead.

Captain Smith, coming down the line, rapped him on the shoulder. "I saw that, Brown. Hold your fire. We won't shoot until they shoot first."

As he walked away, Amos shook his head. "Shooting's already started. We held our fire at the bridge and lost good men."

Proctor rolled his tongue through his cheek and spit. "It's not like he's telling us to let them shoot first, then turn the other cheek."

"I'll say that much for the Reverend Emerson," Amos said, referring to the minister from Concord. "He sure knows when it's time to beat plowshares into swords."

Drums sounded from the western bank of the river. The other four companies of Redcoats had returned from their expedition to the mill. When they saw that the bridge was unguarded and they were surrounded by colonial militia, the front ranks broke into a run.

Proctor aimed his musket at them and discovered that his shoulder was bruised from the four quick volleys at the bridge. He needed to watch his powder.

How four companies of Redcoats marched under the guns of the militia without either side firing a shot, Proctor couldn't say. The Redcoats crossed the bridge, quietly gathered up their dead and wounded, and continued their tense march under the guns of the minutemen until they rejoined their main force.

Amos lowered his musket and took a deep breath. "Can you tell me why we let them rejoin forces like that?"

Proctor wasn't sure. "Maybe when they're all bunched up together they make a bigger target."

Amos nodded. "That makes sense. Some of those old men in the militia, their eyesight's going bad and they need that advantage."

Proctor was anxious to do something more than sit behind a wall and guard the bridge. But now that they'd been stung, the British moved slowly. They milled around town, forming their order of march, stealing carriages for their wounded, and sending skirmishers out along Arrowhead Ridge to protect their retreat. It was noon before the drums beat the call to arms and the Redcoats started back toward Boston.

A sense of relief flooded Proctor. He could reach Emily again, explain to her how the fighting happened. He could tell her about Pitcairn—

Captain Smith came down the line. "Listen here, men. It's been decided that we mean to teach the Redcoats a lesson."

There were somber murmurs at this. "Spare the rod and spoil the child," Amos said.

Smith patted the ramrod attached to his musket. "They're not to make it back to Boston, not one of them if we can help it. That'll put a stop to their bullying."

Proctor wondered how they were going to stop Pitcairn, with his protective charm. If they didn't stop Pitcairn, he'd hold his men together. "Not one?" Proctor asked.

"Not one," Smith said. "The militia's been raised from all over. We're setting up along the road to harry the Redcoats. Our company's job is to get to the curve at the Bedford Road just past Tanner's Creek before they do."

"That's more than three miles cross-country," Amos said.

Proctor pushed his way to the front. "That's out toward my father's farm, and I know the paths between there and town as well as any man."

"You lead the way then," Smith said.

Proctor nodded. If Pitcairn had to be stopped, he was the only one who could figure out a way to do it. Proctor ran, leading the men single-file on narrow trails over rocky pastures and through the woods where the trees were leafing. A cold wind blew steady from the east, striking them every time they passed through the open trees. They saw other companies taking trails that paralleled theirs. As they crossed the old road above Merriam's Corner, fierce gunfire sounded south of them. Proctor turned aside from their path to go join it, but Captain Smith stopped him.

"There're other companies down there, that's their work, leave it to them," he told Proctor. "We've got to be at our station on the curve to do ours."

"Yes, sir," Proctor said. He led the file through the little Mill Brook valley, where they splashed across the creek, and up over the hills, down into the swampy lowlands around Tanner's Creek. Gunfire echoed down the valley in the direction of Brooks Hill. The men were tired from running and eager to fight, but this time when they tried to change their path to join the battle it was Proctor who grabbed them and aimed them over the water and up the hills on the other side.

"To the curve," he told them. "We'll get our chance—go to the hill above the curve."

Proctor reached the top of the hill to find the Concord men taking positions among the trees. The Lincoln men joined them on the upper slopes. Proctor crouched, back pressed against a huge elm, and caught his breath. He stole a glance around the trunk. The Reading militia were strung out low on the hillsides, near the start of the curve. Brown and russet jackets shifted from tree to tree on the far side of the road. Probably men from Woburn.

He almost felt sorry for the Redcoats. Drawn out in a narrow line, penned in by stone walls, with tree-covered hills on both sides—they didn't have a chance.

They came marching around the bend in a line that was much more ragged than it had been leaving Concord.

Across the road, the Woburn men fired first, followed by the Reading militia in their positions at the bottom of the hill. The Redcoats were caught in a vicious crossfire. One or two of the men around Proctor let off a shot, but Smith shouted, "Hold your fire."

Captain Barrett, of the Concord minutemen, shouted the same thing. "Wait till they're closer, and stagger your shots. We won't get them all with that first volley."

Down below, some of the British were trying to fight back, but those who left the road and tried to climb over the wall to reach the men from Woburn and Reading only made themselves easier targets. The smarter Redcoats ran forward through the fire.

"Here's our chance now," Smith said.

Proctor took aim at the Redcoat in the lead, waiting until he'd almost reached the second bend, and then fired. A dozen muskets went off around him at the same instant. There was no way to tell who shot the man, or how many times he'd been shot, but several Redcoats in the front fell.

Proctor stepped behind the tree to reload and heard bark splinter as the Redcoats returned fire. When he stepped out to shoot again, he saw that the Redcoats kept pushing forward. They had to—they were being attacked from either side, and from behind, and a man could only load and shoot so fast. As long as the Redcoats kept moving, most of them would get through safely. Through a second and third volley, they continued marching and their carriages continued to roll, until only their dead and wounded were left.

He had looked for Pitcairn and missed him, probably one of the times he was behind the tree reloading. But the

British troops held together, confident in their leaders, and he knew that the British major hadn't fallen.

"Where to now, Captain?" Proctor asked.

"We're to skip ahead of them again," Smith said.

This was Proctor's land, figuratively if not literally. He lived within a mile and knew every road and trail, every farm and pasture. "The south side of the road is too low and swampy, you get much beyond here. But we could make our way to the Bluffs outside Lexington."

"Then that's what we'll do," Smith said.

Proctor was off and running again without waiting for an order. Looking back, he saw they didn't have a full company anymore. Men who were wounded, or who had family wounded, stayed behind, as did men tired of the fight. Their ranks had thinned, but the Redcoats had been thinned as well.

They crossed the Bedford Road and passed through Mason's soggy pastures. This time when they heard gunfire down around Hartwell's farm, not a man turned aside. In truth, there was no place where they did not hear gunfire, and nowhere they went that they did not glimpse other groups of militia running through the fields and woods. Proctor took a twisting path over pastures strewn with granite boulders. He was panting, and several others were drenched with sweat, but they came to a hill above the road, once again ahead of the British troops.

There were only two or three dozen of them now, mixed men from Concord and Lincoln, but they saw many others hiding down among the boulders and in the ditches, waiting for the Redcoats. Proctor started to lead the men down there, thinking it would be his best chance to get at Pitcairn.

"Not there," Smith said between breaths. "Farther up, on the hill."

It had a steep slope, covered with rocks, and would be harder for the Redcoats to assault. He didn't have the strength left to explain all that, but the men saw it, understood, and followed. Proctor was the last to go.

Smith chose a position on the next curve in the road. A company of men already occupied the hillside, waiting for the Redcoats, but it took a moment for Proctor to recognize Captain Parker and the other Lexington men. A few wore bandages over wounds they'd taken that morning. Many more had faces black with powder.

Parker stood tall, out in the open, listening to the stuttering beat of the British drums and the distant crack of muskets, waiting for the Redcoats to appear. He coughed quietly into his palm, eyes widening in his gaunt face at the sight of Proctor.

"You look familiar," he said, his voice hoarse.

Proctor's throat tightened. Was he going to be blamed for shooting first? "Proctor Brown, sir. Stood on the green with you this morning."

"That'd be it," Parker said, and stifled another consumptive cough. He looked like he was going to die soon, whether a British officer shot him in the back or not. "You look like you've been far today, son."

"All the way to Concord and back," Proctor said.

"That's a long way to go on a day like this," Captain Parker said. "God bless you for coming back to help us a second time."

"I'm sorry for the way things happened—"

Parker interrupted him with a shake of his head that might have been general or specific. "Don't think about it. The situation was bound to come to shooting sooner or later. Either way, the Redcoats owe us a debt for what they did once the shooting started, and we plan to make them pay back every cent with interest."

Proctor stared at his feet. The sounds of drums and muskets were much closer. He opened his mouth, unsure what he wanted to say, but Amos sidled between them.

"Being that's how you are with loans," Amos said, "I

guess I shouldn't ask to borrow lead from you, though I don't have more than three shot left."

Captain Parker laughed at that, and his laugh turned into a cough. Once his coughing stopped, he signaled for one of his men to come over. "We won't loan you shot, but we'll give it to you, how's that?"

"That'll suit just fine," Amos said.

Proctor put his hand into his hunting bag and counted the lead balls—he could fire nine more times if he didn't double-shot. Then he checked his powder horn and saw that he didn't have nine measures left.

Gunfire peppered the road just west of them, and smoke from muskets marked the imminent arrival of British troops. Proctor scooted downslope and took cover behind a tree that none of the Lexington men had claimed yet.

The Redcoats rounded the bend, a jangled mass of men with bare bayonets followed by battle-scarred carriages bearing wounded soldiers trying to return fire despite their injuries.

Only one mounted officer proceeded as if everything were orderly, one man untouched by the hail of shot aimed at him. Even before Proctor saw the golden spark flashing near the officer's throat, he recognized Pitcairn. The major was holding the Redcoats' retreat together by the example of his courage and the sheer force of his will.

"Fire!" Captain Parker shouted.

Proctor aimed but didn't pull his trigger. As the smoke thinned, he saw Pitcairn still untouched, though men around him had fallen.

While the militia reloaded, Pitcairn ordered his marines to take the hill. Militiamen in the first ditch screamed out as they were bayoneted. A thin red line moved into the trees.

Seeing a minuteman die on the hillside below him, Proctor thought about Munroe, and Everett, and that little blond fifer from Acton. As long as Pitcairn stayed mounted, he'd hold the British troops together and more good men would die. And it wasn't right, wasn't fair, not with Pitcairn using witchcraft to protect himself. It was the same way some bullies wrapped themselves in a title like *Lord* and did as they pleased, and it made Proctor's teeth clench in anger.

But Pitcairn could be stopped.

Proctor grabbed Amos by the shoulder. "Pretend you're an ax cutter and clear a lane for me through the trees. I mean to cut the head off that long red snake."

Without waiting for Amos's answer, he started down the steep slope.

A marine, hatless, wild-haired, raging, charged up the hillside with his bloody bayonet. Amos's musket cracked behind Proctor and the Redcoat dropped, shot through the leg.

A second marine lunged at him from the right, bayonet extended, and Proctor discharged his own musket point-blank before he recognized the huge Scot from the British Coffee-House. As the other man fell, Proctor dropped his weapon, ran off the edge of a large gray boulder, and leapt into the road.

He fell short of Pitcairn's horse, stumbling and falling. A marine with a broken bayonet swung the butt of his musket at him; Proctor rolled out of the way, freeing his hatchet from his belt. When the musket butt came at him a second time, he knocked it aside and rose to his feet.

The horse snorted, stamping at Proctor, pushing between himself and the marine. Proctor grabbed the bridle with his free hand and swung the hatchet at Pitcairn; his eyes were blurry, wet from the sting of musket smoke.

Pitcairn caught Proctor's wrist on the downstroke.

Grappling face-to-face, there was nothing extraordinary about Pitcairn—he smelled of sweat and dust and powder, like anyone else. Proctor dragged him half out of his saddle, tearing at his collar. There, beneath the shirt—a gold medallion, hanging from a gold chain. The charm.

Proctor tried to rip it free, keeping his feet as the horse

spun in a panic. Pitcairn let go of the hatchet and grabbed Proctor's other hand with both his own.

Fire flowed through Proctor's palm, and he felt the heat race up his arm with every pulse of his blood. He tried one last time to wrench the charm away, and glimpsed the underside of the medallion—an angel with a shield, and letters, though he didn't recognize them, just like those his mother wrote on the bowl of water.

Light flared in the medallion, and fire speared up his arm, and then it went dull the same moment that his arm went numb.

Pitcairn pried the charm free. "What did you do—?"

A musket fired, striking the horse, which whinnied in fear as it stumbled sideways, tearing Pitcairn from Proctor's grasp.

A fist grabbed Proctor's jacket, yanking him back toward the ditch, and Amos was there, one arm under Proctor's elbow, dragging him up the hillside. He was stumbling, trying to go back, yelling, "I didn't get it, I didn't get it!" But a black man was there, pulling him away, and then one of the Lexington men, and he was halfway up the hillside, with someone shoving his musket back into his hand, which closed on it, even though he couldn't feel it.

"You don't understand," he tried to say.

"I understand you're a damned fool," Amos said.

"Nah, I didn't care for that Lobster either," the black man said.

Turning, Proctor saw that Pitcairn's horse was down. Pitcairn had regained his feet, and, throat naked at the collar, called the marines to him, ordering a full assault up the hill.

Proctor ducked as a round of lead whistled overhead, tearing through bark leaves, and then it was bayonets, and one of the men dodging out of the way for safety, and Amos doing the same, and Proctor running through the trees, from cover to cover, until he was alone, unsure where he was. He paused, back against a boulder, to reload his musket, stopping in mid-action to wipe his bloody hands—where had the blood come from?—across his breeches.

He had his chance and failed. He'd done something to the charm, felt some of the power drain out of it, but Pitcairn was still standing, and the British continued their retreat.

When he peered over the boulder, he saw that he'd become separated from the other men in his company. He made his way carefully back toward the road. With their last mounted officer unhorsed, the British were routed and simply ran, leaving a trail of abandoned cases and clothes and weapons behind them.

He gave pursuit, thinking he might have one last chance at Pitcairn, but he was exhausted and the sound of gunfire always cracked ahead of him, all the way past Fiske's Hill. He made his way down to the road to follow the Redcoats into Lexington.

One Redcoat lay dead in a ditch that lined the road. He looked like a man who'd fallen down drunk on his way home, but the ground beneath him was soaked with blood.

A hundred yards farther, two wounded regulars sat abandoned by the side of the road. Their empty weapons had been dropped nearby, with the bayonets removed and thrust harmlessly into the soil. One man patched the other's bloody leg while the second bound the first one's arm. When they saw Proctor approaching, they put their hands up in the air.

"We surrender," the first man said. "We—"

Proctor stumbled by them. Pitcairn was still ahead somewhere, and Proctor was the only one who knew his secret. He tried to explain that, but the words disappeared before they found his tongue.

A few splashes of red were still running in the distance, surrounded by the crack of gunfire.

This, he told himself, was the scene he'd scryed. His mother had been right, in seeing men dead; and he'd been right in seeing a retreat to Boston.

His legs wobbled beneath him, and he staggered to a

stop. He would never catch up with them now. Thirst sand-papered his throat. He fumbled for his father's tin canteen and lifted it in his unsteady, bloody hands, uncapping it for a drink.

Nothing came out. The metal felt cool on his lips, but it was dry. He shook it, but nothing. A jagged edge snagged his sleeve. He turned it over—shot had smashed through the bottom of it. He had no idea when.

And where did that yellow ribbon come from?

Emily.

He still had to make things right with Emily.

Her house was just ahead, before he reached the burying ground. He willed his legs to move again, forcing himself to run despite the dizzy swimming of the world around him.

His feet pounded across her porch and he beat on the front door, calling her name, asking if she was all right. There was no answer. The windows were shuttered. He peered through them and saw sheets thrown hastily over all the furniture.

He leaned his head against the shutters, slats creased against his forehead, and hit the frame hard enough to rattle the glass. The house was shut up tight. No doubt, Bess and the rest of the household had packed up and headed for Boston and safety first thing that morning, after the shooting on the green.

His heart was as empty as the house.

He rolled over, back to the wall, and slid down into a sitting position. Staying upright became a challenge, and so he gave in to gravity and slumped over. The porch rose up to smack his head.

A few feet away a door opened.

"No, I tell you, it *is* Proctor."

The voice was both hushed and insistent, familiar and far away.

"He's bleeding, Bess. I don't care. Come help me this instant."

His lips moved in an attempt to explain how he'd tried to make things right. It hadn't been enough.

"Shhh, don't try to speak, not now. Hurry!"

Hands grabbed him, fists knotted in his clothes, dragging him inside. He hurried, just like she demanded, kicking his legs to help as much as he could. But he didn't seem to be moving anymore. He hoped it was enough.

Chapter 6

Proctor was aware of cushions and damp clothes, drawn curtains and whispered voices.

From the voices, he gathered that a splinter or piece of lead had cut his neck. He knew from the voices that it had missed the vital arteries though he'd still lost significant amounts of blood. He tried to explain that he was fine, that all he needed was some rest. And a good dinner. He was hungry. Now that the battle was over, he and Emily could be together. The battle happened because of his talent, because of what he saw, but he used his talent to stop Pitcairn too, so he'd tried to do the right thing, and now he could be with Emily, and they could have the farm they wanted. His voice sounded far away to him, and nobody answered him, so he spoke louder.

Emily was there, placing her fingers across his lips, her curls tied back under a plain cap. "You must be quiet, Proctor." Her voice was hushed and trembling. "We don't want anyone to know we're here."

He tried to explain everything to her, wanted to assure her that everything would be fine, that she had nothing to worry about, but then Bess was there, squeezing his nose shut and making him swallow a huge dose of medicinal rum. It burned his throat, and he coughed some of it up, and then it burned his neck. But Bess mopped it up, and then made him swallow more. After a while, he fell asleep.

He woke again when it was dark. Emily and Bess were arguing nearby.

"We must leave in the morning, Miss Emily. We don't dare wait another day."

"But Proctor's not well enough to leave alone yet."

"He'll live, which is more than is likely for me, if any harm comes to you and Mister Rucke lays hold of me after."

"We could send word to his mother at the least."

"And let that murdering rabble know we're here? No, ma'am, not a chance. When that wagon comes around, we're going to get on it, and we'll be on our way out of Lexington before dawn comes and anyone realizes we're still here."

They were afraid because of her father's ties to the governor. He pushed himself up on his elbow. "I'll be fine," he rasped. The words sounded like a file scraped over rough wood, so he wasn't sure they understood him.

"He's awake," Emily whispered. "Light a candle."

"I don't think we ought to be doing that, Miss Emily. And you can see for yourself, he's well enough to leave alone."

Emily came to his side, a shade in the darkness. She smelled like soap. He reached out toward her shadow, but she pulled away and his hand fell back to his side. "I'll be fine," he said.

"It was madness out there, Proctor."

"I saw some of it," he mumbled. The words filled his mouth like rocks. "You'll be safe in Boston with your father."

"They meant to kill all of them," she said, her voice choked with shock and fear. "If Lord Percy hadn't marched out from Boston with the rest of the regular army, every one of them would have been killed."

"The Redcoats started it," Proctor said, and then caught his tongue. He'd started it too. If he hadn't shot at Pitcairn, would they have avoided the carnage that followed?

Bess whispered from across the room, and Emily rose to go speak to her. His throat hurt, inside and out. He reached up and felt a bandage under his fingertips. When she came back, she sniffled before she spoke, as if she had failed in holding back her tears.

"I begged you not to go, I begged you, and you marched out with that mob anyway," she said.

She *had* begged him. But he had to go. It was his duty. And if he hadn't acted, Pitcairn would have shot Captain Parker, and that wasn't right.

"Emily—"

"I don't know how I could ever rely on you if you don't listen when I beg you, for both our sakes, to do the right thing and avoid those rebels."

"I thought it would end peacefully—"

"Because you have *magic*?"

"I have magic." He'd meant to say it as a question, but the last word fell out of his mouth as flat as the truth. What exactly had he said to her? He remembered his driving need to explain things to her, but he couldn't recall his exact words.

"A *witch*. I don't want to believe the things you told me," she said. "You said that you performed some kind of satanic spell to see the future, something with an egg and a bowl, only what you saw isn't what happened. How could you mess with sorcery and expect anything different, Proctor? I don't understand why you're so surprised that the king of lies misled you."

"It's my talent," he said feebly.

"You used that word, *talent*. You raved about us, and our children, and how they'll be poisoned by this magic talent." Her voice was thick with disgust. "Our *children*? You're lucky I sent Bess away, or she might have thought we'd done things I'd never do. I . . . I don't know what to think."

Wheels creaked on the road outside the house, and a door opened, letting in the cool April breeze.

"It's time, Miss Emily," came Bess's voice.

"Emily, please let me explain," Proctor said, trying to rise.

"No," she said. "You have no right to ask anything of

me, not now. Bess says you'll be safe here. There's food and water by your bed. When you feel better, you can go out to your mob and ask them for help. Just don't tell them you believe in the rightful king or they'll turn against you."

"Miss Emily, it's time."

"I'm coming."

"Emily, please," Proctor begged.

"Good-bye to you, Mister Brown," she said, rising. With her voice choked, she added, "This isn't what I expected from you, not after our understanding in Boston."

Then her shadow slipped into the other shadows and the door clicked shut and a moment later the wheels creaked. When the sound of the cart faded, the room was perfectly dark and still again, and Proctor was alone.

Proctor had never been alone in a house before, not that he could recall. His mother was there, or, in the past few years, his father. When they left to go to church, or to go visiting, he went with them.

Lying there alone in Emily's house, he felt like an intruder, like a stranger to himself. Emily left him. She was afraid of him and the men whom he'd risked his life with. She was afraid of who he was, afraid of the talent he was born with, a talent he barely understood himself.

He was still awake when dawn lit the room well enough for him to see it. All the food in the house had been left on the floor at the head of the couch where he rested. A pitcher of water sat next to a pot of cold tea and a jug of small beer. Covered plates of salted meat and cold beans were surrounded by loaves of bread and bowls of butter and jam. At the foot of the couch, they'd left every chamber pot in the house. His shoes and stockings rested at the foot of a sheet-covered chair. His jacket had been scrubbed and patched, and was hung over the back of the chair to dry. All his gear—musket, hunting bag, the shattered canteen with the shredded yellow ribbon—were set in a jumbled pile nearby.

All of it was placed so it couldn't be seen from the windows. Emily had been very afraid.

And now she was gone. He thought he might as well dress and head home, but sitting up made him dizzy and weak, and he knew that it wouldn't be possible. He sipped some of the tea and lay back down to stop his head from pounding. Then, turning his back to the food, he closed his eyes.

What good did it do him to become the richest farmer in Lincoln if Emily hated him? He had shared with her the one deep secret that he had, and she had looked at him with disgust then locked the door behind her. His whole plan to raise cattle and sell the beef in Boston seemed stupid to him now.

He must have fallen asleep because pounding on the door woke him. People called for the Tory's daughter to come outside, saying she wasn't welcome. Feet thumped across the porch, and the shutters rattled as people peered in the window just as he had done.

"They're gone," a voice said. "Covered everything up and left. Good riddance to 'em."

These were Proctor's friends, the men he'd fought beside. If he spoke up and showed them his wounds, they'd make him welcome and help him get home. But he felt that, for Emily's sake, he couldn't speak.

When they left, he took advantage of the things that Emily had left him. He craved meat, so he filled up on the salt pork first, then chased it down with the small beer. For the next few days, he slept and ate and thought about how he could fix what he had done and then ate and slept some more. Every time he heard a noise outside, he looked up and expected Emily to come back through the door again, saying it had all been a mistake.

The door never opened.

Emily didn't return, wasn't going to return.

He finally admitted that he was only delaying. His mother

would be looking for him, and there would be work enough waiting for him. So he shaved and dressed and gathered up his gear and, late in the morning, left Emily's house. He slammed the door shut behind him.

A few other farms along the Concord Road were shut up as Emily's had been, and there were fewer men in the fields than he expected on an April morning. An old farmer at his well saw Proctor passing and pointed in the other direction.

"You're heading the wrong way," he shouted through cupped hands. "The siege is in Boston."

Proctor crossed over to the stone wall along the road. "What's the news?"

The farmer looked at Proctor's bandages and the stains on his clothes, and limped over to his side of the wall.

"The Redcoats are smarting from the bloody nose we gave them," he said. "Now they're blocked up in Boston, waiting for reinforcements, but it won't do 'em no good. All of New England is sending men to the siege. Israel Putnam himself rode in from Connecticut two days ago."

"Putnam's here already?" His father liked to talk about Israel Putnam. They'd both been born in Salem and had served in the rangers.

"Aye, Putnam's here. He knocked the French about in the last war, showed Pontiac the business at Detroit, and helped take Havanna from the Spaniards. He'll see to it that we pick up all those Lobsters and toss them back in the ocean where they came from, you can count on it." He turned his head to spit tobacco, then squinted at Proctor. "You look like you seen some fighting already."

"A few days back," Proctor said.

"You one of the fellows Doctor Warren patched up? They said he came out to Lexington and saved lives after Lord Percy showed up with the cannon."

"No, sir, I wasn't hurt that bad," he said, and he held himself straight to prove it. "But I've got to get home. My folks'll be worried after me and I need to let them know I'm fine."

"Well, turn back around when you're done. We're not finished here yet."

"No, sir, I don't reckon we are," Proctor said. He tipped his hat and walked away, counting the days on his fingers. He thought it was Monday. He'd slept right through the Sabbath, so he bowed his head and said a quick prayer for forgiveness.

As he approached the turn-off to his own home, he had too many things going through his head. Was Emily right? Had he been fooled by Satan? If that were the case, did that make Pitcairn and his magic Satan's work? Because if it did, someone had to stop him.

Or was it even magic? In the light of day, after all he'd seen in the fight against the British, magic seemed like such a fragile, ineffective thing. Maybe Pitcairn was simply brave and lucky. Maybe it *had* been a tinfoil knife at the coffeehouse in Boston. Maybe if he told Emily he'd been dreaming, that everything he said was a dream. He'd never bring up magic again, never have anything to do with witchcraft.

He walked past the turn-off, continuing on in to Concord. He could ask the Reverend Emerson what to do. He wouldn't mention the witchcraft, but Emerson would know how to patch things up with him and Emily.

In Concord, signs of the battle were all around. The liberty pole stood over the town, the burned cannon carriages sat outside the meetinghouse, and at the bottom of the road, the North Bridge was stained and scarred, with bright new wood replacing the planks that had been ripped up in such a hurry by the British.

The Reverend Emerson's mansion rose on the slope beside the bridge. It stood three stories tall, with a handsome brick chimney and a shingled roof. His farm spread out across acres and acres of prime land. Proctor suppressed a pang of envy. His land wasn't watered by a river and would never be as rich, but he might someday build a house as impressive as this one.

Now that he had arrived, he felt tired and weak, unsure what exactly he meant to ask the Reverend. But he had no one else to turn to. Since he'd come this far, he thought he best see it through.

He knocked at the front door and asked for the Reverend. The maid took him to a workshop in the orchard back of the main house. Emerson was seated on a stool, sorting pieces of wood trim, the sort of make-work a man did when he was waiting for someone or feeding a powerful need to think. When she knocked on the door, Emerson looked up and said, "Jedediah?"

His voice was both hopeful and worried.

"No, sir," she answered with a curtsy. "It's Proctor Brown."

Emerson rose and came forward. "Ah, Brown. That will be all, Sarah, thank you. The son of Lemuel and Prudence. We spoke on the hill, before the battle at the bridge."

"That's right, sir."

"How's your father? Come in, come in."

Proctor ducked his head to step through the doorway. "Not well, sir. He had the apoplexy. Mostly we just try to keep him comfortable."

"That must be very hard on your mother," Emerson said. He was a hard man with sharp, intelligent features, the kind who looked more at home with tools than books. "And on you, as well. But it's all part of the good Lord's plan; we must hold on to that. What brings you here?"

"It's Miss Emily." He felt light-headed again. "May I sit down please?"

Emerson fetched him the stool. Lowering his voice, he said, "Is Miss Emily in a family way?"

Proctor's tongue froze in his mouth.

"There's no shame in it. Or not much—these things happen. But we'll have to announce the engagement first," he said, counting off weeks on his fingers. "That means the soonest we could have the wedding would be—"

"No," Proctor gulped, finding his voice. "I mean, no, sir. It's not—it's not *that.*"

Emerson seemed puzzled. "Then what is it?"

"Miss Emily has run off to Boston with her father, behind the British lines. I said some things. I think . . . I think I drove her away."

"Ah." Emerson nodded once and closed his eyes. "That would be Emily Rucke, the daughter of Thomas Rucke, infamous Tory and friend of the royal governor."

"It was the witchcraft," he mumbled in explanation, meaning to say that it was all a mistake, a dream.

But Emerson was already talking past him, glancing at the door and making hurry-along gestures with his hand. "Of course, you didn't mean to drive her away, nor should you trouble yourself with those thoughts again. The war itself is enough to drive people apart, even those with deep and time-honored bonds as friends and allies. Are you quite sure of her intentions? Without intending any offense, Mister Brown, I must say, it seems an unlikely match. Excuse me, did you say witchcraft?"

Proctor's mouth opened again, but he couldn't speak.

"If Emily Rucke is a witch, it could be even more difficult—"

"Oh, no, sir, not her, me."

Emerson stopped, covered his mouth with his hand, and studied Proctor. He stepped to the door, checked outside, looking through the orchard, not toward the house. When he turned back to Proctor, you could almost see the thoughts whirling in his head, like blossoms whipped off a tree in a spring storm.

"Your mother was Prudence Proctor, from Salem, if I recall correctly."

"That's where my father was born too."

"And are you one? A witch, that is."

Proctor tried to answer, but he was scared of lying to the Reverend.

"It would be a very dangerous thing to be a witch," Emerson said grimly. "Do you have the witch's mark on you?"

Proctor tried to move back, nearly toppling the stool. He caught it and said, "What's that?"

"A witch's mark is an unnatural teat, a place for the suckling of your demon familiar." Emerson's face was quite grim. He pressed close, nose-to-nose, so that Proctor could smell the cider on his breath. "You do have a demon familiar, do you not?"

"No," Proctor said, his voice quavering. "No, sir, I do not."

Emerson clasped his hands behind his back, just like Captain Smith did when he was drilling them for the minutemen. He began to pace around Proctor as if he were inspecting for some flaw. Proctor caught himself standing at attention, shoulders squared, eyes straight ahead.

"Of course," Emerson said, slowly, menacingly, "if you did have a witch's mark, or a demon familiar, you'd be compelled to lie about them."

"I . . . I wouldn't lie, sir."

"Is that a lie, Mister Brown?"

"No, sir!"

Emerson stopped in his circuit, right behind Proctor. "You see," he said quietly. "That is the danger with hunting for witches. Once someone is accused, no denial will suffice, and every statement in the positive or the negative is further proof of guilt."

Proctor started to blurt out that he wasn't a witch, then clamped his mouth shut, afraid to be caught in the lie. What if Emerson knew about his mother? Some of the neighbors did. Old man Leary came to her to have his sick cattle healed once, and another time to help find a lamb that had wandered off. His gratitude was part of the reason he was going to sell his fields to Proctor someday, though he couldn't tell Emily or her father that.

Emerson's feet shuffled as he slowly stepped around to the front again. Proctor was sweating, almost as if he had a fever. He was ready to forswear foresight forever, even if it meant never touching another egg as long as he lived. Emerson leaned in close to him.

"Once men start dabbling in witchcraft, the innocent are caught along with the guilty. My advice to you, Mister Brown, is to forget everything you ever heard about witches and turn your thoughts toward the Good Book and God's will."

"I will," he said, nodding.

Emerson sighed and rubbed his chin again, looking away from Proctor. "I know your heart is set on Miss Rucke, but a line divides her from you now that is stronger than any siege line. This war is God's war, and He intends us to emerge victorious. By putting himself on the side of the empire, Thomas Rucke has put himself against God, and dragged his daughter with him."

"She's not like that," he said.

"Perhaps not," he admitted. "But sometimes we are all caught up in forces that are larger than ourselves. Concord is filled with godly young women, and you're still yet very young. My advice to you is this: Go, help your mother care for her farm, and spend whatever time remains in this world with your father. God may have different plans for you. You should be prepared to see them when they're revealed."

"Yes, sir," Proctor said, but without heart. He was convinced he could forget about witchcraft, sure. All it did was reveal glimpses of a future to him that were no better than guesses. But Emerson was wrong about him and Emily.

"And Brown?"

"Sir?"

"Always be prepared to serve your country—"

Someone knocked at the door, and Proctor glanced over

expecting to see the maid. Instead it was an older man in drab clothes and a black felt hat with a broad brim. He had loose white hair and was stocky, with thick forearms poking out of his rolled-up sleeves. Proctor would've taken him for a Quaker, except he carried an old musket and Quakers were pacifists who refused to bear arms. But maybe it was just for hunting. Proctor could not ever recall seeing him at any meeting or muster around Concord before.

"Jedediah," Emerson said, sounding relieved. He walked over to the old man, hands clasped behind his back. Jedediah leaned in close, spoke two words, and nodded his head toward the trees outside.

Proctor's heart pounded like a drum beating to arms.

The two words were, he swore, "the witch."

Chapter 7

Jedediah's whole attention was clearly on something outside, so there was no way he could have overheard Proctor's confession. When Emerson turned back to Proctor, it was clear his mind was elsewhere too.

He looked over Proctor thoughtfully before he spoke. "You made a good choice coming by, Mister Brown. Think on the advice I've given you. Now if you'll excuse me, I have important business to attend to. Do you mind showing yourself out and back to the road?"

"No, sir, not at all."

"I'm very grateful. God bless you and God speed."

Without waiting for Proctor to finish replying, Emerson hurried after the old man. Proctor stood in the rough-framed doorway of the workshop and watched them walk toward the woods. When he looked for the way back down to the main road, he realized the workshop was placed so it could be approached without ever coming in view of the mansion and its servants.

Which this Jedediah just seemed to have done.

Very odd.

As the two men walked away, the taller Emerson bent down to listen to the old man. They whispered to each other, even though no one was near enough to hear them.

Even odder.

The witch.

Had Emerson, who had just lectured him on lying, been lying to him? And if the phrase wasn't his imagination, what did it mean? The musket, and Emerson's enthusiasm for the patriot cause, seemed to indicate some business with the war against the British. Beyond that, Proctor wasn't sure what to think.

Since no one from the house could see him, no one would know if he followed after them. He set off, hanging back on the path and keeping low so they wouldn't notice. He proceeded anxiously, constantly ready to duck behind tree or bush or boulder, but their attention remained fixed on their destination and they never saw him dogging their steps.

Once they were in among the copse of trees that lined the river, he slowly closed the distance between them, if only not to lose them to some sudden turn.

But there were no sudden turns. As the two men proceeded into rougher country outside Concord, Proctor argued with himself that he'd made a mistake. It was his imagination, fixated on Emily's accusation and on the memory of Pitcairn's mysterious charm, which lingered like the taste of copper bit between his teeth. Probably the old man was a farmer who needed Emerson's help with someone dying, or a similar situation. Proctor was glancing back over his own shoulder, checking how far he'd come, when the sound of voices made him stagger to a stop.

He jumped behind the nearest bushes and almost swore when the brambles pricked his hands. He crouched there, sucking blood from his fingertips.

Three people clustered on the path ahead: Jedediah and Emerson joined by a young woman. Like the older man, she was dressed in drab gray and dun browns. Her hair was pulled back under the plainest cap he'd ever seen, excepting Quakers that his aunt had pointed out once in Boston. Not a curl of her hair showed at this distance.

They were too far away for Proctor to make out their whispered words, but the young woman gestured farther down the path. She and Emerson shared a brief conversation, reinforcing Proctor's impression that this was merely some commonplace domestic tragedy calling for a minister's comforting assistance.

Ashamed of himself for sneaking after them like an ill-intentioned spy, he prepared to turn back toward Concord and start home. His plan was delayed when the two men continued down the rough trail, leaving the young woman where she could not miss seeing him if he returned.

He might have risked it regardless, but she folded her hands together and glanced several times in the direction of his hiding spot. Forgetting the other men for a moment, she approached cautiously, leaving the trail and entering the edge of the woods. Proctor was prepared to stand up and explain himself when she stopped some distance short of his hiding spot and bent down among the spring weeds. She stood up a second later with a purple three-petaled flower in her fingers. Sniffing it caused her to wrinkle her nose, an expression followed instantly by a brief flash of utter delight. A smile lingered as she threaded the stem through a buttonhole in her shawl.

Her reverie was broken by the snort of a horse and the creak of wheels. As soon as her head turned the other way, Proctor retreated into a ditch behind the brambles, knees digging into the mud as he hunkered deeper in the brush. He mounded last year's moldy leaves up around him, to hide his mustard-colored waistcoat.

A small, two-wheeled farm cart, pulled by a shaggy old draft horse, rattled through the woods and down a path never intended for wagons. The horse seemed good-naturedly oblivious to this fact, pulling with calm determination over every root and rock. Jedediah led the horse by the bridle, murmuring encouragement, musket in his free hand. The young woman retreated quickly from the approaching cart, staying well ahead of it. Emerson followed behind.

The cart was ordinary—boards on three sides, and a tailboard down in the back—but its cargo was not. As it came closer, the head of a woman became visible over top of the boards. Proctor would've guessed her a widow, wrapped in black cloth, with a shawl pulled over her head, obscuring her face. Her hands were folded in her lap, as if she were pained by arthritis.

If this was the witch they had mentioned, then it could have easily been his mother. Some harmless old farm wife with a talent she barely understood, even if she had courage enough to use it. This was what his mother warned him about, the fate of those accused of witchcraft.

His mother. It had been days since he'd seen her. She had to be worried about him, worried that something had happened to him, either in battle or because someone had discovered his secret.

He lifted his eyes to see if the way was clear, but the young woman had nearly reached his hiding place, and he ducked quickly to avoid being spied by her. He needn't have worried. All her attention was focused on the woman in the wagon. Her lips moved in silent prayer as she led the way down the trail.

The cart was close enough that Proctor could hear Emerson's voice bringing up the rear. ". . . there is no point in persisting in your wickedness any longer. You have been caught. Reveal your purpose in the attack on the farm, and earnestly repent of it, I implore you."

The widow sat silent and unmoving, head bowed, face hidden behind her shawl. And her hands weren't folded in her lap—they were bound with ropes, the hemp knots clearly visible now because they contrasted with the black cloth of her sleeves.

"Thou art wasting thy breath," the old man murmured, just like a Quaker. "She hasn't spoke a word since we caught her."

"We must do the right thing whether she chooses to or not," Emerson replied. "And that includes giving her the opportunity to admit her sins and make amends."

The cart bumped past Proctor's hiding place, and as it did, the widow showed her first signs of life. She lifted her head, sniffing, then tossed her head back, knocking the shawl from her face. Her age was difficult to determine; gray circles under her eyes and a wrinkled throat made her appear old, though her face was smooth and her hair dark like a younger woman's.

An electric tingle shot over the surface of Proctor's skin, and he swayed with vertigo. He thrust out his arm for balance to keep from tipping over.

The cart was directly beside him now, no more than fifteen feet away. From her perch, the widow turned her face to peer over the bushes directly at Proctor. He saw that his impression of her was wrong. It was just as he'd first suspected: the woman on the cart could have been his mother, with gray streaks through her hair and a face careworn before its time.

Only her eyes were different—they flashed, like lanterns in the night, as old as the beacons on the hills that warned sailors off difficult shores. Over the eerily distant tone of Emerson's ministerial voice, she spoke.

"It's in the blood."

The words shaped a smile on her lips, not of joy but of relief. Emerson stopped in his tracks, staring at her as the wagon rolled away from him; the Quaker woman shouted something and hurried back, halting twenty-five or thirty feet short of the wagon; the old man at the bridle turned his head, patting the horse on the flank as he pulled it to rest, and said, "What did she say?"

The widow looked at Jedediah, the fire in her eyes sharp like lightning, bright as the medallion on Pitcairn's chest, and said something under her breath. The words tumbled out, like water over rocks, falling from streams to rapids, and rising into a roar without individual parts.

Proctor started forward, ready to help, though not knowing how, and then the widow glanced at him a second time, still pouring forth the torrent of words in some language he had never heard before.

In an instant, her head flattened and grew a snout and whiskers; the black cloth of her dress and shawl rippled and became a furry pelt; and the roar of words deepened into the snarl of a panther, black and sleek and angry.

Proctor's jaw dropped open and his hand groped blindly for a weapon, a stick, anything, as it would if he had stumbled on a real panther unawares. But to that was added a second layer of panic—if this was true witchcraft, then what else could she do?

On the road, Emerson staggered back, eyes wide in fear, his voice imploring God for aid. Jedediah reached out to grab the panther by its bound wrists, or ankles, whatever they were. But the creature writhed and twisted atop the wagon, snarling and snapping at the rope, keeping its paws away from the old man's hands.

The horse glanced over its shoulder, took a step forward nervously, nostrils flaring. But when Proctor expected it to bolt in blind panic, it stopped again. The Quaker woman rushed forward, shouting, "What have you done? Tell me, what have you done?"

"Nothing," Jedediah said, then shouted at the panther, commanding it to stop.

Emerson, his jaw set grim, came forward cautiously. "What manner of sorcery is this? What do we do?"

The Quaker woman shook her head. "Do nothing! I'm going to retreat, in case she's drawing on my fire. It's an illusion—don't believe what you see."

The panther roared in an attempt to drown out her words. With a shudder through its shoulders, the panther grew in size and bulk, changing shape again into a black bear. Its lips rolled back from pink gums and huge teeth, froth flying from its open mouth as it snapped at Emerson and slashed at the old man with its long, curved claws, still bound together. Both men jumped back.

Proctor's heart clenched, the way it had when he'd gone into battle against the British. His pulse throbbed beneath the bandage on his neck.

"We must do something," Emerson insisted.

"Help me grab her," Jedediah said. "We'll wrap her in the blanket and lay her in the cart."

As he tried to hold the bear's bound paws, it struggled harder. Emerson was hanging back, and he couldn't control the woman or beast or whatever it was alone. Proctor advanced another step, half out of the bushes and up the side of the ditch, ready to lend a hand. Neither man saw him, their attention fixed on the cart. But the bear, or panther, or witch, whatever she was, stared straight at him.

The bear's bare-toothed snarl turned into a laugh.

An invisible fire poured out of Proctor, flowing opposite the direction that it had when he'd grasped Pitcairn's protective charm.

As the fire flowed out, real, visible flames burst out on the bear's bound wrists, leaping from the ropes. The old man muttered under his breath and tried to throw a blanket over the flames. Emerson leapt the other way.

It was wise that he did—Jedediah's coat burst into flames around his shoulders, fire licking at his ears while he spun in a circle, madly trying to pat it out. He knocked his hat off as the flames singed his cheeks. Emerson rushed to help him, shoving him to the ground away from the wagon, and rolling him to put out the fire.

The Quaker woman shouted, "You must hold her." But still she held back.

Proctor didn't understand what was happening, but he knew he was the only one who could help, so he ran to the edge of the road, ready to grab the witch, no matter her shape.

As he approached the cart, though, the bear shrank back into an old woman, who shook off her singed bonds, which fell, smoking, with a thump, onto the wagon.

At the same instant trees all around them erupted with the sound of crows cawing, a din so loud Proctor covered his ears. A black mass rose up from the woods like smoke from the British fires in Concord only a few days before; a murder of crows spiraled into one big cloud of birds, screeching and crying as it circled the sky.

Beneath that ominous black mass, Emerson was still putting out the flames on Jedediah's clothes, Jedediah was shouting that he was fine, and the Quaker woman stalked down the trail, head lowered, chanting.

And Proctor stood there, motionless, uncertain.

The widow rose free and unencumbered in the back of the cart. She spread her arms, and the sleeves of her dress flared out like wings; tilting her head back, she cawed to the sky, echoing the crows in their dark blot overhead.

Then she stared at Proctor for a third time, and the grin vanished from her face. A cold air settled over Proctor, more than the chill of the shadow from the crows. A thin, gray mist rose from the floor of the forest, as if called by the cold.

Her eyes dulled to the color of coals in the hearth. She spoke softly but clearly. "Come and fetch me, darlings."

Proctor thought she spoke to him, but at the call of her voice, the crows ceased their circling and swooped out of the sky, crowded together, hundreds of them, talons snatching at the old woman's outstretched sleeves. As if she weighed no more than a threadbare shift, they lifted her from the wagon, new crows constantly dropping through the flock to clutch at her when she slipped from the grasp of others.

Stunned by the sight, Proctor walked onto the trail and stood there in the open, watching her form rise over the trees.

The Quaker woman reacted first. "Who in God's name are you?"

Emerson rose to his feet, his gaze flicking for a second

from Proctor back to the sight of the old woman dipping over the tops of the trees. "Brown? What have you seen?"

Jedediah ignored him. Bareheaded, his bald skin blistered from the fire, he tumbled across the path, snatching up his musket. He rose and aimed it at his diminishing prisoner. The pan flashed, and fire and smoke jetted from the barrel.

At the crack of the musket, the crows dropped the woman in black. She fell toward the trees and then vanished. The crows suddenly evaporated, like a wisp of smoke in a strong wind.

The air was quiet, empty, and utterly still.

Far away, in a pasture in the hills across a river, a cow lowed. The horse lowered its head and began to nibble at grasses that lined the path.

"Don't stand there," the old man said, reloading his musket and gesturing for Emerson to follow him. "We have to recapture her."

He set off running toward the spot where the crows had dropped her. Emerson followed, but at a slower pace. Proctor would have sprinted too, eager to help, desperate to learn more, but the Quaker woman stepped in his way.

"Wait, something's wrong," she said.

"I don't think any of that was right," Proctor answered. But then, without looking for it, he saw what she meant: a light breeze, coming across the nearby river, had pulled the smoke from the musket one direction. A cloud of mist, low to the ground and no bigger than a person, drifted against the wind and into the forest.

"There," Proctor said, pointing at the mist. As he pointed, he became aware of a slight tingle, like ants crawling across bare skin, that made him certain he was right. "There she is!"

Emerson said, "Where?" and the old man stopped, twisting back around to see. Proctor was the closest to the mist, and without regard to danger, he ran toward it.

The Quaker woman intercepted him, shoving him aside. The contact shocked him. "Stay back," she warned.

"But—"

He sputtered, trying to regain his balance. She came toward him, making him stumble backward, preventing him from resuming his attempt to help. Up close, she was much younger than he expected, perhaps no more than three or four years older than he was. Her face was as plain as her clothes.

"This is your fault," she said. "I don't know how, and I don't know if you're aiding her—"

"I'm not aiding her, but—"

"—or if you're also a British spy, but if any additional ill comes of this, and I find out it is your fault—"

"But—"

"—I will see to it that you itch in places too uncomfortable to scratch for the rest of your miserable life."

"But she's escaping!"

The mist had vanished completely now, and she was only a small, frail woman, a black wraith dodging through the rough brown trunks. The old man sprinted after her. Emerson followed, pausing as he reached Proctor and the young woman.

"Deborah?" he said.

"I'm fine," the Quaker woman replied, more calm now than she had been moments ago. "But she must be stopped until we know what she intended."

Emerson nodded. "This is Mister Brown, one of the local minutemen . . ."

Deborah said, "You know him?"

"I do. He's no British spy, but served well at the battle—his wound there came from a British gun."

"It did," Proctor said, and then Jedediah called for Emerson. The Reverend ran off after the older man while Deborah placed herself squarely in Proctor's path.

The anger had faded from her face, erasing the line in her brow and at the corners of her mouth, giving her face, with its strong cheekbones and narrow nose, a more pleasant appearance.

"Are you a witch?" she asked.

The air disappeared from Proctor's throat. After a second, he said, "No, of course not."

"No, of course not," she mimicked, and anger wrote new lines across her face in an instant. She reached out to touch the back of his hand with the tips of her fingers. A shiver rippled up his spine, but there seemed to be nothing left in him, like a pitcher that had been poured until it was empty.

She withdrew her hand and turned away. "Stay back, and keep out of the way," she said as she walked, not even pausing to look at him. "And forget you saw anything you think you saw today."

"What? But that woman—"

She spun on him, scowling. "But that woman what? She's an old lady, suffering from infirmities, who we are helping on her way to visit relatives."

"What about—?"

"What about what? Go ahead and tell people that you saw an old woman transformed into a catamount, or a bear, tell them that she was carried away by crows." She paused, her eyes moving from side to side, as if she were reading his expression like a page. "Tell people whatever you wish. But it was entirely an illusion, just a fanciful daydream, a waking vision. No one but you will ever admit to having seen it."

He stood there with his mouth agape. This was the second time he had witnessed a stranger's witchcraft. In Boston, Pitcairn, an enemy, had commanded him to spread what he had seen; here, among those he considered allies, he was commanded to stay silent. When he found his tongue, he said, "But you saw it too."

"Go home," she said. "Go off to your militia. Or just . . . just go off to China."

In the distance, the tiny figure of the widow tripped, allowing Jedediah to close on her, with Emerson near behind. Jedediah called out, "Deborah."

"If you'll excuse me," she said. "I have work to do." She hurried over to the cart. Off in the woods, the two men pinned the arms of the widow.

Proctor sniffed the air and caught the lingering scent of burned hemp and seared flesh. He looked over Deborah's shoulder into the back of the cart and saw a rope with charred ends.

"Not entirely an illusion," he said.

Chapter 8

Deborah withdrew a small bag from her pocket and circled the cart, leaning over the sideboards to sprinkle something around the perimeter of the floorboards. Her lips moved, as though she prayed beneath her breath.

Proctor watched her, puzzled. He pressed his finger against the grainy trail that trickled from her fist and touched it to his tongue. Salt.

She saw him and her face went red with anger. "What do you think you're doing?"

He hooked his thumbs in the waistband of his breeches. "Why are you sprinkling salt?"

"You really don't know?"

"No."

"Then stay back and don't interfere again," she said, spreading a fresh line of salt over the spot he'd touched.

The quiet anger suffusing her voice convinced him to step back. He glanced over his shoulder to see what Jedediah or Emerson thought. Jedediah was leading the widow back toward the road, bound at her wrists and this time also gagged. His arm was hooked through her elbow, and her body bent against his hip, so that he was practically carrying her. Emerson walked at her side, silent and thoughtful, making no entreaties to her to repent her sins. Both wore the same grim expression as Deborah.

She circled the cart two more times, spilling her thin trail of salt. When she finished her third circuit, there was so little left that she was forced to brush it from the palm of her hand. She murmured intently the entire time; Proctor could not tell what she was saying, only that every third word or so seemed to be "light."

"Art thou ready?" Jedediah called, his voice strained.

"Not yet," she said, bending over a corner of the cart.

Four large iron nails protruded from the corners of the cart's frame. Proctor hadn't noticed them before. He approached one opposite Deborah and saw that it had been tied with a piece of white ribbon. The knot in the ribbon was burned through as surely as the ropes had been.

"Do you have any ribbon?" Deborah asked over the edge of the cart.

Proctor held a hand to his chest. "Me?"

"No, the more helpful fellow standing next to you."

He reached in his pocket for the yellow ribbon that Emily had given him; he was thinking that he would keep it rather than give it to this surly young woman when he realized it was no longer there, but had been tattered to threads by the same shot that had ripped apart his father's canteen. "I'm sorry, but I don't," he said, more puzzled than ever.

"I'm not surprised." She tugged up the hem of her skirt and ripped it, tearing off thread after thread.

"What are you doing?" Proctor asked.

"You need to step away, much farther away, before they bring her close," Deborah said. She put a string in her teeth and tore it in two, then began knotting it around the first nail.

"Sure," Proctor said to mollify her, but he leaned in close for a better look at what she was doing. The knots seemed perfectly ordinary, even a little rushed.

"Deborah?" Jedediah's voice sounded strained. The skin on the side of his face was red and blistered from the burn.

"I'm hurrying as fast as I can," she said.

Emerson took a few hesitant steps forward, his face pale and his eyes still wide. "Can I help in any way?"

Deborah's glance fell on Proctor. "Your little toy soldier

won't get out of my way. If all your patriots are like him, it's a marvel they did any harm to the British."

"Mister Brown," Emerson said firmly, drawing himself up into formal posture. "Be so good as to obey this young woman."

"Sir," Proctor answered and looked to Deborah for instructions.

"Over there." She indicated with a jerk of her head as she hurried to the second corner and began tying another set of knots around the next iron nail.

With his hands still hooked in his waistband, he took a few casual steps away. She continued to pray as she tied the strings. She seemed to be repeating the same phrases she had used when sprinkling the salt. *Hold in the light, by the light, and with the light.* Whatever that meant.

"You can bring her now," she called out as she finished the fourth set of knots, lifted her tattered hem, and hurried away from the cart. Proctor stepped closer to see again.

The old woman, who had been limp in Jedediah's grip, suddenly lifted her head and stared at Proctor. Her eyes were distant, almost milky like cataracts, with the same absence he saw in his father's gaze, as if they were looking at something far away, over the horizon of the spirit. He felt himself picked up and carried with the gaze, like a bird in the wind, thrown over the landscape to his home, and in through the window: his father sat in his chair, staring back, his eyes clear and focused. His mother lifted her head from the table where she worked, and his vision closed on her face, eyes full of fear and worry. Her face became the widow's face, the two blurred together.

His knees buckled. He staggered back and leaned against a tree for support, never taking his eyes off the widow until he felt a sharp pinch on the back of his hand. His blood raced with anger as he jerked his hand away, but relief followed a second later. Deborah stood beside him, her fingers poised where his hand had been a second before.

"That hurt," he said.

"No, not a witch," she murmured sarcastically.

The widow started to laugh through her gag. Deborah grabbed Proctor's arm and pulled him along the path ahead of the cart. "Come with me," she said.

"Why should I?" he said, bracing his legs and stopping.

Deborah yanked Proctor's arm hard enough to pull him off-balance. "Because I don't want you to get us killed."

"Go with her, Brown," Emerson snapped.

She put her body between Proctor and the cart, and pushed him down the trail. He allowed her to only because of the fear in Emerson's voice.

Jedediah and Emerson lifted the widow into the tip cart. As she crossed the tailboard, she lashed out with her feet at the line of salt.

"Don't let her break the circle," Deborah shouted over her shoulder.

"I know," Jedediah grunted.

The widow kicked and struggled like a spoiled child throwing a tantrum, but both men were strong, and Emerson quite tall as well. As soon as they lifted her clear of the edge, she fell limp, whimpering, into the bottom of the cart, where she lay suddenly still atop the bits of old straw and manure.

A shiver iced through Proctor. "What did I just see?"

"If you're smarter than I take you to be, then you didn't see anything," Deborah said. She continued to push him down the trail away from the cart.

"What kind of witchcraft is this?" he asked.

"There's no—" Deborah started, and then a grunt from Jedediah interrupted them.

The old man stood in the path beside the cart, hands on his knees, breathing deliberately while his body shook. Emerson leaned over him. Proctor started back down the trail toward them.

Deborah grabbed two handfuls of his jacket. "Stop!"

"He needs help!"

"Don't you understand? You're helping *her*."

Proctor twisted, pulling his coat free. His voice wavered as he said, "No, I'm not. I'm not helping her."

"If you didn't help her, I don't know how she escaped my original binding spell."

"That's madness," he said, but he glanced over his shoulder. "What's a binding spell?"

She shook her head in disbelief. "You don't need to know."

"I need to know." The voice belonged to Jedediah. His face was a grimace, his neck and cheek covered with blisters. He stood upright and approached her. "What happened back there?"

"She escaped," Deborah snapped.

"I saw that. But how did she break the spell?"

"Why don't you ask Elizabeth?" Deborah asked.

Proctor shook his head. Who was Elizabeth?

"Oh, wait, you can't ask her because she was nearly killed," Deborah said. "And she's the only one of us powerful enough to understand this woman."

"What did thou do wrong?" he asked, stomping toward her.

"What did I do wrong?" Deborah said, his voice rising sharply. "What did you do at all? You stood by and did nothing until it was too late, the way you always do."

"Deborah," Emerson said, addressing her like a child.

"No, it's fine," Jedediah said, raising his hand to stop Emerson from saying anything further. "Stay thine anger. She has the right to speak her mind, however she truly feels."

"Those burns look painful," Deborah said instantly, more softly, reaching her hand halfway to his cheek.

He turned his head away, then, a second later, his whole body. "I'll go get the cart."

Emerson bristled at Deborah. "I'll treat him as soon as we get to your house," she said.

"I'll have Sarah bring you everything you need," he said sharply before turning away.

"How did she escape?" Proctor said.

"You know as much as I do," Deborah said, pulling him ahead. Jedediah had retrieved his hat and musket, and had taken the bridle in hand again. He was rubbing the muzzle of the horse and speaking to it before leading it on.

Proctor had thought he knew more about magic than nearly anyone, all because he could glimpse the future in the death of an egg or recognize the charmed medallion worn by Major Pitcairn. That was nothing compared with the things he had witnessed in the last half an hour.

"But I don't know anything," he said.

"Then that is the one thing we share in common," Deborah grumbled.

"But what were you doing on the cart? What was with the salt and the knots?"

"As if I would tell you," Deborah said. "What if you are helping her on purpose?"

"I swear I'm not."

She frowned, an expression that looked unnatural on her face, though it seemed that she did it often enough and with enough ease that it might someday become her permanent mask. "I don't trust anyone who swears," she said finally. "The Bible teaches us not to take oaths."

"The Bible also says to suffer not a witch to live."

"Do you make no distinction between how we're born and what we choose to do?"

He opened his mouth, but there were no words to come out of it.

"If we have special talents, it's only because God gave them to us, and He expects us to use them to His glory. Were you given one talent that you've buried, or many talents that you wisely invest?"

Proctor recognized arguments that he had made to himself. "Just like the parable of the talents . . ."

"Exactly," she said, as if surprised that he wasn't as stupid as she'd thought him. "Jesus also commands us to swear not at all."

His head was spinning. "What's that then? Is that also part of some spell?"

"What?"

"That flower in your buttonhole."

"The flower—?" She regarded the blossom in surprise, as if she'd forgotten it. Up close, it appeared as much red as purple, a shade somewhere between blood and bruise. She frowned at herself. "This is a vanity, a distraction from my duty."

"Ah," Proctor said. "My mother calls it truelove."

Deborah sneered. "And I bet she uses it to treat nosebleeds and help with childbirths."

"Nosebleeds," Proctor admitted. "She says that each of the threes in it—the three leaves, three petals, and so on—is for the Trinity."

"I call it stinking benjamin," Deborah said, ripping it from her shawl and leaving the torn stem behind.

"My mother calls it that too," Proctor said. "And wake-robin."

"Three names for everything. It sounds like she and my mother would get along very well." She crumpled the blossom in her fist. He noticed that her pale, slender fingers were bare of adornment. She threw the flower down in the trail, trampling it on purpose. "There's Emerson's house." Over her shoulder, she called out, "I'll go ahead to find Sarah."

Proctor blinked in the light as the old trees opened up on the young orchard. Emerson's house sat near the river below them. Deborah hurried away. What a contrary and unpleasant young woman, Proctor thought. No wonder she was still unmarried at her age. He was glad Emily was nothing like her. Well, except for a certain sharpness of tongue.

Jedediah led the cart toward the isolated workshed where Proctor had met with Emerson. Emerson took Proctor aside, leading him away from the shed and back toward the main road.

"So are you still worried about Miss Rucke's accusations of witchcraft?" Emerson asked.

"What did I see?" Proctor demanded. "How did she do those things?"

"Magic is mostly lies, but lies told to our eyes instead of our ears. If you report the lies as fact, you may do great harm, and bring innocent people to an unfortunate end, like the situation witnessed by our forefathers at Salem. Is that what you want?"

"I just want to understand what I saw."

"Which is it?"

Proctor shook his head. "What do you mean?"

Emerson had shaken off whatever fear had marked him on the trail. "Do you want to shake off Miss Rucke's accusation and find a wife and build your cattle farm, or do you want to pursue forbidden magic and bring the scrutiny and approbation of the community upon you?"

"I—"

"You must choose, Mister Brown." He placed a hand on Proctor's shoulder. "I strongly encourage you to forget everything you saw. Treat it as but a dream that fades as the day progresses, so that by nightfall no memory of it remains. Go home. Do your duty to your parents, and to your country. Become the man you want to become."

Proctor couldn't believe what he was hearing. "But how did she start that fire? That fire was no illusion. That Jedediah fellow is burned, all over his face and shoulder."

Emerson cleared his throat. "Perhaps a bit of gunpowder, and a flint, hidden in her sleeve for such a circumstance. A mere trick."

A laugh formed on Proctor's lips and evaporated just as quickly.

"Do you wish to help us?" Emerson asked.

"Yes, sir," Proctor said. "Of course I do."

"Then run ahead to Amos Lathrop's home," Emerson said. "Tell him to call on me, that it's for the patriot cause."

"Anything Amos can do to help you, I can do as well."

Emerson tilted his head forward and glared down his nose. "Did you mean your offer to help or no?"

Proctor hesitated. Maybe Emerson didn't trust him after all. Maybe he knew somehow that Proctor was also a witch. Maybe, like Deborah, he blamed Proctor for helping the widow nearly escape.

"I meant it," Proctor said.

"Then run to the Lathrop farm and tell Amos to come straightaway to the shed at the back of the property. I'll need him to stay all night."

"Yes, sir." He took a few steps backward before turning to leave.

"Mister Brown?"

"Yes?"

"You've been injured recently. You may be a little light-headed still. It might be best for you to go straight home after the Lathrop farm and rest until you are well."

"Yes, sir," he said, ducking his head, and hurried away.

When his feet hit the main road, he began to wonder if Emerson was right. Did he really have to choose? What if he wanted a life with Emily and also wanted to understand his talent? Why couldn't he have both, one helping the other?

He had to understand his talent better, if only to make Emily understand it. He had to prove to her that his talent was God-given, meant to be used.

These thoughts were still marching through his head when he arrived at the Lathrops' farm. They were glad to see him. Mrs. Lathrop, Amos's mother, wanted to know about Proctor's wound, and then both parents and Amos's two unmarried sisters joined them at the table while he had a cup of cider and listened to them share the same news from Boston he'd already heard from the old farmer. Proctor made agreeable noises around mouthfuls of beans and pork fat, delivered his message to Amos, and begged to be excused because he still had a long walk home.

Amos followed him out to the porch, which sagged beneath their weight. His sisters stood at the window, smiling and waving at Proctor. The younger one kept trying to pull off the cap of the older one.

"Did the Reverend Emerson say exactly what he wanted me for?" Amos asked.

Proctor rubbed his nose, looked away. "I'm not sure. Best that he tells you himself."

Amos nodded. "All right. You go get rested up. And Proctor?"

He paused, already half turned to go. "Yes?"

"I heard that Emily Rucke and her father went over to the other side. If you're ready to start looking for another sweetheart, I might know a couple girls who'd return your interest, if you were serious."

Behind the glass, the older girl covered her mouth and the younger one giggled. Amos winked at them.

"I'm sure it'll work out fine with Miss Rucke," Proctor said. "We just have to give it a chance. But thanks, Amos."

Amos grinned. "Things change in ways we don't expect. Just keep an open mind."

Proctor assured him that he would, but as he headed cross-country for home, he rehearsed the things he planned to say to Emily next time he saw her. To that end, his own ignorance frustrated him again and again. The closer he came to his home, the angrier he grew. How much did his mother really know about witchcraft? What had she been keeping from him all these years?

He climbed over the stone wall and cut across the pasture toward their house. Blankets hung outside on the line to dry, still too heavy to stir with the breeze. Wild ducks milled in the yard with the chickens; they all scattered, quacking and clucking, as he walked through them to the door. He stopped to peer inside before he entered.

His mother must have been cleaning for days. Their normally tidy house was immaculate, every surface clean, every item in its place. His father sat propped by the open window, his face clean-shaven, his hair washed and brushed back to dry, revealing the scar where he'd been scalped.

Proctor went inside and leaned his musket against the wall, hanging up his powder horn and bag. There was something he needed to say, but he was finding himself too choked up. He forced the words out.

"Robert Munroe," he said. The veteran who had served with his father, and the man who had the misfortune to be standing next to Proctor on Lexington Green when he shot at Pitcairn.

His father continued to rock, eyes unfocused.

"He said, what Munroe said was, he said you were a good man in a fight."

The door creaked open and his mother entered one step, pausing as soon as she saw Proctor. She looked away from him and carried the bucket of water over to the table, where she splashed some into their brass cooking pot and scrubbed at it, even though it was already so clean it gleamed.

He cleared his throat. "I'm home, Mother."

Chapter 9

His mother stood there, scrubbing the pot even harder than before. "I see that," she said finally without looking up. "You're home. You're home after running off to play soldier, after being gone for days. After you went all the way to Concord and back, marching right past your own mother's house without stopping. Don't lie or tell me different. Mister Leary saw you on the road this morning."

"I had to go see the Reverend Emerson. He sends his regards." When she didn't answer him, he went over to the hearth and tipped lids on the kettles to see if there was any food left. "We have to talk, Mother. About the scrying. About our talent."

She banged the pot on the table. "We never talk about it! Never! Do you want them to hang me? Do you want them to burn me alive?"

"Of course I don't want anyone to burn—"

She cut off his sentence by banging the pot on the table again. This time his father stirred out of his ordinary half sleep and blinked in vacuous agitation at the room.

"Now see what you've done," she said. "You've gone and woken your father. Today exhausted him and he needs his rest, but you had to wake him up."

Instead of moving to comfort her husband, as she usually did when he woke, she put the pot back in its place by the hearth, hung the rag up to dry, and slammed out the door.

Proctor went over to soothe his father, patting the old man's shoulder until he smiled and slurred some sentence

Proctor pretended to comprehend. He explained that he needed to go help his mother, and his father nodded. When his eyes drifted shut again, Proctor followed her outside. He wasn't sure if she was just afraid or if she was deliberately hiding something from him.

Although the light was fading, she was in the garden with the hoe, where she slashed at the heavy soil and turned it over for planting. "What are you doing?" Proctor asked, trying to control the anger he felt.

"Everything," she said with another slash. "I have to do everything. Your father's too sick to work, and you're running off to wars you have no business with, coming near to getting yourself killed. If I'm going to be here all by myself, I'll have to work twice as hard. Even though I'm at an age where I ought to be mostly taking care of grandchildren."

"Mother, I'm not going anywhere."

"You think you aren't, but I can tell differently," she said, punctuating her sentence with three ferocious slashes of the hoe. She stopped and turned to him. "When you first came to me with your . . . your talent"—she made the word sound like a curse—"that day your friend was shot by British soldiers, what did I tell you?"

He tried to take the hoe from her hand to do the work for her, but she pulled away. "That I must never tell anyone about it."

"Yes," she said. "We have relations who were killed at Salem, who were hanged to death, not eighty years past, because people discovered they were witches."

"That was a long time ago. Massachusetts is nothing like that now."

"If it isn't, it's because those of us with talents have been wise enough to hold our tongues and keep them secret. No one knows outside the family. I would never have said anything to you if you didn't have to bear the same cross." Her voice dropped lower, and for a second he thought her secret was going to spill out. But all she said, in a whisper, was, "I thought with a son, I would be spared." She reached up, as if she finally noticed the bandage on his neck, and peeled it back to look at the wound. "Oh, Proctor, if that ball had been two inches the other direction, it would have killed you for certain."

He folded his hand around hers and pulled it away from his wound. "If it had been two inches the other direction it would have missed me completely."

She turned away, slamming the hoe into the ground again, but this time when he reached for it, she handed it to him. He slowly turned over the soil. "So when did you find out?"

Wiping her hands on her apron, she said, "When I was about the same age as you were. I kept finding things our neighbors had lost—a needle in a haystack was as obvious to me as a dog in the chicken coop—until my mother heard of it and told me what would happen if I didn't keep it secret."

"And that's all she told you?"

She paused, turning partially away from him, before she answered. "What do you want me to tell you?"

"I want you to tell me everything. I deserve to know."

She dropped her head. "My mother," she started reluctantly. "She told me that our people came to America to practice our talents in freedom, away from the burnings and hangings in England and the rest of Europe." Her chin came up, her eyes fierce with anger. "But then the fear spread here. And good, God-fearing people, with no more evil in them than the talents God gave them, were put to death, and all of us were forced into hiding."

Proctor hacked the soil hard. It smelled dry and rich, ready for planting. "There was this soldier," he said. "An officer."

"Yes?"

"He was a Redcoat, Major Pitcairn. He had this medallion around his neck, like a golden coin."

"Was this at Concord?"

"In Boston first, then at Lexington and Concord. No one else seemed to notice it, but it gleamed like the sun to me, and I could tell there was . . ." He was at a loss for words. Charm? Protection? "There was something about it that steered harm away from him."

She bent over as he worked, scooping stones out of the soil as he turned it over. He slowed his motion to match her bending and plucking. "I don't know anything about that," she said.

The phrase came so easily to her lips that he felt sure she would say the same thing even if she did know something.

She carried a handful of stones over to the side of the well and dropped them. When she returned, he said, "Then today, I saw this woman, when I went to see the Reverend Emerson." He started to explain about the shape-changing—the panther and bear—and the crows. But he looked up and saw that the grief and pain in her face made her appear older than even his father instead of many years younger. After turning and starting the next row, he said, with his back to her, "She could start fire with nothing but the air and wind for flint and steel."

His mother slammed a stone back into the dirt. "Proctor, you're the one playing with fire. I beg you, please, to stop before you are burned. Before you have me burned with you."

He kept his eyes on the ground as he continued to hoe. "But we don't just play with fire. We use fire for cooking, for heat, for the forges that make our tools—our lives depend on fire. This is the same thing. I want to know what I'm doing so I'm *not* playing." He lifted his head to meet her eyes. "And who else will explain it to me but you?"

"I beg you to give up your interest in this," she said, her voice trembling.

He stopped, planted the hoe in the ground, and leaned on it. The sun dropped in the western sky, like a stone in a pond that sent out splashes of pink and orange over the blue. She had tears in her eyes but held them dammed back by the rims of her lids, refusing to let them flow down her face.

"I'm afraid for *us,* Proctor."

"I didn't even tell you all of what I saw yet."

"And I don't want to hear it."

Anger flashed through him, and he slammed the hoe into the dirt. It was always the same answer from her. If she knew something, she said she didn't. If he needed to know something, she refused to talk about it.

She dropped her head, covered her hand with her mouth for a moment. "I have prayed on this, and prayed on it, every day of my life. I have to believe that what we have is a gift from God, a blessing, but it is only a blessing if we use it to do His will."

"I've never said I wanted to do anything else—"

"If you use it for personal gain, if you use the gift to harm another, it becomes a curse, and God will punish you for it. Like a man who has great strength, who uses it to bully the weak instead of protecting them."

He paused until her throat stopped quivering. When he spoke, he spoke softly. "Mother, a week ago, I thought I was going to take over this farm, and get married to Emily, and have a life just like the one that you and Father had."

"And what's wrong with that? Why can't you do that still, with someone else? Other young women find you handsome, and you're known as a hard worker. Why can't you forget about the war? Why can't you do what you were going to do before?"

She sounded so desperate, he felt sad. "That's what I want to do," he said. "But I have to understand what's happened and what I've seen."

"There's nothing to understand." She knotted her fists in her apron and punched it at him, then stomped several steps away, back toward the house. "I can tell you're not satisfied, Proctor. I can tell you want more. Well, go look for it if you must, go look at your British officer and your old woman in Concord with their medallions and fires. But you won't like what you find."

"How do you know that?"

"Because when you turn over rocks, all you find are snakes." She forced her hands to relax, smoothed her apron. "I know what happened before, when people with our talents tried to share them with their neighbors, when they dared to speak of them openly."

"I'll be careful."

She laughed, wearily, and looked away, shaking her head in exhaustion. She headed back toward the house, saying, "It's been a long day, and I need to put your father to bed. I have to do that too, just like I do everything else."

At the door, she paused, waiting for him to offer to come help her. But for once he didn't move, and a moment later the door slammed shut behind her.

He tapped the hoe against the ground, thinking. Their conversation left him with more unanswered questions than he'd had before they talked. And one of them was this: what *was* his mother hiding from him?

Chores had their own soothing pace, giving him time to think. He cleaned up, putting the hoe away, chasing the last of the chickens into their coop, splitting tomorrow's firewood. As he worked, he considered that he might be heir to a secret that went back generations, but his mother knew little or nothing more about it than that. She carried the shame and fear of it around like a bushel full of rocks. His mother was afraid of a vision from a cracked egg when at any time she, or he, might make a man burst into flames.

The fire had been no lie—he could still smell the scent of burned wool and scorched skin. He had discovered scrying by accident. Would he discover an incendiary talent the same way? No, it was better if he understood it, where it came from. How to use it.

Yes, how to use it. Imagine being able to start a fire in the winter without barking his numb hands against steel and flint until he struck a spark. It was almost enough to make him feel wickedly lazy.

What if he used it to defeat evil witchcraft? What if he could have undone Pitcairn's charm before a shot was ever fired on the green?

The wound in his neck throbbed. He pulled off the bandage and felt the scab with his fingers. No fresh seepage, that was good.

He went inside as the gloaming fell and found the plate of salted pork and boiled potatoes his mother had left sitting out for him. By the time he finished eating, he was surrounded by darkness and silence.

Emerson and Deborah had avoided his questions. His mother either didn't know the answers or hid them from him. But he knew where he could find someone who did.

He rose and shrugged his jacket on again. The prospect of understanding his talent chased exhaustion from him. For the second time that day, he headed across the fields toward Concord and the Reverend Emerson's great house, this time in the dark, this time in secret.

Lanterns flickered or were extinguished in various windows as he went. Dogs barked at his passing, except for the big sheepdog on the Kagey farm, which ran happily down to lick Proctor's hand and steal a scratch behind the ears. The air grew colder until his breath ghosted in front of him. He would have to lie, deliberately, to do what he wanted. Twice before he reached the Emersons' place, the fear of lying almost turned him back home.

But then he was cutting through the orchard. Near the shed, a dark shape sat across from the shed door. The silhouette of a familiar hat, one side of the brim pinned up, drooped toward its wearer's chest.

"Hello, Amos," Proctor said softly as he came up close.

Amos started up, aiming his musket defensively. "Proctor. You alarmed me."

"Anything happen?"

"Not a thing." Amos lowered his musket and rubbed his eyes. "You know who they have in there?"

Proctor hesitated a moment, then shook his head.

His friend shrugged. "Me either. But I'm not supposed to tell anyone about it, on peril of betraying the patriot cause. It's an odd business."

Proctor swallowed hard. "The Reverend Emerson asked me to come back to relieve you. Decided it was too long to have you stay here all night."

Amos stared hard at Proctor, his expression unreadable in the dark. Proctor had his next lie ready to trot out as soon as he was challenged, but Amos said, "Fine by me. I'm glad he thought of it, because I wasn't looking forward to bedding down out here tonight without so much as a tent. I'll get enough of that when I head down to the siege at Boston."

"Are you going?"

"I reckon so. There's no way to keep the Redcoats bottled up in there, not when they control the harbor. But we can keep them from marching out into the country again." He resituated his hat to one side. "Didn't Emerson ask you to bring your musket in case you need to sound an alarm?"

Proctor swallowed air wrong, which made him cough. "He must've forgotten to mention it."

Amos pulled his bag and horn off his shoulder and offered them, with the musket, to Proctor. "Drop them off by the house in the morning."

"Thank you," Proctor said, trying not to let the straps slip through his sweaty hands.

"If you come by early enough, I'll have my sisters fix breakfast for you."

"I don't care who fixes it, I'll eat it," Proctor said, and then they both laughed.

"Good night, then," Amos said. He trudged past the big house toward the road.

As soon as his shadow faded into the night, Proctor went over to the shed. He saw nails, with ribbons knotted on them, just as in the cart. It was too dark to see if there was a circle of salt on the ground, but he sat across from the door, far enough not to disturb it if there was. He listened for a long time without hearing anything, so he reached over and rapped lightly on the wood slats. "You awake in there?"

A body stirred against the other side of the door. "If I wasn't, I would be now, wouldn't I?"

A woman's voice, exhausted, but with a faint foreign lilt to it, Proctor thought—though his experience with foreigners was limited to a few people he'd overheard in Boston.

"Where are you from?" he asked.

"I reclaim my previous answer—I am most definitely sleeping. Now leave me alone." A rustling sound inside moved away from the door.

He rapped again. "How did you do that?"

Wearily, "I closed my eyes and rolled over."

"On the wagon today—how did you create the illusion of that panther, and the bear? How did you make us see the crows? I could have sworn it was cooler beneath their shadows, that a wing brushed my face."

A pause inside was followed by the sound of her sitting upright and the creak of wood as she pressed against the door. "You're the young one, hiding in the woods, aren't you?"

It was his turn to pause, wondering, now that he was speaking to her, how much he dare give away.

"No, it's all right, you don't need to tell me," she said. "Now that I'm awake, I can sense you clear and fine, a fire bright as daylight, even through the door."

Fire? That was the word Deborah had mentioned. "What does that mean?"

She chuckled. "So you have powers, do you? Talents you don't understand. And there's no one to explain them to you, no one to show you how to use them?"

"I never said that."

"Then why did you come wake me in the middle of the night?"

"How did you do those things? Was it witchcraft?"

A sigh, not wholly muffled by the planks of wood. "Those were illusions, mere tricks of the eye."

"The fire wasn't."

"I had a flint and steel hidden in my sleeve."

"All right, then, if that's how it is, good night."

He was shaking a bit, not that he would have called it scared, what with her inside and him out here. But his skin tingled again, the way it had earlier, and he was afraid it might burst into flame, no matter what she said. So he stood up to walk away.

"Wait. Come back."

He stopped. "Why? You told me what I wanted to know. They were tricks of the eye, and tricks hid up your sleeve. And the salt and the nails, that was all superstitious nonsense."

"Come back, I'll tell you something."

The door bulged and cracked at the edge as she pressed against it. He checked the latch to make sure it was secure. Then he looked to the nails, and saw the ends of the knotted ribbons fluttering in the light breeze.

"You know someone like me, maybe your grandmother, or your maiden aunt," she said. The steam of her breath came out through the crack in the door. "Perhaps it's your mother? No matter. Whoever she is, you know what the mobs do at the first hint of even harmless sorcery. So you know that women like your grandmother or your aunt and myself, we have to lie to protect ourselves."

His jaw clenched and he took a step back toward the shed. "How do you know what I know?"

"I've met young men just like you once or twice before. Where did your mother tell you witches came from?"

"She didn't."

A pause, smug in its silence. "So it is your mother, then."

"Maybe not," Proctor said quickly. He had a sensation of ants crawling all over his skin—he looked down to brush them away, but saw none.

"Do you know your Bible?" she asked.

"Are you going to tell me the 'suffer not a witch to live' passage?"

That won a wry laugh. "Why waste my breath in asking? This is Massachusetts—you know the Bible better than the current news. Do you recall the passage, that 'there were giants on the earth in those days, when the sons of God came unto the daughters of men, and they bare children to them, and the same became mighty men, men of renown'?"

He paused. "What's that to do with anything?"

"Where do you think witches come from? The sons of God slept with the daughters of men, and we are their grandchildren. Some part of the angels lives on in us, giving us the power of angels, the ability to do small miracles."

He gripped the musket with his hands.

"Why are you angry?" she said softly, so muffled by the door that he had to lean closer to hear it.

"That's blasphemy."

"Is it? Do you not know your own talent? Where else could it come from, but from the seed of the angels?"

He slammed the butt-end of the musket against the door.

She swallowed a gasp of pain and moved away from the door. "See now why witches must lie? We have powers that make us giants among ordinary mortals, and they call us blasphemers. They hunt us down and hang us and burn us, because they are afraid of us. Even those who share our talent."

"Is that what they're going to do with you?"

"They are afraid of you too. These people lied to you, didn't they? Give them a reason and they will kill you also."

His neck throbbed. The scab itched; his whole body itched. He didn't want to believe what she said. He didn't know if he dared to disbelieve it. "They don't want to kill me."

"Not yet, they don't. But wait, give them time. Our powers—your powers—are a gift from God. God has made us giants. And every man longs to be like David. Open the door, and set me free, and I will teach you anything you wish."

He took another step back. She was pushing him too hard, reminding him of the traveling huckster who'd come through Lincoln the past summer. "Do you have a familiar?" he asked.

"No," she cried instantly. "What kind of nonsense do they teach you in these colonies? I'm as harmless as your mother. I'm just an old widow that people fear because I'm a stranger."

"I thought they feared you because you were like the angels, because you did magic."

"I have powers, little things," she said. "What does it matter if I do them? I should be able to do whatever I wish, so long as I harm no others."

"You harmed that man you set on fire today."

"An accident. I was just trying to burn through the ropes. Please, you have to set me free."

The darkest part of night had settled around them, thick and cold and heavy, like a winter snow. "I don't think so."

"Just look into my eyes," she pleaded, weak and helpless like a frightened old woman. "Open the door a crack and look into my eyes. You'll see that I'm telling the truth. I just want to go my own way, go far away from here, and I promise I won't ever return."

"I'm sorry I woke you," he said, tipping his hat.

Fingertips appeared on the edge of the door, her bound hands frantically trying to pry it open. The door banged against its latch as she struggled desperately to break out. "You can't leave me here," she begged, close to tears. "They'll kill me, they'll burn me alive, just like a pack of savage Indians. You must help me—you must."

He looked over his shoulder toward the house, afraid the noise would wake someone. A candle appeared in one of the windows. "You have to stop that," he said in a hushed tone. He lifted the musket threateningly. "I said stop."

"Shoot me, please, I beg you," she said, increasing her frantic efforts to break open the door. "I'd rather die quickly than to feel my own flesh on fire. Just open the door and shoot me."

"Nobody's going to shoot you or burn you," he said.

She began to sob pathetically. She sagged to the ground, her hands sliding down to the base of the door, where she pulled back the corner plank. The candle in the mansion window had bloomed into the light of a lantern. He went to the door, bending down to pull loose her hands.

Her fingernails dug into his hand the moment he touched her, and she let out an almost delighted gasp. At the same instant, the powder flashed in his musket, misfiring. The sudden glare blinded him all the same.

He would have pulled away, rubbing the smoke and powder from his eyes, but he felt drained. For a second he wondered if he'd torn his wound open again, and was faint from loss of blood as he had been on the battlefield at Lexington. He felt cold, bone-shaking cold, and empty, and although he wanted to pull away, to rip his hand from the widow's grasp, he collapsed instead. His head banged the side of the shed, his shoulder slammed into the ground, and his mouth filled with dirt.

He twisted weakly to the side, gagging, as she let go of his hand. With a small pop, the latch burst off the door.

Chapter 10

Proctor sprawled on the ground, blinking the way his father blinked, drooling the way his father drooled, as the widow pushed the door open.

She paused in the entrance, as if pressed against an invisible fence. She murmured words in an unfamiliar language, and ribbons fluttered to the ground, unwound from their nails. She crossed the threshold.

He could only follow her with his eyes as she stepped over him. She appeared so small and harmless. She tugged her black shawl about her shoulders, pulled it over her head, and took several steps toward the road before turning toward him.

"If I had my familiar," she said, "then I wouldn't have needed you now, would I?"

He rolled over, trying to rise, but it only made him dizzy. He passed in and out of consciousness, too weak to cry for help, so he had no way of knowing how long it had been when she returned and stood above him, holding a lantern.

"Help me," he wheezed.

"You stupid, stupid boy," she murmured.

His eyes were blurred so that he only saw her as a vague and murky shape. The odd thing was her voice sounded just like Deborah's. Her hands tore open his shirt, searching for wounds. Then as she said something to him, her fingers pinched the skin below his breast and twisted.

That snatched a cry from his throat, and then he blacked out completely.

When he felt water splash on his face and opened his eyes again, it was early morning, with the daylight warming his skin. He was sitting inside the shed, though the door was propped open. The old man, Jedediah, stood above him, face framed by the broad brim of his old-fashioned hat. The burns on his cheek and ear glistened with a greasy ointment.

Emerson stood there also, his hat in his hand. He reached down and touched the sore spot beneath Proctor's breast. It stabbed down into Proctor like an icicle.

"Ah, Mister Brown," he said sadly. "I was mistaken. I see that you do have the witch's mark on you, after all."

Proctor blinked at him and tried unsuccessfully to rise. "My mother will be worried sick."

"Thou art the one who should be worried," Jedediah said.

Emerson placed a hand on Jedediah's good shoulder. "I will go and meet our friend, and give him the bad news. Will you stay here?"

"I will."

"Thank you." Emerson took one last look at Proctor. "I think I shall meditate on my message for this Sabbath. The story of Judas is instructive."

He turned and walked away, stepping over a line just outside the door. Jedediah did the same. Proctor pushed himself on his hands and knees, rising to his feet with the intention to follow; but as he came to the threshold, light landed on his face like a lash, blinding him and knocking him back from the door.

Emerson's long strides were already carrying him away past the house. Jedediah squatted down on his haunches. He looked at Proctor and shook his head in disappointment.

Proctor winced and dug his heels in the dirt, pushing himself into a sitting position, with his back against the wall so he could still see through the door. The effort, or the attempt to pass through the door, combined with the smell of cider soaked into wood behind him, made him nauseous. He twisted sideways, propped his head against the wall, and vomited.

"Art thou all right?"

Proctor scrubbed his hand across his mouth. "I'm fine, thank you."

"How long have thou been in league with the widow?"

"I'm not in league with anyone. Why do you call her the widow?"

"We don't know her name, but she dresses like a widow, so that's what we call her. Twice she was able to escape, both times thou were present. The second time thou lied to gain access to her. Do thou deny this?"

"Yes. I mean, no—" He clamped his mouth shut. Jedediah waited until Proctor grew uncomfortable with the silence. "I came back because I wanted to understand how she did those things in the forest."

"Because thou wanted to learn witchcraft also."

"No." After a moment, he said, "Yes."

"Thou do not seem to know thine own meaning."

"That's God's truth," Proctor said, shifting his position against the wall to be more comfortable. He looked at Jedediah. Stubble showed on his heavy chin where he had failed to shave. The rim of his ear, not covered by the paste, was bright red and blistered. He still wore the long, plain jacket with the fresh scorch marks. The hands that rested across the musket showed the scrapes and scars of years of labor. "At first, I took you for a Quaker," Proctor said.

Jedediah waited a moment, then nodded, a bit reluctantly. "Which would be taking me for what I am. Though we prefer to be called friends."

"I never heard of Quakers carrying muskets or shooting at people."

"There is a time for every purpose under heaven. Some of us feel called to fight back when evil takes up arms first. So thou dost not know the widow?"

"I swear—"

"Do not swear, but answer yes for yes, no with no."

"No, I don't know her." He scooted away from the acid-sweet odor from his thin pool of vomit. "I followed the Reverend Emerson, because I thought I heard you say the word *witch* and I wanted to see. Then I saw what she did, changing shapes and setting fires. I wanted to know how she could do that."

"Why did thou help her escape if thou knows her not?"

"I didn't mean to help her. I was talking to her, she grabbed me, everything went topsy-turvy, and I woke to this."

Jedediah grunted, sitting down and bending his legs in front of him. He rested the musket at his right hand, the barrel aimed through the door at Proctor.

"How do you explain that?" he asked.

"What?"

"The witch's mark." He pointed at Proctor's open shirt.

A loose tab of flesh hung from his ribs. The memory came back to him, sharp and clear. "It was Deborah. She found me, after the widow attacked me. She pinched me, and called me stupid."

Jedediah grunted. "She called thee stupid?"

"Actually, she called me a 'stupid boy.' "

"That has the ring of truth to it." He rubbed his face and sighed. "So thou denies thou art a witch?"

Proctor opened his mouth, snapped it shut again. His hands were balled into fists.

"No, don't deny it," Jedediah said. "I can see thou art a poor liar in the best of times, which is a credit to thee and no shame. In any case now is not the best time to be lying. Thou art a witch, as sure as I'm a farmer's son. What's thy talent?"

He buttoned his shirt with unsteady fingers. So his secret was known. Which would be worse, that they knew the truth about him, or that they thought he was capable of changing shapes and setting fires? When the top button slipped through its hole, he said, softly, "Scrying."

"Scrying, is it?" Jedediah laughed, long and heartily. "Thou must not be very good at it."

"Why do you say that?"

"Because if thou could see the future, the widow would not have bested thee and thou would not have ended up in here."

He hadn't even considered scrying before his visit to the widow. What harm could it do to talk? That perspective seemed naïve now. "Why was she your prisoner?"

His voice rasped, dry from the vomiting and his overnight fast. Jedediah had a waterskin. He lifted the strap over his head and tossed the skin to Proctor, who fumbled the stopper free and swallowed a drink.

"We believe her to be a British spy," Jedediah said. "But we don't know. She attacked us, injured one of us very badly. While she thought she still had the advantage, she asked a lot of questions about how we had broken one of her charms in the battle on the Concord Road."

Proctor felt his mouth go dry despite the water.

"Deborah is more powerful than she admits, and was able to surprise her. She used every binding spell she knew to hold her, once she was our prisoner, but . . ." His words trailed off.

"A British spy?" Proctor asked.

"She was aiding them, but whether to their purposes or her own, I cannot say."

The jangle of a cowbell sounded from pastures beyond the orchard. The thought of his chores waiting for him, of the fence he needed to build along the eastern side of the pasture before he bought a breeding cow later this year, stirred Proctor to stand again. Bracing himself against the wall, he took a step toward the door.

"I wouldn't suggest that," Jedediah said. "Not unless thou wish to be sick again, and too weak to walk for days."

Leaning against the wall, Proctor said, "My mother will be worried sick over me. And I have work to do."

"Friend Emerson will see that someone goes to help thy mother until thou art able to return."

Proctor slid back down to the floor, taking a splinter in his palm as he went. The sunlight was warm on his skin as he pulled at the splinter with his teeth. He thought about what the widow had said, that it was in the blood. He spit out the splinter. "How does one become a witch?"

Jedediah shook his head. "Only God knows the answer."

"So you think it is a gift from God?"

The old man pushed back his hat and wiped the sweat back off his bald head. "All things come from God. We choose what we do with them, for good or ill."

The sound of horses came through the orchard. Emerson was riding with another man, brown-haired, wearing an open-collared shirt and a craftsman's vest. They rode to the side of the shed. Emerson dismounted easily, but the other man moved stiffly, as if he'd been in the saddle a bit long. He hadn't shaved in two or three days, nor, by the look and smell of him, changed clothes either.

"Jedediah, you know Paul," Emerson said.

"Good to see you again," the newcomer said.

"Likewise," Jedediah replied, with a nod of greeting. "But shouldn't thou be back in Boston, where the action is?"

"Don't mistake a siege for action," Paul said. "The action is out here in the towns for the time being. I'm engaged in out-of-doors work for the provisional government, helping raise volunteers to man the siege."

Emerson leaned in the door, careful not to break the line outside it. "Jedediah?"

"I believe the boy was curious, and the widow took advantage of him."

"And the mark?"

"Left by Deborah, to explain why he was inside the shed with the binding spell if we should chance to find him before he awoke. Dost thou have word from Deborah?"

"I saw her on foot, nearly all the way to Charlestown, just

before dawn," Paul said. "She said she was in pursuit of a woman dressed as a widow and asked me if I had seen her."

"And had thou seen her?"

"I've seen many widows on the roads, especially of late. That's why it's such an effective disguise, if disguise it is. Do we know her purpose?"

"I already told him all that we know," Emerson said.

"And there was nothing more to be learned from our friend," Jedediah said, with a nod to Proctor.

"Ah," Emerson said. "Let me introduce you. Paul, this is Proctor Brown, the problem I was telling you about. Proctor, this is Paul Revere."

Proctor stood up and started toward the door, stopping short before he was struck down again. "Paul Revere? I very much liked your engraving of the Boston massacre, sir. My father had it framed and hung on the wall."

"You're too kind," Revere said. "So you are a patriot?"

"Yes, sir. Samuel, one of the boys who was shot by the Redcoats, he was a friend of mine."

"Mister Brown served with courage at Concord and Lexington," Emerson said. "That's how he received the mark on his neck."

"I suspect that his family are the Proctors of Salem," Jedediah added.

"From the witch trials?" Revere asked.

"How did you know?" Proctor demanded.

"The name has not been entirely forgotten," Jedediah said. "And the talent is in the blood."

Revere's eyes lit up. "You have the talent?"

Tongue thick in his mouth, Proctor said, "Yes, sir."

The horses were nibbling the grass around the shed. Revere's mount, sniffing the scent of cider, bumped Revere aside and poked her muzzle through the door. Ears twitching, she nuzzled Proctor for an apple. Revere took her by the reins and pulled her out of the shed.

"He says he can scrye," Jedediah said.

"Ah," Revere said.

Emerson looked grim. "We'll have to send him on the Quaker Highway then."

"That's what I was thinking," Jedediah replied.

"What's the Quaker Highway?" Proctor asked.

Emerson looked either way, and toward the house, before speaking. "After the witch trials in Salem, and all the innocent deaths, Quakers and others in the colony created a secret system of houses and hiding places, each a day's journey apart or less, in order to move witches in secret."

"When someone shows a talent, we move them to another part of the country," Jedediah said, his voice likewise lowered. "We move them someplace where they're unknown, someplace less likely to be inflamed by fear of witchcraft."

"Many have found homes along the frontier," Emerson explained. "Originally in western Pennsylvania, more recently in the territories opening up along the Ohio River. It's good land, a good place for a young man who's willing to work."

Ohio? That was the last place he wanted to go. He'd be starting from scratch, hacking the poorest of farms out of the wilderness, living in constant fear that Indians would do to him and his family what they had done to his father, only worse. Emily would never go to Ohio. There'd be no way to build a cattle farm there, or sell beef to Boston or the other big cities. He would never move to the Ohio River country, and meant to say so, but the words that came out of his mouth were, "You mean my mother has lived her whole life in fear for no reason?"

"Not for no reason," Emerson said. "She's been wise to hide her talent." He turned to Jedediah. "Perhaps we should consider whether to move her also."

"No, she's been smart," Jedediah said. "If she's gone all these years and thou never even heard a rumor. She's been quiet, never shown her talent to her neighbors, never made anyone jealous or suspicious of her. There's no need to move her. But this one will have to go as soon as he is well." Turning to Revere, he said, "Maybe thou can take him with thee south, as far as the house at Uxbridge."

"That's the wrong direction," Revere said.

Finally, thought Proctor, someone was speaking sense. "I can be just as quiet as my mother."

"It's too late for that," Jedediah said. "Even when Elizabeth heals, it's too much for a forgetting spell. This isn't like the demon in New Haven in 1763."

"Right," Emerson said. "And he's shown no ability to resist his curiosity. The next time—"

"No, I mean that he should go to The Farm," Revere said.

The way he said it—The Farm—made it sound, to Proctor's ears, like someplace very specific and nearby. The other two men scowled.

"Are you sure that's wise?" Emerson asked.

"I'm sure it's not," Jedediah burst out, not bothering to lower his voice at all this time. Songbirds in one of the nearby trees went suddenly silent at his tone. "How would we explain him?"

"How do you explain anyone there?" Revere asked.

"Distant feminine relations need little explanation," Jedediah said. "But this fellow is known about the area. Sooner or later, someone local would recognize him."

Revere's hands shaped the air in front of him. He gestured every time he spoke, as if he couldn't think without having them in motion. "But why take a patriot, a trained militiaman, away from the fighting? Dear God, I'm out here in the cold, wearing filthy clothes, not knowing where I'll sleep from one night to the next, trying to convince the men of Massachusetts to fight for their freedom. Here we have someone who's already shown he's willing to fight—why should we send him off to Pennsylvania, or to the Ohio River country, where he can't get a lick in against the Lobsterbacks? It makes no sense."

"It's his witchcraft skills, not his fighting skills, that are at issue," Emerson said. "Even in these times, they can be a danger."

"His witchcraft can aid us," Revere said. "Aren't the other witches at The Farm helping out in our patriot cause?"

"No," Emerson said at the exact same moment that Jedediah answered, "Yes."

They stared at each other.

"Women have no place in the line of danger," Emerson said.

"Danger came and found them when the widow attacked us," Jedediah replied. "She accused us of helping the patriots defeat the British. Think about it—what if the Redcoats are using sorcery to aid their cause?"

"Exactly," Revere said. "The Farm may still be in danger. Why not send a trained minuteman there? If, at the same time, he can see something in the future that will help us defeat the Redcoats, even better."

Proctor didn't fully understand what had happened on The Farm. Maybe his attack on Pitcairn had been more successful than he thought. Maybe the people on The Farm had paid the price for it.

Maybe he could learn how to use his talent.

"I'll go to The Farm," he said. Outside the shed, birds resumed their songs with a few tentative notes.

Revere rubbed his hands together. "Well, that's done then."

"Not so quickly," Emerson said; Jedediah shook his head, saying, "I think it's a mistake."

Proctor would have preferred to do a scrying first, before agreeing to go; but he had done one before marching to Lexington, and his visions had misled him. He'd take his chances this time. "I'll be quiet," he promised. "I'll do whatever I'm told, until it's safe for me to come home."

That would be a week or two at most, he thought. With the war on, everything else would be forgotten in that length of time. Meanwhile, he could make right the inadvertent harm he'd brought on these other people by his actions. Most importantly, if he went, he could learn something about his talent, and how to use it.

Revere started forward warmly, to congratulate him. Emerson stopped him before he crossed the invisible barrier.

"Are you sure you want to do this?" Emerson asked.

Proctor nodded. If Paul Revere and the Reverend Emerson, after all they had done and sacrificed for the cause of liberty, thought he could use his talent to help, then he had to try.

"Besides," he said. "Anything's better than going to Ohio."

Chapter 11

Each time they spied a substantial house atop some hill or saw a cluster of buildings at a fortunate turn in the road, Proctor asked, "Is that The Farm?"

But the shaggy horse bounced its empty cart past each place without slowing. As the two men continued east, they left the gabled homes and sprawling outbuildings behind them. The main road forked into a side road, which dwindled to a trail. They passed through a crossroads hamlet too small for a church or even a tavern, and circled a swamp on a trail that was little more than an ambitious footpath.

As they passed under the shade of a white oak, Jedediah said, "This is it, just up there."

The path curved around a wooded hill where the declining sun splashed light across the budding limbs of the trees. The Farm had to be around that rise. Proctor hurried ahead.

"No, back here," Jedediah called.

He stood beneath the oak, his hand resting on a post that Proctor hadn't noticed.

Proctor retraced his steps, scanning the landscape. The hills around them were topped with trees. Beyond the trees, smoke snaked into the sky, but from a chimney at least half a mile ahead. "Where?"

"Rest thy hand on this stile," Jedediah said.

Proctor did as he was bid: the landscape shifted as if a piece of colored glass had been removed from his eyes. The thick undergrowth along the trail became a wall of field-stones and treefall. The solitary post turned into a gate. A path led between two hills, whose curved lines were broken by the sharp peaks of roofs. A saltbox farmhouse, clapboards weathered gray, sat across from a barn that was larger, more weathered, more gray. A brick well occupied the yard halfway between them. Gardens cascaded down the hillside in front of the house. There was a fruit orchard and pastures behind the barn.

Proctor was unsure what he had expected to see. A mansion like Emerson's perhaps, or maybe even a small castle of dressed stone. A fortress of witchcraft, a temple of sorcery. Instead it looked like, well, an ordinary farm.

When he lifted his hand, the scene disappeared. He touched the post with just two fingers, and it shimmered back into sight again.

"Are you a witch too?" Proctor asked.

Jedediah's smile was not amused. His broad-brimmed hat moved from side to side. "No, friend, I am not."

"But—"

"It's an enchantment. It has the same effect on anyone who doesn't know to see past it."

"So it's called 'The Farm' because—"

"It's a farm," Jedediah finished.

The horse tossed its head and rubbed its muzzle against Jedediah, who led it through the gate and up the hill. Proctor followed him, not wanting to be caught on the wrong side of the enchantment. A dog ran from the barn, barking as soon as it saw Jedediah. It was as shaggy as the horse and stocky like its owner. The dog bounced around Jedediah's legs, and he petted it, saying, "Hello, Nimrod."

Proctor recognized the biblical allusion. "Is Nimrod a mighty hunter?"

Jedediah shook his head as the dog bounded over to sniff at Proctor. "Not so much. But he's a good dog."

They put the horse in the barn. A gray cat rubbed against Proctor's leg while he forked fresh straw into the stall and

Jedediah stowed the gear. Outside the barn, a middle-aged black woman was drawing water from the well.

"Hello, Lydia," Jedediah said.

"Good afternoon, Master Jedediah," she said.

"There are no masters here, friend. We are all free."

"Uh-huh," she said. With the bucket in one hand, she leaned over to pick up a firewood basket with the other. Her sleeves were rolled to her elbows, and her forearms corded like knots of ironwood.

They followed her across the yard, Nimrod trailing them, bouncing happily the whole time. A gray-haired woman in a black cape dress and white cap stood on a bench, using shears to trim young stems from the top of an elderberry tree at the corner of a house. She teetered on her bench, and Jedediah paused to steady her.

"What art thou doing?" he asked.

"I need de pith," she said in a thick Dutch-German accent. "For to treat her burns, but dere is not so many green stems left. Do you know vere dere is anudder elderberry?"

Jedediah scratched his chin. "If it were me, I'd ask—"

"Ya, ya, if it vere you, you vould ask Elizabet. But Elizabet is not vell, is she, so I cannot ask her."

She waved them on. Proctor followed Jedediah onto the front porch; the dog lay down beside the step. A girl about fourteen years old, with long reddish brown hair, tipped back on an old chair. She turned her hand, hiding a small knife in her palm. Proctor followed a nervous flick of her eyes and saw the first scratch of a carving on the corner post.

"Why, hello," she said, putting sugar in her voice the way some folks put it in their tea. "I think maybe my charms worked after all."

"Thou art here because thy charms worked too well," Jedediah said grouchily as he pulled open the door.

She shrugged and smiled at Proctor as he went inside. She rose to follow him, but the gray-haired woman yelled for her. "Alexandra, vere are you? I need your help." Her shoulders slumped in a sulk, and she went the other direction.

"Are these all witches?" Proctor whispered as they stepped inside.

"What were thou expecting?" Jedediah asked.

"I don't know," Proctor said. But he was sure it wasn't this.

The room was small but tidy. Lydia crouched by the hearth, using the poker to adjust the new logs on the fire. She clanged the iron back onto the rack and ladled water from the bucket into the cooking pot. There was a daybed against the wall, and a bandaged figure lying in it, and another woman—dark-haired, about thirty, quite beautiful—seated beside her; her dress reminded him of the yellow dress Emily wore to the coffeehouse in Boston, only much finer.

"It's too warm, you're making it too warm, Lydia," she said. She had a strong southern accent. *It's too-ah wahm. Yewrah makin it too-ah wahm.* "For God's sake, Lydia, she's been horribly burned. The last thing she needs is more fire."

"Yes, Missus Cecily." She scooped water from the bucket to dampen the fire.

"Thou art doing fine, Lydia," Jedediah said.

"Well, of course she is," Cecily said. "I don't know what we'd do without her. I swear, she is the pillar of us all. Don't worry about the fire, Lydia dear, it's fine."

"No, Missus Cecily," Lydia said and set the bucket down.

"I have been here night and day by our Elizabeth's side while you were gone," Cecily told Jedediah.

"How is she?"

"Fire cannot keep her down any more than it could destroy the glory of Rome. I have used every healing spell I know—"

"Mm-mmm," said Lydia, sipping the spoon from the cooking pot. "Needs a pinch of salt."

"We all have been, to be honest," Cecily said. She dropped her voice and held her hand to the side of her mouth. "Except for our young friend from the mountains. If she was my daughter, I would have taught her manners long ago." Then raising her voice again, she said, "But Magdalena has been 'vunderful,' as she would say, and Lydia has been tireless, simply tireless."

The sheets stirred, and the eyes beneath the bandaged face opened slowly. "What happened to thee?" said a slurred voice.

Jedediah touched his scorched cheek. "Same thing that happened to thou. The widow burned me."

"Thou foolish, foolish man."

The old man bristled. "She was escaping. It's not as if I had a choice."

"That horrible woman escaped?" Cecily asked, looking anxiously to the door and windows.

Elizabeth closed her bandaged fist on the hem of Jedediah's shirt. "Was Deborah hurt?"

"Deborah is safe. But she followed the widow toward Boston, trying to discover her destination."

The door opened, and the gray-haired woman—Magdalena, Proctor guessed—entered with a small basket of green stems. Alexandra carried the bench and shears.

"Vat is the news?" Magdalena asked.

"It's frightful," Cecily said. "That horrible woman escaped capture and burned Jedediah—he was lucky to escape with his life. And Deborah, you know how fearless she is, chased after her, la-de-dah—we don't have any idea when she'll return." Turning to Jedediah, she said, "What if that woman comes after us again?"

Jedediah nodded toward Proctor. "I brought a friend to help protect us."

"Ma'am," Proctor said, ducking his head and holding his hat in front of him.

"Thou needn't take thy hat off," Jedediah snapped, glancing at Lydia. "We're all equal here. There's no need to sir or ma'am anyone either."

"Yes, sir," Proctor said.

Elizabeth began to wheeze, shaking her cot. Cecily started, as if panicked, and checked the woman's head and hands to see if she was fine. It took Proctor a second to realize she was laughing.

"Mm-hmm," said Lydia, rising. "Mister Longshanks is going to fit in here, jest fine."

"Mister Longshanks's proper name is Proctor Brown," Jedediah said. "He's a minuteman from Lincoln. Our friend Emerson sent him to us for a time."

Elizabeth had stopped laughing. She grunted as she made an effort to sit. "Proctor, is it?"

"Yes, ma—" He caught himself and stopped. "Yes, it is."

"Come nearer."

He glanced over his shoulder to see what he should do. Cecily frowned—he was certain she was attempting to discourage him—but the others watched him expectantly, waiting to see what he did.

He stepped closer.

Elizabeth reached out with her right arm, which was wrapped in bandages down to her palm. Her blistered fingers shook as she stretched them toward him. Then her fingers touched him and clamped down on him like a vise.

The sensation was the opposite of the experience he'd had when the widow had grabbed him. He felt as though light poured into, fountained into him, until he wanted to burst. Surprised, he dropped his hat to the floor.

Elizabeth nodded and let go.

He bent to pick up his hat, but the girl Alexandra nabbed it first, smiling as she handed it back.

"Thou have the talent," Elizabeth said. "A flame shines strongly in thee."

"Ah, I thought there was something hot about him," Alexandra murmured.

Proctor swallowed and looked around again at the faces staring at him intently. To take his secret, the one his mother said would kill him, and have it discussed in the open felt . . . wrong. "I guess I do."

"That can't be true," Cecily said finally, with a forced laugh.

"It is," Elizabeth affirmed. "Thou should try to sense it thyself. Thou could do it if thou tried diligently."

Cecily blushed. "Oh, not me."

"He takes the talent from his mother," Jedediah said. "She's practiced her whole life in secret, undetected—"

"I should ask him those questions," Elizabeth interrupted. "I understand it better."

Jedediah hesitated, then nodded. "I best go see to the animals."

Proctor turned to follow him out of reflex. A young man didn't stay alone in the company of so many women.

"Stay here," Elizabeth commanded; at the same instant Jedediah told him, "Elizabeth will want thee to stay here."

"I've fed and watered the pigs already," Lydia interjected. "And I let the lambs out to the pasture behind the barn. Nimrod has been watching them."

"Thank you," Jedediah said as he left.

"Thou take the talent from thy mother?" Elizabeth asked.

"Just like Jedediah said. She's never told anyone about it but me, and she didn't tell me much."

"Oh, the poor dear," Cecily said. "I would have simply wilted away without Lydia to sustain me." She patted Elizabeth's hand. "Until I joined you, I mean."

"What is thy talent?" Elizabeth asked. "How did it manifest?"

"Scrying," Proctor answered. He felt like he had to force the word past his lips; but it was so much easier to speak of it now than it had been to explain it to Emily. "A few years ago, I saw something, a death, before it happened. My mother explained it to me, told me I had a talent, then told me I had to keep it secret."

Elizabeth nodded, then leaned back on her bed, exhausted

from her effort. "We'll have no secrets here among us, is that clear?"

"Yes, ma'am," he answered.

Lydia snorted at the sound of *ma'am.*

"If you don't mind me asking, what is this place?" he asked quickly, to cover up his mistake. He swung out his hat to encompass the room. "Why are all of you here?"

"Ve come here to learn," Magdalena said.

"To learn what?" Proctor asked. Could they teach him how to make protective medallions, or create the illusion of changing shapes?

"To learn everything," Cecily insisted. "Elizabeth is simply the best teacher—"

"Please," Elizabeth protested.

"No, you know it's true. Elizabeth knows more than anyone about our sort of talents and how to use them."

"And how to keep us safe," Alexandra added.

"Safe?" he asked.

Elizabeth was too weak to do anything but speak; he had to lean forward to hear her voice. "Talents manifest themselves in specific ways. Someone who is unprepared can be a danger to themselves and to those around them."

"How?"

"I had an older cousin," the auburn-haired girl Alexandra said. "She started hearing voices in her head, when she was still a little girl. Her mother didn't understand what was happening, didn't want to listen to my mother."

"What happened?"

"The voices told her to go drown herself." She looked away, twisting the end of her hair around a finger. "So she filled her rocks with pockets and went down to the millpond."

"The voices told her to drown her little brother first," Cecily whispered to Proctor. "She did that too. It was such a tragedy, you have no idea."

"A necrovocative can hear the voices of the dead," Elizabeth explained.

Magdalena grunted in disapproval. She carried her basket of elderberry stems to a table with a mortar and pestle.

"The dead can be as capricious and misguided as the living," Elizabeth said. "Without proper training, her cousin had no skill to shut out those voices. Thou can imagine what happens when someone is born with a talent for fire."

Proctor shivered. Had his mother known that, and kept it from him when he asked? She knew more than she told him, he was certain. "A man could burn himself up."

"Yes," Cecily said, patting Elizabeth's arm. "It's too bad that didn't happen to the widow when she was young."

Elizabeth winced. "No—we'll wish harm on no one, but will pray that she turns away from the fire, which consumes, and toward the Light, which illuminates. I believe that, whatever her reasons, she can be saved."

Out in the yard, the dog barked cheerfully. "What happens to those who scrye?" Proctor asked.

Elizabeth closed her eyes. "It is easy for them to be misled by their visions, pulled down a path toward darkness."

"Men often become gamblers, I am told," Cecily said, smoothing the sheets around the other woman. "Testing their luck until it runs out and they get shot or go broke or something terrible like that. Are you a gambler, Mister Brown?"

"Voresight tempts men to try to cheat de vill of Gott," Magdalena said in clear disapproval, waving a pith-covered pestle at him.

Proctor remembered the scrying he'd done before mustering at Lexington, and the way he'd been wrong about what it meant, about what would happen before the British marched back to Boston. "And how do we know the will of God?" Proctor asked.

The door banged open.

Deborah stepped inside and slammed it shut again. She had dark circles beneath her eyes, and her clothes were covered with dust. Looking at Proctor, she said, "I could see the two of you when you left the main road. If you ever looked over your shoulder even once to see if someone was following you, I could have ridden home the rest of the way in that cart. Can someone help me with my shoes? My feet are bloody tatters."

She limped over to the chair and fell backward into it. Lydia brought over her bucket and sat at Deborah's feet while Cecily gave her instructions on bathing wounds. Magdalena emptied her pestle, pulled down a bound bunch of mint stems hanging above the worktable, and began crushing them in the bowl.

Proctor ended up standing next to Alexandra in the corner. She crossed her arms and gnawed idly on a fingernail.

"How did you happen to come here?" Proctor asked.

"I drew too much attention to myself by casting love potions." She leaned in close to Proctor so that their shoulders brushed. "Pastor Woodburn accused me of witchcraft, which was fair enough, although I don't think he'd have made so much trouble about it, only his son was involved. He accused me of cavorting with the devil, and denounced me from the pulpit, and that very night I was met outside the house by two women from the next county over, and before I knew it I was walking away with them."

"That seems odd."

"Almost all the women in my family have the Irish powers, which is what we call them. There was the problem with my cousin, just a year before. In any case, my mother told me I had to go away for a while, so I went. It was exciting at first, seeing new places, moving in secret. But I was on the road north for weeks, moving mostly at night, never staying at anyone's house more than a day, hardly getting to know anyone. Many were Quakers, but coming up through Pennsylvania, there was even a free black family that put me up for the night."

"And then you ended up here?"

"I ended up here about ten days ago, right before the widow attacked."

Deborah was soaking her feet in a pan of water, redolent of mint, describing her pursuit of the widow.

"—I had great luck at first, telling people I was trying to find my addled aunt. They were extraordinarily helpful, many of them having seen her pass, a stranger crossing fields in the morning mist. She was in such a hurry to return to the safety of Boston that she made little or no effort to cover her trail. But in Charlestown, only an hour behind her, I lost her. She simply vanished. I searched for her for another whole day without finding her or anyone who had seen her. I'm sure she made her way into Boston."

"But isn't Boston under siege?" Cecily asked. "How could she get past the soldiers?"

"A woman may pass where a man may not," Deborah said. "And old women are, in particular, as you know, largely invisible to men."

Magdalena made a snorting sound.

Elizabeth could not find the strength to sit upright again, but she turned her head to watch Deborah. "Do we have any better idea whom she serves?"

"No," Deborah replied. "We thought it was some gentleman by the name of Nant or Nance. I asked around, when I was searching for her, but no one knew a British officer by that name. The Reverend Emerson and Mister Revere promised to make further inquiries. But we do know something more about her magic."

Cecily stood up, leaving Elizabeth's side. "What?" she asked eagerly. "What did you learn?"

Magdalena was toweling dry Deborah's feet and applying an ointment to them while she said a spell. Deborah grimaced, leaned back her head.

"She draws power by siphoning it off those around her," she said. "I had suspected as much, because I felt weaker when I went too close to her."

"How does she do it?" Cecily said. She reached out to touch Lydia's arm for reassurance; the black woman wore a sickly expression on her face.

Deborah gritted her teeth while Magdalena wrapped one of her feet. Then she said, "She creates a circle without the permission of the other witch. She's powerful enough to do it without contact, although the effort drains her too, once the circle is broken."

She explained how the widow had drawn on Proctor while he was hiding in the woods, breaking Deborah's binding spell. By the time she finished explaining how Proctor had helped the widow escape by going to her shed, the women were glaring at him. Dusk had fallen; their faces were lit only by the glow from the hearth, giving their expressions a malignant orange cast.

"I didn't do it with the intention of helping her escape," he said. "I didn't know better. I don't know about circles and siphons and things like that. No one has ever taught me."

"Vell," Magdalena said, then shook her head, bundling up the dirty towels and scraps of bandages.

"It seems like you might have learned a lesson the first time she took advantage of you, Mister Brown," Cecily said.

"Come here," Elizabeth said, her voice so soft he barely heard it.

He turned and took a step toward the bed. "Yes?"

"Stay here. I will teach thee as soon as I am well."

"Yes, ma'am," he said.

She smiled at the *ma'am,* then gave him a single nod and closed her eyes.

Cecily rushed back to her side. "Everyone out. Elizabeth needs her sleep. We must let her rest."

The women dispersed, quietly going about their different chores, while Deborah limped to the other room and Alexandra climbed the narrow stairs to the second floor. Proctor stood where he was.

"I have my eye on you, Mister Brown," Cecily said. "If you have decided to aid this widow, or be a willing part of her circle, I will be the first to know it."

"You don't have to worry about that," he said. "But I don't know where I'm supposed to go."

Her eyes narrowed, and she smiled slowly.

He climbed into the loft of the barn carrying an extra blanket. His ascent of the ladder woke Jedediah, who was already stretched out asleep on his blankets in the straw.

"Was there a problem?" the old man asked with mild amusement in his voice.

"It's a small house, only three rooms, and with so many women there already, there wasn't a bed to spare for me," Proctor said.

"Mmm-hmm," Jedediah murmured, rustling the straw as he shifted his bedding over to make room for Proctor. "Thou wilt like it better out here anyway."

"Why's that?" Proctor said.

"It's much quieter." He rolled over to go back to sleep.

It was unlikely he'd taken into account his own ferocious snoring. Proctor lay awake a long time, chewing on the end of a straw as he watched the stars through a crack in the board. If these women could be comfortable with the notion of witchcraft, he could find a way to make Emily feel the same way. He grinned in the dark. Emily would like Cecily—he could just hear them comparing fashion, deciding on the best dresses to show off their color and eyes.

He would stay long enough to learn some useful magic, that was decided. And he would have to learn how to control his scrying as well—he didn't want to be misled by it again, the way he had been at Lexington. By the time he'd rolled all these thoughts through his head, he'd flipped over enough times to crush down the straw to make it comfortable. He spit the chewed piece out of his mouth and pillowed his head on his arm.

A hand on his shoulder was shaking him awake almost as soon as he fell asleep. It was still dark outside.

"What is it?" he asked.

"Time to get to work," Jedediah said. "Thou art going to help me take care of the chores, right?"

Chapter 12

Proctor grabbed the top branch of the downed tree and dragged it clear of the woods. He dropped it and paused to mop the sweat off his forehead.

"A trunk that big, I'd have to hitch Mary up to move it," Jedediah said. Mary was the name of his horse.

"Nah, it's been down a long time, mostly dry. It's light enough to shift."

"Maybe," Jedediah said, handing Proctor an ax.

From this spot on the hillside, he could see all fifty-one acres of The Farm occupying two low hills between the swamp and the woods. The buildings and gardens and fields were laid out neatly, and kept in working order; but the sun was bad, the soil was poor, and the pasture pushed up rocks faster than grass.

"You'll never get rich on this farm," Proctor said.

"Worldly riches may be a wall that keeps us from the wealth of heaven," Jedediah said.

"I don't even think you need an enchantment to hide this place. I could live my whole life within a mile of here and never look at it twice."

"Elizabeth says that's why her great-grandparents chose it, right after the witches were hanged at Salem." He tilted his chin, indicating the town nearby to the east.

"They've been at this a long time, then?"

"I reckon the Quaker Highway got its start right here."

"So witches from Massachusetts come through here and are sent somewhere else for safety?"

"Yes, and witches from elsewhere come north. Elizabeth, and her mother and grandmother before her, have trained witches to use their powers quietly, both for their own safety and for the safety of their communities. In the time I've lived here, I've seen dozens pass through, though we have more now than ever before."

"Any men among them?" Proctor asked.

"Well, there's thee."

Proctor turned his head and spit. "Any idea when she'll start lessons again?"

"Any day now I'm sure," Jedediah said. He carried his ax around to the other side of the tree. "Will thou help me cut this tree, friend? Or dost thou expect the wood to split itself?"

Proctor hefted the ax and fell into rhythm with Jedediah, each blow falling in turn to hew the trunk in half. It'd be nice, Proctor thought, if there were a way to do it with magic instead.

So far he'd seen very little in the way of magic.

His first week on The Farm, Elizabeth had been recovering from her burns, and all the women tended to her, lending their efforts to help her heal. For that week and the next, Jedediah kept Proctor busy with all the neglected tasks that could use two sets of hands—fixing the barn roof, rebuilding the chicken coop, digging a new spot for the necessary house.

By the third week, Proctor had been ready to leave. If he was going to work this hard, it might as well be on his own farm. Then a messenger came from the Reverend Emerson. Emerson apologized for his absence, but the siege in Boston and the rebellion against British rule occupied all his energy. He had been able to find out nothing more about the widow, except that she was somewhere in Boston. The messenger brought a letter for Cecily, from her family, and she promptly sat down and wrote one in return.

The messenger also carried a note for Proctor: Emerson

wanted Proctor to know that his parents were well, and that young Arthur Simes was helping out with their day-to-day work on the farm. He praised Proctor for his devotion to the patriot cause and encouraged him to learn anything he could that would help them down the road. Emerson's note concluded by promising that the messenger would deliver any letters Proctor had written to his parents.

Only Proctor hadn't written any. His father was beyond the reach of correspondence, and his mother—had she forgiven Proctor yet, for wanting to learn more about his talent, for turning to someone else besides her for that information? He tried to imagine his mother at a place like The Farm and couldn't do it. A secret shared with anyone outside the family would no longer be a secret to her.

While the messenger waited, Proctor penned a short note to his mother, telling her that he was serving the patriot cause and doing well. He could be reached through the Reverend Emerson. Don't worry about him. He couldn't say more than that without lying or betraying The Farm's secrets, and he couldn't bring himself to do either.

He almost left with the messenger, but Elizabeth had come to him and promised to teach him more about scrying and his talent as soon as she had recovered from her burns. Still, despite Emerson's encouragement and Elizabeth's promises, Proctor wondered about his father's health, and whether his mother could forgive him, and if Arthur knew not to plant corn at the lower end of the field because rain settled there and it tended to rot. If his lessons in magic did not start soon, Proctor would leave The Farm. He did not fit in here, even though all the others were witches like himself.

In truth, it was the most unsettlingly diverse group of people Proctor had ever known. Elizabeth's whole life was witchcraft and the Quaker Highway. She scarcely knew anyone in the community beyond The Farm, though she knew other witches in all the colonies and across the frontier. Her talent was healing, and though her left arm had been badly burned, with her hand hooked back on itself so that it would never be useful again, she had prevented any infection. Her other burns were improving better than Proctor could have ever imagined.

The only woman older than Elizabeth was German-speaking Magdalena Stolzfus, a dour powwow woman from Lancaster County, Pennsylvania, who dressed so plainly—no buttons on her clothes, only simple hooks—she made Quakers look ostentatious. Despite belonging to some small religious group that rejected contact with the outside world, she had made several trips to The Farm over the years to improve her skills at healing. Alexandra Walker whispered a rumor to Proctor that Magdalena had breathed life back into a stillborn baby; the creature that survived had no soul, and a few years later she had to smother it. She had come to The Farm because of the murder.

Proctor never knew when to believe Alexandra, who was just fourteen, loose-limbed and quick to laugh or climb a tree. She liked rumors and anything the least bit scandalous, and had been sent to The Farm from the mountains of western Virginia because she used her talents to cause mischief. She complained to Proctor that she was there not to learn how to do things, but to learn how not to do them. The other women, especially Cecily, tried to keep her on a short leash.

Cecily Sumpter Pinckney would have had them all on leashes if she had her way. She reminded Proctor of Emily in some ways—petite, beautiful, sure of her place in the world. But Cecily was more than that; she was the kind of lady who dressed daily in the type of finery that Proctor had only seen once before on the governor's wife. She wore emerald rings, and an ivory cameo pendant, even when she attended to her chores, though Proctor came to realize that while Cecily talked about her share of The Farm's work as though she did it, all her time was spent attending to Elizabeth. The real labor was done by Lydia.

Lydia was Cecily's slave. According to Alexandra, Lydia had been Cecily's nanny on her childhood plantation in South Carolina. The two of them discovered their talents together. The other residents on The Farm tried to treat Lydia like an equal, but she steadfastly kept her head down and served Cecily without complaint, doing the chores assigned to both of them, often leaving her too exhausted to learn anything from their lessons.

The lessons were taught by Deborah, at least while Elizabeth recovered from her burns. Deborah still disliked Proctor for the widow's escape, and she arranged the lessons so he missed them. She had been on The Farm the longest, had been trained as Elizabeth's assistant. She knew so much about binding spells and other nonhealing magic that it sometimes made the others anxious, especially Jedediah.

Jedediah lacked any talent for witchcraft, but he worked as a trailblazer for the Quaker Highway and kept The Farm running. The latter was easier now that he had Proctor's help, as he did on this day, when they were cutting up dead trees to restock their firewood supply.

By the time they were finished, Proctor was shoulder-sore, with the calluses raw on his hands and a powerful appetite growing inside him. He returned to the house, grateful to see that the trestle table had been set up in the yard and laden with food. Someone had taken time to decorate it with bright arrangements of cut flowers.

Deborah came out of the house with a bowl of buttered greens and placed them among the flowers.

"Are you sure that's going to be enough?" Proctor asked, trying to make friendly conversation with her.

"Who knows? We have to cook more since you came. You eat twice as much as anyone else."

She stalked off immediately. Proctor put his hands to his mouth and called after her. "Maybe that's 'cause I do twice as much of the work."

Alexandra, standing nearby, overheard him. Swinging

her arms randomly from side to side she said, "She's a bit full of herself sometimes, ain't she?"

He shrugged, to say yes without saying yes.

Her eyes sparked. "Watch this. She won't feel so proud in a minute."

Hands behind her back, she strolled over to the house. As Deborah banged out the door with another plate, Alexandra whistled a series of notes and spun her finger in the air.

The bottom of Deborah's skirt rippled as if there were a sudden breeze. She stopped without turning around. Then a dust devil spun on the ground from her feet back to Alexandra, and—with a sound like the wind catching a sail—her skirt blew up, lifting the hem to the top of her head.

Proctor scratched his nose and averted his eyes from her spindly young-girl legs. It was one thing to see a lady's undergarments drying on a clothesline and another thing entirely to see her wearing them.

Deborah calmly walked over and set her plate down on the table while Alexandra screeched and tried unsuccessfully to shove her skirt back into place. Elizabeth came to the door, her left arm in its sling, with Cecily beside her. Lydia and Magdalena stopped their work around the table and watched closely.

With a single word from Deborah, the skirts dropped back into place. Alexandra's face was flushed with anger, her nostrils flaring as she tried to control herself. She started to walk away, and Deborah held out her hand.

"Today's lesson is the simple reversal spell," she said. "Pay close attention."

Proctor took a few steps closer.

"We'll begin by explaining to everyone exactly what you were trying to do," Deborah said.

"You know exactly what I was doing," Alexandra growled.

"You conjured up a wind spell. Fairly impressive, actually. You must have had a good teacher for weather spells. But what was your intent?"

Alexandra kept her lips tight, staring defiantly.

"Your intent was malicious," Deborah said. "To humiliate me."

"I don't think that's possible—you don't have any shame," Alexandra said.

"Be that as it may, I felt your spell and turned it with a simple incantation to give an eye for an eye, with a prayer to spare my own." She turned her head toward Proctor, saying, "We often use Bible verses for our spells, to acknowledge that it is God who gives us our talent."

It was the first useful thing she'd said to Proctor. Instantly, he saw the sense in it. "And using the Bible deflects charges of satanic worship as well."

"Those who fear us are quick to say that even the devil can quote scripture," Deborah corrected. Turning back to Alexandra, she said, "It's our intentions that matter. If you had intended me no harm, no harm would have come back to you."

Magdalena shook her head vehemently. "This is not right. Ve must the other cheek turn."

Elizabeth raised her good hand in a gesture of peace. "Deborah, I am not content to see us harm, or wish harm, even to reputation, on one another, neither in jest nor in turnabout."

"This is not in jest," Deborah said, never breaking her gaze from Alexandra. "I favor violence no more than either of you. But we have recently been attacked by a witch who wanted to kill us. If Alexandra knows how to do this spell, it could save her life."

The color drained from Alexandra's face, and she took a step back. "Will it work against any kind of harm?"

"No," Deborah said. "Only against harm coming from a magical source. An ordinary torch would still burn you."

"What . . . what did you use as a focus?"

"You used a spell for wind, so when I felt the wind, I held it in my head, and sent it back to you."

"Is that why I couldn't make it stop?"

"Not so long as I held the thought."

"I can't do that," Alexandra said, pale now. She held up an empty hand, then made the spinning gesture with her finger. "I need something more tangible than a thought."

"Practice," Deborah told her. "I am sure you can learn to do it."

Proctor held back a whistle of appreciation. Bet that would take some kind of practice. If Deborah could recognize a spell and create a counterspell simply by holding a thought in her head, then she was a natural talent. Deep down, he already knew as much. He had seen examples of the widow's power, and yet Deborah had been able to trap her with a binding spell that only his ignorant intervention undid. How powerful was Deborah really?

He imitated Alexandra's whirling gesture, knowing he would be happy to learn that much.

Jedediah came up and stood beside him. "Might be a bit chilly around the table, come time to eat," he said. "Reckon we could say we had work to do and take our plates to someplace warmer, like the barn."

Proctor shook his head no. This was the first useful thing he'd learned since coming to The Farm. A focus and a Bible verse, just like the eggs and the prayer his mother taught him for scrying. All her rituals were to help her focus. All her prayers were to hold her good intentions.

"Art thou sure?" Jedediah said. "Have thou ever seen a pack of barn cats around one saucer of milk, all that hissing and clawing?"

"I came here to learn about magic," Proctor answered. "If I have to put up with a little caterwauling now and then to learn it, I'll take my chances."

Jedediah shrugged. "It's on thy head."

Despite Jedediah's prediction, there was no caterwauling

over dinner. All the conversation concerned the widow; what were her motives, whom did she serve, how could her magics be defeated.

"I have been neglectful of our safety too long," Elizabeth said as they cleaned up the empty plates. "The enchantment that conceals this place is not sufficient protection. The widow was able to find her way past it. Deborah made a good point this afternoon that we must be prepared. We should establish a spell that will act as a barrier against unwelcome magics." Looking to Magdalena, she said, "Then we will have no need to reverse them."

The old Pennsylvania Dutch woman frowned. Frowning seemed to be her principal mode of expression, but this was clearly a frown of approval.

Elizabeth gathered items from the house and then collected the women around her. Proctor joined them. "I'd like to help too, any way I can," he said.

Elizabeth smiled at him. "This is very advanced magic, a bit too complicated for where thou art now. But I promise I will show thee some of the basic spells tomorrow."

He clenched his fists, ready to demand a chance to participate, but Elizabeth saw his expression.

"Really, this is women's work," she said. "Thou can do women's work if thou want to, but I'll be happy to teach spells more suited for thee. First thing in the morning. That'll be all right, won't it?"

"I guess," he said, and immediately regretted it.

"Lydia?" Cecily said from her spot at Elizabeth's side. She looked away from her slave as she spoke, brushing dust from the lace trim on her sleeves.

"Yes, ma'am?" Lydia answered.

"We don't want to trouble your head with all these complicated things. Would you mind seeing to the weeding?"

Lydia's dark face remained impassive. "As you wish, ma'am."

She peeled away to go over to the vegetable garden beside

the house. Proctor looked at Elizabeth and said, "Tomorrow?"

"First thing in the morning," she said.

He didn't believe a word of it, but he was too polite to say so. Maybe there were other ways to learn what he wanted to know. "I'll go help Lydia then."

He watched over his shoulder as he walked to the garden beside the house. The five women joined hands—Cecily rested her delicate fingers on Elizabeth's crippled arm—and began with a prayer. In their own way, they were just as secretive and fearful as his mother. Hiding The Farm with an enchantment, leaving their families to go someplace safe, reluctant to share what they knew with him.

Meanwhile his own farm was being neglected, putting his plans for the cattle a year behind. And Emily was God knew where, probably worried sick about him. She had left him sick and injured in an empty house. He needed to send word to her soon, to let her know he had recovered and things would be all right between them.

The weeds in the garden were thick-stalked and hearty while the vegetables struggled beside them like sickly younger siblings. Lydia hacked at the roots with her hoe, pausing every few steps to pull them out.

"I'll hoe, if you pull," Proctor said.

She regarded him for a moment, then handed the tool to him. She knelt in the dirt, which blended into the brown check of her coarse cotton dress.

"I thought you had the talent," he said.

She pulled up another handful of weeds and tossed the whole bunch aside. "I might've said the same about you."

"We're all equal here, all free."

"That's what they tell me."

Proctor replied with a friendly laugh. "I still don't even know how magic works. I mean, you know enough you could probably teach me."

"I don't know about that," she said.

In some ways, it was like prying information from his mother. He had to remember to be patient. He hoed steadily, letting her gather the weeds. Finally, she lifted her head to make sure no one else was around.

"Magic is like water," she said. "It's everywhere in the world—in the air, like the rain, and in the ground, like water in a deep well. Magic flows in deep rivers."

That was an interesting way of seeing it. "How'd it flow into me?" Proctor asked.

"Water, it always flows downhill. Magic is the same. Magic always flows downhill to someplace, or someone, that can hold it."

Proctor stopped hoeing for a moment, to puzzle that out, but she quirked her mouth at him so he started again. "I know how to carry water," he said. "How to put out a barrel by the rainspout, or how to pull a bucket from a well. But I have no idea how to do anything with magic, except for a little scrying."

"It's all in the head. Trying to grab magic, that's like trying to pick up water with your fingers." She held up a prickly green stem between her thumb and forefinger. "You need something to carry it—a barrel, a pitcher, a cup."

"So, you have any spare cups lying around?" he asked.

Lydia stood, turning her lean face toward the group of women, who were making a circuit of the property, starting from the gate.

"You take what they're doing, for instance," she said. "They're forming a protection spell. They need a focus. They could use anything—dirt even—to make it. But Miss Elizabeth, she's using white sand she brought up from Cape Cod. Miss Deborah, she uses flowers sometimes."

Proctor leaned on the hoe and watched them in the distance. He thought that he saw Deborah carrying a bag while Elizabeth dipped out handfuls of it. "Why that sand in particular?"

"Because she likes it, that's why. It helps to concentrate her prayers, when she says them."

"Well, what's she praying? Something like, *Dear God, don't let bad things happen*?"

Lydia snorted, turned away as if she were walking to the house, then came back again. "Boy, you got more sense than that or she wouldn't let you within a mile of this place."

"No, really I don't know. Explain it to me."

"Your prayers have to be for exactly the thing you want," she said. "*Dear God, protect me from evil witches sneaking up in the middle of the night and trying to set my house on fire whiles I still in it*. Like that. And you have to pray it without ceasing, just like the Good Book teaches."

"And that works?"

Lydia shrugged one shoulder, bent back down to work. "If you got the power, and the chance to use it, yeah, it works. If you don't got the power, it's like sails with no wind. If you don't have faith, then it's only sand and words."

"So to do a protection spell, I just sprinkle sand—"

"Or dirt, or salt, or sheep shit."

He laughed aloud at the last one. "So I sprinkle whatever it is, something I believe in, and I pray. And then the spell lasts for as long as I'm praying."

"Oh, some of them last a good deal longer," Lydia said. "If what you used for a focus lasts, the spell can last too."

"So when I scrye, I use an egg."

"Works best if you use the same things every time, or similar things for similar spells. The more complicated the spell is, the more items you add, each one to reinforce your focus."

"Will you teach me how to do spells like that?"

"No, sir," she said. "If Miss Cecily discovers I been talking to you, even about this much, I'm in for a world of unpleasantness. So I please to ask you not to say nothing to her."

"Why not?"

She stood up and took the hoe from his hands and hacked

at the soil, showing him how to do it right. Then she passed it back to him and bent to pull up the weeds. "Tell me something. Did you help the widow escape?"

"Not on purpose," he said.

"Mmm-hmm. It's that purpose part that's the problem. Miss Deborah doubts your purpose, and until she's sure of you, nobody's going to teach you a thing worth learning." She straightened and smacked the dirt from her hands. "But you didn't hear that from me."

She gathered up the weeds and carried them down to the compost piles. The group of women was still making their way clockwise around the property, and had reached the pasture behind the barn.

"I didn't hear it from you," Proctor said. "But I hear it loud and clear."

On his way back to the barn, he stopped by the chicken coop, hoping to find an egg. He'd avoided scrying since they'd warned him about it, waiting for a chance to learn to use it better. He pushed the chickens aside, rummaging through their nests, but it was the wrong time of day. There were no eggs.

He kicked the side of the coop as he left it, and the rooster charged him, flapping its wings and pecking at his shins.

"Doesn't matter what I'd see anyway," he said as he skipped out of its way. "I already made up my mind."

Chapter 13

That night, Proctor waited until Jedediah's deep snores echoed off the rafters. He listened for the better part of an hour, until he was sure the older man was deep asleep. Then he quietly rolled up his blanket and climbed to the edge of the loft.

The wooden ladder creaked under his weight, so he jumped, pushing off from the top rung and landing nimbly on his feet. He put on his shoes, shrugged on his jacket, and stopped at the well for a quick drink. He had nothing to take with him but the clothes on his back and a single knife. With a little luck, he could be halfway to Concord by sunrise.

The wind stirred, ringing chimes hanging from a tree.

Nimrod appeared from around the barn. He ran, tail wagging, to Proctor's side and joined him as he walked from the house toward the main gate. The shaggy black dog kept butting his head against Proctor's thigh and nuzzling his hand until Proctor knelt to scratch his chin and rub behind his ears. The dog slobbered happily on Proctor, as if they were old friends.

"I'm going to miss you, boy," Proctor whispered.

A hand fell on his shoulder. "Where art thou going there, friend?"

Proctor jumped at the touch. He took a step back when he saw the musket in Jedediah's hand. The old man stood shoeless and hatless, out of bed in a hurry. Nimrod, tail thumping twice as fast, weaved in circles around their legs, hopping for attention.

"What's it to you where I go?" Proctor asked.

"Well, that depends on how much I trust thee," Jedediah answered. "Thou must admit it is suspicious, sneaking off in the middle of the night."

Anger coursed through Proctor, mixed with sadness. "So am I a prisoner here, then? A slave, like Lydia? Do you plan to shoot me if I try to leave?"

"Nothing of the sort, friend," Jedediah said. He rested the gun against the ground. "I heard Elizabeth's warning chimes ring, so I knew someone was walking the property. I didn't realize it was thee. The last time someone came here in the middle of the night, it was to try to burn us, so I had to be cautious."

Chimes rang again, startling Jedediah. This time Proctor realized that he heard the sound even though the air was still. Nimrod's ears went back against his head. He turned toward the gate and growled.

"What's wrong, boy?" Proctor asked.

Jedediah pressed a finger to his lips to indicate silence and pointed toward shadows below them.

Three heads topped by feathers prowled along the low stone wall at the gate. Even knowing that the days of wars against the French and their Indian allies were over, Proctor tensed at the memory of what had been done to his father. The British had Indian allies as well.

Jedediah loaded his musket quickly. As the metal ramrod scraped softly against the inside of the barrel, Proctor keenly felt the absence of his own weapon. Emerson had insisted that he couldn't return to his house for it, and had said he wouldn't need one on The Farm in any case.

The situation looked a little different now. If there were only three attackers, he and Jedediah might be able to scare them off. If there were more than three, or if they didn't scare easily . . .

Nimrod growled again. He would have charged the men as they came over the wall, but Proctor dropped to his knees. He grabbed Nimrod by the scruff of his neck and held his muzzle shut. Surprise might be the only advantage they had. The men below didn't know yet that they'd been spotted.

"Run to the house and warn Elizabeth," Jedediah whispered to Proctor as he finished loading his musket. "She'll know what to do. If thou must escape, take them out past the orchard and through the swamp."

"But—"

"I'll slow them down as long as I can, but hurry. Now let him go," he said, pulling Proctor's hand off the dog. "Go, Nimrod, hunt!"

Nimrod barked furiously, racing toward the three men who had fanned out and were walking side by side up the path toward the house.

Jedediah raised his musket and followed Nimrod. He called out, "Leave now and live. Take one more step and I'll shoot you where you stand."

All this unfolded while Proctor crouched in the darkness, unwillingly to leave Jedediah's side against three-to-one odds, but unwilling to stand beside him without his own musket.

At the sound of Jedediah's voice, the Indian on the left spewed a string of oaths and yanked a pistol from his belt. Nimrod leapt, biting his arm and dragging it down as the gun discharged. The flash illuminated three faces slashed with red and black war paint, but the brightness momentarily blinded Proctor.

The second Indian raised his musket in the same instant and fired.

The ball made a wet pop as it hit Jedediah's chest, and a noise came out of his mouth like a punctured balloon. The instant after the ball hit him, his own musket discharged uselessly into the air.

Nimrod growled and scuffled with the first Indian. Proctor crouched low, not moving, counting on the attackers to be blinded by the flash from their guns. He would have run to Jedediah's side, only the damage he had seen on Lexington Green told him it was already too late.

The second Indian ran to the old man's body.

Nimrod's growls became more intense, and the first Indian said, in a voice as Yankee as any Proctor ever heard at church, "Help me out, Dick, the dog's mauling my arm!"

"Hang on," called the third man in the same familiar Yankee cadence. They were no more Indians than any of the men who'd thrown British tea into Boston Harbor. Somehow that made Proctor more afraid, not less. These were his neighbors, at least in some sense of the word. And they had come to kill him.

The third man buried his hatchet in Nimrod's skull. The dog yelped and fell back, and the man lunged forward with another whack to finish the job.

"We're damned fools, shooting off our guns," the second man said. He bent over Jedediah's body with a knife and sawed off one of his ears. "We're here to kill them witches. We best do it quick now before they figure out what's going on and cast spells on us."

They knew there were witches here and felt confident enough that they could kill them. The lack of fear distressed Proctor. He wished he had run for the house when he had the chance. There was no way he could beat the three men there—or if he did, it would only be by seconds. And most of the women, maybe all of them, would rather die than use their powers to kill. Deborah might be the only one capable of protecting them.

Proctor's militia training, all the drilling and marching, hadn't prepared him for this kind of battle. But he remembered something his father had told him about being a scout in the war against the French and Indians. If you were in a fight with a man up close, it was best to hit him hard and fast, and then keep hitting until he was down.

Proctor swallowed. If he'd left an hour earlier, he'd be on his way home now, and no one would be the wiser.

Only these assassins would have caught The Farm unprepared and slaughtered everyone inside.

Proctor drew his knife. The first two men passed him in a hurry, and he let them go. The third trailed behind as he tried to bind the dog bite on his arm.

When the third man passed, Proctor reared up and grabbed a handful of the man's hair. He yanked the head back, slashing across the throat the way he would to drain a deer. Warm blood spurted over his hands as he shoved the body aside.

He charged the second man, who was just turning at the sound of his companion's death. Proctor jammed his knife down into the man's shoulder. He grunted and fell, twisting the hilt out of Proctor's blood-slippery hand. Proctor hopped over him and made an awkward tackle of the last Indian, who stank of grease and whiskey.

"Damn, you're just a boy," the man said. Then he smashed his forehead into Proctor's nose.

Light and pain flashed through Proctor's head as the impact knocked him backward.

The other man fumbled for his pistol. Proctor lurched up, blinking through the pain, and grabbed for the weapon as it pointed toward his face. The hammer smashed down on his fingers, and he yelped in pain, but it prevented the gun from firing.

The false Indian jerked the barrel sideways. The cold metal slashed a wound across Proctor's brow, but he held on tight and wrenched the barrel away with both hands. When the man drew his knife, Proctor used the pistol as a club, smashing the butt against his head. The man reeled from the blow, but he charged back at Proctor, slashing wildly with his knife. Proctor dodged the weapon, then jumped inside the man's guard. He knocked him to the ground and pinned his knife hand down, battering his head with the pistol until he lay still.

A voice said something behind him. Proctor spun to his

feet, holding his free hand out defensively. The pistol was still clutched club-like in his other fist.

A lantern bobbed toward him, a group of people, yards away. Elizabeth's voice said, "God have mercy, what's happened here?"

"An attack," Proctor gasped, lowering his club. His eyes searched around for other attackers. "Three men—there may be more."

Deborah came forward, holding the lantern. "You have blood on your hands."

"I just saved your lives," Proctor said, searching for the third man. Two lay dead on the ground, but the third was gone. "They shot Jedediah."

"Jed?" Elizabeth cried, then more frantically, "Jed!"

"He's over there," Proctor said, pointing. "Give me the lantern."

"We need it to treat Jed," Deborah said, searching for the older man.

"One of them is still out here," Proctor said. "He came here to kill you all, and as long as you're holding the lantern, you're an easy target."

Deborah spun, expecting an attack to come instantly.

Alexandra said, "Give him the lantern and I'll go fetch another." Without waiting for an answer, she turned and, holding up her skirts, ran to the house.

Proctor reached for the lantern. Deborah's hand shook as she handed it over. He dropped the battered pistol and pulled the hatchet from the dead man's belt. It still had Nimrod's blood and fur on it.

At the same moment, Elizabeth found Jedediah's body. She knelt at his side, cradling his bald head in her lap while the other women gathered around her. Magdalena shook her head, saying nothing, and Lydia stood with her arms folded. Deborah turned away from Jedediah's body and watched Proctor.

Certain they were safe for the moment, he bent the lantern

near the ground and looked for signs of the other man. He found a trail of crushed grass, some of it slick with blood. He had followed it forty or fifty yards from the house, almost to the gate, when he heard a horse whicker impatiently.

Hand tight on the tomahawk, Proctor proceeded slowly. The lantern made him the easy target now.

The pool of light flowed ahead of him, revealing a man crawling on the ground. The handle of Proctor's knife still protruded from his shoulder. He clutched a rock in his hand as a weapon.

Proctor approached slowly, prodding the man with the tomahawk. "Who wants these women dead?"

The man's eyes were wide and almost blank, staring at Proctor without any sign of recognition. Blood bubbled from his nose as he panted, trying to form words. He would be lucky to get out a single answer.

"Tell me who sent you," Proctor demanded.

Determination flared in the man's eyes, and he swung the rock at Proctor's head. Proctor easily blocked the blow, but the motion made the other man roll. The knife shoved deeper into his shoulder, and he cried out in pain.

"What's that? Are you all right?" cried Deborah's voice from the darkness behind him.

"I'm all right," Proctor called back.

He set the lantern down and rolled the man onto his side, removing pressure from the knife. The man groaned in pain. They needed him alive, if only to find out who sent them, and why.

"Hang on," Proctor said. "We've got the best healers in the colony right here on this farm." Raising his voice, he cried, "Help! Wounded man down here! We need help!"

The man lifted his head and tried to speak.

"Yes?" Proctor asked. He leaned close, his ear almost to the man's mouth. "What is it? Who sent you?"

The man whispered, "Damn you to hell, boy."

Proctor started to shake. Grabbing the lantern, he ran back up the path, calling for help again. The women were all bent over Jedediah. Elizabeth cradled his head in her lap, speaking soothing words; Deborah knelt over him, trying to clean his wounds. Lydia held a lantern for them while Alexandra ran from the house with bandages. Magdalena stood to the side, shaking her head.

"The third one is still alive," Proctor said. "But only barely. Can one of you come help me? I don't know what to do."

Deborah tossed her loose hair back. "Can't you see we're busy here?"

Elizabeth placed her good hand on Deborah's forearm. "Where's Cecily? I'll send Cecily. Cecily?"

"She's hiding in the house, ma'am," Lydia said. "Said she's afraid."

Elizabeth nodded as if she understood, and she pushed Deborah away. "Thou hast done all thou can here. If the other man can be saved, then for the sake of mercy, I beg thee go save him."

Deborah threw down the bloody rags. To the other women, she said, "Help Elizabeth carry him inside. We will be back shortly."

They walked quickly down the path again. "He's got a knife stuck in his shoulder," Proctor said. "Has lost a lot of blood. He's here by the gate."

"Where?" asked Deborah.

She was right. The man was gone. Proctor carried the lantern back and forth, but there was no sign of the man, only a trail of crushed grass through the gate. The horses were all gone too.

"You must be very disappointed," Deborah said. "Not to have killed them all."

Proctor spun, holding the lantern up between their faces. The light revealed both of them covered chest-to-waist, hand-to-elbow in blood.

"These men came here to kill you," he said. "They did kill Jedediah, whose last words begged me to protect all of you. They damned near killed me. So if you don't trust me, if you think I'm your enemy, just say it straight-out, and I will walk away from here and not come back."

Deborah dropped her head. "You're right."

"Because . . . what?"

"No, you're right. I have no reason to judge you. I beg your forgiveness." She turned away and stepped out of the light. "It's just that it is hard to see my father dead like that, lying in my mother's lap."

Chapter 14

Before the attack, the skies had been clear for days, a few brushstrokes of cloud whitewashed on the bright blue but no hint of rain.

The morning after the attack, clouds rolled in slowly from all directions, growing darker as they gathered. The air began to twitch like the skin of a horse bothered by flies.

Proctor was sitting in the loft, sniffing the sharp smell of the air, when the drizzle started. The raindrops pattered a lullaby on the wooden shingles. The gloomy day was made for napping, but he was in no mood to sleep. He had no idea what he should be doing. He was still a bit shaky from the fight the previous night.

Elizabeth and the other women had already cleaned Jedediah's body and laid him out to rest. When Proctor went inside to see if he could help, Magdalena had snapped that she did not want to share a room with a killer, and Cecily had asked him to leave. He returned to the barn like a hired hand. Until last night, he had thought Jedediah was some kind of hired hand, and not the master of the farm.

A scrap of weeping slipped through a crack in the house's windows and reached his ears through the rain. Proctor felt bad for Elizabeth, and for Deborah too, no matter how she treated him.

Nobody, especially not Proctor, wept for either of the dead men wrapped in old horse blankets and tucked into the stall below. They were drunks and murderers, sent to kill a house full of women, and they deserved what happened to them.

The flies had already started to find them; whenever the rain lessened its patter, he noticed their buzz. The milk cow complained about the smell and the flies, banging the side-boards of her stall from time to time.

Two men dead, but one had escaped. Proctor doubted that the survivor made it very far, or would long outlive his companions. Whoever sent the widow had sent the false Indians, and next they would send somebody else. Proctor couldn't leave the women unguarded until somebody else arrived to protect them. He made up his mind to write a letter to the Reverend Emerson and find some way to post it.

These thoughts paced familiar paths in his head, like a dog leashed to a post. He fell into a fitful sleep, with dreams of fighting Indians and being scalped like his father had been. Something startled him awake, and he bolted up, plucking straw from his hair and rubbing his eyes. He heard the noise again, a dull chopping sound.

Proctor grabbed his weapons and jumped from the loft. A few steps outside the barn, he slipped to a stop. Even with the rain blurring his eyes, he recognized Deborah at the edge of the orchard behind the house. Her skirt was pinned to her knees, and she hacked away at the ground with the garden spade.

He set Jedediah's musket down in a dry spot inside the barn and went to help her. She slammed the spade into the ground over and over again.

"Miss Deborah," he said.

Her eyes were puffy and red from crying, her face blotched, and her hair plastered to her head from the rain. But her lips were tight, her tiny chin firmly set. Without a word to him, she turned back to her work, deliberately marking out the edges of a grave.

"Let me help."

She shook her head and slammed the spade into the ground harder.

He stood out of her way. The rain soaked through his

clothes to his skin in moments. It was bad enough feeling useless while a woman did that kind of work, but he was starting to shiver from the cold. He returned to the barn, to the spot where Jedediah hung his tools, and found a pick and shovel.

Without asking her permission, he began to scoop away the soil from the rough rectangle she had marked out. He could tell in moments that she had done physical labor on their farm before; the two of them fell into a comfortable rhythm without speaking. She moved around the edges, spading through the turf and levering up the larger stones. Proctor followed half a plot behind, breaking up the soil and shouldering shovel after shovel of rain-sodden mud into a pile beside the grave. The rocks weighed the same no matter what, and he began to be glad for them. The work warmed him enough that after a while, he unfastened the top button of his shirt.

Finally the hole grew deep enough that Deborah could no longer help without climbing down inside it. Proctor stepped into it first. There was an inch of brown water in the bottom, and the mud sucked at his shoes as he shifted position for a better angle. Deborah paused. The work and rain had washed away most of the sorrow from her face. He wasn't sure what it had left behind, beyond a certain grim determination.

He jammed the shovel into the ground, folded his hands over the top of it, and met her eyes. "Don't you have family or friends to help out with this?"

"No, there's just us."

"What about folks from your church?" he asked. "Can't your pastor gather the deacons or someone else to help out you and your mother?"

She was silent for a long moment while he squinted against the rain and listened to its steady splash in the puddle at his feet. "We're Friends," she said.

"Well, sure, that's why I'm out here helping you."

She opened her mouth to explain that Friends meant Quakers, and then saw—he hoped—that he was teasing her. "The Society of Friends has no pastor or deacons for our meetings," she said. "We all come before God equally."

"But there's somebody like that," he said, believing there had to be. If they came to help, whoever they were, he could pass the responsibility off for the safety of the women onto them, and he could head home. "Elders. Or somebody."

"There isn't. The Friends aren't organized like that. But it wouldn't matter if we were—my mother and father were read out of meeting years ago."

"Read out of meeting?"

"It means that the other members of the meeting asked them to leave." She sighed, letting the spade drop. Her shoulders sagged. "I don't know if it had more to do with my father's beliefs that the colonies ought to be free of British rule, or with my mother's . . . practices. I was too young to remember and my parents never spoke of it. Are you thirsty?"

He was still trying to understand the idea of being read out of meeting. "I'm sorry."

"I said, are you thirsty?" She lifted her head to the sky and emitted a short, sad laugh. "As if one could be thirsty in all this wet."

"I am," he said.

"I'll be back in a moment." She turned and went to the house.

Proctor dug vigorously while she was gone, emptying the grave of soil and rock. The sides constantly caved in around his feet, and he had to shift from one side to the other. He was almost chest-deep when her shadow darkened the rim of the hole again.

She handed him a crust end of black bread and a slice of sharp cheese. "I put on water for coffee, but it will need another moment to steep. I thought you might be hungry too."

He swallowed the bite of cheese that already filled his mouth and said, "Thank you kindly."

"No, thank you." She stood there patiently silent, soaked by the rain, while he chewed and swallowed.

He went to brush wet crumbs from his cheek and tasted the mud on his hands. He was trying to spit out the flavor when Elizabeth came and stood by her daughter with two steaming mugs in her one good hand. The older woman's face was marked with all the grief that had been written in Deborah's features, and for the first time Proctor saw more than a casual resemblance between them. Deborah handed a mug to Proctor.

He looked up at the rain. "I better drink it quick before it's watered down too far to taste."

Deborah took her cup and tilted her chin at the rain. "Mother, you must stop this now. Our neighbors' crops will rot in their fields with all this rain." She spoke low enough that Proctor didn't think he was supposed to hear.

Thunder rumbled in the sky beyond the trees and past the hill. "Thou art welcome," Elizabeth said, and turned away. The rain did nothing to lessen.

After a few sips, and then one long drink from his mug, Proctor passed it up to Deborah. "I should keep working."

"I don't know how I would've finished this without you," she said.

"Oh, it's not finished yet," he said. The deeper he went, the slower he worked, as he had to lift each shovelful up and over the edge of the grave. Several times the pile of mud collapsed and flowed back into the hole, and he had to toss it out all over again. By the time he had dug the hole as deep as his chest, he was soaked through to the bone, sore from shoulders to feet, and covered in a layer of mud from toe to waist. He tossed the shovel over the edge and climbed out, slipping back twice before he finally pulled himself to his feet. Standing hands on hips, he caught his breath for a moment and felt good about his work.

Deborah picked up the spade and took a few paces to one side. "Let's dig the next one here."

"What?"

"We've got two more men to bury. If you don't keep working, we'll never be done by nightfall."

"Shouldn't we tell the authorities?" he asked. "Have them come out and identify those men." If he had thought to offer to do that this morning, he wouldn't be digging now. He might even be on his way home.

She marked the outline of the grave with the spade. "We don't want the attention. Not if we don't know who sent them out here."

"Well, it's obviously the British," he said. "Wait a minute. How do the British know you're all witches? Have you been putting curses on them?"

She stopped her work. "Let's be clear about one thing up front. No woman here, no student of my mother's, would ever use magic to make a curse or bring harm in any way to another."

"What exactly do you do here?"

"We teach women how to use their talents to be better midwives and better healers. Sometimes we have a preacher's wife come stay with us for a while, or someone else with the talent. But we do God's work. We make sure the women use their talents to help their communities, and that's all."

He shoved his hands into his pockets, the rough fabric sore on his work-raw knuckles. "If you say so."

"I say so," she said.

"So you've done nothing to draw the attention of the British?"

"My father was outspoken against the Parliament and their taxes, true. He did not want his taxes used to support any wars, and I may share some of his opinions. But we had never done anything to antagonize them. And there are many other people around here who have been eager to harm witches in the past."

"But you said the widow came after you because of what

you did to one of their officers." He tried to ask the question casually, as if he didn't know his own part in it. To disguise his unease, he shoveled mud out of the area she had marked.

"That's what we gleaned from the few things she said."

"What happened?"

"We were lucky, much as we were last night. We would never have known the danger, except Cecily woke in the night and went outside. Lydia followed her and spied the widow using some kind of compulsion to force information from Cecily. That's why she was so terrified when we were attacked again last night."

"I don't blame her," Proctor said.

"Cecily doesn't remember anything about the widow, but Lydia heard angry questions about some British officer. She woke my mother for help, and when my mother ran to confront her, the widow tried to set the house on fire."

"How did you escape?" This spot of soil had more rocks in it, and larger ones, and Proctor had to stop frequently to toss them out of the hole.

"My mother drew all the fire into herself and then sent it down the well." She smiled. "Steam rose from the well for a day. Even though it took only seconds, she was badly burned."

"And then she put a spell on the widow, to bind her?"

"No. Then my father came out of the barn and hit her on the head with a shovel while she wasn't looking. I put the binding spell on her while she was unconscious. We sent word ahead and then set out at once to see friend Emerson."

He knew the rest of the story from there, but he couldn't shake loose thoughts of the fire. He had seen animals burned to death in a barn fire once, and the thought of that happening to this houseful of women disturbed him greatly. The thought that it might all have been his fault, because of what he did to Pitcairn, disturbed him even more. "I saw her start fire from nothing, no steel or flint or spark, just a word from her lips and flame."

"Yes."

"How did she do that?"

"I don't know," she said. The way she shuddered made him believe her.

The two of them worked with the same easy rhythm again, and the hole grew steadily deeper. When he stepped inside it, she walked over to the same spot on the opposite side of her father's hole.

Proctor stopped digging. "If we make this one big enough, we can put both men in it."

"It's not right to elevate one man above others," she said, indicating her father's grave.

"Seeing as how they're the ones who came to kill him, it seems just fine to me."

She shook her head and started turning the soil with the spade. "No, we are all made equal in the eyes of the Lord. They deserve to be mourned too, as much for the loss of their souls as for the loss of their lives. I'll do it by myself, if the work's too hard for you."

"I bet you would," he said grudgingly and went back to work. He didn't dig the second hole quite as deep. By the time he finished digging the second grave, she was more than knee-deep in the third hole, shoveling away the mud and rocks in small, slow, steady scoops.

The rain continued steady. All three holes were filling up with water. He couldn't get any wetter. Mud coated his entire body, and his waterlogged hands had the texture of prunes.

"I can finish that," he said.

"Thank you," she said, clearly tired. She slipped as she tried to climb out of the hole, so he offered her his hand.

"I'm sorry about the mud," he said, seeing his handprint on her sleeve.

She looked at it, then laughed, and he laughed too. She

stood and watched him for a while, then went up to the house.

The sky, dark all day from the clouds, was descending into truer darkness by the time Proctor decided he had shoveled enough mud from the third grave. It was the shallowest hole, little more than three feet deep. His arms nearly gave out as he climbed over the edge of the pit. He sat on the ground, arms folded across his knees, head leaning on his arms.

Deborah had been moving back and forth between the house and barn, but when she saw him finished, she came over to his side. After he said nothing to her, she picked up the shovel where he had dropped it. Holding it out to him at arm's length, she said, "One more."

He lifted his head and stared at her blankly. "What?"

"One more."

"For who?" he said, not hiding the weariness in his voice. "Did we find the third Indian?"

"For Nimrod," she said.

The dog. Of course, the dog had to be buried too. He pushed himself to his feet with a grunt. When he reached out for the shovel, she snatched it away.

"I was just joking," she said. "You have no sense of humor. There's some water for you in the barn."

He looked up at the sky, at the puddles around them, at the water standing in the graves. "I have plenty of water out here."

"Clean water," she said. "And I brought out some of my father's old clothes for you to change into. He won't be needing them anymore."

"As long as they're dry, they could be your clothes for all I care." He walked stiffly toward the barn.

The first thing he noticed in the barn were the two "Indians," wrapped in sheets with knots at their heads and feet. Their clothes had been stripped off them and piled outside the door, waiting to be burned to kill the lice. Assuming the lice didn't drown first.

His gaze encompassed all that in a split second and then was drawn to the steam rising from the tub. She'd heated a tub full of water for him, a pot at a time, and carried it out while he was deep in the graves. If he hurried, he might get not only clean but warm.

He stripped to his waist and plunged his face into the water and decided to hold it there for as long as he could keep his breath or stand the heat. The former won out, and he pulled out with a gasp a moment later, shaking the water from his hair. By the time he'd scrubbed clean and changed into the dry clothes—who cared if they were too short in the ankles and sleeves, they were dry!—he noticed the smoked ham and pork puddings and fried potatoes set out for him beside a pint mug of beer.

With his belly full, and his body tired, he didn't think about going any farther than someplace to sleep, at least for the night.

In the morning, beams of light fell through a threadbare curtain of clouds. Proctor walked to the house, his feet squishing in the mud.

The women were all dressed in their daily clothes except for Cecily, who had found a black dress somewhere. Jedediah was wrapped in a sheet that knotted at head and foot, just like the two "Indians" in the barn.

"When's the minister coming?" Proctor asked.

"Our faith makes do without ministers," Elizabeth said.

"Oh." Proctor had been planning on asking the other man for help carrying the body. His arms and shoulders were sore from yesterday, but he wasn't willing to admit it. "Well, it's no problem—I'm sure I can carry him by myself."

As he bent to pick up the body from the floor, Deborah went to the feet and took hold of the knot. "Don't be full of foolish pride. I'll help you."

Proctor was going to argue, but he saw the look on her face and realized how far it would get him. "That's fine, thanks." He hooked hands under Jedediah's shoulders. "Ready? Up."

She pulled up as he lifted but the knot slipped out of her hand, and her father's feet slammed the floor.

"I'll be glad to help," Alexandra offered.

"Don't be ridiculous, girl," Cecily said. "Lydia was born to labor, it's in her nature, isn't that true, Lydia?"

"Yes, ma'am," the black woman said quietly. She positioned herself opposite of Deborah and said, "Are you ready?"

The three of them carried the body out to the first grave and lowered it as far as they could. It splashed at the bottom, and the sheet immediately began soaking up the mud. Proctor looked to Elizabeth for a reaction, but she only sighed and nodded. Then she said, "Let's show the same respect to the others."

Deborah had started toward the barn, Lydia in her wake, and Proctor had to stretch his legs to catch up. They took the man with the mauled arm first, lowering him a little less gently into the second grave. The second Indian was dropped at the side of the shallowest grave when Deborah asked to catch her breath. Proctor put his foot on the body and rolled it into the hole, splashing mud and water up around their ankles. Being this close to them, remembering how they'd tried to kill him, made his hands start to shake again.

To Elizabeth, he said, "I'm sorry I didn't dig a separate grave for Nimrod. I'm not sure where you want him."

"He can go in with Jed," she said. "He was a good friend to us."

Her throat was thick by the time she choked out the last words. Proctor went and carried the bloodied dog back, getting mud all over his clean clothes. He gently lowered the animal over his master's feet.

He stood up and stepped back from the grave. Elizabeth stared at her husband's body, while Cecily rested a hand on her crippled arm. The southern woman leaned close and murmured something into Elizabeth's ear, producing a wan smile. Elizabeth covered the other woman's hand with her own, patting it for reassurance.

Magdalena paced nervously back from the edge of the graves. Lydia placed herself opposite Cecily, standing next to Alexandra, who glanced from face to face looking for clues.

Deborah cleared her throat. "Friends, we are gathered here today to remember Jedediah Walcott, my father, a good friend to all of us here." She wiped the corner of her eye, quickly, trying to hide the gesture.

"Amen," Lydia said under her breath.

"We will also remember these two strangers who killed him. We hope they have found a better peace now than they knew when they were living. We should remember that all men are equal in God's eyes, if not our own." She looked at Proctor and Alexandra. "For those of you not familiar with our ways, we have no set hymns to sing or prayers to say. We begin with silence. Anyone who is moved to speak may do so. You can share a memory or a prayer about any of the men we bury here today." The longer she spoke, the harder it was to get the words out. She paused to regain her composure.

"May Gott have mercy on us—this whole thing is terrible," Magdalena said.

Cecily spoke immediately. "Well, I, for one, am grateful—"

"Please leave a few moments for contemplation between contributions," Deborah said.

Cecily squeezed Elizabeth's arm sympathetically. "But of course, forgive me." She waited a brief moment, and when she spoke it was in a softer voice. "I, for one, am grateful that it wasn't worse." She looked around at their faces. "I mean, it's terrible that Jedediah was killed, he was a good man, a very noble man. But God was watching out for us."

Elizabeth tried to speak and couldn't. Clouds passed in front of the sun. Proctor shivered.

"I'll miss him," Deborah said. "He sacrificed himself for something he believed in, trying to protect us."

A spattering of raindrops pelted out of the sky. Elizabeth said, "May the Light guide the souls of these two strangers, who also died for a cause they believed in."

Proctor shook his head at that. He figured their true cause was cash and whiskey.

The rain came down harder. Cecily and Magdalena began to glance to the shelter of the house. Lydia stood with her hands folded in front of her. Alexandra fidgeted, twirling her long red curls around her fingers. No one else seemed inclined to speak. Proctor cleared his throat.

"Jedediah was a good man to work with. He labored without rest, never expecting anything in return." His hands began to shake. "On the night he died, he only expected to be able to delay his attackers long enough so that all of you could escape. I suspect that he didn't have the smoothest intercourse with all of you"—he knew the words were wrong even before Lydia hid a smile and Deborah glared at him—"but he didn't think twice about giving his life to save you. I hope that someday, if I have to, I can be as brave."

After a moment's silence, Deborah said, "I think that's enough, Mother. Let's go inside before we're all soaked."

The women stepped away from the grave in a slow procession back toward the house. Elizabeth stopped when she reached Proctor, and patted his arm. "That was very moving, dear boy. Do come inside and join us once thou art done."

"When I'm done with what?"

"When thou art done filling the graves," she sniffled, as if he should have known. "They can't stay uncovered."

Of course. He should've known. He was their hired help now. Their Jedediah.

"Do thou want us to stay and help thee? We can stay and help thee," she said.

Cecily shielded her face against the sky. "Maybe it would be better if he left it until tomorrow."

"No, I'll take care of it now," he said.

He filled the graves quickly, packing the mud into Jedediah's first. The second he filled with loose soil. The rain was pouring again by the time he turned to the shallow grave. He tossed a few shovelfuls across it, just enough to cover the body, and then went to clean up.

Deborah pressed a warm mug of coffee into his hand as soon as he went inside. Food sat uneaten on the table. The women were discussing their attackers, wondering who had sent them and what they wanted.

"Why don't you ask them?" Proctor asked.

The conversation stopped. Cecily stared at him, and said, "Are you touched in the head? They're not alive to question."

"Didn't you say that witches can speak to the dead? Necrosomething."

Elizabeth shook her head. "It's not that easy."

"It's in the Bible," Proctor said. "Saul and the witch of Endor, speaking to the dead. If you want to find out why those men wanted to kill you, summon them up and ask them."

Chapter 15

The women debated the rest of the day, trying to reach a consensus on Proctor's proposal.

"Necromancy is evil," Magdalena insisted. "Ve should have no part of it."

"No one is suggesting necromancy," Deborah insisted. "No one wants to raise the dead, or ask the spirits to foretell the future. We only wish to speak to them about the past."

Magdalena spewed sentences in German, ending with, "*Totenbeschwörung*, necromancy, vhatever—it is all the same. It is evil, the verk of Satan."

"No, it isn't," Deborah said patiently. "We are only going to ask them for information."

"I don't understand how we can do that spell," Cecily said. "Not that I know as much as Elizabeth or you, I'm not claiming that. But I thought, at the very least, you needed to know someone's name to summon them. We have no idea who those terrible men are."

"One of them was named Dick," Proctor said, recalling the name he heard during the fight. "He's the one who killed Nimrod."

"And we have their things still," Alexandra interjected. "Their clothes, the weapons they were carrying—that should help."

Deborah nodded. "Those are exactly what we need. All we want to do is find out their purpose in coming to kill us.

Who were they working for? Is it the British governor or one of the generals or—"

She stopped in mid-sentence. That was the part that bothered Proctor the most. Who wanted to kill these women and why? With the militiamen strangling the Redcoats in Boston, it made no sense at all for British officers to care about a few women outside Salem.

"They knew how to see past the enchantment," he said. "So whoever sent the widow also sent them."

That wasn't a very comforting thought, and the others glided right past it.

"Their disguises link them to the attack," Deborah said. "That's the important thing, because that's all we wish to ask them about."

"But Magdalena makes an excellent point too," Cecily said, and the older woman nodded agreement. "We should consider how dangerous it may be. We all want answers. I want answers. But if we summon the spirits of the dead, especially dead men burning in hell, where they ought to be if there is any justice at all, then we draw the undesirable eye of Lucifer himself—"

"Aie, don't mention his name," Magdalena shouted, smacking her hands on the table and making a hex sign to ward herself as she rose.

At the end of the day, Deborah and Alexandra were in favor of Proctor's plan, Magdalena was vehemently opposed, and Cecily alternately affirmed that it was a good idea then sowed caution and doubt. Lydia remained silent, whether because she had no opinion or did not feel free to speak, Proctor wasn't sure. Elizabeth also said nothing, but you could see her weighing the opinions for and against. Finally, after dark, she rose wearily. "Let us sleep on it and pray for a clearer path tomorrow."

The debate resumed the next day. Proctor, having already made his decision about what was right, escaped to do the work of the farm. He tended to the animals and split firewood. When he returned to the house around noon, Deborah met him at the well. "It's decided," he said. "We all agreed to try to talk to them."

"Even Magdalena?"

"Elizabeth persuaded her that it would be safe, if it even worked at all, since we don't know their names. We agreed that we would not call Jedediah, since he can't tell us anything that he didn't know in life."

He noticed how *Mother* and *Father* two days ago, when they were digging graves, had been transformed back to Elizabeth and Jedediah. "And Cecily too?"

"She was the last to be convinced. She is more afraid than she lets on, but I think it is mostly for Elizabeth's sake. She thinks we will not find out anything useful, and it will only make Elizabeth sadder, even if it doesn't bring any direct harm."

He nodded thoughtfully at that. Cecily was smarter than she sometimes seemed. "So are they doing it now?" It was his idea—it seemed too much to expect that they would give him a chance to see it done.

"No, we need to wait for twilight," Deborah said.

"Why?"

"The spirits are most accessible at dusk. At twilight, the world is caught between day and night, just as the spirits are caught between life and death."

"Have you done this before?"

"No."

They both fell silent. Proctor hauled up a bucket of water and offered a ladle to Deborah. She shook her head.

"Will I be allowed to watch?" he asked. His voice was tight, sharper than he intended.

"Yes, positively." Her voice was uncertain. "I convinced Elizabeth that your presence is essential, simply for the role you played."

He supposed that he should thank her. But the words that came out of his mouth had a different edge. "Essential because I killed them, you mean?"

"However you wish to have it." She turned and walked away a second before he would have done the same.

That afternoon, he cleaned tools, straightened up the barn, and hiked the fences. He avoided the graves, although he knew he'd have to finish filling them tomorrow. He was having second thoughts about calling up the dead. This was exactly the kind of witchcraft his mother would oppose. The kind that made ordinary people so afraid of witches they were willing to kill them.

Elizabeth came looking for him late in the afternoon. "Can thou help us gather any of the items the dead men left behind?"

He showed her the items in the barn. "It's mostly their weapons."

"That'll do fine, since we mean to ask them about their intention to kill us. Can thou sort out anything that belonged to the one called Dick?"

"I think these are his boots. This is his hatchet, I'm sure, and the bloody pistol belonged to him."

"Keep them separate, and bring it all inside."

A space had been cleared in front of the hearth for the trestle table and plank benches. Five candles had been arranged on the table at the points of a star, but they were unlit. The room smelled of soap and herbs, the floors and walls scrubbed clean.

Elizabeth directed him to place the dead men's items on the table. "Dick's stuff on this side of the candles," she said, "and the other one's over there."

At first he piled the items randomly, but on reflection he rearranged them, laying them out the way he would if he were going to get dressed. He didn't explain that to anyone, because he didn't want to feel foolish. But he thought the spirits would be more likely to recognize them that way.

Cecily hovered around the table, fidgeting, touching things. "I think this is the right thing to do," she told Elizabeth. "But we shouldn't do it tonight. You're not ready. Let's sleep on it another night. We can still try tomorrow."

"No, tonight is the night to do it," Elizabeth said. She sat down and massaged her crippled arm. "These men are not well known to us—no more than half of one's name, and it might not be his real name at that—nor are they bound to this piece of land. Their spirits will want to wander back to more familiar places. This will be the third night since their death. I fear if we do not attempt it tonight, we will have no chance at all for it to work."

"But look at you, dear heart—you haven't eaten for several days, much less slept." She frowned at the table and rearranged items, putting weapons together on one side, clothes on the other. "Your hands are shaking even now as we speak. What difference will one more day make?"

"I am also vorried," Magdalena said. "Ve could pray on it for anudder day."

"We all agreed this morning that we would try," Elizabeth insisted. "We were led to believe it was the right thing."

"I want to know why people are trying to kill us," Alexandra said sulkily. "Frankly, I would feel safer back home with my kin, even if folks there did want to burn me for a witch."

They fell into uncomfortable silence. Elizabeth rose and left the room, followed by Cecily. As soon as she was gone, Proctor quietly moved all the dead men's items back to their original positions.

A moment later Elizabeth bustled back into the room as if she were trying to escape conflict by outrunning it. "Do thou not want to know who's trying to kill us?"

"Of course I do," Cecily said. "But don't you see, we need you, Elizabeth, to guide us and help protect us. What good can you do us if you're completely drained?"

"The power should flow through the circle to me, not away from me. I won't be drained."

Cecily's hands moved, sketching possibilities in the air. "What if something bad happens and you're so tired, you can't react fast enough to protect us the next time?"

"I thank thee for thy confidence, but if thou art all so helpless without me, then I have done a poor job indeed."

"Oh, my dear Elizabeth, perish such thoughts. None of us would have near the skill we have without you. But could anyone else here capture fire and channel it the way you did when the widow attacked?"

Elizabeth looked at Deborah.

"The hour is upon us," Deborah said. "If we are in agreement to do this thing, let us begin now."

Her mother nodded. She took Cecily's hand and chose seats on one side of the table. Deborah and Alexandra took seats on the other side.

Elizabeth looked at Magdalena. "I cannot do this without thee. In the name of the God we both love, I beg thine assistance. If it does not work, I will forgo the attempt and not try again."

Magdalena's jaw worked as if she were chewing over some unpleasant phrase. Finally, she went and sat at Elizabeth's right hand.

"Ya, I vill help you this vunce," she said. "But I vill do no more than join the circle. I have seen the dead summoned back before and do not vish to see it again."

"That will be enough. I thank thee. Lydia, Proctor?"

The two of them were standing to one side. "Yes?" Lydia said, and Proctor said, "Yes, ma'am?"

"A circle of seven is stronger than a circle of five. Both are in the sequence of holy numbers. Join us, please."

Proctor's heart pounded. They took seats across from one another on the ends of the benches, Lydia next to Cecily, Proctor next to Deborah. The circle was formed with Magdalena, Elizabeth, Cecily, and Lydia on one side of the table, with Proctor, Deborah, and Alexandra going up the other.

"Let us join hands," Elizabeth said. Deborah's hand felt

smaller than he expected. He tried to hold it gently. He reached across the table and took Lydia's hand, finding it large, and rough, and callused. Cecily rested her hand on Elizabeth's crippled arm.

"May the Light lead us to do Thy will, O God," Elizabeth said. After a moment of silence, she said, "Girl, if thou please?"

"Yes, Mother," Deborah answered. She slipped her hand from Proctor's grasp and fetched a taper from the coals, returning to light the five candles. She sat, holding out her hand for him.

He looked at it a moment before taking it.

"A really powerful witch can draw on another's power by proximity," she said. "But we require touch."

"Shhh!" Elizabeth said. "The time for lessons will be later."

Proctor took her hand. He felt a tingle moving through him clockwise, through his right arm and out his left. Then it faded and disappeared.

"Ah," Elizabeth said softly. "Yes."

The light of sunset through the windows slowly matched the glow from the candles. When the quality of the lights seemed indistinguishable, Elizabeth spoke.

"We are ready. Proctor, call the name of the one thou heard addressed."

He pulled back. "I don't know what to do. Shouldn't there be a, a prayer, or a ritual, or something?"

"Let the Light flow into thy heart and guide thee," Elizabeth said. "All miracles are performed by the grace of God. Open thy heart to God and call the name of the man who attacked us."

Proctor sat quietly for a moment. He felt too self-conscious to speak aloud, but to himself he recited the prayer his mother had taught him for scrying, asking the Father for guidance and knowledge. He was no calmer or surer when he was done.

"Dick?" he asked uncertainly, looking around to see if something happened.

They waited a moment, and nothing did.

"Which items are his?" Elizabeth asked.

Proctor nodded toward the pile in front of him. "Hold his items in your mind as you call him," Deborah said. "Let the power flow through you to the rest of us, to Elizabeth. We'll do the work."

"I don't know how to do this," he whispered.

"Maybe we should wait until tomorrow," Cecily whispered to Elizabeth.

Deborah squeezed his hand. "You can do this. First, close your eyes, as if in prayer." He did. "Now feel the pulse in your right hand, your pulse. When you sense it, feel the life pulse of the other person, beating in your palm."

He slowed his breathing and relaxed until he thought he felt it. He opened his mouth to say so, but she interrupted him first.

"Now feel it pulse out of your left hand," she said in a low, soothing tone. "Like the double beat of your heart, in, then out, in, then out."

As her sentence dropped to a murmur, he felt both hearts pulsing. A light burst inside him, like the heat from a flame. It coursed into his right arm, through his chest, and out his left, the next wave starting as soon as the first one was gone. He opened his mouth in delight, but Deborah interrupted him again.

"Call to him now," she said softly.

"Dick, are you out there?" Proctor said, waiting for a response. He opened his eyes and lifted his head. "Dick?"

Again, nothing.

Deborah squeezed his hand more firmly. "You could always try calling as though you actually expected him to answer."

He recalled the phrase the man had used. " 'Help me out, Dick, the dog's mauling my arm!' "

Quit your whining. We'll bind it up after we kill the witches up at the house.

The candles flared, and smoke twined up from all five of them, forming the torso and head of a man. The smoke seemed to capture the light and reflect it, giving the shape a glow from within. Proctor forgot to feel the pulse going through him and a bolt of ice shot up his arm through his shoulder. But Deborah gave a tug on his hand that drew the next pulse through, and he felt the spirit flowing freely again.

"Who sent thee, Dick?" Elizabeth asked. The candlelight on her face in the dark gave her a similarly ghostly appearance. "Dick, answer me, who sent thee?"

Old Nance sent us, the ghost shape said. *Wait, who are you? You're not Billy.*

"What did Nance send thee to do?"

To kill them witches, just like it says in the Bible. Nance said they must be killed, paid us to do it. Who are you? Where's my brother, Bill? Bill?

"Dick," Elizabeth said. "Thou must tell us who Nance is."

But the ghost twisted its head from side to side. The smoke had started to dissipate and the glow was fading.

They hadn't learned anything yet. Proctor shouted, "Hey, Bill! Get your sorry ass in here!"

Deborah twitched at his yell, but the second man appeared immediately. His face and body, suffused with light, formed out of the smoke. He was staring at his shredded arm. The first image solidified again. The pulse grew stronger through Proctor's hands.

I don't know what happened, Dick. The dog bit me, and then we were running toward the house, and then it all went black. His chin lifted and he looked blankly around the room, then he looked down. *Hey, there's my gear. Where are we?*

Hell if I know. It's all so black and cold.

"Thy souls may still go into the Light if you make amends

for your evil deeds," Elizabeth said forcefully. "Where dost thou come from? Who is Nance and why does he want us dead?"

Both faces turned toward Elizabeth. Finally, Dick said, again, *Who are you?*

Why are you talking to her? Bill asked.

"Do rightly here," Elizabeth said. "Tell us who Nance is."

Proctor wanted to scream at her. These were rough men, backwoodsmen—he knew the type well. "So did you fellows take the road up from Boston?"

Bill looked over his shoulder, shook his head. *No. Nance arranged it. We boarded a smugglers' ship at Hancock's pier, and he sailed us up the coast to Salem. Didn't hear his name, didn't want to either.*

Shut up, Bill, I don't think we should be talking to him either.

"Nance wanted me to check up on you," Proctor said. "Find out where things went so wrong. You two mucked it up pretty bad, didn't you?"

He felt a sharp pain flow into his right hand, like a needle red from the flame, and he winced.

Wasn't me who mucked it up, Bill said.

Nance promised it'd be easy. Said they were witches and Quakers, traitors to the Crown, spies for the rebels. Said they were already headed to hell so we weren't doing no wrong.

Bill's ghost nodded. *We just had to speed them on the way. We were supposed to spare—*

The pulsing through Proctor's hand stopped abruptly. The light drained from both figures, and they were only dusty shadows lit by the natural candlelight.

Cecily had covered her mouth, and she was pale and shaking. "God forgive me," she said. "They were going to spare no one."

Elizabeth whispered, "Take Lydia's hand. Now, please."

She did so reluctantly, only when the ghosts had almost faded away. Outside the house, darkness had fallen. Proctor immediately called to them, "Finish your report."

That's all there is to report, Bill said. *What do we do next?*

Dick closed his hand on Bill's mangled arm. *Come on, we're done for. There's nothing left for us here.*

They stared off into the distance beyond the dark horizon. "Thou art welcome to stay here awhile," Elizabeth said. "Make amends for what thou did."

It's cold here, Dick. It's so cold it burns.

That's all right, brother. If it gets cold enough, we'll just fall asleep and then we'll forget everything.

They started to fade. The ropes of smoke unraveled. The candles sparked, flames flaring, and then guttered back to normal. The ghosts were gone.

Around the table, it was as though everyone finally remembered to breathe.

Elizabeth said, "Let us keep our hands linked, and our hearts and heads clear a moment longer. Proctor, call them back."

He nodded. He didn't think it would work, but he would try.

"And do not cheat them vith the lies this time," Magdalena said.

He wanted to argue with her—this whole calling forth spirits was a lie, making dead men believe they were still alive. But he held his opinion for now. "Dick, Bill, come back here. You haven't been dismissed yet. Dick! Fall in to muster!"

The candles flickered, but the smoke failed to coalesce, so he called out again. Again, nothing.

"Call back the dead men now," Elizabeth said, her voice sounding desperate.

Proctor thought about the tone of voice his captain used in militia training. "Get your ass in here now."

The flames shot up, consuming the candle wax in a second, and then they all fell dark. He felt his pulse flowing both ways, out both arms. A ball of light appeared above the center of the table, unshaped by any smoke. It had a warm, honeyed glow that illuminated the faces around the table with a holy light.

"Hold on to one another," Elizabeth said, her voice shifting from desperation to fear.

Proctor felt pulled both ways. He squeezed both hands tight.

Across the table, Lydia's head flung forward and then snapped back. When she opened her mouth, the voice that came out was old and masculine, and spoke with a New England accent.

"I am sorry for the way things happened, Elizabeth. I do not like to see thee hurt. Keep faith that this is as God intended it to be."

"Jed?" Her voice wavered. "Jed, is it thee?"

"Tell Deborah I'm sorry that I won't be around for her." Proctor couldn't take his eyes off Lydia's face, or the glow that floated above the table, but he heard Deborah swallow beside him. "Tell her that I'm sorry I won't see her marry, and won't have a chance to bounce her grandchildren on my knee. I had always looked forward to that."

A sob strangled itself in Elizabeth's throat. When she spoke, she sounded young and vulnerable. "Oh, Jed, what are we going to do without thee?"

The room fell silent and the glow intensified, as if it were drawing all light into itself and emitting none. The faces around the table fell dark, invisible to Proctor's eye.

"Don't worry, my dear Elizabeth, we will be reunited soon."

An icy wind swirled around the table, stirring their hair and goose-pimpling their skin.

"What do you mean?" Deborah asked. "Lydia, what does he mean?"

The spirit ignored her. "I loved thee so much, Lizzie, and never told thee often enough."

"I've always known," she said.

"That's why I'm sorry the end will be so painful for thee. Trust that the pain will end quickly and thou will go to a better place."

Proctor couldn't see her face. He was glad he couldn't.

"Tell Deborah she will be safe for a little while if she sticks close to the Concord boy."

Elizabeth's voice faltered. "I . . . I will."

"May the Light shine upon thee."

With those words, the glow faded, leaving them all in the dark. The smell of singed wood and melted wax filled the room. Lydia's hand went from rigid to limp in Proctor's grip. Her body slumped unconscious across the table. Deborah jerked her hand away.

"I'll get another light," she said softly.

Proctor nodded, feeling so dizzy he thought he would collapse just as Lydia had. He wiped the sweat off his forehead and took deep breaths to rein in his galloping heart. Everything had been so vivid and immediate when the ghosts were present. Now that they were gone, the room around him seemed pale and far away, a scene from a dream. Only the women in the circle were real, as present in this world as they were in the other.

Elizabeth sobbed softly. His heart ached for her.

Deborah's feet padded across the floor. Iron scraped on iron as she pulled the poker from its holder and stirred the last dull coals of the fire, adding tinder and wood to build the flame. Soon there was enough light to illuminate their faces once again. Cecily held Lydia's hand and stroked her hair; Lydia looked like an emptied cup, her eyes rimmed with fear, her limbs slack and unresponsive. Elizabeth sat with her hands folded in front of her on the table, her head bowed.

"What do you think they meant," Proctor said, "the

ghosts, when they said they were supposed to spare someone?"

No one answered at first. Cecily turned the emerald ring on one of her fingers, clearly shaken by the encounter as all of them had been. Finally, she said, "Likely enough they were supposed to spare no one, unless it was for questioning. Or something unspeakable and vile."

Proctor hadn't considered that. Women had to fear things that he did not.

"How did you summon Mister Walcott?" Alexandra whispered. Her face looked young in the firelight, more child than woman.

"I don't know," Elizabeth said.

"He may have summoned himself," Deborah suggested. "This is his home, all his worldly possessions are here. If that"—she indicated the piles of items taken from the dead men—"is enough to summon them, then surely there is enough of him here to summon himself."

"Perhaps," Elizabeth said.

Magdalena rose from the table, trembling with fury. "You promised me there would be no *totenbeschwörung*."

"I did not cause that to happen," Elizabeth said.

The old woman squeezed a fist against her mouth, saying some prayer. Then she stomped off to the other room.

"What's wrong?" Proctor asked Deborah. He meant, besides the obvious.

"She didn't mean to, but she asked my father's spirit about the future," Deborah said, watching her mother with sorrow written on her expression. "The dead tend to see death more clearly, so that's what they speak of when they speak the future. Sometimes the dead want death for the living, so they mislead us. To act with knowledge from the dead leads us away from the will of God."

Alexandra waved her hand at the two of them. "So what are you going to do?"

"What do you mean?" Deborah asked.

"Do you trust your father's spirit?" She nodded at Proctor. "Will you stay close to him or not?"

Proctor shook his head, not wanting that obligation, afraid of what it meant. When he saw the miserable, forlorn look on Deborah's face, he regretted the gesture at once.

"I'm not sure," Deborah said.

Chapter 16

Proctor opened his mouth to apologize to Deborah. Whatever their differences were, she didn't deserve that kind of rude rejection from him, not after losing her father, nor after hearing the warning from his spirit.

But she had already turned away.

"So what do we do now?" she asked her mother.

"Whatever thou wish," Elizabeth said, wiping the tears from her face with a burn-scarred hand. "What difference does it make to me?" Her face was vacant, as if part of her went with the light when it faded. When she sighed, her shoulders seemed to collapse inward, like an empty sack.

"I'm getting rid of these things," Deborah announced, gesturing at the items on the table. "Alexandra?"

"Yes?" the girl asked.

"Will you help me carry them?"

"I can help too," Proctor said.

Deborah jumped at the sound of his voice. She started to say no, but changed her mind. "Thank you."

Proctor gathered the weapons—the two pistols, the hatchet, a wickedly curved fascine knife, and other knives. It was clearer to him now that they meant to make the murder of these women a close and personal thing. Deborah and Alexandra gathered the clothes and boots.

As they turned to leave, Lydia forced herself to stir from the table.

"Shh, shh, darling," Cecily said, stroking her hair. "Rest easy now, just rest easy."

But Lydia ignored her. She reached out and grabbed the hem of Proctor's jacket, her eyes wide and frightened, her mouth still slack. "When you go," she gasped. "Just keep going."

"What?" Proctor asked. "Why?"

But Lydia was too exhausted to speak again. Cecily clutched the black woman's head to her bosom and rocked her. "The poor, poor woman," she said. "That must have been terrifying for her."

Proctor nodded. Alexandra and Deborah stood at the door waiting for him. They'd heard nothing.

There was a fire pit for burning waste downhill from the barn. Deborah threw the clothes into the pit. "Alexandra, will you go fetch tinder, as much as you can find?"

The girl brought twigs and dry grasses while Deborah piled wood to create a better flame. When she turned to go to the house, Proctor pulled a flint and steel from his pocket.

"I want to destroy all of it, every piece," she said as she struck sparks to the tinder. "Especially their weapons."

"They won't burn so easily," he said.

"Then I'll smash them."

She took the hatchet from him and hacked at the first pistol, destroying it. Behind her, the fire spread from the tinder. A burst of orange flame knocked the logs back, made them all jump. It flared high, shooting off sparks and hot ash.

Proctor took both women by the shoulders and pulled them back. "I guess you didn't take the gunpowder from their bags, did you?"

Deborah's hair had come unpinned. It tumbled wildly down her cheeks. She stopped to brush it out of the way, and laughed, then seemed surprised at the wildness of the sound.

"I guess I didn't," she said soberly.

They took turns destroying the weapons. When the firing pins were broken, the barrel ends smashed, and the stocks splintered, they threw the pieces into the flame. They broke the knife blades and destroyed the hilts the same way. When all that remained was the hatchet, Proctor used two huge stones to break the hickory handle, and tossed it into the fire.

"Do you feel better?" he asked Deborah.

"No," she said. "I don't."

"What are we going to do now?" he asked.

Deborah didn't say anything for a minute, so Alexandra spoke. "I want to go home, where my brothers are."

"Yes," Deborah said. "My first thought is to send everyone away. But then I wonder if that will be what causes my mother's death, and I don't want that hanging over my head forever. But then if I have everyone stay here, and that causes her death, it will be just as bad."

"Maybe your choice, your intentions, won't make any difference," Proctor said.

She shook her head angrily. "If I believe that, then I'm powerless, and that is unacceptable to me."

"Magdalena would call it the will of God."

Deborah snorted and wiped the hair away from her cheek again. The fire, which stank of clothing and gunpowder, was already burning low. She stooped to add another log to the flames.

"So does this mean I'll be able to go home?" Alexandra asked. She fought back a yawn and rubbed her eyes.

Deborah rested her hand gently on the young girl's back. "Yes, it does."

Proctor revised his first impression of Deborah. She was not as harsh or rough-edged as he originally thought. With the ordeals she had been through—a lifetime of secrecy, the attack on her mother, the murder of her father—she showed remarkable steadiness and courage. A lot of her strictness with Alexandra was only because she knew too well the dangers in the world abroad and worried about the girl's safety.

He cleared his throat. "If you two want to go back up to

the house, I'll clean up the fire and check the farm, make sure everything's safe."

Deborah's face turned toward him with an expression of relief and gratitude. "Do you mind?" she asked.

"If I minded, I wouldn't have offered."

She reached out and squeezed his forearm. "Thank you. I wish I had something more to say—"

"That's enough," he said.

She rose and led Alexandra inside. He watched them go, shaking his head. He could not figure Deborah out. Underneath that brusque manner, behind that sharp tongue, there was a smart, thoughtful, hardworking woman. But she seemed determined to prevent anyone from seeing it. The same way her Quakerish dress hid how pretty she could be too.

He let go of those thoughts and made a circuit of the farm. They were worried about Nance, whoever he was, but there were more ordinary threats. If a fox got into the chicken coop, they'd all go hungry. He went to the coop first, but there were no eggs in the nests, nothing to scrye with, so he continued his round. As he checked the last of the buildings, he called the dog out of reflex. When Nimrod didn't respond, Proctor remembered he was dead.

"Damn it, Nimrod," he said, trying hard not to choke up. "All those other dead fellows showed up. You could have come and barked at us once or twice."

There was one more thing to do before he went to sleep, but he wanted the shovel for it. He looked in the barn and realized that he'd left it up by the graves. He was getting sloppy, leaving tools outside. There was no excuse for it.

As he walked to the orchard, he realized that he still needed to finish filling in the graves, which were tumbled, as if the mud had started to settle. As he picked up the shovel, a chill shivered through him, and he wondered if their ghosts remained nearby.

He shook off the chill as he walked back to the fire pit.

He meant to try a protection spell tonight, fashioned out of what he had gleaned from Lydia and the others. They might not teach him, but that didn't mean he couldn't learn.

First, he needed a material to focus his magic. Deborah used salt, and Elizabeth used sand from Cape Cod. He didn't have either, but ash would work just fine, especially ash taken from the items of men who had already attacked them once and failed.

He shoveled the dim coals out of the way and scooped cold ash into an old bucket. When the bucket was full, he smothered the rest of the fire. Easy labor compared with the digging a couple of days before, but it took away some of the skin-crawling unease that had settled on him ever since they called up the dead.

"All right now," he said to himself. "Let's see if I remember how this was done."

He stood at the eastern corner of the barn and began with the prayer that his mother had taught him for scrying. Taking up a fistful of the ashes, he lifted his hand and said, "Merciful Lord, if it be Thy will, please keep all harm from men or magic outside this circle." Then, because that didn't seem like quite enough, he remembered Deborah's use of Bible verses and added, "Ashes to ashes, dust to dust, and all that, amen."

The ashes trickled out of his palm as he paced clockwise around the barn. Afraid that drifting would make the circle broken and inefficacious, he bent as he walked, leaving a solid gray line. Recalling what Lydia had told him about praying without ceasing, he repeated the prayer his mother told him. When the words got so jumbled from repetition he wasn't sure what he was saying anymore, he switched to the Lord's prayer, tossing out a hasty, "I'm sure it's all one prayer to You, Lord," as he went.

The bucket was empty before he completed the circle. At first, he was going to spread the last ashes thinner, but then, praying vigorously and aloud, he ran back to the dead fire for more. He finished by pouring extra ashes along the gap, to be sure.

When he was done, he wiped his forehead on the inside of his elbow. Anything near his hands would have smeared ashes on his face. He stepped back to admire his handiwork, if *admiration* could be used for work that he surveyed so anxiously. Either it would work or it wouldn't; if he didn't need it, he would never know, and if it didn't work, he wouldn't find out until too late.

Out of habit, Proctor washed the bucket and put it and the shovel away. Then he splashed water from the trough on his hands and face. When he could no longer smell the smoke, he took himself for clean and went into the barn to sleep.

The straw, fresh as it was, was less comfortable than his mattress at home. Part of him hoped that Deborah did send everyone home tomorrow. He was eager to sleep in his own bed again. He'd never been away from his mother and father this long either, and while he didn't miss them the way Alexandra missed her folks, he wondered how they were.

Part of him was not quite ready to go, and that puzzled him. There was nothing to keep him here, not really. Maybe he could get to the chickens first thing in the morning and snag an egg or two for scrying. If he didn't use it to see the future, maybe it wouldn't be as evil. He could just use it to see where Emily was, what she was doing. That was a good intention, right? He missed their conversations, the way they used to plan out the future they wanted together.

He rolled over. He missed Emily. He missed Jedediah and his thunderous snoring. He missed Nimrod, whining for attention because he couldn't climb up to the loft.

A dog barked outside, over the hills, on the other side of the woods, at some distant neighbor's farm. Finally it howled. Proctor rolled over and looked through the hay door. There was no full moon, no reason for it to howl. Other howls sounded from farther away, carried across the acres of swamp and wood by a rising wind.

Proctor's skin crawled.

He tried to shake it off, attributing it to the shadow cast by the attack the other night. But he checked to make sure Jedediah's musket was at hand, and he suddenly regretted the destruction of the pistols.

He wrapped the blanket around himself and squeezed his eyes shut. Asleep or not, he dreamed. Dead men dressed like Indians attacked him, and he was powerless to defend himself. A knife slashed at him. He felt his own blood spurting hot across his helpless hands, and he jolted upright.

Outside, it was still dark.

The wind rushed through the farm buildings like a mob of hands, rattling doors and slamming loose shutters. The milk cow lowed in agitation, banging the sides of her stall.

Proctor shuddered, his skin tingling.

The house door creaked open, a sound he recognized at once. He thought it caught by the wind, only the sound of it swinging open was followed by Deborah's voice.

"Mother! Magdalena! Cecily!"

The wind crumbled her words into pieces like the fragments of an eggshell and tossed them away. Another "Mother" sounded like it was ripped from her mouth and dashed against the nearest wall. He bolted up and grabbed his weapons.

A shrill scream cut through the wind.

Barefoot and jacketless, he leapt from the loft and ran outside the barn. A stench like rotting flesh choked him.

Magic shot through the air like a cannon blast, so powerful all the hairs on his body stood on end. So that's what magic felt like. He wondered if women like Elizabeth or Deborah could feel it all the time.

He was past the well when he saw Deborah on the porch in her nightdress. She was frozen with fear. Her eyes looked past him, toward the orchard and the graves.

A second scream, mingled with prayers, came from the darkness. Proctor ran toward it. The stench grew so thick that bile rose in his chest, burning his throat and nose.

As he rounded the corner of the barn, he staggered to a stop, overwhelmed by fear and the urge to vomit.

A mottled corpse, its pale skin bruised black, moved like a puppet on invisible strings. The white shroud was tangled around its left leg, dragging behind it like a filthy afterbirth. Magdalena lay sprawled on the ground. Elizabeth crouched protectively over her, holding up her burned arm to ward off the creature's attack.

How . . . ?

Proctor stood still, fighting the urge to run away. His indecision gave the corpse a chance to lunge at Elizabeth, using its arms as crude cudgels to bludgeon her head. She fell over, her neck bent like a broken stalk.

Magdalena whimpered, pulling herself hand-over-hand on her belly through the mud. The corpse took a step toward her.

"No!" Proctor cried. He raised the gun by the barrel, ready to use it like a cudgel, but his legs were shaking too hard to carry him foward.

The corpse tilted its head at him. The front of the skull was smashed in where Proctor had battered him with the pistol butt. The eyes were dead and closed, the mouth open and slack.

It rushed him, fists raised.

Proctor dropped the gun and cowered, forgetting to breathe, forgetting to move, braced to die—only to see the corpse stop abruptly two feet short of reaching him.

He looked down.

The dead thing's toes were at the line of ashes that marked his protective spell.

Proctor began to recite the spell again, unsure whether he was performing magic or praying to God for deliverance.

He stumbled over the words, taking a step away from the creature.

The door creaked at the house, and Alexandra joined Deborah on the porch. The corpse turned toward them.

"Go," Proctor shouted. "Lock yourselves inside!"

They didn't need his advice, bouncing against each other in their rush to safety. The door slammed, and there was the sound of tables scraped across the floor to block it.

The corpse was already halfway across the yard when Proctor realized they weren't safe in the house. The door might be blocked, but the windows were unshuttered. Whatever force directed the creature would find a way inside. Proctor wiped cold sweat off his forehead and swallowed hard. Unless he did something, Alexandra and Deborah were as good as dead.

He looked down at the line of ashes that kept him safe. Then he took a deep breath and jumped over it.

The corpse was at one of the windows, and Alexandra was screaming, when Proctor reached it. He grabbed the tail end of the shroud, still wrapped around the creature's ankle, and yanked on it.

He had intended to drag the creature away, but the sudden snap upended the corpse and flipped it on its head with a sickening crunch that would have crippled a living man.

The creature rolled over and pushed itself upright with its clumsy hands, staggering to its feet. Proctor searched desperately for the musket, forgetting where he'd dropped it. Instead his eye lit on the stump where he split wood. He'd left the ax outside. *He'd left the ax outside.*

Proctor ran to the stump and yanked loose the ax. The corpse was halfway through a window when Proctor smashed the heavy blade into the creature's shoulder.

The blow would have killed a man, but this creature was already dead. It rolled out of the window as Proctor swung the ax again. The corpse fell to the side and the blade smashed into the clapboards, lodging in the wood.

One of the corpse's arms hung uselessly, destroyed when the shoulder was shattered. It swung the other arm at Proctor, missing him but knocking the ax out of the wood.

Proctor was lucky to keep hold of it. As the corpse lurched toward him, Proctor swung the blade wildly. The flat edge of the iron crunched through the creature's skull and knocked it down.

The creature wriggled on the ground, with one arm hanging loose by a flap of skin and its head lolled forward on its chest, the top of the skull split open, spilling damp gray brains.

Proctor stepped back on shaky legs. His skin screamed as if it were on fire. Something inside him laughed in denial. This was wrong, all wrong—the slack face with its shut eyes, the deep gashes with no blood, the dead limbs intent on harm.

The creature stumbled upright like a broken puppet.

The laughter inside Proctor bubbled out of his mouth as a scream. He swung the ax at the creature's knee. The blade made a heavy sound as it sliced through meat, chipping bone as it severed the joint. Proctor staggered off-balance one way as the corpse toppled the other and smacked into the ground.

Proctor wobbled, fiercely gripping the ax. His breath came in quick gasps as tears welled up in his eyes. His pants were wet, soaked all the way down his legs and running off his bare feet.

But it was done.

The dead thing's head rolled suddenly to the side. The one good arm swung over its head, slamming into the mud. The good leg twitched as its foot sought purchase.

Proctor shuffled away, tears streaming down his cheeks.

Hand and foot, pulling and kicking, the corpse crawled toward him. It wasn't stopping. It would never stop.

There was no plan, no intention, only blind fear and a helpless rage. Proctor raised the ax above his head and struck, again and again and again, until nothing remained but pieces too small to pull anything anywhere.

"Stop, you can stop," said a voice, piercing through the storm-loud noise that raged inside Proctor.

He lifted his head, like someone woken abruptly from sleep, and saw Deborah and Alexandra standing in the doorway of the house.

"You can stop," Deborah said. "It's done."

"No, it isn't," Proctor said, his voice thick and foreign to his own ears. He looked toward the orchard and the other graves.

Ax in hand, he went behind the house and up the hill.

He checked Jedediah's grave first, relieved to find it undisturbed. The one that he had only partly filled lay empty, the ground churned from within.

The dirt on the third grave bumped and rose.

Proctor shook his head. This wasn't happening.

The dirt bumped and rose again. A mud-crusted hand thrust through and began flinging dirt aside, clearing the way for the rest of the body.

Grim now, the rock of fear hard in his throat, Proctor slammed the ax down, driving it through dirt and flesh and bone to cut the hand off at the wrist.

The dirt lay still for a moment, then bumped again, furiously, frantically, as another hand thrust clear.

The things Proctor did next, he did in a frenzied haze. He sprinted to the barn for the shovel and some oil. Later, he would have a vague memory that he must have dug up the second grave, hacking the corpse as he worked, burning the pieces. But all that remained vivid to him was the sound of sizzling, crackling flesh, and the way the burned-corpse smell of the smoke hung in his hair. When he finished in the orchard, he went back down to the yard and doused the pieces of the corpse littered there, burning them also.

As the sun rose, the black plumes of smoke drew the silhouettes of the neighboring farmers to the horizon. Once they assured themselves that no building burned, needing their aid, their silhouettes melted away. Had any come across the hillsides and passed the barriers hiding the farm, Proctor would have collapsed gibbering at their feet.

Instead, he found himself sitting on the ground across from a fire as it burned down. His knees were drawn up to his chest, with the handle of the shovel across his lap. Smoke and dirt covered his skin and clothes. Mud and ashes were crusted between the toes of his bare feet.

Deborah came and stood behind him. Softly, she said, "You saved our lives. Thank you."

He didn't say anything for a long time. When he finally spoke, his throat was raw. "What was that?"

"Necromancy of the most evil kind, black magic, the most evil thing, against all nature." She spit out the words, as if they were a curse. She paused for a long moment, then said, more softly again, "My mother's dead."

He nodded; he had guessed as much when he saw the creature attack her outside the barn. He was too weary, too numb, to express his sorrow. Sorrow seemed inadequate.

"But you came to Magdalena's rescue in time," Deborah said. "She's barely clinging to life, but she is alive. Alexandra is doing everything she can to heal her."

"Good," he said. He rested his forehead in his hands, covering his face. "What about Miss Cecily?" he asked. "And Lydia, how are they?"

Lydia had saved his life by explaining spells to him. He needed to thank her.

"They're gone."

He looked up, turning his head around as if he expected to find them. "Killed?"

"No, they left in the middle of the night, before the attack, using some kind of concealment spell," she said.

He didn't understand. "Why?"

"Cecily left a black altar in front of the hearth before she went. She's been working with the widow all along. She's the one who sent the corpses to attack us."

Proctor shook his head in denial. "No. No, that's not right."

He looked at Deborah's face for the first time. Her cheeks were drawn, but her jaw was firm. Instead of fearful or sorrowful, she looked angry. So angry that he felt sorry for anyone on the other end of her temper. She held her hands at her sides, but they were clutched in fists.

"The border around the farm would have kept the corpses alive inside, giving them a chance to kill us all," she said. "Magdalena woke and found the black altar and panicked. She woke Elizabeth, then fled the house terrified. My mother chased after her."

"Why did Cecily want to kill us? What did we do?"

"I don't think it's about us. I think there's something bigger at stake. I intend to find out what it is."

Pitcairn, the widow, Cecily—they were all connected some way, Proctor realized. But he didn't know how.

Leaning down, Deborah slid the shovel out of his lap and set it aside. Then she walked behind him and put her hands under his arms to lift him to his feet.

"You don't want to do that," he protested. "I'm frightful dirty."

"It's all right," she said.

She led him to the house. He didn't think he had enough strength left to lift his feet up the step or over the threshold, but somehow he made it inside. Magdalena lay on the cot beside the hearth, her face bruised and bloody. Alexandra sat beside her, dabbing her skin with a fragrant ointment. When she looked at Proctor, her eyes were still wide and frightened.

He wanted to say something to her to make it all right. Too aware of the stench of fire and death on him, he nodded at the ointment. "That smells like heaven."

Her hand jerked protectively to her chest. Her eyes and cheeks were red from crying, and she didn't say anything.

"This way," Deborah said, carrying a pitcher of water to the basin in the other room. She sat him on a chair and washed his face and hair. It felt glorious, and he meant to thank her, but then she called to Alexandra for a fresh pitcher of water. When the girl brought it, Deborah pulled off his undershirt, pressing her finger to his lips to silence his protest. It was the same gesture Emily had made, when he was lying injured in her house. He shuddered. That felt so far away, as if it had happened to a different person and he had only heard about it. How would he ever explain this, what had happened tonight, to Emily? He couldn't. He would have to hold it secret, and never let her know.

While these thoughts raced through his head, Deborah scrubbed his neck and shoulders and arms, lingering over his hands, laving his palms, cleaning under each nail. Another pitcher and clean washcloths were brought for his legs and feet. When she cleaned between his toes, rubbing his soles, he began to cry. He sat there, sobbing, with his face in his hands, feeling so ashamed but unable to stop.

She pushed him into the bed. He looked around and realized that it was her room. An old rocking horse sat in the corner, with tassels of real hair for its mane and tail. A rag doll sat in a tiny chair.

"I can't—" he protested.

She pressed his lips shut again. "We won't feel safe unless you're in the house."

He nodded that he understood.

She started to leave the room.

"Deborah?"

She paused in the doorway. "Yes?"

"If I knew this is what it took to get me a bed around here, then—" She smiled at him, but it was so sad and forced, he couldn't finish the joke. "Then I'd be happy to still be sleeping in the barn."

The corners of her mouth twitched toward a genuine smile.

"I'm sorry about your mother," he said.

"It was God's will," she said, but the words stuck in her mouth as if she didn't really believe them. "You get some sleep now."

"All right. But leave the door open."

"Don't worry, we'll keep watch." She propped the door open with an iron and went to help Alexandra.

He couldn't shut his eyes without seeing the image of the corpse rush at him, so he lay there awake for a long time, watching Deborah and Alexandra tend quietly to Magdalena. The smell of mint and clove from their lotions soothed him.

When he did fall asleep, he had nightmares of the corpses coming for him over and over again, no matter how many times he hacked apart their limbs. But he was too exhausted to wake up and escape.

Chapter 17

On the morning of Elizabeth's funeral, the sky was a high pale blue, unbroken by even a hint of clouds.

Proctor sat at the table with his head in his hands. Deborah put a plate of hot oats and molasses in front of him. "Are you sure you're up for this?"

"The sooner the better," he said. Alexandra brought in the pail of milk from the cow and set it down. He ladled warm milk over the oats. Between bites, he said, "Where do you want me to dig?"

"Next to my father," Deborah answered.

Proctor thought about the two empty holes nearby, where the assassins had been raised. He glanced across the table at Alexandra, her face drawn and tired. She had been tending constantly to Magdalena, who lay on the bed against the wall. He saw the same discomfort in Alexandra's expression that he felt in his heart.

"I don't mean to argue," he said. "But that ground, it don't seem fit for good folk anymore."

"It's where she'd want to be," Deborah said. "Next to my father."

"We could move him," Alexandra offered softly.

Proctor took another bite to cover up his frown, figuring that he'd be the one doing any moving. And he didn't think he could dig up a grave again without adding to his nightmares.

"We'll reconsecrate the ground when we bury her," Deborah said. Pushing her plate of uneaten food aside, she rose and went to stand on the porch, leaving Proctor and Alexandra alone.

Spoons clinked against crockery. After a few moments, Alexandra said, "Do you know how to consecrate anything?"

Proctor didn't look up from his plate. "Do I much resemble a minister to you?"

"Not much, no," she admitted. "But then I wouldn't have taken you for a sorcerer either, and you defeated a powerful magic the other night."

"That wasn't sorcery," he said, rising, plate in hand. Some of the leftover milk splashed on the table, and he smeared it up with his other palm. "That was butchery."

He wiped his plate clean with a rag and stepped outside to look for Deborah, but she was nowhere to be seen. He walked by the charred pile of the bonfire and picked up the shovel where he'd dropped it the other night. Deborah wasn't in the barn either, but he grabbed the pick and spade, and headed toward the orchard.

The ax rested on the ground by the second grave, wet mud already eating at its smooth finish. He shuddered at the memory of using it, then cursed himself for being lazy. He'd have to sand the blade down later to keep it from rusting, but the task at hand was refilling both graves. He jabbed the shovel into the ground and started. Sometimes simple work was an act of consecration.

He was done sooner than he expected. That left one new hole to dig. He chose a spot on the hillside near Jedediah's grave under the shade of an apple tree. He kicked the spade in the ground. The work had its own logic, demanding a level of attention that kept his thoughts from spinning too far or too fast. By the time he finished, muddy and sweaty, the sun burned down on him with the promise of summer. As he climbed out of the hole, Alexandra and Deborah arrived, carrying Elizabeth's body wrapped in its shroud.

Proctor tried to brush the mud from his hands, so he

could help them without dirtying the white sheet. But Deborah marched right past him, and on the count of three, they swung the body over the grave. Deborah tried to lower it, but the sheet slipped from Alexandra's hand and the body thumped into the mud.

"Friends," Deborah said, and she met each of their eyes as if the word were more than just a figure of speech, "we are gathered here to remember Elizabeth Walcott."

Proctor looked at Alexandra; she gave him only a grim shake of her head that told him not to argue with Deborah this morning.

"Elizabeth Walcott was a friend to all who knew her," Deborah said. "And those who knew her stretched from one end of the colonies to the other—"

"I'm sorry," Proctor interrupted. "But—"

"Yes?" Her mouth was a thin, tight line.

"I'd like to clean up," he said. When she stared at him as if he needed to offer further explanation, he added, "Out of respect to your mother and all that she did for folks."

"My mother had great respect for the honest work that men and women do with their hands," Deborah said. "And there is no more honest labor than the work you just did for her. I am sure she would be satisfied with you in your present condition, even pleased."

Alexandra lifted her eyebrows, as if to say to Proctor, *I told you so.*

It didn't feel right to Proctor, so he had to try one last time. "It won't take me long to wash up, just my face and hands."

Deborah's mouth grew even tighter, if that were possible. "We face a terrible enemy. They may be satisfied with the damage already done, and, indeed, they may think us all dead, not expecting that anyone should escape the terrible creatures they loosed upon us, but I don't think we should rely on that."

"You think we should do something about this enemy immediately?" Proctor said.

"I do, and I also believe it is what my mother would want. She would not be content to let such an evil magic go unopposed. I would like to finish here and start that work."

She was right. Proctor released his reluctance and nodded.

Deborah held out her hands. Alexandra took hold of one, and Proctor gripped the other in his own muddy fist. The sun pressed down on them while birds jumped from branch to branch in the nearby trees, calling out to one another. After a moment of silence, Deborah lifted her head.

"I'll miss her," she said, choked. Looking at her father's grave, she said, "I'll miss them both."

"I didn't get the chance to know either one of them as well as I'd've liked, but they were good to me," Alexandra said. "Your mother taught me more about my talent, and about helping people, than I ever dreamed of knowing."

Deborah responded to that with a firm nod.

"I liked your mother too," Proctor said. "She didn't make me work as hard as your father did, and she fed me better."

Deborah hiccupped a laugh in spite of herself. When the tears flowed after that, they were happier tears than they might have been. She squeezed his hand hard. She must have done the same to Alexandra, who also smiled.

"May the light of God always shine on this ground as bright as the sun shines today," Deborah said. Letting go of their hands, she picked up the shovel. She tossed the first shovelful in. The dirt pattered across the shroud.

"Here, let me finish that," Proctor said, taking the shovel from her hand. The two women stood there quietly, holding hands, while he filled the grave. When he finished, he looked at Deborah. "So is that all then?"

"No," she said, letting go of Alexandra's hand. "Now it's time to wash up and get to work. Meet me back at the house."

Alexandra met Proctor's gaze with another *See, I told you so,* then followed Deborah.

"Well, that's good," Proctor said aloud to himself, looking up at the afternoon sun. "Because I haven't done enough work to satisfy myself yet today."

He gathered up the tools and carried them back to the barn, taking time to clean them thoroughly before putting them away. When the tools were clean, he washed himself.

Inside, bowls of vegetables and berries were spread on the table. Alexandra slouched sleepily in a chair, picking at a plate of greens. Deborah moved like a hummingbird in a flower garden, flitting from one corner of the room to the other and back again, cleaning, scrubbing, and putting away.

Proctor spooned himself a bowl of strawberries and poured the rest of the warm milk on it. Alexandra looked up from her plate, so he nodded toward Deborah and said, "I'm tired just watching her."

Deborah heard his voice and finally noticed him. "Oh, good, you're here." She put down her rag and wash bucket and came to join them.

"You're allowed to slow down," he said. "It's all right if you need to grieve."

She made a plate of greens and then methodically cut them into smaller and smaller pieces. "There will be time enough for grief later," she said.

"If I could get my hands on Miss Cecily Hoity-toity, I'd give her grief enough for all of us," Alexandra said.

"I should never have been fooled by her," Deborah said.

Alexandra nodded. "I knew there was something wrong with her from the very beginning."

"How?" Proctor asked. He would have liked to have said he felt the same way, but he hadn't noticed anything evil about her, not beyond her use of the slave woman.

"She always held her light under a bushel," Deborah said. "Never letting her real power shine through, no matter how often my mother tried to help her unblock it. But it was all an act."

"I noticed just the opposite," Alexandra said. "I felt her draw on my power the very first day I was here."

"Really?" Deborah asked.

"Yeah, it made me feel weak and sickly. I got so I avoided her as much as I could."

"I thought that was because of her sharp tongue," Deborah said.

Alexandra shrugged. "Well, yeah, that too."

"If you felt that way, why didn't you say anything about it?"

"I was too scared to say anything."

"You? Scared?" Deborah asked.

"Yes." Alexandra leaned forward on the table. "I didn't know how things were supposed to work here. One week I'm accused of witchcraft, the minister saying I cursed the wife of another man and made her die, with people working themselves up for my own blood. The next week I'm here, must be a thousand miles from the only home I ever knew. And every woman here is a witch fit to turn my blood to ice if I make so much as a misstep."

Deborah reached across the table and took her hand. "I should have thought of that. I forget how intimidating my mother can be." After a pause, she amended herself, "Could be."

Alexandra lightly squeezed her fingers. Proctor smiled, because he was sure it wasn't Elizabeth who was most intimidating to Alexandra. "I think you're both walking backward when you ought to be running forward," he said.

The women let go of each other's hands. Deborah picked up her knife and fork again. "What do you mean?"

"The last couple of things I heard you say were *could have, should haves*. It's like my father told me when I miscut a piece of wood, there's no going back to do it over. You have to set the bad piece aside and do it better."

"My daddy always told me, measure twice, cut once, so I wouldn't have that problem," Alexandra said.

The corner of Deborah's mouth twitched up. Given the past few days, it made Proctor glad to see any kind of cheerfulness.

"Well, your daddy's a smart man," he said. "It seems like it's time to take a second measure of Miss Cecily, and then decide how we're going to cut her down to size. For one thing, I'd like to know what the real connection between her and Lydia was. Lydia tried to warn me twice, once that Miss Cecily couldn't be trusted, and once that we were all in danger. But I didn't know enough to hear what she was saying."

Alexandra nodded. "She took me aside a couple of times and told me to think about going home to my folks. I didn't listen to her because she didn't have any real authority here."

"I've been thinking about this a lot," Deborah said. "I think Cecily was using Lydia as a kind of familiar, channeling much of the magic through her in order to stay undetected. We all could feel powerful magic in Lydia, but we thought it was her experience as a slave holding her back. Now I think it was Cecily, using her as a channel."

"Poor Lydia," Alexandra said.

"Normally, when witches form a circle, even a circle of two, the magic is open to flowing both directions. When the widow drew on you, Proctor, you could've drawn back, if you were powerful enough. I never dreamed that Lydia would let Cecily draw on her without drawing back, but maybe she couldn't."

"That makes sense," Proctor said.

"Well, that's just it," Deborah said. "It doesn't make sense. Cecily sought us out almost a year ago, telling us that her magic was blocked, trying to get Mother to teach her to release it."

"All right," he said.

"It's not all right." She reached out and rested her hand on Alexandra's arm. "Most women who have come here over the years are like Alexandra here, who need to learn to control their talents—I'm sorry, dear, but it's true."

"No, I see that now," Alexandra said.

"Or they're like Magdalena over there. Magdalena was sent to my grandmother when she was a young girl, about Alexandra's age. She's come back a few times, usually to try to learn something new. There's never been anyone come here like Cecily before. My mother was so flattered."

"But why did she come? To spy on Elizabeth?"

"Maybe, yes."

"But that doesn't make any sense," he said. He started rearranging cutlery on the table, thinking of tactics he learned in the militia. "If you already have Cecily here, why do you need to send the widow, or those Indians? Or was Cecily the mastermind?"

Alexandra sneered. "She's no mastermind."

"I think she reported to the widow, whoever she is," Deborah said. "That night the widow came, she only wanted to meet with Cecily."

"Lydia was the one who sounded the alarm," Alexandra said.

"Yes. She was trying to warn us even then." She slammed her hand on the table, startling Magdalena. "How could I have been so stupid?"

"Run forward," Proctor said. "The rest is obvious. Cecily was meeting with her superior. Lydia tried to warn us. Your mother surprised them, and the widow defended herself. But there was never any plan to kill you until that moment."

"Maybe," Deborah said.

"No, think about it—if Nance, or whoever is behind this, wanted you dead, or wanted Elizabeth dead, then Cecily could've killed you at any time. She could've poisoned your mother while she treated her burns."

"She's too much of a coward," Alexandra said. "Face-to-face with anyone, she tries to please them."

"And there's no way anyone could slip an herb or poison past my mother," Deborah said. "No one in the colonies knows—knew—as much as she did."

"But that brings us back to—what did they want?" Proctor asked.

"I think I know the answer to that," Deborah said. "My father was a strong supporter of the patriot cause, and I have lent my talents to the Reverend Emerson and Mister Revere and other patriots. If Nance is British—"

"I just bet Cecily's a secret Tory," Alexandra interjected.

"And those three Indians," Proctor said, "they were rangers or scouts who served with the British regulars during the French wars or I'm a monkey."

"Right. So if they're supporters of the royal governor, and are using magic in their cause, then they would suspect us of doing the same. The widow came to see Cecily just days after the battles at Concord and Lexington. Something must have happened there to frighten them."

The three of them fell silent. Deborah and Alexandra appeared to be thoughtful, examining all they knew about Cecily and the widow for a clue to the event.

Proctor cleared his throat. "I know what happened."

He expected it to be hard to confess, that they would blame him for what had happened to them. In a rush of words, spilled too quickly for them to interrupt him, he told them about his chance encounter with Pitcairn in Boston, about the protective medallion, and about the way he broke the spell during the battle at Lexington. When he was done, he felt like a burden had been lifted from his shoulders, whether they blamed him or not.

"Now I know why you weren't afraid," Alexandra said. "When those men attacked us, or when . . . when the other thing happened. I was so scared."

"Believe me, I was plenty scared too," Proctor said. "I just did what I had to do, is all."

Deborah had dropped her head and was shaking it sadly. "So that's why," she said.

"That's why what?"

"That's why you were so eager to follow the widow and

speak to her. You weren't trying to help her. You had just encountered magic—real sorcery—for the very first time, and you needed someone to help you understand it. And no one else was available."

"That's about the size of it. I had no idea anything like The Farm existed. I never knew that witches met with one another and shared their knowledge. All I knew was the fear and shame my mother taught me."

"I grew up around this, and it's so easy to forget that it's not that way for everyone."

"Vater, please, some vater."

Magdalena stirred on her cot. Alexandra rose to give her water while Deborah fetched her a cup of broth and induced her to sip it to regain her strength. Proctor stood behind them, feeling his body tense; the poor old woman's face was battered so black and blue she could barely speak or swallow liquid. Deborah sat at her side, saying a spell for healing, until Magdalena finally drifted back to sleep. The three of them returned to their seats at the table.

"She looks like she's improving," Proctor said.

"If she is, it's because of her power, not mine," Deborah said. "That's one mighty woman."

"What exactly did she find that upset her so much she ran outside?"

Alexandra wrapped her arms across her chest and turned away. Deborah licked her lips. "Cecily killed two of the farm cats, probably for a focus to animate the corpses. She left their bodies in front of the hearth, on an altar made out of a table—"

"That one I saw outside?"

She nodded. "She wrote curses against all of us with their blood, calling for our deaths. The longest curse was written against my mother. We were just lucky the corpse didn't come to kill you first."

"I created a protection spell that night," Proctor said, and he explained how he had surrounded the barn with ashes, and how the corpse had stopped when it reached the line. Deborah stopped him several times to ask him specifics about the spell, and nodded at his explanations.

"The thing I don't understand is, why didn't any of your mother's protection spells work?"

"That's easy," Deborah said. "Cecily insinuated herself into all of Elizabeth's routines. She revealed the enchantment that hides The Farm from casual travelers, and she must have gone around undoing the protective spells."

"Now that you mention it, I saw her trying to ruin the spell where we called the spirits of those dead men."

"What?" Deborah asked.

"Your mother wanted each man's items separate. When Cecily thought no one was looking, she mixed them together. I thought she was just nervous—you know how she's always touching stuff—so I moved them all back."

"It was deliberate," Deborah said.

Alexandra leaned forward eagerly. "She must have been terrified that they were going to reveal her."

"Yes," Deborah said. "She didn't undo Proctor's spell before she left, because she didn't know about it. We should all have been taking steps like that to protect ourselves."

He grabbed her hand and held it. "That's enough with the second-guessing. It's no good."

After a moment, she nodded.

"What do we do now?" Alexandra asked. Her face and posture were those of a girl again, helpless, wanting someone else to solve her problems. Proctor tried not to be surprised: she was on the cusp of adulthood, one moment a child, the next a woman.

"I have written letters to the Reverend Emerson and others asking them for information about this Mister Nance," Deborah said. "But there wasn't time to post them, and now it seems rather pointless to proceed in that direction."

"Why do you say that?" Proctor said. "It seems like this Nance is still the hinge that swings all the doors."

"He is, but I don't think we'd receive a reply quickly enough. The time for waiting has passed."

"I could always go and see Emerson directly," Proctor said. And that would let him check on his parents as well. "I'd be back in a couple of days."

"No," Alexandra blurted at the same moment that Deborah said, "I think not."

"Why not?" Proctor asked.

"You need to stay here to protect Alexandra and Magdalena," Deborah said. "It was only your quick action—and your spell—that saved all our lives two nights ago."

It wasn't quite all their lives, but Proctor didn't want to draw her attention to that. "How can we take action and stay here at the same time?"

"We aren't all staying here," she said. "I'm going to Boston—to find Cecily, or the widow, or Nance."

"And what exactly do you think you'll do when you find them? Invite them to hold hands and pray with you, the way Elizabeth did, talking to those spirits?"

"That's uncalled for," she snapped.

"No, he has a point," Alexandra said. Deborah glared at her. The girl fidgeted uncomfortably and wouldn't meet Deborah's eyes, but she continued to speak. "Don't think I care for the idea none, but he has a point. We can't sit here and wait for them to make another attempt to kill us, especially when we don't even know why they're trying. But you can't go haring after them alone. They'll tear you to pieces."

The criticism made Deborah bristle, so much that when Alexandra reached across the table to squeeze her hand, Deborah pulled hers away.

"I'm not trying to run you down, believe me," Alexandra said. "Because I know how powerful you are. But this is a fight, and this fellow here is the only one of us who has experience fighting."

Proctor swallowed hard. Sure, he did his duty, but he

didn't think of himself as a fighter. It's not who he had ever wanted to be.

"He doesn't have enough experience using magic," Deborah said firmly.

"It was enough to protect us two nights ago," Proctor snapped.

"That's why you both need to go," Alexandra said. "You know the magic. You were born to it, and your mother, she taught you everything she knew."

"I wish that were true," Deborah said. She leaned back in her seat, resigned.

"And him"—Alexandra pointed to Proctor—"he's shown he has a trick or two in a fight. I figure he'll need all of them if you run into this Nance or whoever he is."

Proctor rubbed his head, trying to think clearly. There didn't seem to be anyone else to turn to, or any better solution. "So you'll stay here and take care of Magdalena?"

"Hell, no," Alexandra said, and when the two of them stared at her, she added, "Excuse my language, and let me explain before you say anything. The way I figure it, we've got a little window here."

"What kind of window?" Deborah asked.

The word drew Proctor's attention to the window outside, where the summer light was already fading amid the buzz of insects and the occasional call of a bird.

"For all this Nance knows, we're all dead right now," Alexandra said. "Miss Cecily, she's not the type to stick around to see what kind of mess she made."

"She's probably halfway back to Charlestown and her fine house already," Deborah said ruefully.

"Right. So it may be a few more days before they send anyone up here to find out different. We can use those days to our advantage. The two of you to go after him, whoever he is, and me, well, I plan to make Magdalena comfortable in that horse wagon and head toward home."

"She's too sick to travel," Deborah said.

"She's too weak to stay here if someone else comes after her again. I can go slow, keep her comfortable on the road. I can hitch a wagon and take care of myself just fine."

Deborah leaned forward to argue, but Proctor spoke first. "If you go by way of Emerson's first, he'll set you back on the Quaker Highway. You can go from crossroads to crossroads until you get back home."

"I'm not sure," Deborah said.

"You'll find healers along the way, who can help Magdalena recover faster," Proctor added. To Deborah, he said, "It's a good plan. She's right about taking advantage of the days while they think we're dead."

After a long hesitation, she finally nodded her consent.

Proctor stood. "You two better get some sleep, so we can leave first thing in the morning. I'll go set a protection spell and take first watch."

Chapter 18

The walk to Boston took two days down the coastal road through Lynn. They stopped twice, the second time to spend the night with a family whom Proctor suspected was part of the Quaker Highway. The first time had been to sell the milk cow.

"We can't leave the cow behind," Deborah had said. "The chickens can fend for themselves, but it'd be cruel to leave her unmilked."

The reduced price they sold her for seemed crueler still to Proctor. But when they resumed their journey on the second morning, they used the coins to cross the penny ferry at Charlestown.

"You can tell we're close to Boston," Deborah said when they disembarked on the Charlestown side of the river. "I see soldiers everywhere."

"They're not soldiers," Proctor corrected her. "They're militia, just ordinary men trying to do their duty." He was short-tempered from lack of sleep. Every time he closed his eyes, he had nightmares about corpses attacking him.

"Whatever you call them, all I see are men with guns," Deborah said disapprovingly.

Proctor carried Jedediah's musket. He would have snapped at her, but he knew that the loss of both her parents had taken a toll on her. When he thought about all she had gone through, about the horrors she had seen, he was amazed that she stayed as pleasant as she did. She was strong-willed, that was for sure, but in the good way that carried a person through a bad harvest followed by a difficult winter. There was genuine kindness in her as well. If she ended up a spinster, it would likely be because she couldn't meet many young men in the isolated life of The Farm. He'd have to think about it, see if he didn't know a good fellow for her.

"If we can get past the men with guns and into Boston, we can rest at my aunt's lodgings," he said. That was their plan: get into Boston, find his aunt, then start hunting for the person who'd done all the terrible things to Deborah's family.

"If you really need to rest that much, you should have let me spell you to sleep last night," Deborah said.

"And then not be able to wake if we're attacked again? No thanks."

They fell silent as a group of militiamen passed them. By their rough appearance—with beards and hunting caps—and the backwoods sound of their voices, they'd come all the way down from the Maine territory beyond New Hampshire. The men stared at Proctor, who, after several sleepless nights and a day without shaving, looked just like them. Several of them nodded greetings to him.

Either the heat of the sun or the lack of sleep caught up with him. As he nodded back, two of their faces turned to bone-white skulls shining through translucent skin.

He stumbled. Deborah reached out to grab him, and the men laughed as they walked by.

"What just happened?" she asked in a hushed tone.

"I tripped over a rut in the road," Proctor said, pulling his arm free and staggering forward to regain his balance.

"That's nonsense," she spit back, chasing after him. "I saw your knees buckle—I felt the surge of power through you."

"I haven't been sleeping well," he said. "I think I'm falling asleep on my feet, dreaming while I walk."

"What kind of dream?"

He described the vision of the skulls, how it was specific to two of the men.

"Sometimes the talent surges through in a dream state," she said. "Maybe you're still agitated about . . . what happened. And since you're sleepy, it pushes through."

"Maybe you're right," he said.

"You'll have to rest before we get to Boston. I'll need all your energy and strength when we find this Nance. You must let me perform a spell to help you sleep tonight."

He thought about it for a moment. "If you show me how you do it, so I can do it too. And if you promise to stand guard."

She nodded and immediately slipped into other thoughts. Her cheeks had dust on them from the road. Proctor wanted to reach out and brush it off, but her head was bowed in such serious contemplation that he let it go.

The Charlestown peninsula was dominated by two large hills that overlooked the little city at the water's edge. Across the narrow bay stood Boston. On his last visit, he had gone to Charlestown and taken the ferry to Boston. He thought they might do the same this time, but they found the road down to the water blocked by militia.

A dozen or so farmers and tradesmen lounged about on a couple of stumps and an old fence, laughing and talking. At Deborah and Proctor's approach, they picked up their weapons and blocked the way.

"Excuse me—" Proctor said.

Their leader was an older man in a buckskin hunting shirt—he grew pale and washed-out before Proctor's eyes: his face became a skull and his flesh hung dead and bruised on his skeleton like the walking corpses on Deborah's farm. Proctor's knees buckled and he jammed his musket in the ground for a crutch.

The men aimed their weapons at Proctor. "What's the matter?" the old man asked.

"Nothing," Proctor said, forcing himself upright. "We're just trying to find a way into Boston."

The old man looked Proctor up and down, then spit. "Nobody but Tories is trying to go into Boston."

Deborah stepped forward and placed her hand on his bare wrist. He could feel the power flowing into him, giving him strength to stand. The strength didn't erase the vision before his eyes: the old man was still a skeleton covered with rotting flesh. Now that Proctor looked, he saw that several of the other men were too.

"We're sorry to bother you," she said. "But our aunt is trapped in the city. We want to bring her out before the Lobsters do any more harm."

Our aunt sounded wrong to Proctor, even though he and Deborah had agreed on the pretense of being brother and sister.

"Doesn't she have a husband to look after her?" the leader asked suspiciously. Proctor winced and averted his eyes because the talking skull unnerved him.

"Not since our uncle died," he said. "She rents a small house, does laundry for folks."

"If she does laundry for people, she's doing it for British officers," said one of the young men.

The leader answered, "Now, now, Elias, just because you never wash doesn't mean no one else does."

The men laughed at this. Proctor said, "My name's Proctor Brown, and I served with the Lincoln minutemen on April nineteenth, all the way from Concord to Lexington. We'd really like to help our aunt."

The leader looked at him sideways. "So you served under Captain Lamb?"

"No, sir, that'd be Captain Smith."

The leader smiled. "Sorry, about the deception there, but I had to be sure." He offered his hand. "The name's Nehemiah Johnson, and I wish I'd been there with you to give the Redcoats a licking."

"You'll get a chance soon enough," Proctor said.

Johnson's hand waited for him, all bone and rot beneath the translucent sheath of his visible skin. Proctor hesitated, then took hold of it—the touch turned his stomach. He shook it quickly, then let go before he puked.

"If you head around and cross The Neck, you might get in that way," Johnson told them. "Good luck with your aunt."

Deborah was already tugging on Proctor's arm, pulling him away. "It happened again, didn't it?"

"Yes," he said, mopping the cold sweat from his forehead. "I don't think it's from lack of sleep or nightmares."

"But they look just like those fellows we saw on the farm, all dead, even though they're up and walking. Could you see that too?"

"No, I can't see anything but by the effect it has on you. What do we do now?"

"We go around to The Neck," he said. They walked in silence for a while, Proctor trying to control the shakiness he felt in all his limbs.

When they left the peninsula and turned down the road toward Cambridge, Deborah said, "I don't know what's going on. But both times it happened, I've felt a strong surge of magic. All the hairs on my body stood on end at once, like when lightning is about to strike."

Proctor wasn't ready to talk about it quite yet, so he said, "You've seen lightning strike? I mean, close enough to feel it."

"Yes, when I was living with friends of my mother's down in New York State," she said. She paused, tilting her head up at the sky, as though she was making up her mind to continue. After a bit, she said, "The storm was coming in over the other side of the valley, black thunderheads down there and clear skies right above us, just like a line separating light and dark, drawn right through heaven. I went outside to watch the storm develop. I was holding Sissy, their cat, in my arms—I was probably the same age as Alexandra. While I was standing there, listening to the distant thunder and watching the rain fall in torrents a mile or two away, my skin tingled and all the hairs stood on end, and then thunder went off right beside me, and lightning hit the barn roof not twenty feet away, set it on fire."

Proctor shook his head. "That's something."

"Yeah." She rolled up her sleeve and held her arm out for him. Pale white scars, thin as a cat's claw, marked her skin. "The cat was terrified. Of course, I was scared too, so my first instinct was to hug her tight. Her instinct was to get away. She tore me up pretty bad trying to escape."

They walked farther while Deborah rolled down her sleeve. "Why were you living with friends of your folks?" Proctor asked. "Couldn't they take care of you?"

"Oh, they could take care of me fine," Deborah said.

When she didn't elaborate, he asked, "Why then?"

She had a thoughtful look to her eyes, as if she was making up her mind again how much to say. "Mother said there was only so much she could teach me, so she sent me off to stay with friends."

"Do you mean *Friend* friends, or just friends?" Proctor asked.

"They weren't Quakers, if that's what you're asking," she said. "Her name was Margaret, and she was Methodist, though not especially devout. On Sundays, we were as likely to be in the tavern as at church." She frowned at some memory she was unwilling to share. "It helped me learn to make my own choices."

"My father never said much," Proctor said. "But my mother seemed to think the fewer choices I made, the less trouble I'd get in."

Deborah kept walking, refusing to say anything about getting into trouble.

"So that's why you don't talk like your folks?" he asked.

"You mean with all the *thee*-ing and *thou*-ing?"

"Well, yeah, that's what I mean."

"Yeah, that's why. When I arrived at Margaret's, all her children mocked me. Later I learned that her two boys got in a fight with some other boys who were making fun of me, but I didn't know that then. I learned to talk like Margaret's family so I could fit in there. I didn't go back to the old way, not even when I came home."

"I am glad thee don't talk like thou parents anymore," Proctor said in an approximation of her father's tone.

"*Thou* don't and *thy* parents," she corrected him. Then she saw that he was mocking her. She frowned at him, but the corners of her eyes crinkled. Then the mention of her parents hit both of them, and they remembered how they had died. All the humor drained out of Deborah's face in an instant.

"I'm sorry," Proctor said.

"Stop that," she replied. "Just stop."

"Stop what?"

"Stop apologizing every time we mention my parents. It's not your fault that they're dead."

"But if I had only—"

"Stop it!"

He fell silent. She was so strong in the face of losing her parents. He didn't how he would handle the same thing. He knew his father wasn't there much in spirit anymore, but he still dreaded his passing.

"It is solely the fault of those who killed them," she said. "And they will be called to judgment for it."

They were far away from the militiamen now, headed toward Cambridge and the Harvard College buildings. Even though there were no men in sight, Proctor still felt ill. His limbs were rubbery and his stomach churned.

"So we could be looking for the widow, or Miss Cecily, or this fellow Nance who's behind it all," he said. "No matter how you cut it, I'm not sure how we're going to deal with them once we find them."

Privately, he hoped it was Nance. If they were attacked

with magic again, and their magical defenses failed, it might come to killing. He was sure he couldn't kill Cecily or even the widow, not even if his own life depended on it. He might not even be able to kill Nance. After the past week, he'd thought he might have lost any taste he had for fighting and killing. He was afraid to tell that to Deborah.

She'd been working through their options too. "There's a spell my mother taught me," she said tentatively. "A severing spell."

He covered his mouth, fighting an urge to retch. "You mean, to cut them up, in pieces?"

"No! A spell to sever them from the source of their magic. Mother never used it, because a simple reversal spell can turn it back on the sender. But after the widow's attack on The Farm, she taught it to me. She thought it was important to know it, in case a witch was ever using her talents for harm."

They stepped off to the side of the road to let a wagon pass. They exchanged a glance as they fell back in behind it. With all the people around, they would have to be circumspect with what they said.

"The risk is so high," Deborah said. "The idea of being cut off from my talent forever frightens me. Are you all right?"

His head was bent down between his shoulders, and he covered his mouth again. "I'll be all right," he said. "I just need to concentrate a bit, walk it out of my system."

As they passed through Cambridge and crossed the bridge over the Charles River, they began to see signs of the siege. High on a hill to their right, cannons aimed their dark muzzles at the road. Behind the cannons there were squat barracks of rough-hewn logs, surrounded by rows of tents that shook in the breeze. The wind carried the smell of the waste pits down the slopes, along with scraps of voices from the men in the camp.

Men closer to the road looked up from their work or conversations to stare curiously at Proctor and Deborah as they passed. Some of their faces began to flicker if Proctor glanced too closely at them. At first he thought it was a trick of the light, but the longer they walked, the more he grew to realize it was their skulls, grinning at him beneath an onionskin of flesh.

"It's happening to you again, isn't it?" she asked.

"What makes you think that?"

"You mean, besides the way you're staggering like a drunk?" Her face was pale with worry. "Are you sure you're all right?"

The images of skeletons draped with rotting flesh and eyeless skulls were all around him. It was as if an entire cemetery had coughed up its dead, and not just a pair of graves.

"If we stop, I think it's going to get a whole lot worse," he said.

"It's definitely a spell." She dropped her voice as a wagon loaded with baskets of radishes and sweetpeas passed them. "I didn't realize it at first, because it's the largest spell I've ever felt."

"What do you mean?"

"You know how you would walk around the barn, or Elizabeth would circle the farm?"

"Yeah."

"This surrounds everything from Charlestown to Cambridge to here. It's strongest since we crossed the bridge, so we must be near the heart of it."

He tipped his hat to a pair of women carrying baskets of laundry away from the camp. Their faces were normal. "It's only the militiamen I see that way."

"Maybe it's meant for the militiamen."

The road curved through Brookline and passed under Roxbury Hill, which was also heavily fortified. The farther they went, the harder it became for Proctor to talk. It took all his effort just to keep walking upright. They were getting close to The Neck; that's where the largest concentration of militia would be.

Boston sat on a peninsula that swam away from the mainland like a tadpole leaving its sac of eggs. The fat body of the city was connected to the rest of the land by just its tail, a long narrow stretch called The Neck. The solitary road that ran down the neck toward the city was barricaded by colonial troops. In sight of their goal, Proctor staggered to a halt.

"Can you do this?" Deborah asked.

"Just give me a moment."

There were hundreds of men around them, and they all looked like skeletons inside clear sacs of jellied, putrid flesh. Proctor was ready to admit defeat, ready to leave the way they'd come, when a man broke away from the main group and jogged toward them. He yelled Proctor's name.

Deborah tightened like a bowstring. "Who is that?"

"Friends from my militia unit there."

"Proctor!" cried a familiar voice. "We were just wondering what happened to you!"

Proctor tried to look directly at the face, but it was bone-white in the late afternoon sun, so painful he had to avert his eyes. "Amos Lathrop, is that you?"

"Live and breathing, in the flesh," he said. The collar of his shirt was open under his jacket, and his sleeves were rolled up to his elbows. His hat was tipped at an angle. "Where have you been?"

"I had to go help out at my—" He couldn't call Deborah his sister—Amos knew better, he'd have to call her his—

"Cousin," Deborah suggested.

"—friend," Proctor said. "I mean, cousin."

"Cousin?" Amos asked. "But I thought you didn't have any relatives except for your aunt."

"She's a distant cousin," he said.

"More of a family friend," she explained.

"Pleased to meet you—"

"Deborah Walcott," she said.

"Pleased to meet you, Miss Walcott. I've been a neighbor of Proctor's all my life. You can't ask for a better man."

"I know," she said. "He's been a good friend to my family in a very difficult time."

"That sounds about like him," Amos said. Proctor still couldn't look at Amos's face. The vision of his talking skull made him sick to his stomach, and thinking about what it might mean made his heart want to shrivel up. Through blurry eyes, he saw his friend lean forward. "You don't look very good, Proctor."

"Well, thanks."

"He's had a fever," Deborah explained.

Amos took two quicks steps back. "We've been seeing the first signs of camp fever around here already. Maybe you've got that, but I hope not."

"What's camp fever?" Proctor asked.

Amos shrugged. "It's the phrase they use to describe a fever you get when you spend time in camp."

Deborah stepped toward him eagerly, but that pushed him farther away. "What sort of symptoms does it have, beyond the fever?"

"It leaves a fellow weak and shaky, kinda like Proctor there," Amos said. "Only it gets worse, to the point where a fellow has a hard time standing up or knowing which way to march. The worst of it is, food shoots straight through you, like you're a bucket with a hole in the bottom. Begging your pardon, ma'am."

"It's all right," Deborah said.

"I haven't had anything like that," Proctor said.

"So far," Amos returned skeptically. "They say it comes from filth, that we aren't cleaning up properly. But even where we're as clean as a whistle, men are falling sick with it." Turning to Deborah, he said, "Ma'am, if you want to do us a favor, you'll talk Proctor out of staying and take him somewhere he can rest until he's better."

"I wasn't planning on staying," Proctor said.

"Oh," Amos said. "Here I thought you were showing up to muster. Rumor has it the Redcoats are going to try to break out of Boston any day now. With so many men getting sick, we need reinforcements."

"No, we came down to fetch our aunt—" Deborah started.

"My aunt," Proctor interrupted.

"—out of Boston," she finished.

Amos looked at them, puzzled.

"We want her out of the way before the fighting starts," Proctor explained. "If it goes into the city, door-to-door, the way it did in Lexington, we don't want her getting hurt."

"That makes sense," Amos said. "But I don't think there's any way the Redcoats would let you pass the road, not even if you were well. They've got the city closed on their side too, to keep spies out. They might let you send a message to her by one of their couriers, though. There's boys hanging out by the barricade, most days, will run errands for a half a pence."

"Thank you," Proctor said.

Amos backed away, gave Proctor a casual wave of his hand. "It was good to see you again. You take care of him, Miss Walcott."

"I will," she promised.

Amos turned to leave, then paused. "By the way, Proctor, I wanted to tell you personally how sorry I am."

"Sorry?"

His friend shuffled his feet awkwardly. "I can see you don't have any idea what I'm talking about. I thought for certain your mother would have sent you a letter."

"Maybe it didn't arrive yet," Proctor said. Deborah stepped closer to his side again.

"Well, she needs to be the one to tell you, not me. I'm sure your aunt knows too. But it wouldn't be right to hear it from me, so I won't say another word."

"I already heard it from you, Amos Bigmouth Lathrop. What is it?"

But he shook his head. "You'll be home tomorrow, right? It can wait until then."

Proctor considered pushing harder, but he felt so weak and sick, he wanted to be away from Amos and all the camps as fast as possible. He wished Amos farewell, and then staggered down the road.

"Let's turn back," she said. "You're too sick."

"I have to keep going."

"No, you don't," she said, sounding worried.

"You know what my vision means for those men." He didn't want to see it come true for Amos, not if he could do anything to stop it.

She sighed in resignation. "Yes, that much is clear to me now. The Redcoats are getting ready to break out of Boston. Whoever our opponent is wants the colonials to lose. So he's cast a spell on the camp to make men sick. You're susceptible because it's aimed at you—young, healthy militiamen—but the effects are amplified because of your talent."

He sweated profusely and his knees wobbled if he walked too fast. "So I can see it happening the same way I saw Pitcairn's medallion."

"It seems like. Maybe it has something to do with your militia training. You're more attuned to it, the way my mother was to healing spells."

The great mudflats of the back bay at low tide spread out on their left; the colonial barricade across the road was directly ahead of them. Deborah pulled Proctor to the side.

"Here, I have an idea."

She took his hand, bare skin touching bare skin. She shuddered and squeezed her mouth shut with nausea, but he felt power flow into him, making him stronger. Then she tugged his collar up, yanked his coat down on one side, and mussed his hair.

"What are you doing?"

"Making it easier for us to pass," she said.

He grasped instantly what she intended. "An illusion, like the widow used?"

"Something very similar. Lean on your musket, as if it's a cane."

"As if I'm an old man."

"Something like that."

He hunched his shoulders, trying to think how his father looked—broken and nonthreatening. "How's that?"

"It's almost right," she said, scrutinizing his face one last time. "But let me do all the talking when we approach them, otherwise the illusion could be shattered."

She poked her finger in the corner of his eye.

"Hey, that hurt!"

"It made you squint—keep doing that." Turning, she smoothed her skirts and took a deep breath. "All right, then, let's go."

The barricade was guarded by militiamen, most in their ordinary work clothes, half without jackets. They lounged around, even as Deborah and Proctor approached. When Proctor saw them up close, he had to lean on his musket to support himself—it was no act.

"Our aunt is trapped in the city," Deborah explained. "We hear there's fighting coming, and we don't want the Lobsters to hurt her once it starts."

"They won't hurt a woman, not if she doesn't cause them any trouble," a young captain answered.

He glanced out of the corner of his eye at Proctor, and some of the other men stared openly. Sweat beaded on Proctor's forehead and ran down his face.

"I need her to help take care of my brother," Deborah said.

"I can see that," the captain said sympathetically. He looked over his shoulder. Farther on, a wall manned by Redcoats blocked The Neck from one side to the other. "Even if we let you pass, the Lobsters probably won't. They're scared to death of spies right now, don't trust nobody they don't already know. But you're welcome to give them a try."

He gestured to his men. Two of them lifted the log that blocked the road, grunting as they pivoted it to the side to let Deborah and Proctor pass.

"Thank you," she said. She dragged Proctor with her—her grip on his arm was as firm as a shackle.

As soon as they passed the men, the log thudded back into place. Proctor leaned his head toward Deborah and said, "What do I look like? It's no old man!"

She shushed him, squeezing his arm. "Stay hunched over, and shuffle more."

An empty causeway, with mud on either side of it, stretched between the colonial barricade and the city wall.

"Halt where you are, in the name of the king!"

They stopped in the middle of the causeway just outside the wall. The British soldiers were quite the opposite of the colonists. They dressed in identical uniforms, a bit dusty but still tidy, and presented as a single row over the top of the wall. They were stiff and bristling with pent-up anger.

"Please, sir, we want to enter the city to fetch our aunt," Deborah said. "Her name's Sarah Bowden, and she lives above a wig maker's shop, off King Street."

Proctor grimaced at hearing his aunt's true name and address given, in case it brought trouble on her. But he and Deborah had discussed it at length, deciding that they must use the real information in case the soldiers sent anyone to check.

"I'm sure that's nice for her," the guard said. "But it don't mean a thing to me, so off with the both of you."

"She sent us a letter—she's too sick to take care of herself, and she doesn't have anyone else. She needs us to look after her."

"Plenty of extra folks in the city right now, rich merchants and their families, all looking for safety from that rabble over there," the guard said, with a nod at his counterparts beyond the other barricade. "I'm sure someone will look after her."

"But—"

"Sorry, miss, but you can't enter." The bayonet was affixed to the end of his musket; he gave her a move-along gesture with it that would have easily gutted either one of them were they close enough. "Now be on your way."

She made further remonstrance, but to no avail—the soldier would not be persuaded. The longer they waited, the more frustrated and restless Proctor became, until finally he opened his mouth to speak. Deborah's hand shot out, clasping his, digging her nails into his palm.

Relenting, she returned with Proctor in tow to the colonial barricade where the militiamen offered her sad shakes of their heads and heaped abuse on the Redcoats. When she and Proctor disentangled themselves and retreated from sight, Proctor straightened his shoulders, patted his hair into place, and righted his clothes.

"What did I look like?" he demanded. "It was no old man."

"No?" She wouldn't meet his eyes, but kept looking around to see if they were followed.

"No, or you would not have referred to me as your brother."

"I made you appear like a simpleton to them. I'm sorry if it hurts your pride, but I thought it easier, and a good explanation for our need to reach our aunt."

Proctor counted off ten steps before he spoke. "And it's not the sort of thing to elicit comment either."

"No," she said. "I'm sorry I didn't tell you, but we didn't have time to argue."

"I'm fine with it. It was a good plan. I would've gone along with it. I did go along with it."

"But it doesn't matter," she said. "We failed. There's no way into the city."

"Yes, there is," Proctor said. The Redcoat's comment

about rich merchants and their families reminded him of something. He started back the way they came, eager to escape the skulls and skeletons as fast as he could.

Deborah caught up with him. "What is it? What's the way into the city?"

"I'd tell you about it," he said. "But I'm just a simpleton. Probably a mute."

Chapter 19

"When you get ready to move your cattle toward Boston market," Thomas Rucke had told Proctor once, months ago, during their meeting at the coffeehouse in Boston, "you might want to begin by contacting a man named Elihu Danvers. Danvers has a house near the mouth of the river, across from Cambridge."

Though Rucke never said as much, Proctor came away with the impression that Danvers was a smuggler. Used to eluding the customs men at any rate, the sort of sailor who could help a young man just starting out make a bit more in trade.

The sort who could find a way into besieged Boston.

The only trouble was that "house near the mouth of the river, across from Cambridge" described a great many houses.

"Are we going to knock on every single door?" Deborah asked.

"No," Proctor said. "I reckon we'll stop once we come to Danvers's house."

She rolled her eyes at him, and at the first house they tried she asked for directions. The girl who answered the door had been displaced by the rebellion and didn't know where Danvers lived, but the old fisherman at the second house knew Danvers well and pointed them in the right direction.

Danvers's house was a tumbling sprawl of makeshift room additions overlooking the Charles River. Though it was late in the day when Proctor and Deborah found it, the house stirred with at least a dozen children from toddlers to husky young men.

Danvers answered the door when they called. He was a broad-chested man in a gray peacoat, topped by a hat so threadbare it was almost the ghost of a hat. He had a thick beard sticking out at all angles, but a clean upper lip. Between the two, he held a pipe clenched firmly in his teeth, even when he spoke. He spewed a constant stream of blue smoke.

"What makes you think I can help you?" he asked.

"Thomas Rucke recommended you," Proctor said. "A couple of months ago, in early April. We were talking about transporting cattle."

Danvers peered over Proctor and Deborah at the road behind them, then puffed on the pipe and blew out a cloud of smoke. "I don't see any cattle."

"We're here for a different reason, but we still need transportation."

"I do seem to recall him mentioning you to me, right before the current trouble started." Danvers watched Deborah closely. "Something about a connection to his daughter."

Proctor shuffled his feet, uneasily. "Yes, sir, that's how I know him, sir. He and Emily are behind the siege lines in Boston now, and we need to reach him."

Danvers puffed again. "Are you taking him some beef?"

"No, sir."

"That's a shame, because there's a shortage of fresh meat in the city right now, and we could get a prime price for it. What are you taking then?"

"Just the two of us, sir."

A pair of boys, maybe ten and twelve, peeked out from the open door. Without looking back, Danvers closed his fist around his pipe and jabbed it in their direction. The boys jumped back. Danvers stepped away from the house and crossed the yard to the edge of the garden. He rolled from side to side as he walked. He gestured at the colonial military lines visible from the hillside. Beyond the militia lines, across the glassy sheet of the bay, the steeples of the Boston churches spired into the sky, fixed points against the drifting masts of the British ships.

"So you're Tory loyalists, going over to the British side?" he said. "You realize that means I'll have to report you to the local militia."

"No, sir, we're not planning to stay there—"

"It's a personal matter," Deborah interrupted. "We only plan to deliver our message and then make our way out again."

"You may not have noticed," Danvers said. "But there's a war going on. The militia don't want anyone going into the city, and the British don't want anyone coming out. That's a narrow channel, with shoals on either side. There's nothing in it for me to pilot you through those waters."

If Danvers couldn't smuggle them into the city, Proctor wasn't sure they could make it. "Sir, you're the only recourse we have left."

Deborah pulled a small purse from one of her pockets and retrieved a gold coin. "Will this make it worth your while?"

Danvers stared at the coin, although he didn't reach to take it. "If I were the sort of man who could help you, and I'm not saying that I am, that would be enough to ferry one of you under the circumstances. And one of you is all I'm likely to be able to help in any case."

Proctor stared at the coin also, unaware that Deborah had that much to spend. He regretted the price they got for the milk cow a little less.

She reached in her purse for a second gold coin and a silver piece. "Both of us need to go. This is all we have."

Danvers sucked on his pipe and looked at her purse as if he could judge its weight simply by the way it sat in her hand.

"The British boats patrol the bay looking for so much as

a canoe or a skiff that moves across the water without their permission," he said. "The officials give writs to fishing boats to sail out from the Boston wharves because they're short of food and they need the catch. Each writ is for a specific number of men per boat, say four or five. When the boat returns to dock, the British inspectors count the men getting off again, so that no spies can get into the city undetected."

Proctor turned away. "So you're saying it's hopeless. There's no way to get us inside."

"That's not what he said," Deborah interceded. "Only that's it's difficult."

"Aye," Danvers said, and he drew on his pipe again. "The boy here, he wouldn't be much of a problem. One could meet a fishing boat in the bay and exchange one of their crew for him. Do you know how to fish, lad?"

Proctor shook his head no. "Never been on a boat, except a ferry."

Danvers frowned, as if such an admission made one a bit less of a man. "Then we'd best make the exchange later in the day, after they've already hauled in their catch. Fish are too valuable to forgo the help of a crew member right now. But the lass—"

"I could hide on the boat, under a blanket or something," Deborah said. "The inspectors wouldn't see me."

Danvers frowned again in frank disapproval. "Maybe if you hid her under a blanket of fish you'd escape the first inspection. But it wouldn't do you much good after they unloaded."

Proctor could go alone, but he didn't know how to do the spell that Deborah planned to perform. He turned to her and lowered his voice. "I can do this, if I have to; you just need to show me—"

"Captain Danvers," Deborah said. "Could two men be exchanged for two crew members, if such were the case?"

A puff on his pipe, and a nod. "Maybe."

"Then, as I understand it, the problem is not that there are two of us, but that I'm a woman."

"I've got nothing against the fairer gender, as Mrs. Danvers can attest, but yes, young lady, that about sums it up."

She opened her purse a third time and placed her fingers inside without withdrawing anything. "Mr. Danvers, tell me, would it be possible to buy some boy's clothes from you? About my size."

His eyebrows rose, his mouth hinged open, and he held his pipe there for a long moment before clamping down on it and puffing again. "I thought your purse was empty."

"Is that a no, sir?"

Danvers looked over at Proctor, who had straightened and taken a step back. "I've a dozen children, ma'am. It's difficult to keep them all clothed, as they're constantly outgrowing things or wearing them out. A contribution toward the purchase of new clothing would make Mrs. Danvers extraordinarily pleased."

Behind them, the door flew open and out stepped a woman half Danvers's age and twice his considerable size. "Elihu Zachariah Danvers, your devil-bred sons were jumping on the bed and broke it—what are you going to come do about it?"

He held up his hand and waved to her, then puffed silently on his pipe until she stormed back into the house. "So we have a deal then?"

Proctor had too many misgivings and not enough options. Deborah didn't even glance at him for approval before she answered. "We do."

"Meet me here tomorrow morning before sunrise." He held out his hand for the coins.

Deborah dropped the coins back into her purse and shoved it into her pocket. "Not a shilling before we're aboard the boat. And only half then, the other half when we reach our destination."

"Leave me the musket as a down payment," he said,

puffing vigorously on his pipe. "You won't be able to take it with you anyway."

Proctor's fist tightened on the weapon. "No, sir."

Deborah said, "We'll give you half a shilling now, and you send the boy out with the clothes."

"Another half a shilling when he brings the clothes?"

Deborah nodded, and Danvers nodded back, the equivalent of a handshake. She placed a half-shilling coin in his hand. Danvers walked back toward the house, humming and trailing a cloud of smoke behind him.

Proctor lowered his voice as soon as they were alone. "You don't have to spend all your money to get us into Boston."

"It's not really mine," she said. "My father earned it, a shilling here, a penny there, and my mother saved it. This is the only way it can still do them any good."

A mop-haired boy of about ten ran out of the house with a bundle of clothes so worn Proctor would hesitate to use them for rags. He was about to say so when he saw that the clothes the boy was wearing were no better.

Deborah gave him the coin and they hurried away. "I was afraid he wouldn't send out the clothes tonight, and then it would be harder to change his memory."

Proctor looked over his shoulder. Even though he felt so sick he wanted to find someplace to lie down, he said, "Slow up. The boy is following us. Let's let him grow bored."

Deborah, lost in thought, looked back, startled. It was late in the day and already growing dark. They meandered, drifting from one side of the road to the other until the boy gave up and ran back toward his house. Proctor found a ditch covered with brush and pulled Deborah down under the branches, where they found a dry spot, relatively flat, and sat down.

Deborah said, "I expected you to put up more of a fuss about me dressing in boy's clothes."

"No," he said. He was sweating less, breathing easier

now that he was at rest. "If you're dressed like a boy, I won't feel as bad when I spell you into a squinty-eyed hunchback simpleton. What did you mean, *change his memory*?"

"If I have a different appearance tomorrow morning, I can convince him that's how he saw me today. Make him think it was two young men who came seeking his aid all along. It's not much, but it may throw off Nance or anyone else if they come looking for us."

"How can you do that?"

"Memory is malleable as clay in a potter's hand." She passed him half the cheese they had packed, but it was no more than a few bites. "We all like to think we remember things exactly, but the fact is memory has to be shaped, like a bowl or a pot, until it can hold something without it spilling out. If you shape the vessel, you can limit what it holds, or how it spills."

The thought made Proctor vaguely uncomfortable. He shifted, pulling another New England stone out of the dirt beneath him, and tossed it aside. "So you're saying that, if we tried, we could change my memory of the attacks this week? I could remember them differently."

"If you wanted to, we could even try to make you forget them. It might help you sleep better."

That kind of talent, in the wrong hands, could do an awful lot of harm. That Deborah had so much power, and never tried to use it except for good, left him a little awestruck. As if he knew he ought to hold himself to higher standards. It wasn't enough to want to raise cattle or become a rich farmer. A man ought to stand for something, make a positive difference in the world.

As much as he hated the memories, he decided he ought to keep them, just to remind himself of who he ought to be. "No," he said. "But thanks."

"You should get what rest you can right now," she said.

He found it awkward, being in such close proximity to her, but at least they wouldn't be sleeping at the same time.

He carefully placed the musket between them, rolled up his hat to use for a pillow, and closed his eyes.

His dreams mixed memory and fear. The images of the corpses from that night on the farm blurred with the skeletal visages of the men from the militia companies. Then Amos stood before him. Flesh melted like candle wax from Amos's bones. He kept handing Proctor a bowl, which Proctor smashed, then a cup, which Proctor shattered, over and over again. Every time he smashed something, Amos handed him something else.

He woke to the sound of feet crunching in the brush nearby. It was still, and he bolted up not knowing where he was, fists pulled back, heart pounding, ready to fight.

"There," a man's voice whispered. "I heard something."

Deborah put a hand over his mouth and pressed against him, holding him down. The sensation of her body against him produced a different kind of agitation, but then a knife hacked through branches just a foot from their heads.

"Where?" asked a second voice.

"Over here, maybe," the first said. They moved off, randomly cutting their way through the culvert until finally they gave up and left.

When it had been silent a long time, Proctor whispered, "It's a good thing you did a concealment spell."

Deborah's face was drawn, her eyes wide. "But I didn't."

"Deborah!" he whispered, quickly scanning the brush around them.

She pulled away from him. "I fell asleep and forgot. We were lucky."

"Do you think it was Danvers?"

"It was a couple of his boys, that's for sure. I recognized the younger one. But whether he sent them, meaning to rob us, or they came on their own, I can't say."

Proctor rubbed his face, trying to wake up, trying to clear his mind of sleep. "Maybe that's why he wanted the musket, so we couldn't defend ourselves. We should be cautious today. We won't be lucky again."

His eyes had adjusted to the darkness. Deborah had already changed into the boy's clothes. They were huge on her slender frame, so she had rolled up the cuffs on the breeches and sleeves. She didn't look like Deborah to him anymore. More like young Arthur Simes back home.

"You already did the spell," he said.

"I wasn't sure how I was going to do it, so I worked on it for hours before I fell asleep." She had removed her cap and unpinned her hair. "You still need to help me cut this shorter."

"I can barely see it," Proctor said.

"It doesn't have to be perfect, just short," she insisted. "Saw it off as best as you can."

She turned her back to him, holding her long hair out to the side in one hand.

"I'm not sure I can do this," he said.

"Hack it off already!"

Her hair felt heavy and soft in his hand, like folds of silk. He held it tight and, after a short sigh, began to slice through it with his knife.

"Proctor?"

"Yes?"

"Who's Emily Rucke?"

The knife jumped, nicking the tip of his finger. He shook several locks from his hand, then sucked on the wound. "She's, um, Thomas Rucke's daughter. He's a sugar merchant, someone I met once in Boston. We talked about the cattle business. He was going to help me get started."

"Ah," she said.

He finished cutting her hair, doing about as credible a job as he would have for Amos or another fellow. After tucking the knife in his belt, he brushed the loose hairs from his hand and shirt, reaching out to catch the largest lock as it fell. He held on to it a second, thinking to keep it.

"We're lucky they came by to wake us," she said, tucking her hair under a boy's cap. "Are you ready to go?"

His hand closed around the lock, and he slipped it into his pocket where she couldn't see it. "Yeah, I'm ready."

He unrolled his hat and jammed it back on his head. Climbing to his feet first, he held out his hand and helped her up.

Danvers waited for them exactly where he said he would, the coal in his pipe like a beacon in the night. "Aha," he said. "I was wondering if you two boys would show."

As soon as he called them *boys*, he pulled his pipe out of his mouth and stared closely at Deborah as if he knew something was wrong. Then he shook it off, like a dog spraying water after a bath.

"I have to admit, I don't like a fellow with a gun aboard my boat," he said to Proctor. "You won't be able to take it with you on the other boat nohow."

"It's unloaded," Proctor replied, and showed him. "I'll leave it in the boat when we make the transfer."

Danvers accepted this and led them down to the water's edge, which smelled green and fishy. A white slash appeared in the predawn sky, and a seagull screeched overhead as they climbed aboard a little one-mast boat. Danvers pushed it offshore, splashing knee-deep in the water before climbing aboard. Though he rolled awkwardly when he walked on dry land, he was perfectly in balance the minute they set off. His legs barely moved except to keep him steady, but his upper body coiled rope, raised anchor, and hoisted sail, reminding Proctor of the way his father used to work in the barn.

In moments they were away from shore and gliding into the harbor among all the other boats. A British man-of-war sat just offshore of Charlestown, with the gentle rise of the hill outlined against the sky behind it. Dozens of other ships were anchored around Boston.

Proctor felt better as soon as they left land. The constant

sickness in his stomach lifted, and he didn't feel as wobbly. He turned at Deborah to tell her, but her boyish, Arthur-like face disturbed him; he looked away as fast as he had from the skeletal militiamen.

"There seem to be a lot of British ships," she said.

Danvers blew out a cloud of smoke and shifted the stem to the corner of his mouth so he could speak around it. "Troopships have been arriving from Britain the past few weeks, bringing thousands of soldiers. Any day now, I expect they'll march out to teach the militia a lesson."

Proctor recalled what Thomas Rucke had told him about the city of London compared with Boston, how it was hundreds of times larger, and he wondered if there was any limit to the number of troops they could send.

By sunrise, they sailed around the north end of Boston with its great steepled church, past the hay fields of Noodle Island, and beyond the mudflats that surrounded some of the other harbor islands. They saw more British men-of-war, at anchor like sleeping dogs. Through the morning they bobbed on the water, drifting east into the sound, amid a diverse collection of fishing boats and cargo ships. The rocking motion of the boat lulled Proctor to sleep, and for the first time in days, he slept without nightmares.

Deborah shook him awake. Her face was green with seasickness. Fishing boats were coming back to harbor with their catch. Clouds of gulls dived toward the decks, stealing guts and cast-offs.

Danvers steered toward a two-master with *Laughing Jenny* painted on its prow.

"'Hoy, there," Danvers called. "Two to board."

The captain was a young broad-chested man, with a trim beard, a clean upper lip, and bloody hands. Without a word, he stepped away, checking the horizon, looking at other ships through his glass, then beckoned two of his crew.

"What are you waiting for?" he barked at Proctor and Deborah when they sat waiting.

Deborah handed the coins over to Danvers, who held them up to examine them. He tucked one into his vest pocket and handed the other back to her. "Give it to the cap'n." He pulled a packet of letters from inside his jacket. "Would you mind handing these over to him as well?"

Proctor snatched the packet from Danvers's hand before Deborah could take it, wanting to see if any were addressed to Mr. Rucke. Then he clambered up the side of the boat, slipping as soon as he put his foot over the side. There were stacks of cod on the bottom of the craft, and the deck was slimed with the guttings. He reached over to help Deborah, and the captain gave him an odd look—of course, he thought it was another young man and not a woman. She remembered herself better than Proctor, and ignored his proffered aid. She made it on to the deck and stood there while two men climbed down into Danvers's boat and pushed off.

Proctor pulled out the letters to peek at their addresses. But the captain stepped beside him, holding his hand out. Except for lacking the pipe and about twenty years, he was the spitting image of Danvers.

Proctor smacked the packet of letters into his empty palm. So much for that plan.

"We'll pay you the money once we're safely in Boston," Deborah said. Her voice was almost a squeak.

The captain folded back the corners of the letters, examining their addresses; he grunted something that might be consent, or might be disinterest, before tucking the letters away inside his own coat. "Have either of you been cod fishing before?"

"No," Proctor said. Deborah opened her mouth to speak, but, overcome by the rocking of the boat and the stench of the fish, shook her head instead.

"You're of no use to me then, so stay over there, out of the way, until we get into dock."

They went aft and sat on a locker. The one remaining crewman grumbled about the workload until the captain told him to stow it. The sailor, a swarthy fellow with a black goatee and a slight French accent, glared at them as if he could force their help through shame or discomfort.

But they refused that bait, and he worked alone, cursing from time to time in French, gutting the rest of the cod and stacking them in the center of the boat. Gulls dived at them constantly. The French sailor laughed when Proctor kept ducking them. Deborah was too ill to notice. After a while, she leaned against Proctor just to prop herself up. He put a clumsy arm around her.

"Your little brother hasn't been sailing before?" the captain asked from the spot where he steered the ship.

Proctor looked at him blankly a moment, then shook his head. The captain laughed at that, looked at her, then laughed some more.

Deborah's jaw set. She scooted away from Proctor, holding herself upright even if she was too sick to speak.

They approached the harbor. Now that it was daylight, Proctor saw a hundred ships, all flying the Union Jack. It was an odd sensation, to see the red, white, and blue banner and think that it might no longer be his flag. He'd always felt a stronger connection to Massachusetts than to England. But until now he'd had the dual sense of being part of something local and also part of something larger. If the rebellion succeeded, he wondered if he would ever feel part of something so powerful again.

The shadow of Boston formed a hedge of peaked rooftops in the distance. The waves grew choppy as they passed among the wake of larger ships, and Deborah ran to the side of the boat and leaned over.

"We're coming into the dock, if you can just hang on," the captain said.

She gripped the gunwale until her knuckles were white. The ship sailed past one large wharf and then another larger one, both crowded with British merchant ships. As they sailed south, they passed a series of smaller docks and wharves until they rounded Fort Hill and the captain aimed for one of the smaller wharves. The captain and the cursing Frenchman ran back and forth to steer the craft into position, where it slammed hard against the pier. The crewman jumped over the side with a rope and began tying off while Deborah staggered to starboard. Her vomit splashed into the water below while Proctor ran to her side.

"Wot, someone sick?" a voice said roughly.

Proctor looked up as one of the British dock inspectors thumped onto the deck.

The captain shrugged and handed over his papers. "My nephew—brought him aboard as a favor to my wife's sister, but he's been useless. You want to take him? We had to do all the work ourselves."

The inspector, who walked stiffly, started toward Deborah, who stepped away from the side and made a quick gesture toward the dock while murmuring a prayer. The inspector stopped.

The captain picked up a slab of the finest cod, twenty pounds of meat or more, and said, "Would you mind holding on to this for me?"

The inspector tucked the papers back into the captain's jacket. "And how am I supposed to hold that?"

The captain grabbed a piece of sailcloth to wrap it in. The inspector stood over him as he wrapped it.

"You should be careful," he warned. "The rebels have been trying to secret spies into the city. If we catch any, we'll make an example of them and anyone who helped them."

"If I see any, I'll call for the city watch."

The inspector grunted in reply, took his fish, and climbed back onto the dock. A fish merchant with two boys rolling barrows came down the wharf and argued with the Frenchman about unloading their catch.

Deborah wiped her mouth, not quite as pale as before, and pulled out the second coin to give to the captain.

"You owe me the price of that fish as well," he said.

She swallowed and reached for her purse. But Proctor took her elbow and steered her toward the side of the ship. "I left payment for it in Elihu's boat," he said. "You can collect it from him."

He led her down the wooden planks. The water that lapped against the piers was filled with dead fish and trash and sewage. The British inspector was already aboard another fishing boat, using his staff to poke among its catch while the captain argued loudly with him over British policy in the siege.

When they came to dry land once again, Proctor hesitated before stepping onto it. He closed his eyes and put one foot forward. Nothing.

"Whatever was affecting me," he said, "I think the water washed it away."

"Good," she said weakly.

Now that he was no longer nauseous, no longer tense with worry about betrayal, he felt hungry. "We'll go to my aunt's lodgings and spend the night there. She'll have something to eat," he said.

"I . . . I don't want anything to eat right now." She clamped her hand over her mouth as she said it.

She stumbled away from him until she found a stoop to sit on outside a barrel maker's shed. He went to comfort her, but she waved him away.

"It's getting dark," he said. "We need to find my aunt's lodgings."

Swallowing hard, she forced herself back to her feet. "Where does she live?"

"The big wharf we passed is Hancock's, which connects King Street. She lives above a wig maker's shop on Pudding Lane, just off King Street. If we head that way, I know I can find it."

"Can you find me fresh water first?"

"Yeah, I'm thirsty too."

He could see Fort Hill rising on their right, so he led her

away from the water and into the city. He thought he might be able to find a well or even a rain barrel outside someone's house, but a ropeyard ran the length of the first street he chose. The long open grounds smelled of pitch. A handful of men were still at work; one of them stood by the street tapping a hickory bat against his palm. Everyone seemed on edge. Feeling like one of the spies the inspector had warned about, Proctor decided not to speak to anyone.

Despite what he'd told Deborah, he didn't know the southern end of Boston at all. So he led her from street to street, peering around houses, looking for a public square with a well, like the north square he was familiar with from his previous visits. Instead, they saw several open pastures, some with cattle. He finally led her to a trough at the edge of one of the pastures, and they scooped water from it, drinking with their hands.

"This looks like Orange Street," he said when they were refreshed. "I think it leads toward King."

Deborah looked at the darkening sky. "We better hurry," she said.

He could tell they were headed the right way now. The streets were narrower and dense with buildings. As they wandered from street to street, looking for a landmark Proctor recognized, a shutter banged open above them. A bareheaded man in a nightdress leaned from his second-story window. "It's after curfew—I'll call the watch on you, you damned troublemakers."

They hurried away as he yelled after them, cursing all apprentices and boys with loose morals.

After that, they moved from shadow to shadow, dashing across the streets, staying out of sight. They didn't dare allow themselves to be caught after dark without papers.

Proctor thought they were close to King Street because he could faintly smell the peculiar mix of odors—fish, tobacco, tea, and rum—that defined the wharf when a voice shouted one street over.

He dodged into a doorway, pulling Deborah after him. At the corner closest to them a light appeared, then two lights. It was the night watch, two men in long coats and broad-brimmed hats, carrying heavy staves and lanterns.

"Nine fifty pee em," the first voice said, and the second added, "And the wind is blowing from the north."

They held the light up to the doorways as they passed, stopping to check the lock on a small bakery directly across the street.

Proctor's hand searched all his pockets, looking for sand, for dust, for anything he could use as a focus for a quick spell. His heart began to pound as he realized he had nothing.

Deborah lifted her head to him and silently mouthed a warning: *We can't be caught.*

He answered her with a small nod. Too much was at stake. They would have to outrun the men if they approached. He braced himself to knock them down.

Instead, the watchmen stared in the window at the counter with its baked goods and talked about coming back for fresh bread when the baker opened shop in the morning. The thought of warm bread made Proctor's stomach growl, loud as a shop dog, but they didn't hear it and moved on. They turned the corner, and Proctor heard, distantly, "Nine fifty-five—"

Deborah's fist, closed on the hem of his jacket, finally relaxed. Proctor whispered to her. "I think I recognize that bakery—we're just around the corner from my aunt's."

When they rounded the next street and turned down an alley, Proctor's heart leapt. He not only recognized her lodging but saw a light burning in her window, despite the late hour.

"Come on," he said, taking Deborah by the hand.

He tapped lightly at the door.

It cracked open instantly, and his aunt's thin face peered out at him. "Proctor," she said, hardly sounding surprised. "Well, come in."

She stepped back, holding the door open so they could enter. Proctor watched the street while Deborah entered first, then he slipped inside and shut the door behind them.

When he turned around, he saw his mother sitting in a rocking chair by the fire, wearing all black, hands folded in her lap.

"I knew you were coming, Proctor," she said. "I scryed it. I saw your arrival at this very day and hour."

Chapter 20

Proctor was so stunned, all he could do was yank his hat off his head and stand there. "Hello, Mother."

She looked as though she had aged ten years. Her already careworn face was thinner, the circles under her eyes darker, her hair grayer.

"Two months," she said. "Two months gone from the only home you've ever known, two months gone and your own loving parents needing you, two months gone . . . and all you can say to me is *Hello, Mother*?"

His aunt moved quietly to the far end of the room next to the door, as if she was ready to block his potential escape.

"But the Reverend Emerson—" he started.

"The Reverend Emerson," she said, "called on me for about an hour one afternoon, told me how you were off to fight the war, and when I asked him who was to take care of your family while you were gone, he told me not to worry, it wouldn't be long, and then he was off to go do his own part, and days went by, and turned into weeks, and I didn't hear a word, didn't even receive a scrap of letter from you."

"Mother—"

"Let her have her say, Proctor," his aunt scolded. Then muttering to herself, "God knows as much as I've had to listen to it, you should too."

"Don't you dare criticize me, Sarah!" His mother's head turned to look at her sister, but her hand raised from her lap, finger extended at Proctor, as if to pin him where he stood. When she looked back to Proctor, the finger stayed aimed at him.

"Didn't I teach you your letters? Didn't I spend winters with you practicing your writing, over and over, until you could spell as well as boys raised up in fine houses with their own schoolmasters trained at Yale? And to what end? You left without a word, for months, and you couldn't even write me a single letter to let me know where you were or that you were still alive?"

"I sent you a note—"

"This?" She pulled up his note to her from some weeks past, and flapped it at him. "This is barely a note. I've seen bills of sale that contained more information. There's nothing in here about where you were, why you were gone, when you'd return—nothing!"

"It had to stay a secret," he said.

Her voice went very cold. "Boy, another word for secret is *lie*. I don't want to hear any more lies."

"But I haven't lied."

"That's a lie right there," she snapped. "You told the Reverend Emerson you were going off to fight the war, but I went to see Captain Smith, of the minutemen."

"My captain?"

"Yes, your captain! Because if my son was off to fight this . . . this God-damned war!—"

That was the first time Proctor had ever heard her take the Lord's name in vain. He took a deep breath.

"—you'd think his captain, the man he signed a covenant with, the man he reports to, you'd think *that man* would have some idea, maybe a general inkling, even a notion, where one of his minutemen was assigned. Or where he was off volunteering. But no! Your captain had no idea at all! He said he hadn't seen you since the fight on the road to Lexington."

Proctor's mouth set. She must have been worried sick

about him, and he couldn't blame her. He was going to stand here and take it, let her get it out of her system, before he tried to explain things to her.

Deborah shuffled uncomfortably behind him.

"So then"—she looked over to her sister for confirmation, as if Sarah had been witness to all of this—"I go back to the Reverend Emerson. And he tells me not to fear, that God is looking out for you, and I ask him, 'Who is looking out for me? With my only son gone and his father ill?' And he promised that God would provide, but I can tell you God didn't provide me with nothing but heartache. Because it was just like you were one of the men shot dead on the green, only there wasn't nothing left of you to bury."

"But I thought Arthur Simes came over to help you out. Emerson said—"

"Arthur Simes helped himself to dinner and that was about it." She leaned forward, the crease showing in her brow. "Are you a Tory?" she asked.

"*What?*"

"Have you been hiding in Boston with the Ruckes this whole time?"

"No, I just arrived tonight."

"Because I couldn't figure out where you'd gone or where you were. I never scryed so often or so hard as I scryed looking for you, and God did not answer one of my prayers, not once in all the rest of April, nor in May. I couldn't see anything! It was like you were wrapped in a shroud, as if you were dead—"

The image of a dead man wrapped in a shroud made Proctor shudder.

"—until three days ago, when I scryed and there you were again."

Her voice cracked, and she paused to wipe her cheeks and restore her frown.

They'd left The Farm three days ago. The concealment

spells must have hidden him from her. Softly, he said, "I'm sorry."

His apology only infuriated her. "So there I am, my only child has left me, and God and His angels have left me—"

"Now, Prudence," Sarah said.

"That's what it felt like. And then, then—" Her voice cracked again, and she couldn't speak for a second.

Sarah walked over to her side and rested a hand on her shoulder. "There now, it'll be all right."

His mother reached up to squeeze her sister's hand, but she continued to stare directly at Proctor. She tried to speak again, but her voice broke before any words came out, and she turned her face away and pressed it against her sister's hand.

Proctor shuffled his feet, feeling sick to his stomach again. "Mother, I'm sorry. I shouldn't have gone off without saying anything, and I should've sent you a letter, but when it was all happening—"

She lifted her head again, just long enough to say, "And then your father passed on."

Proctor stepped back as if he'd been kicked by a horse, bumping into Deborah. She touched his elbow and whispered, "Oh, Proctor, I'm so sorry."

He yanked his arm away as if her touch were fire, and started toward his mother, wanting to comfort her, wanting with all his heart to make things right. A look of reproach from his aunt stopped him dead in his tracks.

"And who did I have then?" his mother wailed. "My husband was dead. My son, my only child, who I loved and depended on, was missing, without a word, without a letter, no way to reach him. Even the Reverend was gone, off to help raise troops."

Her sister patted her shoulder and kissed the top of her head, murmuring to her. "There, Prudence, there, now, if I had known, I would have come."

"I couldn't even send word to you," she sobbed. To Proctor, she said, "The only family I have left in all the world, when I need her most, and she's trapped behind a fort, behind a wall of soldiers, all because some fool started shooting at the Redcoats back in April."

Proctor came forward, and bent down on one knee at his mother's feet, hanging his head as low as he felt. "I have no right to expect it, but I beg your forgiveness. I should have been there for you, and I wasn't. I let you down."

His mother sniffled, but her face, red-eyed and wan, was set hard against him.

"You must never let her down again," his aunt scolded.

"I won't," Proctor said.

"You've always been a good boy," his aunt said. "A little headstrong, yes, maybe a little too sure of yourself, but it never brought you to any harm."

"No, ma'am. I mean, yes, ma'am."

"But your mother is no spring chicken anymore—"

"Hush, Sarah," his mother said.

"It's true. You were past thirty when Proctor was born." Turning to Proctor, she said as an aside, "And it was no easy birth, I don't have to remind you—thirty-six hours in labor, and the midwife and I both thought she was going to die."

"No one thought I was going to die," his mother said.

But Sarah was on a roll now. "You almost died to bring him into this world, and then you sacrificed your own ease and comfort to give him the best." As an aside to Proctor she said, "Like that linen jacket she gave you two years ago, that was a fine jacket, with those silver buttons. And you hardly ever wear it, then rip it when you do." Then, addressing her sister again, she said, "You sacrificed everything."

"I know how much she sacrificed for me," Proctor said.

"Do you?" his aunt snapped. "Then you shouldn't have acted such a prodigal, should you?"

"I'm going to make it right," he said.

"Your mother has no one else to depend on now, no one

to provide for her," Sarah said. "She's an age where she should be a grandmother now, looking after her grandchildren, not running a whole farm by herself."

"I don't need grandchildren," his mother said, swallowing the last of her tears. "But it's not just me. Sarah needs you too."

"Shush now, Prudence," his aunt said.

"But it's true," his mother said, sitting straight again. "With the war going on, and the siege, there's no work left in the city."

"I'll get by somehow," she protested.

"There's no food left," his mother said. "I tried to buy meat today, in the market, and there was nothing but dried fish available."

"You can still find a bit of lamb at the market every few days," his aunt said. "Enough to make a pie or two."

His mother looked down at Proctor, who was still on his knees like a penitent. "She has to come live with us. The farm is yours now, like you always wanted. We can sell off some of the timber to buy those calves you wanted, and we can start raising cattle, like you always said you wanted to do."

"That's what I always wanted to do," he said. But the words left a bad taste in his mouth, like a spoiled egg.

"Good," his aunt said.

His mother said, "We'll have to make some excuse to get you past the gate. Three days ago, I finally scryed you here and came down to find you. The Redcoats let me in only because I begged them. But if we go tomorrow, they may—"

"Wait, wait, wait a moment," he said, rising to his feet. "I can't leave tomorrow."

His mother and his aunt stared at him with so much focused anger, he thought he might be struck.

A gentle voice behind him said, "No, Proctor, it's all right. They need you, and you should go take care of them."

He spun around. Deborah stood there, her own cheeks

wet where she'd wept quietly. She scrubbed at them with the back of an oversized sleeve, while her cap slouched down over her poorly cut hair.

"Who's your friend?" his mother asked, as if truly noticing this odd young man for the first time. His aunt bustled away from his mother's seat, saying, "Forgive the lack of a proper introduction, but—"

"No, no, Miss Sarah, forgive me for intruding on your family in such a difficult hour."

"Deborah," Proctor whispered, and she gave him a tiny shake of her head to warn him not to speak. His aunt turned her head, having caught the name but unsure what she'd heard.

"That looks like Arthur Simes," Proctor's mother said. "Is that Arthur Simes?"

"No, ma'am, I'm no one you've met before," she said, speaking low, trying to hide the femininity of her voice. "Proctor—your son—graciously came to help me and my family, because of the war. The Reverend Emerson brought him to us."

"Deborah," Proctor whispered again, more urgently, but this time she just talked over him.

"We were in a desperate hour of need, and he risked his own life and well-being several times to protect us. I am"—she glanced at him—"I will always be grateful to him for that."

"Oh, you poor boy," Proctor's mother said, and Proctor thought she was speaking to him, but he saw that she was addressing Deborah.

His aunt pulled one of her chairs away from the wall and pushed it forward. "Please, have a seat. Tell us everything."

"I would love to," Deborah said. "He was as brave as any man I've ever seen. He faced horrors no man should ever face—"

"Oh, my," Proctor's mother said, covering her mouth with her hand. His aunt hemmed skeptically.

"—but I can't remain, and he obviously belongs here." She walked to the door and put her hand on the latch. "Thank you, Proctor. For everything. I wish you all luck in escaping the city. But do it soon. Please do not delay."

Proctor rushed to the door before she could pull it open, and pressed his hand against it. He thought of all those skeletal faces he'd seen on the other side of the siege line, especially of Amos.

"I'm going with you," he said.

"I can finish this by myself," she said, her voice now genuinely low, viscerally harsh.

"No, I mean to see it through."

"Don't be foolish, Proctor," his aunt snapped. "You've already done good for their family, but now it's time to see to your own."

"They need you, Proctor," Deborah said. "You got me into the city—I couldn't have done it without you."

"But—"

"Now I need to see the rest of it through myself. Clearly, divine providence has a hand in this. You were meant to be here, your mother was meant to find you because she needs you. You got me in, you can get them safely out, before the fighting starts again in earnest."

"They can wait a day, a few days—"

"The fighting will start again, and they need to be gone before it does. What if the British burn the city? What if the militia sets fire to it, to burn out the British? You can't leave them here to burn."

"Proctor?" his mother pleaded. "Proctor, you can't leave me alone again."

He kept his eyes on Deborah.

Her eyes never wavered from his.

"You can't leave me alone, Proctor," his mother said again, rising to her feet, so weak she almost fell over. She braced herself against the table to stay upright. "I went to your father's funeral alone, with no family at all to stand beside me.

I can't go on alone, Proctor. The farm is yours now, you can do whatever you want to with it, only come home, please come home."

"Honor your mother, boy," his aunt said. "And honor the memory of your father. Ask yourself what he would want you to do. He'd want you to look after your family."

He continued to look into Deborah's eyes; she continued to look back.

"Your father died of a broken heart," his mother said. "You were the world to him, Proctor. After you left, whenever he had a lucid moment, he would sit up in his chair and call for you, he would call your name, and it broke his heart that you never came running."

Her voice cracked, and she started crying pitifully. Proctor felt a lump form in his own throat.

Still, his eyes and Deborah's eyes had not wavered.

"Go home," Deborah said. Her face was dry now, her voice firm and strong.

She had lost both her parents, to murder and to worse, and their killers were still free. Proctor could have saved them—he was right there at her father's side and had failed him. He swallowed the lump in his throat, wanting to speak, but it stuck there.

"Go home, to the people who love you, who need you," she said. "It's where you belong. You've earned it."

"It's the only right thing to do," his aunt said. "Everyone will understand that you must take care of your family first, no matter what other wars and disturbances are going on. There are plenty of other men who can do the awful fighting."

Other men to do the awful fighting? Proctor remembered the way Amos's skull appeared behind his flesh, the way the militiamen guarded their posts unaware that they were merely skeletons waiting to discover they were already dead. And he was the only one who could see that. Who could maybe do something about it.

So much more than his family was at stake. And there were no other men.

He reached down and took hold of the handle. Turning, he said to them, "It's not done yet, and there isn't anyone else to see it through."

"Don't be selfish, boy," his aunt said.

"Proctor—" His mother's voice quavered.

"I'll come back for you when we're done," he said, then added, "if I can."

"Proctor, if you walk out that door," his mother said, "don't bother to come back. You'll be dead to me. I'll sell the farm—Lucas Bundam is interested in buying it, he came to see me after your father's funeral. I'll have to sell it, to take care of Sarah and myself."

"I understand," Proctor said. "You best do what you need to do then."

"Don't be a fool," his aunt said. "Here, you've had a hard night, clearly. You're not speaking from reason. Rest until morning, and then it will all look different."

"It won't look any different in the morning," he said. "Unless it looks worse."

He thumbed the latch and cracked the door open.

"I'm sorry, Mother, for letting you down, and for missing Father's funeral. If I don't see you again, I hope you will not think too poorly of me."

Her hands were balled in fists, hanging like knots on the ends of two thick ropes. "No loving son would ever walk out that door. If you do it—"

Unable to listen to the rest of her threat, not wanting to remember her that way, he walked out the door.

A wail came from the room behind him, followed by the mixed voice of his aunt, trying to calm his mother, and calling back after him.

Deborah was right behind him in the street. He didn't know where he was going, so when he reached the corner he stopped.

"It's not too late to go back," she told him.

"It was too late to go back the night they sent those men dressed as Indians to kill your father."

"But *your* father—"

"My father lived a long life and died peacefully in his sleep. Others haven't been—won't be—so fortunate."

"But your mother needs you, and I know you've always looked to the day when you could claim the farm as your own. This doesn't have to be your responsibility."

He raised his fist, wanting to punch a sack of grain, even a wall—anything to expel the furious energy built up inside him—and saw the he still had his hat, crumpled in his hand. He'd forgotten to put it on when they left the house, just like Deborah, used to wearing a cap, had forgotten to take hers off inside.

"Those people, whoever they are, who did that to your mother and father, they're evil, Deborah," he said. "Somebody has to stop them."

"I will."

"And you think you can do it alone?"

She paused. "I don't think your help will make any difference in the end."

"Maybe not," he admitted, and the need to hit something drained out of him a bit. At least, the need to hit something random. "But all those men out there, Deborah, they don't know that." He lowered his voice. "Something magic is killing them, but they have no idea, and wouldn't believe it if you told them."

"But—" she said.

"No, let me finish—they wouldn't believe it, but I know, because of things I've seen. Yeah, I'd like to go back to the farm, and the life I had before. My mother, my aunt, they'll find some way to get by. But now I see there's something bigger, and I have to try to do something about it, even if I fail."

"Proctor," Deborah said, "I understand. I just wanted to say—"

Another voice across the street called, "Proctor?"

Someone stepped from the shadows. The silhouette was familiar, but he couldn't put a name to it. He stepped protectively closer to Deborah.

"Oh my God, Proctor, that *is* you."

Her voice trailed off as she came nearer. A young woman in clothes as girlish as Deborah's were boyish, her dark curls spilling from under her cap.

"Emily," he said. "What are you doing here?"

"Father received a letter from Captain Danvers. It said you had been smuggled into Boston. I knew your aunt lived here, so I came looking for you. I know it's after curfew, but—"

"Oh," Deborah said in a small voice, the pieces finally clicking together. "You're Emily Rucke."

Emily didn't hear her. Words were tumbling out of her mouth. "—I haven't been able to stop thinking about you, Proctor, not for a single day. I don't ever want to go that long without seeing you again."

Deborah stepped quietly away from him.

"Deborah?" he said.

Proctor never finished his explanation. Half a dozen men ran out of the darkness at them. The screams of the young women were cut off by rough hands. A stave glanced off the side of Proctor's head. He swung back, feeling one satisfying impact of his fist with someone's face before the other staves hit him, and then the fists, until he was compliant enough to let them gag him and bind his wrists and throw him into a carriage.

Chapter 21

Deborah's body slammed into his. He twisted, trying to pry himself upright, but they were wedged between the two seats. Someone grabbed their legs and folded them inside, them slammed the door.

He was bent in half, with Deborah's elbows in his ribs. She tried to rise, crushing his chest and shoving the breath from his lungs. He groaned through his gag and she stopped. He sucked air through his nose and tried to think clearly, find some way out.

Outside the carriage, a man spoke to Emily. "Miss, you were mistaken, this isn't your friend."

"But I saw—"

"What you saw was a rebel spy, pretending to be someone your father knows. But he is nothing of the sort. He's a cold-blooded murderer who killed two of His Majesty's soldiers on a farm outside Salem."

The voice sounded familiar to Proctor, but he couldn't place it. Something about the tone or tenor of it had changed.

"But the other boy, he called him Proctor—that's Proctor Brown, I know him."

"Shh, now, miss, you want to keep your voice down. It's dark out, isn't it?"

"But—"

"You don't know what or who you saw, not in the dark, not truly."

There were other ways to reshape memory, and not all of

them were magic. Proctor began to shift and twist away from Deborah. If he could just free his legs—

"He looked like the Proctor I know."

"Only because you wanted him to be your friend, Miss Rucke. In reality, he is an evil man, abusing your friend's good name to take advantage of your father's reputation."

Proctor tried to shout through the gag, *"Emily, it's me,"* but his words were unintelligible.

"My father received a letter," Emily said. "From Captain Danvers—that's how I knew to come looking for him."

"I'm afraid this murderer deceived Captain Danvers too."

"If I could just see him in person—"

Yes, thought Proctor. He tried to shout again, and kicked his feet against the sides of the coach to draw her attention. Deborah grunted as he kneed her accidentally.

"I'm sorry, miss, but he's too dangerous."

The door swung open, and a fist came at him like a blacksmith's hammer. He twisted his head from side to side to avoid it, but one blow clipped his jaw, sent his head cracking into the edge of the seat.

"—see, if he was your friend, would he be fighting that way? No, he does that because he's a spy and he knows the penalty for spies is hanging."

A hand slapped a horse's rump, the wheels creaked, and the carriage lurched into motion. Proctor struggled one last time to scream out around his gag.

"—Duncan will escort you back to your father's house. A young lady such as yourself shouldn't be out after curfew—"

The voices faded in the distance, hidden by the steady clop of hooves as the carriage rolled through Boston's streets. He stopped struggling and fell still, except to continue panting through his nose. The tight confines of the carriage pressed in on three sides. He was suddenly aware of the weight of Deborah's body on top of him, the way her legs were tangled in his, and the faint scent of rosewater on her throat.

He shifted his shoulders, pushed his head back, and turned his neck so that he could see her face. The gag was drawn so tight it cut gouges in her cheeks. Her eyes were wide with apprehension.

They bumped along, their faces inches apart, unable to speak. The pace of the carriage slowed—too soon! Proctor had no chance to think of escape, to conjure a way free. He chafed his cheek on the edge of the seat, trying to loosen his gag, but to no avail. He couldn't pull out of his bonds, so he felt around for Deborah's hands, trying to undo hers. She grasped the idea at once, and rolled to the side to try to do the same for him.

The hooves clopped slower but with more determination. The carriage tilted uphill, and Deborah rolled back onto Proctor, dislodging his fingers almost as soon as they found purchase in her knots. She shifted from side to side, scooting down for a better position. Her hand slipped past his ropes and closed around his fingers.

The door opened and a man reached in, grabbing her by the back of her collar and yanking her out. A moment later, hands grabbed Proctor by his ankles and dragged him half out of the vehicle before fists closed on his vest and jerked him to his feet.

They were near the summit of the largest hill in Boston, Beacon Hill. A low stone wall stretched along the road. The wooden fence that lined the wall was smashed; only a few broken pickets remained, sharp and stark, atop the stone.

Behind the fence rose the largest mansion Proctor had ever seen. Brown stone walls rose three stories, fortress-like. Shutters hung open, exposing shattered windows with a few shards of glass standing like the pickets on the wall. An empty balcony with an iron railing extended over the main entrance like an abandoned watchtower.

He turned to find Deborah, relieved to see her silhouette standing but a few feet away. She was hunched forward a bit, but otherwise appeared unharmed.

One of their captors held a lantern, the light moving as he walked around the coach. As this source of illumination fell on Deborah's face, it revealed a streak of bright blood pouring from her nose, staining the rag that filled her mouth. She was struggling to breathe.

He started toward her instinctively.

A man behind him grabbed his jacket, pulling him short. A hard shove sent him toward the tall wooden gate that hung broken on its hinges.

"That rebel John Hancock, he don't have much use for it now, so we thought we'd borrow it," one man taunted Proctor, chuckling.

"Shut your mouth and take them to the cabin out back," the familiar voice said. It was less respectful than it had been to Emily, and Proctor almost felt he could place it. It was too dark to see the man's face. Three or four others were similarly hidden by shadow. The man who held the lantern was thick-featured, with piggish eyes, a stranger to Proctor.

Using hands and sticks, the men shoved Proctor and Deborah up the steps in front of the house; herded by blows and cuffs like dumb animals, they stumbled around the main house and its wings, past the huge carriage house, and across the gardens to a few small cabins.

The man with the lantern led them to the first of these and opened the door. Proctor ducked his head as he passed through the low frame into the single room, and Deborah followed. Mud caulked the log walls, all of it dull brown in the lantern light. The room was empty, even the cold, ashy hearth, but the room still felt close and stifling.

A man put his hand in Deborah's back and shoved her across the small room—she tried to cushion herself with her bound arms, but she banged into the wall and fell toward the floor.

Proctor lowered his shoulder and slammed the culprit into the door frame. He brought one of his knees up into the man's groin and watched him double over.

The second beating was worse. He dropped his chin to his chest, tried to cover his face, but in an instant he was on the ground, with shoes pounding his thighs and back and shoulder.

"Hold off that, you fools," called the familiar voice, and the man waded in, tossing others aside. "Nance wants this pair, and Nance'll have 'em."

The door closed before Proctor could roll over for a look at his face. He and Deborah were alone in the dark cabin.

Deborah crawled over to him, gripped her gag with her bound hands, and, with a suppressed grunt, pulled it over her chin. "Are you all right?"

His reply was muffled until she removed his gag the same way. "Been better," he said between deep breaths.

They worked at the knots for what felt like hours, not daring to speak, twitching at every sound at the door or outside. The air changed outside as they worked; the sky shone through chinks of missing mud.

Deborah's ropes came off first, pulled loose enough to slip over her small hands. With shaking fingers, she undid Proctor's bonds. As soon as they came off, he helped her to her feet and they ran to the door.

His hand chilled to ice when he touched the latch to open it. He couldn't budge it, and the longer he tried, the more numb his hand became. But he couldn't stop trying either. His thoughts grew very fuzzy—he needed to open the door, but he couldn't remember why. He kept shaking the latch.

"What's wrong?" she whispered.

"I'm not sure," he said.

"Let me try," she said, pushing him aside. As soon as contact was broken, his head seemed clear again. She touched the latch then pulled back her hand as if scalded.

"It's spelled," she said.

She shuffled over to the cabin's one small window. She touched the sill more tentatively than she had the latch, but the reaction was the same, and she jerked her hand away.

"What kind of spell is it?" he asked.

"Binding spells," she said. "More than one, and more complex than any I've ever attempted or heard described. There's something insidious about them."

"Once I tried to open the latch, I couldn't stop trying," he said.

"I felt that too, like a pin drawn to a magnet—I think it would have held you in that same spot until Nance returned to release you."

They searched the room carefully, every crack and corner, every board on the floor, every beam of the ceiling. Any attempt to find a way out would freeze or paralyze the person attempting it. Hours passed, with sunlight rising in the sky. The view out their window was of the orchard, where only birds came and went. Through a crack in the wall, they saw a boy driving Hancock's flock of a hundred turkeys out of the barn for the day. When they tried to call to him, their tongues froze to their mouths, like Proctor's hand had frozen to the latch.

Deborah grew panicked. She pried mud out of the wall and pounded it to dust, trying to use it as a focus. She spread it in a circle around the door latch. When she started to speak an opening spell, something knocked her down and left her groggy.

When she came to, he forbid her from trying to cast a spell again, and got a glare for his concern. He cast the next spell, with the same result. More attempts left them exhausted and hopeless, and they lay down on the floor, apart from each other, and tried to sleep.

By nightfall, hunger, thirst, and hopelessness were the only sensations left to them as they sat, propped against the walls, in the corners opposite the door.

"Maybe Nance means to leave us here until we die," Proctor said.

"It's cruel," Deborah said. "I was cleaning out the barn one spring and found an old butter churn with two dead mice in it. They had climbed inside and then couldn't climb back out. We're nothing but mice to Nance. Maybe he's already forgotten us."

"No, he'll come," Proctor said. His throat was dry, and speaking made his lips crack. "Otherwise, he could have just cut our throats. When he comes, how can we defeat him? The severing spell you mentioned?"

"If he can cast binding spells like this, if he can cast the sickness spell on the militia, I—" She shook her head, then covered her eyes and crawled away from Proctor.

They sat silent for a while. The scab on her lip, where her nose had been bleeding, was dark and cracked. Finally, Proctor said, "Deborah, if . . ."

"If what?"

He didn't want to bring himself to say *if we die*. He didn't want to die yet. But he felt like there were things he had to explain to her, just in case, especially about Emily. He didn't know how to say them.

"Your mother," she said.

"What?"

"Is she always like that?"

He had to think about it for a moment. The conversation with her seemed to have happened weeks or months before. "She was a bit distraught."

Deborah choked back a laugh. "She really would have gotten on well with my mother. What a pair." Tears welled up suddenly in her eyes, and her voiced dropped. "Light help me, I only pray it's quick, when it comes."

He nodded in numb agreement.

They heard voices outside, in the distance, and, after a little while, the sound of drums. Boston Commons sat below the hill; the Redcoats were stationed there. Neither Proctor nor Deborah stirred to see what they were up to, not even when the noises continued.

The latch rattled, and the door opened. A man stepped inside, holding a lantern in one hand. The other aimed a shotgun at the two of them. "Stay where you are," he said. "Don't try to get up, or you won't be able to ever again."

They both sat where they were, but Proctor started to make plans to take the gun from him. If there was some distraction—

A second man carried in an ornate chair and set it in the corner near the door. It had a stuffed cushion covered in dark green velvet, and gilding on the carved arms. A third man brought in wood and tinder and put it in the hearth, though he did not light it. Then all three stepped out again, the man with the shotgun leaving last. He set the lantern down as he left; it cast a feeble light across the planked floor.

The door remained cracked open. Proctor met Deborah's eyes, saw wonder and confusion in them, and then, without a word, pushed himself to his feet.

An elderly woman dressed all in black stepped through, a long-stemmed pipe in her hand. Proctor froze, his heart thumping.

It was the widow.

Proctor launched himself across the room at her.

She flicked the pipe stem at the pieces of rope and the gags they'd left abandoned on the floor. In midair, Proctor felt his hands drawn together against his will, his tongue pushed back in his mouth. He fell to the floor, bound as surely as he had been in the carriage. He rolled over to his side.

Deborah sat in the corner, trembling, knees drawn to her chest, her wrists crossed as though bound, her mouth pulled back by an invisible gag.

The widow walked languidly over to the chair and arranged herself in it. She flicked her pipe stem at the hearth, and flame leapt from the tinder and jumped to the logs.

"Jolly," she called, and Proctor thought she meant her mood, but one of her men stuck his head in the door.

"Yes, ma'am," the familiar voice said.

Now that he saw the man's face, Proctor recognized him at once: he was the escaped "Indian" from the attack on

Deborah's farm. His left shoulder was wrapped, his left arm bound up in a sling inside his jacket. He glared at Proctor as if he'd be more than happy to kill him then and there. Proctor started to laugh behind his gag, convulsing on the floor. The first part of their plan was working to perfection: they'd come into Boston and found their enemies, the people who wanted them dead.

"Fetch the other items now," the widow demanded, giving Proctor a curious sidelong look. Jolly ducked his head and started to withdraw, but she called him back. "And take that lantern with you. I prefer an open flame."

"Yes, Missus Nance."

Proctor's eyes met Deborah's and they both understood. *Mrs. Nance.* The widow was not the servant of the person who'd been hunting them; she was the master.

When Jolly left, she rose from her seat, went to the door, and closed it. Then, reaching into the deep pockets of her simple dress, she pulled forth a string of dried meats, pork rinds or something similar. Proctor's mouth began to water, and his stomach clenched.

Holding the string aloft, the widow paced the circuit of the room, stepping carefully around Deborah, murmuring in a language that sounded like a wind in a desert. When she stepped around Proctor, he saw that she was holding a string of severed ears.

He choked on the gag, trying not to retch.

She slipped the gruesome strand back into her pocket and, with a brief glance at Proctor, turned toward Deborah. A smile struggled upward at one corner of her mouth.

"The advantage of dead languages," she said, "is that it's harder for other witches to steal your spells. It will be a little while before Jolly returns. That will give us a bit of privacy, so that I may speak openly to you. Now, let's see what we have here."

Reaching out with her left thumb, she flicked the scab off

Deborah's lip. Deborah winced as fresh blood flowed, but the widow closed her eyes and inhaled deeply.

"It's in the blood," she said.

Anger shot through Proctor as he saw the fear on Deborah's face. The widow just laughed.

"And they thought you were a boy. 'We followed Emily Rucke just like you said, and she led us to that fellow from the Quaker farm,'" she said mockingly. "'But he's got a boy with him.'" She drew out the vowel: *boooooooy*. "'What do you want us to do with the boooooooy?'"

She tugged the cap off Deborah's head, and her hair tumbled out; either Proctor's haircut had been bad, or Deborah's spell was broken, but she didn't look at all boyish. Deborah tried to twist away. The widow wrapped one hand around the back of her neck and scrubbed her face clean with the rough fabric of the cap.

"Too proud to cry, are you? That's a good sign, my friend." She chuckled at her little joke. Even when she smiled, the corners of her mouth strained down. "*My friend,* that's a good one."

When she turned and walked back over to her chair, she looked like any other old woman. Taking the seat, she arranged her skirt as carefully as if she'd been sitting in the receiving room of the finest palace.

She put the pipe to her mouth. With one word it was filled, and with another word, a coal flared and it was lit. She puffed on it meditatively. The scent of the smoke was sweeter than regular tobacco, making Proctor's empty stomach churn in protest.

After a moment, she released a deep sigh that spun out in a wisp of smoke.

"We can call this a conversation, if you please, or even an interview, if you prefer," she told Deborah. "But the simple fact is that I'm going to talk and you're going to listen. Then, depending on the course our conversation takes, I may permit you to make a choice regarding your own fate. Or then again, I may not. Did you have any luck trying to escape?"

Proctor pushed himself upright and sat against the wall. He looked at Deborah, but her eyes were fixed on the widow, less afraid now and more angry.

"I would have been very impressed had you been able to escape. But as you may have guessed, these are Hancock's slave quarters, and slave quarters make a powerful focus for binding spells. Much better, for example, than ribbons and nails."

She pronounced *ribbons and nails* contemptuously, though Proctor recalled they had bound her well enough.

"Of course, Hancock's *mansion*"—again, the word dripped contempt—"is a hovel compared with the palaces I've been in—it's barely fit to house the meanest servants at West Wycombe Park. But you pitiful bumpkins, stinking of horseshit and pig fat, have no idea where West Wycombe Park is, and you wouldn't recognize Baron le Despencer if he showed up in a golden chariot with angels trumpeting his arrival."

Proctor used her speech to scoot along the wall toward the fireplace. If Jedediah had knocked her unconscious with a shovel, he might be able to do the same with a log—

She made a low clucking sound with her tongue. "Don't even think about it, boy."

Shock must have registered in his face—was she truly reading his mind? Deborah's glance pleaded with him not to do anything foolish.

The widow chuckled and blew smoke rings at him.

"With but one word to Lord Percy," she said—and Proctor wondered if she meant a word in the sense he had always known it, or a word of power, like the one that compelled her pipe to light—"we could be having this interview in the comfort of Hancock's parlor. But I prefer his slave quarters. There's a certain lingering stink sweated out of men and women who never have their freedom, a misery that soaks into the wood and soil, even the very cloth, that touches their daily life." She inhaled deeply. "It smells like power."

The widow rocked back and forth in her chair, puffing on her pipe.

If he ran at her, knocked her down or knocked her out, or got on her chest and pressed his weight against her until she couldn't breathe, then he could find a way to free himself and Deborah. They would only have to get past Jolly and any other guards outside, then flee to some other part of the city.

She lifted her head and stared him straight in the eyes, daring him to try. His blood turned to slush. Speaking to Deborah, she said, "You could have that kind of power, if you want it."

Deborah recoiled against the wall.

"Don't pretend to be so righteous and pure. Cecily told me about your wild youth, some of the things you did, nearly ruining your mother's precocious little industry."

Proctor could look only at Deborah, but she carefully avoided returning his gaze.

"The thing is, you stupid, uneducated puritan farmers have deflected my blows three times. First, by undoing the protective medallion I made for Major Pitcairn. It was a minor charm, easy to repair, but it brought you to my attention. Cecily thought your mother incapable of that, but she knew of your association with the rebels and swore to me that it was you. I was very impressed. It's the only reason you're still alive. Otherwise, I'd be happy to be rid of your entire bunch of pathetic healers."

Deborah's gaze avoided Proctor now for a different reason. He watched the widow to see if she noticed.

"Second, I know that it was your mother who drew my fire into her—nice trick, that. But it was you who saw her burning, and sent it down the well."

His gaze whipped back to Deborah—she had done that?

Deborah gave her a weak shake of her head. The widow laughed.

"Yes, it was you." She snapped her fingers. "I saw you do it just that quick, with no other focus than the power of your will. If I hadn't been distracted by that, the way you did it, that stinking pig farmer never would have cracked my skull. I would have defeated your binding spells in time, even without the help of your familiar." She indicated Proctor with a lift of her chin. "But they were good work too, for someone essentially untrained."

She leaned back in her chair.

"Anyone can be lucky twice, but you beat me a third time. Cecily performed her master's piece for me, animating Jolly's companions so they could finish the work your lumpkin wrecked. But once again, that spell was undone. Very impressive work, girl. Once may be chance, twice may be luck, but three times is skill."

Deborah shook her head more vigorously this time, stealing a glance at Proctor.

"Girl," the widow sneered. "I can sense the magic you're attempting. Don't even try it, or I will smack you down like a puppy that nips its master at the table. I could sever you in an instant, but I want your skill."

The fire in the hearth flared, shooting sparks into the room. The widow stood and went to the window.

"Do you want to live your whole life in this dirty country of pig farms and ramshackle villages? Or do you want to take your rightful place in the world? Do you want to be a master or a slave?"

She had her back turned, giving Proctor the chance he'd been waiting for. He ducked his head like a battering ram and charged her.

Without looking up, she flicked her pipe stem to one side and he was flung across the room, banging his chin on the rough log wall, filling his mouth with the taste of blood.

"The Covenant of Witches belongs to no country, girl. We exist in every country, spreading our invisible empire across the globe. My master sent me here to put down this simpleton's backwater rebellion. It is not in our interest to see the British empire weakened. But I found something in this pitiful barbaric country that I did not expect: I found power. Cecily has some, but you have so much more."

She walked over and grabbed a handful of Deborah's poorly cut hair, arching her head back.

"Cecily has ambition too. The question is, do you? Do you have the will to become one of the Twelve who serve me? To become one of the masters instead of one of the slaves?"

Proctor watched Deborah closely for her response. Deep in his heart, he knew the alternative was death, so part of him hoped Deborah took the widow's offer. If she survived today, she could escape tomorrow, or another day.

There was a tap at the door. The widow tossed Deborah's head aside almost casually and went to answer it.

Proctor stared at Deborah, trying to catch her eye. *Accept the widow's offer,* he pleaded with her silently, hoping she understood. *Do what you must, but stay alive.*

Deborah lay still, breathing hard, her eyes closed.

Chapter 22

The widow opened the door. Jolly stomped in, unshaven, smelling like whiskey. His good hand clutched a bayonet as well as a struggling, kicking ten-year-old boy. The boy's curly hair was tangled and unkempt, his secondhand shirt hung almost to his knees, and his feet were bare and dirty.

"Lemme goooooooo!" he howled.

The widow slapped the boy hard across his face as casually as she'd tossed aside Deborah. "Quit your whining," she said calmly.

Putting a hand to his reddened cheek, he stared up at her wide-eyed, mouth shut. Proctor wanted to scream at him to run, but he couldn't force the words past the muffle of his gag.

"Will he suit?" she asked.

Jolly nodded. "He's orphaned, father dead at sea, mother dead of a fever this year past. He's been a servant in three households, but ran away from the first two. Hancock took him in as an act of charity, put him to work in the stables, left him behind when he left town."

"I still do my chores," the boy said.

"Good," the widow answered, but whether to Jolly or the boy was unclear. She nodded absently, already turning away. Jolly shoved the boy toward the corner opposite Deborah, and he stumbled to the floor.

Proctor struggled to one knee—if he couldn't touch the widow, he could at least knock down her bully. But Jolly punched his chin, sending him to the floor.

"That one was for me," Jolly said, pulling his fist back to hit him again. "This one is for my mates—"

"Enough," the widow cried. "I need him sensible and whole for my spell to work."

"Yes, ma'am," Jolly said.

"Where's the rest of it?"

He reached outside the door and carried in a bowl, balancing it against his chest. Inside the bowl was a small embroidered bag and several candles.

"Set it by the hearth," she said. She pointed her pipe stem at Proctor. His skin tingled, and a knot shifted low in his belly. She swept the pipe through the air, pointing it to the center of the room, and Proctor's body slid across the floor to the exact spot.

He lay there, panting through his nose, feeling sick again. He'd taken too many blows, gone too long without food or water. He didn't know how much longer he could keep fighting.

Jolly watched Proctor's movement with a wild gleam in his eye, something like lust, Proctor thought. Keeping his gaze on Proctor, he went and pulled another bag through the door, then shut it, taking up a guard's position beside it.

The curly-haired boy gulped a few times, cowering in the corner. Deborah sat quiet and helpless in hers.

The widow set her pipe on a ledge by the fire, lifted the bag, and undid the drawstrings. She plunged her hand inside and removed a scoopful of salt, glittering and crystalline. "Pay attention," she told Deborah. "This is salt from the sea, for an empire that spans all seas. It was very clever of you to use my own salt to bind me before."

She poured it in a circle around Proctor, stretching out almost to the edges of the room. That much, Proctor thought, was no different than Deborah's mother had done with her magic on the farm.

When she was done, she knotted the bag and placed it

back by the hearth. Taking the large bowl, she stepped over to the boy cowering in the corner.

"That's a good lad," she said. "Are you a wicked boy, or a good lad?"

His knees were drawn up to his chest. He nodded hesitantly, eyes wide with fear. "I'm a good boy."

She smiled toward Deborah. "He's a good lad." She placed the bowl in front of the boy, saying, "Behave just a moment longer, and we'll be done with you, all right?"

He nodded again, more enthusiastically.

"Good, that's a good lad. Now lean forward for me, so I can see your pretty hair. You have very pretty hair, my lamb. Have you been told that before?"

"Yes, ma'am, my mother used to say so." He uncurled his knees and rose up straight, tilting his dirty face up so she could see it.

"Bend forward a bit, so I can see it better," she said. "We're almost done."

As he bent forward, she removed a knife from her sleeve. Deborah's muffled cry of anguish pierced the room as the blade slid across the boy's throat. The widow held up his head as his blood spurted into the bowl. He kicked once, then twitched, then hung limp and still while she drained him. She did it calmly, and smoothly, wasting no motion and spilling no blood but in the bowl. The knot in Proctor's stomach twisted again: he was sure she'd done this before.

The blood in the bowl reminded Proctor of the eggs his mother used for scrying. Both represented a sacrificial offering of life . . .

While the blood poured, an image began to form in front of Proctor's face—militiamen on a hillside—gunfire, smoke—their backs as they ran away, retreating—he looked down and he saw blood on his hands.

Jolly chuckled and inched forward for a closer look at

the widow's work. "Don't break the circle," she snapped at him, and he fell back.

The images dissipated and disappeared. Proctor didn't know what he was supposed to see. Blood on his hands? He still didn't trust his scrying, and he especially didn't trust anything touched by this kind of evil.

Finished with the boy, the widow bent him back into the corner and stroked his curly hair. "Such a pretty, pretty lamb," she murmured.

His paled face stared up at the sky, seeing nothing. She wiped the knife on his shirt, leaving long red streaks in the dusty linen, then tucked it back into her sleeve.

Rising with the bloody bowl in her hands, she stepped over the line of salt, carefully so as not to break it, and stood inside the circle. She set the bowl down again, a few feet from Proctor's head, where he could not reach it to spill it. Then she removed a small wand from her other sleeve. The wood looked like blackthorn, worn smooth with age and use. There were several unnatural twists in the middle.

Tilting her head toward Deborah, she said, "This is the blood of a servant, that all the world may be bent to serve us."

So saying, she dipped the wand in the bowl and cast a line of blood across the floor. She dipped and cast again. The third line splashed drops across Proctor's cheek. The liquid was warm when it hit him, and he felt it run, leaving a trail down his throat.

As she continued to work, the widow explained to Deborah, "This is the five-point star signifying the force of our will. Each point breaks the edge of the circle, so that our will might break the natural order and cycle of events to create a new order."

Again, she moved carefully and precisely, her wand rising and falling as she cast the lines of her drawing. Although his head throbbed with pain, Proctor's vision had cleared, and with it his thoughts. When she came to him, he was not going to go as easily as that poor boy had.

She finished and moved the bowl outside the circle, pausing to wipe her wand on the boy's shirt just as she had the knife. Picking up her pipe, she gestured with it and the coals stirred in the hearth until a few blazed red. Then she held a taper to the coals; when it flamed, she lit a candle and placed it at one point of the star.

Proctor held his breath against the odor as she lit the next three candles. They didn't smell sweet like the candles his mother used; instead, they reeked of something like whale oil, but less wholesome. Perhaps the fat of some other animal.

She held the fifth candle to Deborah as she lit it. "The fire carries the will of our spirit, by light and smoke, into the world to make our will take flesh."

Deborah grimaced and shut her eyes, turning her face away. Proctor was glad to see her struggle.

But the widow only chuckled and placed the candle in the last spot. "I also turned my face away, the first time my master showed me the rites. But once I witnessed her power, and saw the futility of my own life wasted, I changed my mind. Jolly?"

He seemed startled by being directly addressed. "Yes, ma'am?"

"Where are the other items I requested?"

"Here," he said, indicating the spot where he'd dropped them by the door. Proctor twisted his head around. He saw a flint bag, like the one he carried in the militia, and the bayonet, and a scrap of paper.

"I mean hand them to me, the musket ball first," she said. "And mind that you don't break the circle."

He knuckled his head, as if saluting a superior officer. Retrieving a ball from the flint bag, he leaned over the circle and held it out to the widow.

She rolled up Proctor's sleeve before taking the lead ball. "I'm so glad you came," she whispered to him. "Before now, I was relying on my spell to make the colonials sick, too weak to fight. But now that I have a real minuteman in my grasp, someone who's already fought the British, I have the focus I need to break them utterly. And a witch, no less, someone with the power in his blood."

Proctor wanted to fight, wanted to protest, but he could feel her draw on him, pulling on his power. Then fire shot down his forearm—she'd slashed his skin with her knife.

He had intended to struggle, but weakness flooded him, the way it had when she'd touched him through the shed door on Emerson's farm. Deborah made a muffled cry and struggled against her bonds in the corner.

"You feel that, do you?" the widow asked, with a glance at Deborah. "I am borrowing your strength now too. Pay close attention. This is a difficult spell, cast to affect men who are not present, on land that is at some distance. If Boston were not connected to the mainland by The Neck, it might not work at all."

She pressed the lead ball into the top end of Proctor's slashed forearm and slowly rolled it down the length of cut toward his hand. His breath came in ragged nasal gasps. Sweat rolled off his forehead, stinging his eyes.

"This English ball is bathed in rebel blood—in the coming battle, may it draw all balls from English muskets toward the blood of the rebels, to strike them down in their insolence and insubordination."

She dropped the lead ball. It thumped on the wooden planks and rolled a foot away. Proctor had to force himself to breathe, despite the stench of the candles, in order to gather his strength.

"Jolly, the bayonet."

He held it out for her as she rolled up Proctor's other sleeve. This time he made himself watch as she pressed the tip of it into his skin and slid it along his forearm, splitting his flesh. He grunted and tried to twist away, but he was as weak as a baby.

The bayonet had three edges, to create a wound that wouldn't heal. She pressed each sharp edge, in turn, into the open wound. His vision blurred and spots swam before his eyes.

"This English bayonet is bathed in rebel blood, so that in the coming battle, every thrust of an English bayonet may find blood, to pierce the heart of rebellion and by the piercing end it."

More than weakness had taken root in Proctor now. A chill surged through him, like winter winds pushing through the cracks in a bad window. He shivered, and only the invisible gag in his mouth kept his teeth from chattering.

An image came back to him like an echo from some distant mountain: a hillside, defended by the militia, as musket balls filled the air around them.

He could see the men falling under fire.

He could see their fallen bodies bayoneted.

He saw the survivors fleeing.

"The commission," she said.

"It's a blank commission," Jolly said, handing over the paper. "Copied from an original."

The paper crackled in her hand as she unrolled it and studied the writing. "Perfect," she said. "If it were a specific commission, the spell would work only for that one man."

The paper ripped loudly as she tore it in half, pressing each separate piece into one of Proctor's bleeding wounds. She turned and fed the first bloody piece into the flame of the nearest candle, holding it up as it burned. When only a corner remained, she flicked it into the air and the ash spun around until the flame burned it to nothing and vanished. She did the same with the second piece.

"Let those who hold commissions be the first to fall. Let them be soaked in blood, and then be destroyed. Let the army be leaderless, like a ship without a rudder, unable to steer itself toward any shore."

Her face was beatific, as though she had prayed for a blessing of rain and saw the clouds form overhead. She smiled down at Proctor, and he could not tell her age. Though her eyes seemed as old as his mother's, or older, her face was free of wrinkles but for the corners of her eyes, and her mouth curved like a young girl's.

"This is the last part," she said, softly, stroking Proctor's hair just as she had stroked the boy's. He tensed to kick her, hoping for a lucky strike with his knee or foot, but the life force drained from him more completely than ever before. She was drawing on him, drawing on his magic, every drop of it, for her next act. He could feel it flowing out of him, but he didn't know how to stop it.

She held the killing knife in her left hand. Up close, it was shorter than he expected, and curved like a sickle.

"With the death of this rebel, let there be fear of death among all rebels," she whispered to Proctor, still smiling.

Energy poured from him now, like water gushing through a broken dam. She tugged open his shirt, and he tried to drive his elbow into her, but it lay dead against his side.

"When this knife pierces his heart, let fear pierce the heart of all the rebels." She placed the point of the knife between his ribs, and pressed one hand on the hilt to push it home. "As the soul flees this mortal shell, let men flee the battlefield in fear for their own flesh and souls."

This was his last chance. He grunted with all the force of life left in him and rolled away from her, thrusting his knees at her side, hoping for something that would give him even a momentary advantage.

He landed a mere six inches away from the tip of her knife. His knees bounced off her and rested still on the ground while he panted through his nose for more breath. He looked for Deborah, but couldn't see her. Maybe he had caused enough of a distraction to allow her to escape.

"Good," the widow murmured, focused entirely on him, drawing on his magic until the pond inside him was dry and the ground beneath was cracked and split. "The greater your courage, the greater their fear."

She leaned forward again. And stopped.

He panted, his eyes wet with tears, so at first he thought he was mistaken. Wrinkles appeared at the corner of the widow's mouth. Her cheeks grew sunken while she stared at her hands, now bent and arthritic. Gray roots appeared at her scalp.

The gray roots lengthened. The hair seemed to flow out of her scalp, like water pouring from a fountain, dusty gray tresses that fell in abrupt cascades about her shoulders, draining toward the floor. Her hands withered and her fingernails grew, first to sharp points, then to cracked edges. The knife fell from her hand with a clatter to the floor and the nails kept growing, curling back on themselves like yellowed snakes, nine or ten inches long, making her hands useless for work.

"You slut," she screamed, turning toward Deborah, who cowered in the corner directly behind her, but the words came out of her mouth like a puff of dust. "You whore, you miserable fat sow!"

The last was no more than the croak of a small frog.

Deborah sat upright, her eyes fierce and fearless, fixed on the widow. Though it was night, she seemed to glow, as if the sun had been poured into her.

The widow, ashen-faced and filthy, like a figure drawn in charcoal, turned toward Deborah. Too weak to rise, she fell forward on her hands and knees. Unable to use her deformed hands, she wriggled forward like a snake, smearing the blood of her star, breaking the salt of her circle, tipping over a candle and extinguishing the flame.

Deborah leaned forward, prepared to meet her, but the widow's body grew smaller with each inch she crawled until she collapsed in a pile of rags at Deborah's feet.

Deborah's face lifted to meet Proctor's eyes, searching to see if he was all right. He felt life flow back into him like the first drops of a welcome rain.

He pulled himself up, tipping away the bloody bayonet between his knees. With that gesture, he realized his hands were free, and his mouth. He crawled toward Deborah, gasping for air through his unblocked mouth.

She stared at the rags, saying, "I didn't mean to. I didn't mean to kill her."

"You did that? Was it a severing spell?"

"Because of you," she said. "She grew so focused on you when you tried to roll away that I was able to pull her magic into me—a circle always flows both ways. But there was so much of it."

"She was far older than she looked," he said, watching the blood run down his slashed arms and over his hands. "Magic must have been the only thing keeping her alive."

"It was horrible," Deborah said. Proctor held her elbow and tried to help her to her feet. "And glorious."

She stood, took a step forward, and collapsed, her body shaking as she vomited. Although her stomach was empty, she heaved again and again, dry spasms that racked her body. Proctor touched her forehead—she was burning with a fever.

"Where's Jolly?" she asked, wiping her mouth.

He followed her gaze and saw the open door. Outside, the boom of cannons echoed from across the bay.

"This isn't over yet, is it?" Proctor asked.

Numbly, Deborah shook her head.

Chapter 23

Proctor looked at the room—the broken drawing, the tipped candle, the pile of dusty rags. He lurched to his feet, kicked over the other four lights, scattered the salt, and stamped out the lines of blood.

Without the candles, the room was dark again, lit only by the glow of the coals in the hearth.

He turned back toward Deborah. The curve of her face glowed red in the light. He held his arms open to her, pleading, as the blood ran from his cuts and dripped from his palms. "Isn't that enough?" he asked. "The widow's dead—won't that break her spell?"

Deborah tried to sit up again, but fell back dizzy, leaned against the wall.

"My mother used to say that the good we do dies with us, but the evil lives long after. She was talking about magic, and this is evil, so evil." She looked at the body of the stable boy, who lay there openmouthed, surprised. "I think this could live much longer."

Outside, the cannons boomed again.

"What can we do?" he said.

"You have to go," she said. She turned her head frantically around the room, crawled to the stable boy and took hold of his shirt, then let go. "You have to go warn them."

"Warn who?"

"The militia." She tugged off her jacket and scrambled across the floor, groping in the near dark until she found the widow's knife. "They won't have a chance unless you do. Come here."

He knelt beside her. "What?"

"Hold out your arms," she said, slashing her lightweight jacket into strips. "Let me bind them up."

Her hands were steady as she wrapped the cloth around his arm and knotted it. She pulled the sleeve down to his wrist when she was done. "There, that'll pass in the dark."

"It itches—"

"A healing spell, the best I can do, I'm sorry it's not more. Give me the other arm."

He didn't want to interrupt her spell, but as soon as she tugged down his other sleeve, he asked, "What difference will a warning make?"

"You're right. A warning's not enough." She sat back, wiping her face, smearing dark lines of his blood across her cheeks. Looking at the scattered pieces of the spell, she said, "The fear—they won't feel any fear, that part of her spell was interrupted, never completed. But we have to counter the rest of it."

Proctor thought of Pitcairn's golden medallion, the one he'd received from the widow. "We could make charms, something to keep them safe."

"But then we'd have to get them there, to the men."

"I can do that," he said, looking around the room for something to charm. He saw the lead ball the widow had dropped on the floor—he didn't want to touch that. But the bag of flints still sat by the door. He ran to it and pulled out a handful of lead balls.

"Can we make these into charms?"

"Those will work," she said. "They'll work perfectly, countering the ball she used for her spell."

Outside, the ship's cannons boomed again. From the commons nearby, they heard the British regulars answer it with a huzzah.

"We don't have much time," he said.

"Give them to me."

He poured the musket balls into her cupped hands, which dropped from the weight. Wrapping his own hands around hers, he helped lift them to her mouth. She whispered into the gap at her thumbs.

"May Thy light shine on these simple balls of lead. If it be Thy will, let them become shields of life rather than takers of life, let no man who bears them fall before his appointed time."

Light flowed down her arms and into her hands. Proctor's skin tingled and all his hair prickled. Inside their cupped hands, the balls glowed for a moment like coals.

Sweat beaded on Deborah's forehead and her eyes blinked, unfocused. It passed, and she leaned back to support herself against the wall.

"Are you all right?" Proctor asked. "Should I find a doctor?"

"I'm fine," she whispered.

"You don't look fine. I'm worried."

"It's just the widow's magic still swimming in me, and all of it tainted like bad water," she said. "Look."

Her hands were open. The lead balls had been transformed into tiny skulls, the irregularities in their surface forming the divots of eyes and noses, lines scored like teeth.

"These will work," she said, thrusting them at Proctor. "They will protect whoever carries them."

He took them and turned them over in his palm in amazement. The enormity of the task ahead hit him then, and he shoved the little skulls into his pocket. "All I need to do now is find a thousand more. At which point, I will be so weighted down that when I try to swim across the bay, I will sink to the bottom, unable to rise."

"There are enough to protect the officers. They're in the most danger from her spell. You must find a way to the battlefield and give them these charms. Protect them."

Proctor nodded and rose. She was right, of course. He offered her his hand to help her up.

She shook her head. "I'm too weak to go anywhere right now. You'll have to do it on your own."

"But—"

"You can do it." Her voice was weak, but full of conviction. She beckoned him close, and he knelt beside her to hear her better.

Placing her hand on his, she leaned her mouth up to his head.

"Keep one charm for yourself," she said, her lips brushing his ear. And then she kissed his cheek.

He felt himself blush. "Do I look like the sort of fellow who's going to put himself in the way of danger?"

Before she could answer, before he could change his mind, he ran out the door.

Cool air washed over him, blessedly fresh.

Cannons boomed at his back and he jumped—the sound traveled clearer out here, the cannons seemed closer. The noise came across the water, from Charlestown, not from the militia lines at Roxbury.

He looked toward the road. Down at the bottom of the hill, British troops marched in formation, the lights they carried glinting off their bayonets. They were headed into the city, not toward The Neck, which meant a staging area for boats. That made sense—the colonials were no match for the Royal Navy.

So he had to get to Charlestown, and the quickest way there was through The Neck.

He smelled horse manure, and where there was horse manure, there had to be horses. He spun around until he saw the stables—so large that at first he took them for an inn or another home.

Inside, they were nearly deserted. He walked from stall to stall, trying not to think of the curly-haired stable boy, never mind the restlessness of the horses. There was a sturdy animal in the first stall, the kind he'd like to have on the farm, but it nipped at his hand. If he had more time, that wouldn't be a problem. The horse in the second stall was a gelding that looked to run like the wind, but the cannons boomed again and it whinnied and shied from him. The sorrel mare in the third stall was swaybacked, built more like the plow horse than the gelding, but she'd have to do.

He spotted the tack at the far end of the stable. He had it in his hands and was carrying it back to the stall when he realized he had nowhere to ride to—if there was a battle tonight, they wouldn't let anyone cross The Neck. Assuming he could talk or force his way through the town gate, by the time he rode the miles around through Roxbury and Cambridge, it might already be too late.

He hurled the saddle down in frustration, and kicked up the straw.

There must be some other way—

He spotted it by the door. He sprinted over and took the broom in his hands, then thrust it between his knees, like a child playing horsey.

"Up!" he said, trying to focus. "Up, up, into the air!"

The broom did nothing.

"Giddyup?" he said, adding a hop.

The mare in the third stall stamped at the ground and craned her neck toward him.

"What're you looking at?" he asked.

The horse snorted.

He leaned the broom against the wall. Maybe he needed a stronger focus—

The door slammed open—a British junior officer stepped in, lean, with a long chin and his hat in his hand. His face was as red as his coat. Proctor balled his fists, prepared to knock down the officer and make his escape before an alarm was raised.

"Stable boy!"

Caught in mid-step, Proctor said, "Yes?"

"That's *yes, sir,* you insolent colonial trash," he said, noticing the saddle on the floor with an air of disgust. "Colonel Jack's horse just threw a shoe. We're requisitioning one of these."

"If you say so."

"Saddle up the best horse and bring it down to the boats or I will return and see you whipped."

As he turned to go, Proctor called out to him, "I'm sorry, but which boats where?"

"The North Battery, and hurry, we're due to embark in half an hour."

"All right," Proctor said.

Lifting his rifle butt, the officer started forward to strike Proctor, probably to make him obey more quickly.

"It'll be harder to do your bidding if I'm lying bloody on the floor," Proctor said.

The officer stopped. "Half an hour—if the colonel has already crossed, you must send the horse after him."

The boats were the quickest way across, maybe the only way. Once there, he'd have to find some way to escape the British and reach the colonial lines without being shot.

The officer was running out the door to rejoin his company on the road. He left the barn door open behind him. The cadence of drums drifted into the room, and then the cannons boomed again, echoing over the water.

Proctor toyed with the notion of saddling up the edgy horse, hoping it might throw its rider. Instead, he went to the third stall and stroked the neck of the mare. "How would you like to go for a ride?"

The horse shook her head as if she understood. In the next stall, the gelding shuffled restlessly and batted the stall door.

"Maybe next time for you," Proctor said as he went to work with the saddle, double-checking each buckle and stay until he was satisfied with it.

When he was done with the work, the mare sidled up next

to him, expecting to be mounted. Proctor shook his head and took her by the bridle instead. "I better lead you to the boats—we don't want to get there too soon."

The horse nudged his hand for a treat.

Proctor rubbed her muzzle. "I'll have to owe you a carrot."

The strength of the horse lent Proctor power as they walked to the docks. The wounds on his arms throbbed, and his head still felt muzzy, his legs weak. Somehow he had to push all that down and keep on going.

It helped that the city was wide awake, with lights in every window and people lining the streets as if it were a parade. The closer he came to the battery, the more the road was packed, slowing his progress. Other boys led horses to other officers or ran forgotten equipment to ordinary soldiers. A plump young woman in an apron, red-cheeked from crying, walked alongside the troops, holding a newborn infant in her arms and encouraging him to say good-bye to his papa.

Proctor started asking for directions. "Where's Colonel Jack? I'm supposed to meet him at the boat."

He repeated the question several times before a squat sergeant with a scar across his face answered him. "He's at the docks—they should be embarking now, if they haven't gone already."

Proctor dallied just enough to give the boats time to depart. As he neared the water, the *boom-boom* of the cannons shelling Charlestown grew louder. Across the dark bay, the masts of the *Lively* lit up in orange relief each time fire jetted from her sides. One boom sounded when the cannons fired, and another when the shells hit, sending up debris and flames onshore. Even across the water, he could see fires spread from one wrecked home to another.

He fell into a line where he saw other horses, making his way down to the shore. Barges loaded with twenty-five or thirty soldiers pushed off and disappeared into the darkness; others came back empty but for the sailors rowing.

His turn came, and he stepped up to the boat. Soldiers pushed past him, jostling the mare in their hurry to board. Cannons boomed at the same instant, and she snorted, pulling away from Proctor.

A sailor in a striped shirt was supervising the boarding. He saw Proctor struggling to calm her, and yelled, "Who's her officer?"

"Colonel Jack," Proctor said

"He's already gone over."

"I'm supposed to take him this horse."

"If he went over without one, he can do without," the sailor said. He held out his hand to block Proctor, and used the other to wave the next group of soldiers aboard.

"If I don't get this to him, his lieutenant is going to come back and beat my hide."

"It's your hide, not mine," the sailor said, shoving a hesitant soldier forward. "Keep moving."

The cannons boomed again and the sound of a great beam cracking echoed across the water.

"Please, sir," Proctor begged.

One of the officers waiting to board stepped forward. "You better give him a hand," he told the sailor. "I saw Colonel Jack's horse back up on the main road—it threw a shoe."

The sailor tossed up his hands in submission and stopped the line, ordering the soldiers off the boat. "Keep her to the center and keep her still," he ordered Proctor.

"Will do," he said.

The mare had been transported by boat before, if only by ferry. She was hesitant to step aboard, but when Proctor backed her up and gave her a few steps' start, she hopped over the low side. The boat rocked, and he struggled to keep his balance. But she stood steady in the center as soldiers packed in around her.

"Push off!" the sailor shouted.

The mare snorted as the boat lurched forward onto the

water, but Proctor stroked her flanks and kept her calm. Maybe he was just keeping himself calm—getting to the other shore was only the first step in stopping the widow's massacre.

"That horse doesn't look like it fights anything, except to get into the oats," said one man.

The young officer, who looked all of seventeen or eighteen, laughed. "It's for Colonel Jack. He'll need a comfortable horse to set upon, all gentleman-like, as we chase the rebels back to Concord."

That brought a few laughs, and a group in the back of the boat shouted "Huzzah!" loud enough to make the horse snort and start forward, rocking the boat. The sailors shouted in protest, the men were shouted down by their fellows, and Proctor gripped the bridle firmly and patted her side, the way he would a plow horse after a long day.

The horse stayed calm for the rest of the ride, even when they passed within a few hundred yards of the booming guns of the *Lively.* They reached the shore, and the sailors were quick to unload Proctor and his charge. The young officer thrust out his hand as Proctor climbed ashore.

"Lieutenant Parry," he said.

Proctor took his hand, too surprised to make up anything. "Proctor Brown."

"You're no horseman—that beast must be the most gentle creature in the world, or it would never have come across for you so easily."

He opened his mouth to answer and Parry laughed at him.

"Still, it shows good sense that you'd picked it for Colonel Jack. He needs a gentle creature. You, however, look like you're made for rougher work. Come call on me at The Grapes in a couple of days, after this rebellion's set to rights, and I'll find something for you in our unit."

"I'm not sure—"

"Of course, but think it over," Parry said. "It'll be a chance to see the world."

With a grin, he was gone and yelling at men who were his age and older, some much older, directing them into their line.

Off to Proctor's left, the town of Charlestown burned in the morning's first light, columns of smoke climbing into the sky like ropes to heaven. Ahead of him, a long slope rose gradually from the water's edge to a peak that overlooked the river. The colonial redoubts, made of hastily thrown-up dirt, could be seen on the peak.

He tugged the bridle gently, pulling the horse's face closer to his. "This is it," he whispered. "Ride like the devil for me, and there's a soft life and all the carrots you can eat until we get you back to your master."

The horse nickered and bent her neck to nudge Proctor's hand and sniff his pockets.

"After we get to safety," he said. He put his foot in the stirrup and pulled himself up into the saddle. Tugging the reins around toward the hilltop, he kicked the horse's sides.

The horse leapt forward and then promptly slowed to a walk. Proctor kicked her sides harder, but the more he kicked, the slower she went.

British soldiers began to look at him. "You there," one shouted. "What are you doing?"

Proctor looked down. "I was commanded to deliver this horse to Colonel Jack. Do you know where he might be found?"

"Do I look like his bloody keeper?" the man said, striding forward.

The soldier next to him held him back. "Colonel Jack's unit has gone toward Charlestown to hold the left flank."

"Thank you," Proctor said, turning his horse in that direction without waiting to be dismissed. He could find a road from Charlestown to the top of the hill. If he got that far, he could make a break for it.

The closer they came to the sound of the cannons, and the haze from the fire, the slower the mare plodded.

"If I used you to plow, I'd still be breaking ground when it was time to harvest," Proctor said. She was a good horse, strong, could probably pull a carriage all day at that same pace without tiring. It just wasn't the pace he needed.

He passed down the line of British regiments, wondering if it would ever end. There were thousands of men—thousands of the best-trained, best-fighting men in the world. As he passed face after face, some grim, some laughing, some angry, he wondered if the widow even needed her magic to help them win. He began to feel sick.

Then Charlestown was rising up in front of him—literally rising, as the fire turned it into a pillar of smoke. He would have to steal his chance to make it to the colonial lines soon.

Another cannon boomed. This time he was close enough to hear the whistle of the shell and feel the ground shake as it hit its target in the city. Another set of stone walls tumbled in a cloud of dust.

The mare didn't like that at all, and tried to turn back. "That's a good girl," Proctor said, aiming toward the hill. "We'll be far away from the cannon if we go up there."

Then hands were reaching up and taking the reins from him. It was the officer from the barn, now considerably less angry.

"Good work," he said.

Proctor thought about pulling the reins free and making a break for it, but he knew it would be a losing gambit with this mare.

"Gentle is the word for her," he said, dismounting.

"This is for you," the officer said, and handed him a shilling. "We're moving cannons up to cover the road, so we can rake the colonials when they start to retreat. Report to the quartermaster over that way, and he'll find a duty for you."

"All right," Proctor said.

When the officer led the horse away, Proctor turned toward the hill. Without meeting anyone's eyes, he simply strolled past the British lines, which were still forming, and headed up the long slope. He could almost feel the guns aimed at his back—his stomach knotted and his knees felt rubbery.

He was less than a quarter of the distance when the shout went up, "Hey, who is that there?"

"Halt! You there, halt!"

"Shoot him before he reaches the rebels!"

With half a mile to go, he started to run.

Chapter 24

The first musket cracked behind him.

More shouts went up, this time from the colonial barricade, as more muskets fired behind him. The balls buzzed past his ears, just like bees. The slope grew steeper just before the summit, the ground filled with rocks and roots and ankle-breaking holes. A ball smashed into the dirt beside him. When his hat fell off, he didn't look back for it—he could find another hat.

He reached the wall, thrown up hastily out of mud and logs, and rough hands reached out to help him.

Balls slammed into either side of him, kicking up mud and splinters. As he tumbled over the top, he saw musket barrels rising to reply.

"Hold your fire," someone shouted. "Hold your Goddamned fire!"

Proctor looked up to thank his rescuers and fell back—skeletons and talking skulls, covered with a veneer of jellied flesh, packed all around him.

"But—" said one of the colonials.

"Don't argue with me," the officer interrupted. His face was a skull with eyes like smoke trapped in ice and light brown hair tied back in a knot. "We've only got seven rounds per man. We'll hold our fire until it can do some good. If you can't follow that order, you need to take yourself home right now."

Proctor sat, back against the wall, gasping. He fumbled

in his trouser pocket—one of the charms, if he grabbed one of the charms that Deborah gave him—

The muskets lowered and the men repeated the reasoning to one another, reassuring themselves of its wisdom.

—and his hand closed around something unexpected, the lock of Deborah's hair. He wrapped it around his finger, and, with his eyes closed to shut out the sight of the skeletons, pressed it to his lips, and said a silent prayer. *Let her healing heal me.*

The itching spread from his arms to his legs and belly, but the nausea, the weakness fled.

He opened his eyes and saw worried faces. Bright eyes. Ordinary, healthy flesh. The officer watched him, the same pale brown eyes and hair tied back in a knot, now set in a young man's face, with a hairline scar along one cheek. Breathing easier, Proctor slipped the lock of hair back into the same pocket.

There was a yelp and a small figure came tumbling back over the wall with something in his hand.

"You dropped this on the way in," the boy said. He was about twelve, with a shaggy mop of hair and a big grin on his face. He handed over Proctor's hat.

Proctor dusted it off and put it back on his head. "Thank you," he said. "What's your name?"

"Tobias—I'm the drummer."

He reminded Proctor a little of Arthur. Or, if he thought about it, the fifer with the Acton minutemen, the one who taunted the Redcoats at Concord with his songs. Proctor reached into his vest pocket for the shilling the British officer had given him. Instead his hand closed on one of the lead charms.

He pulled the charm out anyway and handed it to the boy. "You've got my thanks, Tobias. You carry this for luck, and it'll see you through the day."

The boy took the musket ball and rolled it in his hands.

If he saw anything unusual in it, he didn't say so, but he dropped it in his pocket with a thank-you-sir.

The leader held out his hand. "That was a brave run there. Who are you and how'd you end up on that side of the line?"

Proctor got to his feet and took the hand hesitantly—no new wave of nausea passed through, nothing made him sick. "Name's Brown—I'm a minuteman with the Lincoln militia, but then I got stuck in Boston. You the captain here?"

"Not as such. What were you doing in Boston?"

A crowd of men had gathered around him to listen. A few of them moved behind Proctor.

"A fisherman took me into the city," he said, and then, because he didn't want to appear to be a spy, he added, "so I could check on my aunt. I was going to try to get her out, but with the attack coming, I thought I should get myself out first. I convinced the Redcoats I was one of their stable boys and they brought me over. Then I made a break for it, to get up here."

As he spoke, he looked around at the faces. They were similar to the British faces below—some grim, some grinning, some angry. Most young, about his age. But they were wearing the same clothes they'd wear to work in a field, they stood about as they pleased taking their ease, and they argued with their officers when they didn't care for an order.

The vision he had, the scrying when the boy's blood was spilled, came back to him.

This hillside. Smoke. Relentless fire. The dead. The survivors fleeing.

Blood on his hands.

His failure.

"I need to find my commanding officer and report," he finished.

"Soon enough," the man said. "You say you're from Lincoln—we got any Lincoln men nearby?"

"Not that I know," one man answered.

"Lincoln's 'tween Lexington and Concord," another said.

"I was at Lexington," Proctor replied. "Captain Parker, from Lexington, he'd remember me, if he's here. He loaned me shot at the bloody corner."

Just saying the names evoked memories of that day, only two months past. Was it only two months? He felt like he lived in a different world now than he did then, like he'd become a different man. And this—looking at the fort, the lines of the colonial militia, the lines of the British below, protected by the guns on their warships—this promised to be a different kind of battle.

"I recognize 'im," a voice said. It was a black man, the one who'd pulled him free of Pitcairn's guards when he'd tried to take the medallion.

"Who're you?" a surly man asked

"That's Peter Salem," another answered. "I know him."

"I know him too," the leader said. "Hi, Peter."

"Hi, Will. He was in the thick of it on the Concord Road," Salem said with a nod at Proctor. "There was one last Redcoat riding a horse, and this fellow went down to the road and knocked him clean off."

"So you know him?" Will asked.

"I don't know as I can say I know him, because we've never been introduced," Salem said. "But that was something, taking that officer off his horse, and I'd recognize the man who did it anywhere, even I saw him dressed up like a Turk in Timbuktu."

The men laughed at that.

Will held out his hand. "It's good to meet you, Brown. I hope you'll forgive the questions."

"No problem. There's a war on, I understand."

"Major Israel Putnam is in charge."

"Only a major?" Proctor said.

"After the way we whipped them in Lexington, I guess we figured we don't need a general to beat 'em here."

The men laughed again, and Proctor was struck by the similarity they shared with the men on the other side. He put his hand in his pocket and felt the lead balls. It seemed like a small shield against so much bloodshed.

"Old Put's the one you'll want to report to," Will said. "You'll find him down at the center of the line."

"Thank you," Proctor said, and he took off at a quick pace. The British had aimed their cannons at the fort now, and a plume of dirt shot up in front of him as a ball struck just outside the wall. He waited until the dirt settled and then kept on going, asking for Putnam. There were so few men up here, maybe no more than a thousand, about a quarter of the number he saw among the British.

Putnam was older and more rotund than the other men in the redoubt, but no one looked more like an officer or moved with more purpose and energy. He was taking reports from half a dozen men, stopping every so often to mop his brow with a handkerchief. When it was his turn, Proctor repeated the story he told the other men.

"The British are moving cannons up to cover the road," Proctor said. "They're planning to rake us, if we have to retreat."

"That's excellent, Brown, excellent." Turning toward one of his men, Putnam said, "Have them throw up some defenses along the Charlestown Neck to cover our retreat."

The man, who looked exhausted the way that only a man who has been digging all night can, saluted briskly and ran off to see to it.

Putnam turned back to Brown. "Do you have a musket?"

"Not here—the Lobsters would have been suspicious if I carried it along their lines."

"True." Putnam chuckled, mopping the sweat from his forehead. "The fact is, we've got more men than guns."

"How're you on shovels?"

Another shell whistled in and hit the wall nearby, throwing up dirt and shards of wood. A man fell down, pierced.

"We're short on shovels right now too," Putnam said. "Truth is, most of the digging's done and it's time to fight. If you stay back and help any wounded men away from the wall, we'd appreciate it. You'll be able to pick up a musket and fill in a hole on the line at some point."

"Yes, sir," Proctor said. As Putnam turned away to his next task, Proctor said, "Sir?"

"What is it, Brown?"

Proctor pulled one of the musket balls from his pocket. "If you would take this for luck, sir, it would honor me."

Putnam saw it was a musket ball and dropped it in his bag. "You don't have any powder to go with that ball, do you?"

"No, sir," Proctor said. "That's why it seemed like I ought to give it to someone who might use it."

"Powder would have been luckier for us all. But thank you."

Proctor moved along the line, asking after officers and finding few senior men there. He gave the charmed musket balls to a few captains. They looked at him oddly, but if he handed it over with some excuse, and moved on quickly, no one looked too closely. Suddenly, he found himself wishing for the widow's sickness on him again. If he could see the skulls behind the flesh, he'd know for certain which men to give them to. Instead, he watched for anyone else who acted like a leader and passed a lead ball on to them. It was the best he could do.

The sun was high overhead: it was past noon. All of Charlestown was aflame, the wind pushing the smoke over the hilltop so that their eyes constantly stung. British mortars fell along the fort so often that the sound of explosions no more startled him than the sound of his own heart. But when he looked over the wall and saw the lines of the British regulars, thousands of them, ready to attack, his pulse skipped a beat.

The attack would begin anytime now.

A cheer went down the line as a single man, followed by

a dozen others, approached Putnam. He was tall, fair-haired, and handsome.

"Who is that?" Proctor asked a man nearby.

"That's Doctor Warren. He was just appointed major-general of the whole army yesterday."

"Ah," Proctor said, recognizing the name. Dr. Joseph Warren was considered about the finest man in all of Massachusetts—intelligent, brave, and the best physician in the colonies. He pushed closer to hear his conversation with Putnam.

"—I wouldn't think of it," Warren was saying.

"By rights you should be the commanding officer here," Putnam said.

"Nonsense," Warren replied. "My commission hasn't taken effect yet. It's dated for tomorrow."

"A mere formality."

"Not at all," Warren said. "You were here first, you threw up the defenses, you've taken all the reports, and you understand the situation. I'm here as a volunteer, and I'll serve like any other."

"Are you certain?" Putnam asked, though he was clearly flattered by the younger man. "There is no ego involved. I would be honored to pass the command to you."

"As I am honored to serve under you," Warren said. The way he said it, Proctor felt that he wasn't merely being polite or affecting enthusiasm. He really meant it. "Now, I have my own musket and enough shot and powder to share," he added. "Where should I go?"

Several company commanders spoke up at once, and not just for the chance at an extra round or two of powder. Warren was one of the great leaders of the colony. Proctor thought he had never seen a more gracious man. He needed one of the charms, if any man did.

As Warren moved away from Putnam, Proctor shoved his hand in his pocket and pushed forward. "Doctor Warren, if I may trouble you. Doctor Warren?"

And then his footsteps faltered. His pocket was empty. He had no charms left.

"Yes?" Warren said, puzzled.

Proctor pulled out his empty hand and offered it to Warren. "I just wanted to shake the hand of one of the finest men in Massachusetts."

The men around them laughed at that, but Warren took his hand and shook it heartily.

Another shell whistled over the wall, and a few men ducked as it exploded. But Warren held his head up, and the others were quick to mimic his example.

"They're coming!"

The line of Redcoats had started marching up the hill. The drummers beat out the call to arms and men ran to defend the wall, taking any spot that was empty, regardless of where they might be assigned. Proctor grabbed a tall, thin fellow as he ran by. "Can you spare one lead?"

The man opened his mouth to say something, but his fellows were calling for him to join them.

"Please," Proctor said.

He thrust his hand in his bag and pulled out one round, slapping it into Proctor's palm. Proctor retreated from the front line, back among the drummers and fifers and the other unarmed volunteers.

He sat down and looked at the lead ball. It seemed like such a small thing, that could snuff a man's life. It seemed smaller still, that it could act as a protection. He cupped his hands around the lead ball, holding his lips to the gap between his thumbs.

"Dear Father in heaven," he prayed. "May Thy light shine on this simple ball of lead. If it be Thy will, let it become a shield of life rather than a taker of life. Let no man who bears it fall before his appointed time."

He opened his hand. Nothing had happened.

Clasping his hands again, he prayed more fervently, repeating it three times under his breath. But he didn't feel anything flow through him—no tingle of energy, no warmth, no difference at all.

The lead ball sat in his palm. It was still no more than a lead ball.

Maybe he couldn't do it without Deborah. Maybe she had drained all his magic too. All his power had flowed into the widow, and all the widow's power flowed into Deborah. Maybe he had nothing left.

The British fired as they advanced, the front line shooting, the second line marching up and doing the same while the first line reloaded. One man fell nearby, struck by a musket ball, and lay still.

"Hold your fire!" Putnam shouted. "We have to make every shot count—don't fire until you see the whites of their eyes."

"If they get that close, we can stab them and save the powder," a man called back, and they all laughed.

"Be firm, men," Putnam shouted.

Another series of mortars fell, smashing parts of the wall and throwing back the defenders. A round of musket fire followed. A man fell nearby, clutching his shoulder and moaning as he tried to crawl back up to his position.

"Can we have a hand?" a captain called.

Proctor dropped the lead ball and ran forward to help, hunched over to duck the musket fire buzzing overhead. The wounded man's shoulder was smashed, his right arm hanging bloody and dead. With one hand under his left arm and the other on the man's belt, Proctor hauled him back from the line and loaded him on one of the horse carts that were waiting to remove the wounded.

"Hold," Putnam shouted, and the call went down the line.

Proctor ran to drag another injured man away from the wall. Halfway to the carts, he realized the man was dead. At that moment a shell crashed over the wall, and Proctor instinctively covered the body with his own.

The British soldiers were less than a hundred yards away. hey had the range with their cannons. They had numbers n their side.

The colonials had the high ground and they had courage. t least that part of the widow's curse had failed.

The British came within fifty yards now, and still the olonials held their fire. Another round of musket fire came ver the ramparts and more men fell, but none ran.

And none, Proctor saw, were officers, even though they tood exposed to harm as they marked the progress of the ritish line.

Maybe it was just luck. There were so few officers among hem.

Maybe it was Deborah's charm.

He glanced over the wall. The British regulars were less han fifty yards away. Putnam cried, "Fire!"

Fire flashed in firing pans down the row of the wall's deenders, flame jetted from their musket bores, and a cloud f smoke rolled off their weapons.

When the wind tore away the smoke, the British were till advancing. Their next round of fire knocked down nore of the defenders, who, spread out over a line only one nan deep, were now frantically reloading.

Proctor looked down at the dead man in his arms, at the lood on his hands, and suddenly he knew what his scrying neant. He knew that the little boy's life blood had told him vhat he needed to know as it flowed out of his body into he widow's bowl.

Taking the blood on his hand, Proctor cast it in a circle. Let this man's sacrifice not be in vain," he said in a rush, urrying to finish before the Redcoats came over the wall. Ie groped for words, trying to remember it the way that Deborah had taught it to Alexandra. "Let his blood, shed o defend this ground, defend all men who stand their round. Reverse the widow's spell."

The New Englanders had reloaded their muskets.

Putnam, standing at the wall, yelled, "Fire!"

The colonists' weapons jetted flame and smoke again, firing for only the second time since the British had begun the battle.

Chapter 25

Proctor ran to the wall. When the wind sheared away the smoke, the British were in disarray, many of the men fallen, others dragging them back from the American position.

Tobias, the little drummer, appeared on the battlements beside Proctor. "We beat them! We beat them—huzzah!"

The cheer rose in Proctor's throat and escaped the lips of others. But Putnam and others were there to shout it down.

"Don't be fools," Putnam raged. "They'll take our measure with their cannonades and march again against us before an hour's passed."

Tobias's jaw hung open for a long second. "But they can't stand against us. We whipped 'em."

"They can and they will," Proctor said, having been among them such a short time before. He tousled the boy's head and was glad he'd given him the ball.

"Take a drink, if you have water," one of the captains shouted. "And if you have food or water, share it with those who don't."

A long day, then. Just like the day at Lexington.

"Sir," a voice said nearby. "Sir?"

"Yes?" Proctor turned and saw a young black man in better clothes than he'd ever owned himself.

"I saw you helping the wounded. Some of us are acting as orderlies, and wondered if you could give us a hand."

"Of course," he said.

Dr. Warren knelt beside a bloody man, knotting a tourniquet on a wounded leg to stem the flow of blood. A dozen others were bleeding and groaning nearby. Others lay senseless, like the man Proctor had pulled away.

"What is the butcher's charge so far?" Putnam asked.

Warren lifted his fair face. "Two, maybe three dozen dead. That many more wounded. Some won't make it." He patted the man on the leg and indicated that he should get on one of the carts.

"We gave as good as we got," Putnam said. "That last fire raked them. They were dragging dozens away with them."

"Yes," Warren said, moving on to the next man. "Can I have a compress for this chest wound?"

Proctor stood nearest the pile of lint and bandages. He grabbed some of each and handed them to Warren, who applied a compress to stanch the flow of blood.

"They're forming up to make another assault," someone cried from the wall.

Farther down the line, someone yelled, "Here they come again."

"We'll take 'em this time," the curly-haired boy said, his drum slung over his shoulder.

"That's right, Toby," Will said. His cap was off when he stopped to muss the boy's hair, and Proctor saw the family resemblance at once.

At the same instant, a cannonball whistled over the battlements, struck Will, and knocked him over the drummer. His face and chest were a bloody mass.

"William?" the boy said, his eyes as wide as shillings as he squirmed free. "William?"

"Here," Proctor said, pulling him out of the way.

"They've found our range too," Putnam said. "Back to the wall."

Warren watched the death of Tobias's brother, his face registering no more than a clinical curiosity. He crouched over a different wounded man who was fighting to control the spasms of pain. Warren grabbed Proctor's hand and pressed it into the man's wound.

"Hold that here, hard, even if he complains, until the wound stops bleeding," he said.

"I promise I won't complain," the injured man gasped, "as long as the bleeding stops."

Warren smiled and gently squeezed the man's shoulder. To the black man, he said, "Gather the wounded and help them retreat. Have them make their way to Cambridge."

"Sir."

Warren wiped his hands clean on a rag and picked up his musket. As he returned to defend the wall, Proctor wished more than ever that he had one more lead charm.

"Back to the wall," someone yelled. "Where's the drum?"

The curly-haired boy was still standing there in shock. At another call for the drum, he began a trembling beat. He closed his eyes, avoiding the sight of all the dead and wounded, and the beat grew stronger.

The officers were shouting at the men to hold their fire until the Redcoats reached fifty yards or less.

Proctor looked down, seeing the blood soak through the lint pad that he pressed into the man's wound. Lifting one hand, he shook a drop from his fingertips onto the soil. He held an image in his head, of Redcoats falling, their officers cut down, their will to fight fading—

The black orderly returned. "Can you move?"

"Me?" Proctor asked, shaken from his spell.

"I think he means me," the wounded man said. "And yeah, I'd rather be gone if the Redcoats come over the wall."

"Can you help me get him into the wagon?" the orderly asked Proctor.

When they had moved him and the cart rolled off, Proctor turned to the wall. The triple line of Redcoats marched resolutely up the long slope while shells fell with greater intensity among the colonial defenders.

Proctor looked around for another injured man; his eyes fell on the body of Tobias's brother, Will.

He grabbed the body by the feet and he dragged it out of

the way, where the defenders would not trip over him. When he dropped it, he dipped his fingers in his blood and cast it upon the ground.

"Let his death hold hallow here," he whispered, and he held an image in his head, reversing the widow's spell.

A few hairs tingled on the back of his arm.

He ran to the wall, where another dead man lay hanging half over the ramparts. Musket balls whizzed past his head from the advancing British line as he climbed up to retrieve the body. The men there nodded to him, shifting their small cannonade to break the line ahead and cover Proctor.

The other defenders saw what he was doing and helped him lift the body down. A thick man, with shoulders like wooden blocks, had tears on his face as he dropped the dead man's weight into Proctor's arms. "His name was Matthew, and he was the finest tip-cat player in Menotomy."

The men nodded respectfully to Proctor as he carried Matthew away and lay him beside Will.

Once again, he pressed his fingers into the hole in the dead man's chest and shook blood onto the ground, saying, "Hallow this ground."

He closed his eyes and imagined the widow's spell reversed.

His hair stood on end, from his wrists to his shoulders but the sensation faded instantly.

The first volley of the British had turned into a steady fire by the time Proctor laid the third body next to the first two The militia had their heads down against the swarm, waiting while their officers peered over the wall, marking the advance of the British. Although shells rained down on them, the men held their positions.

This was not the running fight outside Lexington, where men knew the ground better, and fought from behind cover against an enemy surrounded on every side.

"Return fire!"

The British advance up the long slope was less than fift

yards from the wall. The colonials rose to aim. As the fire flashed and the shots went off, the man with the block shoulders fell, hit by a British round.

A few yards away, another man flew backward. Men were falling all along the line.

The survivors kept their heads down, reloading, and as soon as the next British round was fired, they popped up over the wall to take aim and shoot back.

Proctor ran to Block-shoulders, who'd taken a round in his hand. His musket was smashed, the end of his right arm a ruined mess. He was groaning, kicking the ground as he tried to tie off his arm one-handed.

"Let me do that for you," Proctor said. He took the handkerchief from the man's left hand and pulled the torn sleeve down over the smashed stump.

"God help me, that hurts," the man grunted.

Proctor nodded, unable to speak. He racked his brain for a healing spell, something useful he might have learned from Deborah's mother, but there was nothing to do except knot the tourniquet as tight as he could. There was blood everywhere now; his arms covered with it, the men were covered with it, the ground soaked with it.

"What's that?" Block-shoulders asked, his voice shaking.

Proctor looked at him, puzzled, still trying to remember something useful.

"What you just said, as you shook your hand to the ground? It sounded like *hallow this ground*."

Proctor's skin tingled over his whole body and all his hair stood on end. He felt the magic surge through him, as sure and powerful as it had ever been. He had reached the point where he was praying without thinking. There was so much blood on the ground, he had a constant focus for his spell.

"It was a prayer," he said, pulling the man to his feet and dragging him back from the line. "A prayer for all of us."

Block-shoulders grunted in reply, but he was wobbly on his feet, dizzy from loss of blood and pain. When they got to the back of the lines, there were no more carts left for the wounded.

The curly-haired drummer boy stood there, beside the wheel ruts, his drum across his shoulder, his drumsticks hanging down to the ground. He saw Proctor, and he said "I wish I had never signed up to volunteer."

"We needed your drumming," Proctor said.

"My brother's dead." He swallowed hard. "And Mister Silsbee got hit too, shot in his face, he's gone."

"I want you to help me," Proctor said. "Can you do something to help me?"

The boy started to shake his head—

"This man's lost a lot of blood, he's a bit dizzy. Can you take him by his good hand and lead him back to Cambridge? Make sure he gets to someplace safe."

"But I have to stay to beat the drums, so the men know what to do—"

"The men here know what to do from this point onward," Proctor said. "You've done your duty. Now you can help in other ways."

Block-shoulders stirred himself enough to speak. " might have to lean on you a bit, to steady myself."

"You can leave your drum, I'll look out for it," Proctor said.

"Well, all right, then," the boy said. He lifted the strap over his head, dropped the drum, and took Block-shoulders by the hand. They fell in beside another pair, one man dragging his leg, limp and bloody, helping another whose head was wrapped in a dripping rag, all part of a train of wounded.

Proctor spun back toward the fighting. He shook the blood from his hand and ran to help another man tie off his wounds.

That one hobbled away, using his musket for a crutch.

He pulled another dead man off the wall.

The shooting stopped; even the cannons were still. Proc

tor looked up, stunned by the silence. The cloud of smoke from Charlestown rose up to the sky, casting a dark haze over the sun. The sound of gulls crying from the bay floated up the hillside.

Proctor saw some of the Concord men, resting with their backs against the ramparts. Thirsty, out of breath, he went and sat with them. "I think it worked," he said.

"What worked?" Amos Lathrop asked.

Proctor started from his seat. "Hello, Amos."

"You seem surprised to see me," he said. And Proctor was. There was no skull grinning at him behind Amos's familiar face this time, no skeleton moving rotted flesh. "What worked?"

Proctor couldn't answer that his spell had worked. "Our defense of the hill."

Peter Salem grunted skeptically. "Maybe it did, and maybe it didn't."

A distant cannon boomed and a shot sailed over their heads and down the length of the rampart, thumping into the wall. The men sat up.

"They lower the angle on that, and bring it around a bit more, and it'll clear the length of this line," Amos said.

Proctor felt a pain in his heart. Maybe Salem was right, maybe it hadn't worked.

"How much powder do you have left?" Amos asked.

"One round," said Arthur Simes. Proctor hadn't even recognized him, he was so different from the boy he'd seen on Lexington Green.

Amos shook his head and said, "Me too."

"I've got a few rounds left," Dr. Warren said nearby.

The cannon boomed again and another shot sailed over their heads; a bit lower this time, it bowled down a group of men farther down the wall.

One of the captains came running from Putnam's command position, pausing to speak to the nearby cannon crew.

A few seconds later, he crouched by the Concord men. "They're coming back for a third try. We're going to break open the shot canisters and distribute the powder."

"How much?"

"Maybe another round apiece," the captain said, and he ran to the next group.

The cannon crew already had their cartridge box open and a canister cracked. They were doling out powder to the first men there with their horns. The Concord men rose to get a measure.

Dr. Warren stayed behind with Proctor. "I've seen what you've been doing."

Proctor thought only of the spell he'd been trying to work. It was odd—he'd spent his whole life hiding his talent, following his mother's example. And he felt no shame or fear anymore. "I don't even know if it made any difference."

"It made all the difference to the men you helped," Warren said, and Proctor realized he was talking about the wounded. "You have a skill for it."

Proctor looked at the bloodstains on his hands, so different from the kind of blood he thought he'd have on his hands, and shook his head. "I guess I have several skills I never expected to have."

"The only thing harder than staying on the front line is returning to it over and over, the way you've done today," Warren said.

There was a volley from the slope and the thud of lead rounds smacking the wall. It seemed like such a fragile barrier. The other men crouched back into position with their extra measure of powder.

"This is it, men," Warren told them. "They won't have the stomach for a fourth charge up that hill."

"And we won't have powder to shoot them if they do," Amos said, drawing an unexpected smile from Proctor.

Another volley fired from a bit closer, and more lead pocked into the dirt and wood. There was the sound of shots popping from the colonial line now. "How close are they?" Arthur asked.

"Hold a moment longer," Warren said.

"I'll see," Amos said, peeking over the barricade. The shot hit him in the forehead, knocking his hat off and throwing him back, his arms and legs twisted all wrong.

"Amos!" Proctor grabbed his shirt to drag him to safety. He had him ten feet back from the wall when he tripped and fell. He scrambled to his knees, reaching for Amos, and stopped. The body lay exactly where he had dropped it. Nothing in the world, no medicine or witchcraft, could help Amos now.

Kneeling in the churned earth, next to Amos's dead body, Proctor lowered his head and folded his hands. He prayed. He prayed that it was worth it, all these deaths, all the suffering. He prayed that these were birth pangs, delivering a world where greater peace was possible. Because he did not know if he could keep on going in the old world anymore.

He lifted his head. "His mother makes flatcakes for me. How am I going to tell her about this?"

Warren picked up Amos's loaded musket and thrust it into Proctor's hand. "You'll find the words when you need them, but it'll have to wait. The time has come to put your other talents to use."

Proctor's hands closed around the musket stock and barrel. "Yes, sir," he said, and together they crouched back to the barricade.

The instant the next British volley whistled overhead, Proctor and the others lifted their muskets over the wall, took aim, and—

Something gold caught Proctor's eye as he fired. He jerked his barrel toward it but a moment too late.

Major Pitcairn led the marines straight toward their position. He still had the protective charm the widow had given him. It wasn't a coin, or a faint shimmer now; instead, it blinked at Proctor like the eye of some malignant giant caught on a chain.

A hand on his collar pulled him down as the next Britis volley fired.

"You might want to reload," Warren suggested, jam ming his ramrod into his barrel.

Proctor reached for his flint bag—and realized he didn' have it. He reached over and grabbed Amos's horn an bag. He was still pouring powder into the firing pan whe the men around him looked over the wall and shot agair

"Thirty yards away and fixing bayonets," a man yelled.

"That was my last round," Arthur said. "I think I'll b going." He nodded to Proctor, then hunkered off.

"Me too," said the first man, and others followed.

"God be with you," Warren said as he reloaded. He an Proctor and Peter Salem were among the last men defend ing that part of the wall. "One more round," he said.

A British volley cracked and Proctor lifted his muske and aimed for Pitcairn. From the corner of his eye, he sa British soldiers down everywhere, their lines as broken a the lines of the colonial defenders.

As he sighted down the musket, he saw a bright spot c Amos's blood on the end of the barrel.

He thought back to the counterspell Deborah had taugh them on The Farm, the one that turned a spell with ba intentions back on itself. There could be no intentions wors than the widow's. With the blood for a focus, he formed th thought of the widow's spell in his head, just as Deborah ha done.

"An eye for an eye," he whispered. "Reverse the widow' spell."

He squeezed the trigger. Fire erupted from the barrel.

The wind whipped away the smoke from his gun and h saw Pitcairn's sleeve torn. Pitcairn stopped, fingers on th bloody wound, as red as his jacket. He seemed surprisec

Proctor ducked his head again.

His spell had worked. He had, at least, broken the widow's protective spells. Pitcairn could be hurt. He took another shot from Amos's bag and lifted the horn to pour.

But there was no powder left.

He looked over the wall, hoping to see the British charge broken. Pitcairn had been wounded—he had to know his spell no longer protected him. But he still marched at the front of the line, his sword drawn and raised above his head, urging his men onward.

Warren and Salem were both loading their weapons. Salem tilted his head toward Pitcairn. "I've been saving my last round for him."

"Really?" Proctor asked.

"Naw," Salem replied as he put his ramrod away and jabbed a thumb toward one of the dead bodies. "But I saw him on the field at Lexington. He's got too many airs to suit me."

He rose up behind the bulwark, aimed, and shot. Pitcairn fell, his sword spinning in an arc through the air away from his hand. A cry went up from his troops as he went down and Proctor saw his son William, the young officer who'd tried to make amends to him outside the coffeehouse in Boston, rush to his father's side.

Warren tugged at their shoulders. "Well done, men. We're out of powder—it's time to go."

Proctor nodded, relief washing through him. They had paid a terrible price, but he had broken the widow's spell. Whatever was settled on that hill today was settled by men, and not by witchcraft.

They were four steps away from the wall when another volley cracked behind them. Proctor ducked as the shots zinged past them. Warren lurched a step ahead.

"Oh," he said. "That's not good."

He pitched forward, head turned to the side, eyes already empty.

Salem kept running. Proctor hesitated for a moment,

then chased after him. They were the last stragglers, racing to the narrow road that led across the Charlestown Neck.

They stopped there, protected by a wall of hay bales, and looked back down the double slope to see the tiny figures of the Redcoats climbing over the redoubts.

Salem shook his head, disappointed. "A couple more rounds per man would have made all the difference," he said. "It's a shame we had to lose this one."

"I'm not sure we did lose," Proctor answered, seeing the carnage among the Redcoats. A trail of bodies led down the slopes to the bay, and the trampled grass was slick with blood. The soldiers occupied the redoubts, but their enemy had fled before them, able to fight another day. "What's the name of that hill anyway?"

"Which one?" Salem said. "Breed's Hill or Bunker Hill?"

A cannonball smashed into the wall of bales, showering them with bits of hay, and they both ducked, covering their heads. When they looked up, Salem tipped his hat to Proctor, then ran to join the rest of the retreating colonists.

Proctor lingered a moment longer, trying to pick out Amos's body or Warren's among the scene below. But the walls were jumbled, and with the Redcoats milling about, he couldn't tell where he'd fought or which bodies were theirs.

"Never mind," he said to no one in particular, answering his own question. "It doesn't make a difference."

Chapter 26

Proctor spent the rest of the day behind the colonials' fallback line in Cambridge, waiting for the next wave of the British assault, but it never came.

That night he went to work, helping the wounded where he could. Though he knew no healing spells, he changed dressings and prayed for every injured man he met.

A week later, with no further British advance, he sought out Elihu Danvers, hoping to find a way back into Boston. He wasn't sure if he was looking for Deborah or his mother.

"The British won the battle but they've lost the will to fight," Danvers said between puffs on his pipe. "They sacrificed almost a thousand men to take that hill, and all their best officers killed. A few more victories like that, and they're done for."

Proctor sat at his table while Mrs. Danvers stirred the cooking pot and the smallest children aimed sticks at each other, pretending to be minutemen and Redcoats.

"And no," Danvers said. "I can't arrange for you to go back into the city. They're so frightened now, they've shut it up tighter than a nun's drawers."

Mrs. Danvers smacked him on the back of his head. His pipe popped out of his mouth, and he caught it in his hand. He put it back to his lips and blew a ring of smoke after her.

"If you're worrying about a certain relative," Danvers said, "I wouldn't. With the siege on, the British are eager to let anyone out of the city who wants out, so long as they've no value as a hostage."

Neither his mother nor Deborah had any value as a hostage, not to anyone but him. Emily could go anytime she wanted, if she made up her mind where she wanted to go.

Mrs. Danvers served him a bowl of pork and beans, flavored with molasses. His favorite meal. He thanked her and laid into it with gusto.

That night he set out for home.

The roads were full of men, coming from every colony in New England. Word had it that there would soon be forty thousand men to shut up Boston. The war was just beginning.

He wandered by back roads, carrying the musket and bag he had taken from Amos, and thinking about his talent, and what it meant. His mother was right about one thing: there would never be any place for it in the open. But that didn't mean there wasn't any place for it. Even Emily, who had feared his talent at first, had come looking for him, ready to make peace with it. That was something to think on. Maybe there wouldn't be any more witch hangings. Maybe someday, there wouldn't be a need for the Quaker Highway anymore.

But there would always be a need for someone to train witches. No one should ever be left as he had been, ignorant of his heritage, without knowledge or guidance for his talent.

It was midmorning when he cut across the rocky fields toward the familiar farmhouse.

She stood waiting for him at the front door. He paused below the step and bit his cheek to keep from smiling.

"What took you so long?" Deborah asked, hands in her dress pockets. After all they'd been through, he expected her to appear older, harder. More like her mother, or his. But a softness touched her eyes and a slight smile turned the corners of her lips.

He looked off in the other direction. "Didn't you see me coming?"

"I might have scryed it," she said. She pulled her hand from her pocket and opened it to reveal a speckled egg.

He laughed and followed her inside.

Acknowledgments

Thanks, first of all, to Saul Cornell at the Ohio State University for employing me as a research assistant on his Langum Prize–winning history *A Well-Regulated Militia*. I was buried up to my neck in primary source material about muskets, minutemen, and the Revolution when the character of Proctor Brown and the idea for the novel came to me. Any history I get correct is because of skills Saul taught me. Esther Forbes is best known for her novel *Johnny Tremain*, but she was also an excellent historian. I kept her book *Paul Revere and the World He Lived In* at hand whenever I was writing, along with *Paul Revere's Ride* by David Hackett Fischer.

Matt Bialer, my agent, and Chris Schluep, my editor at Del Rey, nurtured the idea until it grew into several books, for which I will be ever grateful. Gordon Van Gelder, editor of *The Magazine of Fantasy & Science Fiction*, bought the initial story about Proctor Brown and the Battle of Lexington and Concord and let me know that I was headed in the right direction.

James Walker and Dr. Lisa Tuvelle-Walker won the chance to name a character in this book at a charity auction for St. Joseph Montessori School. Thank you for the generous donation. If Alexandra is not quite the character you imagined, I can only plead that she is willful and did not want to be the character I originally imagined either.

Traitor to the Crown has been powered by Luck Bros' Coffee. For all the early mornings and late nights, I must acknowledge Ed and Andy and their cheerful, funny, creative baristas.

Finally, I have always depended on the kindness of writers. Catherine Morrison and Amber van Dyk got me on track with the early drafts. It's *all* about the egg, Amber. Special thanks to the 2007 Blue Heaven writers, especially Holly McDowell and Greg van Eekhout. Sarah, I'm sorry about the tick. Tobias Buckell and Paul Melko kicked me in the butt when I needed kicking, the way they always do. Thanks, guys. Lisa Bao read the whole manuscript on short notice and helped me nail Deborah and Proctor's relationship. Rae Carson Finlay read every word critically, from the first paragraph of the first draft to the final correction in the copy editor's notes. This one's for you, Rae.

Read on for an excerpt from

TRAITOR TO THE CROWN

A SPELL FOR THE REVOLUTION

by

C. C. FINLAY

Published by Del Rey Books

Chapter 1

August 1776

Proctor Brown urged his horse into the shallows and forded the Potomac River an hour before sunset. Water splashed up and soaked his shoes; after ten days in the saddle, with his stockings almost as stiff as his legs, he hardly noticed wet shoes. If he found the Walker farm tonight, he'd have a chance to dry off and clean up. Assuming he was welcome.

The jarring lunge up the far bank reminded him that he was more accustomed to being behind a horse, hitched to a cart or plow, than on top of one. He grunted, shifting weight from his sorest parts to those parts almost as sore. A day of rest could be a good thing. It might take that long to convince Alexandra Walker to return with him to The Farm outside Salem, Massachusetts. It depended on how vividly she remembered the assassins sent to kill them during her last visit.

Proctor wanted her help, in case the killers came again. It took a witch to defeat witchcraft, and Alexandra was stronger and more experienced than any of the other witches he'd been able to find this past year.

When they reached the road, Proctor's sturdy little bay mare turned toward the smoke and rooftops a mile away. "No, Singer, the other way," he said.

With a weary toss of her head, Singer circled onto the cart road that led south into the Shenandoah Valley. Even this late in the day, the August air lay on them like a damp wool blanket, one that had been warmed by a fire and filled with biting insects. Land stretched out around them, lush and green, all the way to the mountains.

So this was Virginia, the home of General Washington and half the leaders of the Revolution. Last night about this time, Proctor had arrived in McAllister's Town, Pennsylvania, where the innkeeper at The Sign of the Horse bragged about Thomas Jefferson's visit last April. Jefferson had praised the inn's sausages, which were made by the innkeeper's cousin. The sausages were good, but Proctor doubted that he'd slept in the very same room as Jefferson, no matter what the innkeeper claimed. Still, it had been worth the extra half a shilling to get that close to the author of the Declaration of Independence.

Proctor pushed back his hat and wiped the sweat from his forehead as he scanned the landscape. He was a bit twitchy, wary even. This was the farthest he had ever been from home. The crickets chuckled at him from the safety of the tall grass that lined the trail.

Something rustled through that grass, startling him from his thoughts. Proctor reached for his musket, but by the time he sighted down the barrel, whatever had been there was gone.

He tried to convince himself that it was only a stray dog, or maybe a pig loose from some nearby farm. He'd been jumpy ever since the battles with the Covenant last year. Being this far from home only made him jumpier.

Not that he needed more reasons to be jumpy. As a young man in Massachusetts, he'd been forced to conceal his talent for magic lest his neighbors turn on him. But ever since the battle at Lexington, he'd needed that magic to spoil the plots of the Covenant, a mysterious group of European witches who wanted to crush the American rebellion. The Covenant's ultimate purpose remained hidden, but the stakes were so high that they'd murdered other American witches and had tried several times to kill

Proctor. Not just kill him, but turn the magic in his blood into a curse against American soldiers.

He rolled down his sleeves to cover the pink scars on his forearms, a memento from that particular encounter. Thanks to Deborah, he'd survived and they'd reversed the Covenant's spell before the battle at Bunker Hill.

Deborah Walcott. Prior to the war, he'd been engaged to Emily Rucke, the beautiful daughter of a West Indies merchant, the kind of young woman everyone noticed. These days only Deborah filled his thoughts, though she kept herself plain as a Quaker and tried, like every witch he knew, to go unobserved.

What Deborah couldn't hide was the spark inside her. When the Congress signed the Declaration of Independence, she perceived the new danger.

"The Covenant will strike back hard," she told Proctor. "Only a third of Americans support the rebellion. If the Covenant can make a mockery of independence and break our will to fight, people will go running back to Mother England like chastened children."

Which was why they needed every witch who could detect or break a spell, including Alexandra Walker, who, when they saw her last, wanted nothing to do with magic ever again.

One of the farms ahead, rooftops silhouetted against the sky, must be hers. The sudden return of his thoughts to the present caused him to tense. Something was wrong.

The crickets had fallen silent.

A figure loomed suddenly beside the road, and Proctor raised his musket. Then he realized it was only a scarecrow, made real by the twilight.

As he relaxed, a small flash of light revealed the creature's distorted face, with intense, malevolent eyes and a sneering mouth.

Proctor started in the saddle, jerking on the bridle, and

Singer flared her nostrils and came to a stop. The figure that he'd taken for a scarecrow emerged from the shadows as a man, his face lit red by the hot coal of his pipe.

"Good day," the stranger said, lifting his pipe stem. He wore a pair of calfskin gloves, even in this miserable heat.

"Good night is more like it," Proctor said. It was no wonder he had mistaken the man for a scarecrow. The stranger's jacket was of foreign cut, plum-colored with relics of silver embroidery on the cuffs and pocket-flaps. A golden velvet waistcoat was mismatched to a red silk scarf tied about his throat. His tattered wig was topped by a ragged bicorn hat sporting a cock's feather. The feather was surely the freshest piece of the motley ensemble.

"It's good to see a young man heading away from the war, instead of rushing off to join the rebels," the stranger said. His voice was hollow, his accent as odd as his clothes.

Proctor bristled. He'd risked his life in the war, and he had been cut off by his mother for using magic to fight it. He believed it was the right thing for the country and was glad the Declaration of Independence had been issued, even if it meant renewed fighting.

"I've served as a minuteman and would rather be thought a patriot than a rebel," Proctor said. "Do you have something against independence?"

"No, just against"—he puffed out a cloud of tobacco smoke, pausing as he searched for the right word—"*pointless* bloodshed. No offense intended, young man."

"None taken," Proctor said, though the *young man* felt irritated. Singer stamped her hooves aggressively, the way she did when strange dogs came too close. It would be best to move on. "I'm looking for the Walker farm. You wouldn't happen to know where it is?"

"The Walker farm?" A smile spread slowly across the stranger's face. "That's a coincidence. I've just come from the Walker farm. Follow the trail up to the big oak with the blaze on it. Then turn to the left and climb over the hill. That's where you'll find it."

"Is it far?" Proctor asked. He wondered how the stranger knew the Walkers. The way Alexandra talked, her parents and brothers were all ardent patriots.

"It's a mile, maybe a bit more," the stranger said. "Be careful or you'll miss it in the dark."

"May I have your name?" Proctor asked. "So that I may remember your kindness to me to the Walkers."

The stranger puffed on his pipe again and blew out another small cloud of smoke. "Bootzamon," he said finally. He chuckled, as if at some private joke. "Folks around here call me Bootzamon."

"Thank you, Mister Bootzamon," Proctor said. With a tip of his hat, and more than a bit of relief, he kicked Singer's sides and headed up the trail.

A hundred feet on, he stole a glance over his shoulder. For a second, Bootzamon once again appeared to be a scarecrow standing at the edge of the road. Then the coal flared in his pipe, destroying the fancy, and Proctor turned away from the strange man.

He followed the ruts of the road to the blazed oak standing on the little knoll just where Bootzamon said it would be. Proctor tried to stand in the saddle to look through the trees for some sign of a house, but soreness constrained him to craning his neck. The wind shifted and brought to his nose the scent of cheap tobacco. It smelled like Bootzamon's pipe; the stranger had probably refilled his tobacco pouch at the Walkers'.

He rode down the trail until the dark shape of a primitive house emerged from the trees. Rough-hewn logs, chinked with mud and stones, supported a roof with a single chimney. The plank door stood wide open, but no light shone within.

The hairs tingled on the back of Proctor's neck. He

reached into his pocket for a handful of salt, in case he needed to cast a quick protective spell.

"Hello," Proctor shouted. "Alexandra. Mister Walker Missus Walker." His voice carried past the house, bringing back no reply but the chirping of the crickets.

Nothing appeared wrong. The garden looked well tended as much as he could see of it in the twilight beyond the split-rail fence. So did the field of corn just past the house

He dismounted slowly, grunting as he hit the ground After tying Singer to a narrow stump that seemed meant for that purpose—it was next to a trough made from a dugout log—he limped over to the house.

"Hello," he cried again, leaning into the open door.

Something smelled wrong, sharp and metallic, but the smoke-stench from the hearth overwhelmed it. It was too dark to see anything without a light. He suddenly wished that he'd done a scrying before continuing his journey today, but he hadn't seen a need and he hated to risk doing magic where he might be caught.

He stepped cautiously inside.

"Hello! Is anyone home?"

Nothing.

His nose wrinkled again at the smell. The shadows inside marked out two rooms. He stepped into the one on his left and slipped in something on the floor. His shoulder banged the wall, but he caught himself before falling.

He rubbed his sore shoulder. A few coals glowed red in the hearth, enough to start a fire for some light. He still had that wary itch at the back of his neck, but he dismissed it. That odd Bootzamon fellow had just been here, and he'd mentioned nothing wrong.

Proctor shuffled forward, moving his feet carefully to keep from slipping again or tripping over some stray piece of furniture. When he reached the hearth, he groped in the dark until he found the iron poker. He repeated the effort until he located the basket of tinder and wood. Using th poker to stir the coals, he blew on them and fed them dried twigs and branches until they leapt into flames.

Outside, Singer whinnied. Proctor knew he needed to go out and remove the mare's saddle and rub her down. Or maybe it was the Walkers returning.

"Hello in here!" Proctor called. He added wood to the fire and prodded the coals until the room glowed orange and red.

Singer whinnied again. Proctor turned his head toward the door, conscious that the crickets had fallen silent.

His gaze shifted from the door to the room.

Not all the red was cast by fire.

He jumped back. The iron clattered off the stone hearth as he dropped it. Blood was smeared everywhere. He checked the bottom of his shoe—he'd slipped in a pool of wet blood on his way in. It was fresh. A woman's body lay under the table. The top of her head was missing. A man's broken body, cut to bloody ribbons, was folded against the wall.

"Jesus," Proctor whispered.

"Funny, that's who they called on too," said a voice that made Proctor jump again.

Bootzamon stood framed in the doorway. For just a second he looked like a scarecrow. Then his pipe flared, and he blew out a stream of smoke.

"Mister Bootzamon," Proctor said, trying hard to keep his voice steady. "What happened here?"

Bootzamon shook his head sadly. "It appears to be an Indian attack. Exactly how old are you, young man?"

"Turned twenty-two this past month," Proctor answered in reflex. He looked for a way past Bootzamon, remembering that the Covenant's assassins had come to The Farm dressed as Indians last year. "What makes you say it's Indians?"

"See, that's too bad," Bootzamon said. "My master wants young witches only. 'Catch the young ones, kill the old.' I couldn't find the Walker girl, but I got to thinking you might be young enough to take her place."

His cockfeather brushed the lintel as he stepped through the door. One arm hung at his side, the gloved hand casually dangling a bloody tomahawk.

Proctor saw the tomahawk, but he felt *magic* tickle the back of his neck. Worse than murder had been done here already. He reached into his pocket for his bag of salt while his thoughts raced for the right protective spell. Keeping his eye on Bootzamon, he sprinkled salt in a quick circle around himself. "The Lord is my rock and my fortress, my deliverer. Deliver me from my strong enemy—"

"Bosh," Bootzamon said around the pipe stem in his lips. He removed the pipe and blew smoke toward Proctor. A wind slammed through the house, banging open the window shutters and scattering Proctor's circle of salt.

The wind died, and Bootzamon stood there, tapping the tomahawk against his palm.

"You're a witch," Proctor whispered, and then felt foolish for saying it. His own use of magic was too slow, too useless for this kind of fight. He bent down quickly and snatched up the iron.

"Not precisely a witch," Bootzamon said. "But I may be a ghost—boo!"

Proctor twitched.

Bootzamon chuckled and danced closer to Proctor. "Or I may be an Indian." The last word came out with a sneer as he swung the tomahawk at Proctor's head.

Proctor banged the tomahawk aside with the iron, then reversed his swing and slammed the metal bar into his attacker. It was like hitting a bag of sticks and straw. The tomahawk flew one way and Bootzamon the other. He hit the far wall, crumpled to the floor, and then popped up again, pipe in mouth. He reached up and recocked his hat, then licked his gloved finger and ran it along the edge of the feather.

"What are you?" Proctor asked.

"What are *you*?" Bootzamon retorted. "I'll tell you what you are—you're nothing but a miserable bag of snot and bones, piss and *Scheiße*. And, sadly, too old to be of use to me."

Bootzamon stretched his hand toward the tomahawk. The weapon slid toward him across the floor, the blade scratching a line through the blood, and flew up into his hand. The flickering light from the fire cast a sinister glare over his features, distending and exaggerating them.

He blocked the only path to the door . . .